P9-AOM-018

DOING HARM

DOING HARM

KELLY PARSONS

THORNDIKE PRESS

A part of Gale, Cengage Learning

GALE
CENGAGE Learning·

Farmington Hills, Mich • San Francisco • New York • Waterville, Maine
Meriden, Conn • Mason, Ohio • Chicago

GALE
CENGAGE Learning·

LIBRARY OF CONGRESS CATALOGING-IN-PUBLICATION DATA

Parsons, Kelly.
   Doing harm / by Kelly Parsons. — Large print edition.
     pages ; cm. — (Thorndike Press large print thriller)
     ISBN 978-1-4104-6956-4 (hardcover) — ISBN 1-4104-6956-5 (hardcover)
     1. Surgeons—Fiction 2. Surgery—Patients—Crimes against—Fiction.
  3. Psychopaths—Fiction. 4. Large type books. I. Title.
    PS3616.A78263D65 2014b
    813'.6—dc23   2014005150

Published in 2014 by arrangement with St. Martin's Press, LLC

Printed in Mexico
1 2 3 4 5 6 7 18 17 16 15 14

For Genevieve, Leah, and Nathaniel

ACKNOWLEDGMENTS

The publication of this novel resulted from a series of improbable and lucky events, perhaps none more fortunate than when an early version found its way into the miraculous hands of my agent, Al Zuckerman. I am forever in your debt, Al, for your hours of coaching, coaxing, and cajoling. It is a singularly humbling and gratifying experience to have joined your orbit. Thank you for taking a chance on me.

Judy Katz was another serendipitous link in the chain and, early on, one of the most enthusiastic cheerleaders for this book outside of my immediate family. Judy, you are a passionate bibliophile and the person most responsible for leading me directly to Al. Thank you so much for your time and encouragement.

Then, of course, there are Jennifer Enderlin and the terrific folks at St. Martin's. Jen, thanks for your razor-sharp advice, infectious energy, expertise, and — most important — your belief in me. Our next project will be even more fun than the first!

My gratitude goes to Howie Sanders at UTA, another early advocate for this book who has always fought the good fight on its behalf. Thanks, Howie, for all of your efforts and support.

I dragged some old friends along for the ride. Rich Dandliker provided encouragement and schooled me in the basic principles of computer security systems. And to think, Rich, you thought your tutoring days had ended in college once you got me through physics and organic chemistry. I can't say I was always the best student, but I tried: the clever, accurate computer stuff in the book is yours; the not-so-clever, not-so-accurate stuff is definitely mine. Chris McKenna, one of the funniest people I have ever met, delivered serious professional advice and selflessly went to bat for me several times in my quest for representation. I owe both of you guys a beer. Several, actually.

Gideon Rappaport first planted the seeds for this novel when I was in high school, and then generously gave of his time to help cultivate them twenty years later. Thank you, Gideon, for your constructive critiques, confidence-building conversations, and invaluable insight that Steve's journey needed to be, above all else, one of redemption.

Amy Halushka, another professional writer willing to humor a rank amateur, read an early draft and diplomatically rendered some of the most astute criticism I received. Thanks, Amy. If this novel looks nothing like the clumsy version you read, it's in no small part thanks to you.

Many thanks also go out to Dr. David Caparrelli, cardiac surgeon extraordinaire, for lending me helpful medical advice. Dave, now you know why your urologist friend was so interested in learning how to stick big needles into people's chests.

The Parsons, Riekers, and Noones — you guys are the best extended family ever. Thanks to all of you for your love and support. And Riekers — your book-signing event will *always* be my favorite!

This book certainly would not have been possible without my parents, Lowell and JoEllen, who over the years gave me every opportunity to succeed . . . yet also wisely let me stumble. I love you, and, like many parents, never realized how hard you guys had it until I had children of my own.

Speaking of which: Leah and Nathaniel, I

love you guys. You are extraordinary kids, and I learn something new about the world from both of you every single day. But when you reach the end of this page, please stop reading and put the book down until you're eighteen. Okay, maybe sixteen.

And then there's Gen.

Best friend. The most superb doctor I've ever known. Patient. Supportive. Unflinchingly honest in her criticism. Unsparing in her praise. My moral compass.

Did I mention best friend?

More than anyone else, this book is for you. I love you.

PROLOGUE

My patient is dying.

And it's all my fault.

I watch as the code team swarms frenetically over the naked, frail body lying on the bed in the center of the bare, otherwise unremarkable hospital room.

One of them forces fresh air into the patient's lifeless lungs with a thick, plastic balloon the size of a large grapefruit; another shoves jerkily on the sternum, rhythmically compressing the heart, squeezing the blood out of it like juice from an orange; still another stands close by, defiant and eager, manual defibrillator paddles held aloft, ready to deliver additional electric shocks to the tired, cold flesh.

I stare at this grim tableau, transfixed and helpless, watching dumbly as a life slips away.

And it's all my fault.

One of the patient's hands slides off the

side of the bed and dangles in the air over the floor, swaying slightly in time with the chest compressions, like some macabre metronome. Back in medical school, one of my anatomy instructors had pointed out to us how the hand is one of the most recognizably human parts of the human body; how, unlike the anonymous organs inhabiting the abdomen and chest, it can trigger instant recognition and empathy. To prove his point, he sawed a hand off one of the cadavers and passed it around the class, followed by the spleen of another.

He was right, of course. The hand creeped everyone out much more than the spleen, which was like a big, brown sponge left out to dry in the sun for too long. It was a woman's hand, I remember. Slight and small. Delicate-looking, despite the ghostly pale skin, pickled by the formalin preservative. It made me curious about its owner. What had she been like? Was she old when she died? Young? What did she do? Had she accomplished everything in life she had wanted? What *had* she wanted out of life? Did she have children? Grandchildren? Had she died surrounded by family and friends, or anonymous and alone?

And now, as I study the wrinkles and ridges of my patient's hand as it hangs in space, my eyes traveling over the bony hills of its knuckles and the creases of its palm, I wonder at the lifetime of activity: imagining that hand lifting a forkful of food to the mouth; or balled in anger; or drying a tear from a child's cheek; or playing the piano; or stroking a lover's hair.

But that's all over now.

I feel . . .

How *do* I feel? Like I've been punched in the stomach. Sure. But, really, how to take stock of the emotions generated by the certainty of knowing that you've caused the death of another human being? That through your stupidity or incompetence or whatever, a person who willingly entrusted their life to you will never again draw another breath?

There's guilt, naturally. Shame. Sadness. Disbelief. And, lurking beneath its more compassionate brethren, a selfish sentiment that slips unbidden into my consciousness, calculating and cruel.

Self-pity.

Everyone's going to blame me for this.

I shake my head, as if to clear the thought away, repelled that it would even materialize in my brain. My career should be the last of my worries right now.

But it gnaws at me. I can't help but worry.

I've worked too hard for too long, and it's not fair, really. This shouldn't be happening. This patient shouldn't be dying.

But now . . . here we are.

So, knowing that I can't possibly undo what I've done, I try to wrap my mind around the unlikely series of events leading up to this singular, horrible moment in my life.

And I wonder, *Well — how the hell did I end up here?*

CHAPTER 1

Saturday, July 11

"Steve?" Sally's voice floats down from our bedroom at the top of the stairs. "I'm almost ready. Are the girls okay?"

"They're fine," I call back automatically, staring into the downstairs bathroom mirror. I give one final tug on my tie, walk out of the bathroom, and step over the baby gate that guards the living-room entrance, separating that space from the rest of our small house like a barbed-wire fence around a POW camp. I survey the scene.

Katie is hunched over her play stove in a corner of the room, rummaging through plastic pots and pans and muttering to herself. Her five-year-old face is set in fierce concentration, and I glimpse what family and friends often comment on but that I myself rarely acknowledge out loud: Except for her dark black hair, which today is set in pigtails, Katie is the spitting image of me —

green eyes, an elongated face, and prominent ears. Meanwhile, a short distance away, Annabelle observes Katie serenely from her baby walker, thinking about whatever it is that ten-month-olds think about. She looks every bit as much like her mother as Katie looks like me, with straight, dark black hair, matching dark eyes, and a small nose.

Annabelle spots me, smiles adoringly, bangs happily on the narrow plastic shelf in front of her, bounces up and down, and waves like she hasn't seen me in months. I wave back like an idiot, pumping my hand back and forth with childish enthusiasm. The waving thing never gets old at this age, and I love it. "Hi, 'Bella. Hi, sweetie."

Katie spins around. "Daddy!" she shrieks, running over and wrapping herself around my leg. I love that, too. Who wouldn't? Sure, they're a pain in the ass sometimes — okay, practically *all* of the time — but I can't imagine why anyone would not want to have kids. "I'm making dinner!"

"Oh, boy. Show me."

She disengages herself from my leg, takes me by the hand, and leads me to the play stove. She solemnly spoons some white Styrofoam peanuts, the kind used as packing material in shipping boxes, from a plastic pot and into a small bowl, which she then hands to me. I poke its contents suspiciously and hold up one of the thumb-sized pea-nuts.

"Where did these come from?"

"Mommy's box." She gestures toward an open cardboard box sitting near the front door, a recent purchase from an online store. A few of the peanuts lie scattered on the floor around it, carelessly strewn across the cracked linoleum. "Eat, Daddy."

"Katie, you shouldn't be playing with these. They're too small for Annabelle."

"But 'Bella likes them."

My stomach does a queasy flip. "What do you mean, ' 'Bella likes them'?" I turn sharply to face Annabelle, realizing that she hasn't made a single sound, not so much as a gurgle or a raspberry, since I came into the room, and that her cheeks are puffed out, like a chipmunk with a bunch of nuts tucked in its mouth. She smiles at me again, and her lips part slightly, revealing a glimpse of white Styrofoam.

Annabelle bears my frantic plucking of all of the peanuts — and there are *a lot* of them — from her mouth with grace and equanim-ity, never once crying or resisting. When I'm done, I hand her a plastic rattle, which she shoves in her mouth as if nothing happened, and squat down next to Katie, who's flipping calmly through a picture book.

"Katie. You shouldn't have put those things in 'Bella's mouth."

"Why?"

"Because they could have hurt her."

"Why?" A hint of defiance has crept into her voice.

"She could have swallowed them and gotten sick."

Her lower jaw juts forward. " 'Bella's not sick. She *liked* my dinner."

Hard to argue with that. I'm trying to frame a suitable but firm response that doesn't involve complex descriptions of human-respiratory-tract anatomy when the doorbell rings. I check my watch. Right on time. As usual. "Just . . . don't do it again, Katie," I say lamely, rising to my feet.

"Okay." She's already flipping pages in her picture book.

I grab the box full of the Styrofoam peanuts, shove it in a nearby closet, and open the front door to find my mother-in-law staring up at me, steely-eyed and unsmiling.

"Hi, Mrs. Kim."

"Steven." She steps across the threshold. I hesitate, and then awkwardly bend over to hug her. She wraps her arms around my waist and lightly pats my back once before quickly withdrawing. She steps back and stares at me coldly.

I shift my weight and cough. "I, um . . . We really appreciate you watching Katie and Annabelle tonight for us, Mrs. Kim."

"You're welcome, Steven."

Like a knee-high rocket, Katie launches herself at my mother-in-law, grabbing her by the leg and screaming with laughter. Annabelle beams and bounces furiously up and down in her walker.

Mrs. Kim's face blossoms into a broad smile. "Oh my goodness! What a wonderful greeting!" With Katie still affixed to her leg, she gingerly steps into the room and, with a strength that defies her petite frame, scoops up Katie in one arm and Annabelle in the other. They giggle happily as she whispers to them in rapid-fire Korean.

Sally appears at the bottom of the stairs, her slim figure tucked into a sleek black cocktail dress, looking harried but elegant as she snaps a pearl earring into place. "Hi, Mom. Thanks for coming over." She pecks her mother on the cheek, and they confer briefly on bath, dinner, and bed for the girls. "We should be back by ten."

"Where are you going tonight?"

"We're going to a cocktail party for Steve's work before grabbing some dinner."

Her mother nods approvingly. "Good. You deserve a night out." I'm standing right there, but Mrs. Kim addresses Sally as if they're the only two people in the room.

"*Good-bye,* Mom." We hug and kiss Katie and Annabelle good night, and a short while later we're in our sky blue Toyota Sienna minivan headed for my boss's house.

"I think your mom is really starting to warm up to me."

"Why's that?" Sally flips down the passenger-side sun visor and starts applying lipstick in the cosmetic mirror fixed to the back of it.

"She didn't mention my weight."

"Uh-huh."

"Or my hairline."

Sally sighs. "Why are you letting her get to you tonight?"

"I'm not." *Yes I am.* "It's just . . . I'm a doctor. Aren't mothers-in-law supposed to, you know, appreciate the doctor thing?"

"She does. It partly makes up for your not being Korean." She's done with the lipstick and is fluffing her black, shoulder-length hair.

I glance at her, chagrined. Such blunt, casual acknowledgment of the only ongoing source of tension in our marriage — her parents' displeasure with their daughter's decision to marry outside the Korean community, a displeasure that two well-adjusted grandchildren and years of stable marriage have done little to diminish — is unusual.

"But not completely."

"No. And never will." She snaps the visor back into place and gazes out the window. "But I think you know that already. Can we talk about something else?"

"Sure." She must be in a philosophical mood or something. As bad as it's been for me with her parents, it's been ten times worse for her. But she's always stood her ground with them. It's one of the reasons I love her so much.

Sally is many different things, most of them synonyms for success, and all of which I absolutely adore: smart, driven, witty, confident. I know most people wouldn't call hers a pretty face — on some objective level, from a purely aesthetic standpoint, I know it's quite plain, really; maybe even erring on the side of unattractive. Thick lips. A nose that's too small for her broad cheeks and wide-set eyes. But I can honestly say without a trace of sentimentality that I think she's absolutely beautiful. She has an indefinable charisma that belies her looks, an enviable, innate ability to walk into a crowded room, instinctually size it up, and win over every single person in it with smooth-talking charm. She doesn't even have to try. People like her. All kinds of people. To me, it's a mystical talent, something I wouldn't be able to do if my life depended on it. And a talent that she's always put to good use: Before she had Katie and decided to stop working, Sally had a very successful career as a high-ranking assistant to the head of Human Resources at my hospital. That's how we met.

I try to think of something else to talk about, and my mind drifts back to the Styrofoam-peanut incident with Annabelle. I relate the story, playing down the part about me actually being out of the room when Katie shoved the packing material into her sister's mouth — like a mother bear defending her cubs, Sally can be extremely touchy about anything that even remotely threatens the health of the girls, and my relatively more laissez-faire approach to parenting has gotten me into trouble with her more than once. But when I'm finished, Sally simply throws back her head and laughs. " *'She liked my dinner.'* You know, Katie reminds me more and more of you every day."

I think about the way Katie looked earlier tonight, bent over that stupid toy kitchen, so intent on what she was doing. "Because she's so smart?"

"Nice try. No. Because she's so stubborn."

"Oh." I grip the steering wheel a bit more firmly.

Sally pats my shoulder affectionately. "I know. You hate hearing that. But it is what it is. Besides, it's not all bad. Being single-minded is what's enabled you to succeed. I mean, you *never* give up. I love that about you. But it is a *real* pain in the ass some-times. Once you've made up your mind about something, no force on the planet will get you to change it. Even when you're wrong. *Especially* when you're wrong. You know what I'm talking about."

"You're seeing the same thing with Katie?"

"Every single day."

"Surgeons are pretty stubborn. Maybe she'll become a surgeon someday."

"God, I hope not." She smirks.

"Yeah. Well . . . you know what they say about surgeons, right?"

"Sometimes wrong, never unsure."

"Shit. Have I used that line before?"

"Just a couple of hundred times. Where did you first hear it?"

"I'm not exactly certain. Probably from Collier."

We ride together in silence for a few

minutes before she says, "Your meeting with Dr. Collier is next Monday. Right?"

"Yep."

"What are the chances he's going to offer you a job?"

My insides suddenly bunch up into a little ball. "I don't know."

"Still? Haven't you talked to him about it yet?"

"No."

"We *really* need to stay here in Boston, Steve. Our whole lives are here."

"What do you want me to say?" We're launching into a variation of a conversation we've had countless times before. I *know* how much she wants to stay in Boston. "The opportunity hasn't come up to talk about it. Besides, I think Northwest Hospital is getting ready to make a firm offer."

"But . . . you don't want to work at Northwest."

"The money's good at Northwest."

"That's not what I said. It's not a medical school. It's not what you want."

"I know."

"How about Harvard, or U Mass?"

"They're not hiring right now." What's left unsaid is that there's only one job I really want anyway, more than I've wanted just about anything else in my life, and Sally knows it: to work at University Hospital and be a professor at University Medical School.

"Why don't you ask Dr. Collier about it tonight? He'll be relaxed. Sociable."

"I'm . . . I don't know. Maybe."

"Since when are you so indecisive? You just got through saying how" — she lowers the pitch of her voice an octave — "*never unsure* you are."

"You don't just go waltzing up to my boss and ask him for a job. It's not the way it works. We're talking about *University Hospital.* You don't *ask* to work at University. You're *invited.* Between med school and residency, I've spent the last nine years of my life busting my ass there —"

"All the more reason for you to be proactive about the whole thing."

"— and I don't want to blow it now."

She drums her fingers along the armrest. "If you don't ask him, how are you ever going to know for sure? Maybe he's waiting for you to show some interest."

I stare at the road and purse my lips.

"Honestly." She sighs, turning back toward the window. "Sometimes I don't know who's worse: you, or the five-year-old."

Dr. Collier and his wife stand in the spacious foyer of their home in Wellesley, underneath an elaborate chandelier, informally greeting their guests as they enter through the front door. It's been an unusually dry spring and summer, and the mosquito population is light, so the heavy oak front doors are thrown wide open to admit both a pleasant early-evening breeze and the guests streaming across the threshold.

Each year in July, Dr. Collier, the chairman of our department and my boss, has a cocktail party for all of the surgeons that work for him. He and his wife throw a pretty decent party. Beyond the foyer, in a living room with vaulted ceilings seemingly as high as a cathedral's, faculty and residents from my department stand around with drinks in their hands, clumped into groups of varying size and composition. They chat amiably as servers — nubile young women wearing identical white dress shirts and long black pants — circulate with blank smiles and hors d'oeuvres laid out on silver platters. Along one side of the room, a string quartet plays classical music; on the opposite side, a bartender pours drinks from the Colliers' ornate, marble-topped wet bar.

Dr. Collier himself is the spitting image of the actor Charlton Heston. Not the young, square-jawed, noble, 1950s Charlton Heston from the movie *The Ten Command-*

ments, but the older, crankier, more blustery 1960s and 1970s Charlton Heston from movies like *Planet of the Apes* and *The Omega Man* and *Soylent Green*. It's much more than just a passing resemblance, and I often wonder if Dr. Collier puts any conscious thought into imitating him. Tall, lanky, muscular, and uniformly bronzed even in the middle of January, his sinewy virility and biting cynicism are matched only by his propensity for spontaneously launching into bombastic speeches.

About the only non-Hestonesque thing about him is his musical preference in the operating room: show tunes. He's especially partial to *West Side Story*. Imagine watching Colonel Taylor from the original *Planet of the Apes* cut out somebody's kidney while humming along to "I Feel Pretty," and you'll have some idea of what it's like to operate with Dr. Collier.

Tonight, he's wearing a light brown linen suit and pink dress shirt, no tie, with a pink paisley silk handkerchief neatly folded into the left breast pocket.

Sally and I approach Dr. and Mrs. Collier just as they're finishing speaking with one of the other residents. "Steven," Dr. Collier says, shaking my hand briefly before focusing all of his attention on Sally. He smiles warmly and kisses her on the cheek. "Good evening, Sally. Welcome to our home."

Mrs. Collier is a thin, graceful woman with long brown hair flecked with gray, friendly eyes, and a genteel Southern accent. Looking stylish in a sleeveless silver dress, she takes my hand first, then hugs Sally. Sally gushes over a console table that dominates the foyer ("This wasn't here last year, was it?"). Mrs. Collier beams her approval and responds that no, she only bought it just last month, and launches into a detailed description of the antique store in which she discovered it.

Dr. Collier takes the opportunity to talk shop. "So. Steven. How does it feel to be a chief resident?"

"Terrific, Dr. Collier. I've been looking forward to it for so long, I can't believe it's actually, finally here."

"Excellent. I've been out of town at a conference recently. I understand that you started on service last week, with Luis Martínez as your junior resident."

"Yes, sir."

"Well, you won't find a more industrious resident than Luis. I'm sure the two of you will make an excellent team."

"Thanks, Dr. Collier. I've enjoyed working with him so far." I don't know if *enjoy* is exactly the right word — I hardly know the guy — but we've had a productive professional relationship over the past week.

"Is he coming tonight?"

"No. He's on call."

"Well. Someone needs to mind the store. In any event, Steven, we're expecting great things from you during your chief year."

"Does that mean you're going to hire him on after he graduates next June?" Sally interjects coyly, clutching my arm. She's finished her conversation with Mrs. Collier, who's now chatting with another guest. "I'm hopelessly biased, of course, but I think he's a great catch, Dr. Collier."

Dr. Collier chuckles. It's a little annoying. He never laughs like that in front of me unless I'm with Sally.

I feel the blood rushing to my cheeks.

What the hell does she think she's doing?

"I'm sure he is, Sally. And we're certainly grateful for the work he's done for us thus far. But we normally don't offer faculty positions to . . . let's see." He places his hand on his chin and studies me intently. "Your undergraduate degree was in . . . computer science. Right, Steven? From the University of Chicago?"

Dr. Collier prides himself on knowing the educational and personal backgrounds of

29

each of his residents. "Yes, sir."

"Yes. Computer science. Well. Chicago is a fine school and all, but I don't know if we need any computer scientists in the department," Dr. Collier says, winking at Sally. "Especially ones who grew up in Philadelphia. You know how I feel about the Phillies."

I'm about to respond, but then Sally beats me to the punch.

"But don't forget, Dr. Collier, he also minored in literature." Sally pats my arm. "He's a true Renaissance man. You can tap both sides of his brain. Besides, he was an excellent computer hacker in his day. You don't see that very often in a surgeon."

"Was he?" Dr. Collier arches an eyebrow in a deliberately exaggerated way. "That I was *not* aware of. Hmm. Hacking. Nothing *illegal,* I hope, Steven."

"That depends," Sally interjects before I can answer, her hand on my arm. "On the kinds of things you need him to do for you."

Dr. Collier throws back his head and laughs heartily. "So he can operate on patients, break into computer systems, *and* recite Shakespeare? Impressive. That *is* quite a skill set." Sally laughs merrily at his dumb joke while I stand there forcing a grin, watching stupidly as my boss and wife talk about me in the third person.

"Dr. Collier, I'm sure he'd recite anything you'd like him to."

"I bet he would." Dr. Collier chuckles again. "Well, I'll see what I can do." His attention abruptly shifts to one of the other guests behind us, a senior doctor in the department. "Enjoy yourselves, you two." Still smiling, he guides his wife by the elbow away from us and toward the other doctor.

"What were you doing back there?" I murmur in Sally's ear as we walk the short distance from the foyer to the living room.

"Trying to help you." She nonchalantly plucks a salmon-topped cracker from a passing tray and bites into it.

"I thought we agreed to do things my way. In the car."

She swallows the salmon cracker and wipes the crumbs off her fingers with a cocktail napkin. "We never agreed on anything. You simply stopped talking. Remember? I saw an opportunity and took advantage of it. Did you see Dr. Collier's reaction?"

"Yeah. He made fun of me."

"But in a *good* way, Steve. I bet you he talks to you about a job next week."

"I bet you he throws me out of his office."

But she's spotted one of the other resident's wives, a friend of hers, and is moving away from me, smiling and waving. She's already begun to work the room.

A catering girl walks up and offers me a bruschetta. I take it, shrug, and follow Sally into the crowd.

CHAPTER 2

Monday, July 13

It's 6:45 A.M., and I'm sitting in the cafeteria of University Hospital, cradling a strong cup of coffee. The early-morning rush is under way. I watch idly as nurses and medical technicians, bleary-eyed and blank-faced, stumble into the cafeteria on their way to the 7:00 A.M. change of shift. They grab coffees and juggle paper plates heaping with scrambled eggs and bacon and hash browns to take with them to their jobs upstairs on the patient wards. A few doctors also mill around, mostly other surgery residents wearing long white coats over hospital-issued scrubs — members of surgical teams who have finished their morning rounds and are tanking up before heading to the operating rooms for the rest of the day.

A boisterous group of surgery residents sits at a nearby table, huddled over their meals, swapping stories about patients. At one point, the table erupts into raucous laughter, and one of them accidentally spills coffee onto his white coat. Cursing, he grabs a napkin and starts wiping at the ugly brown spot spreading toward the embroidered University Hospital emblem stitched in bold maroon across the right breast: a caduceus with the words PRIMUM NON NOCERE printed underneath.

I idly finger the University Hospital logo on my own white coat.

University Hospital.

I love being a doctor; I especially love being a doctor *here.*

Who wouldn't? A sprawling, eclectic complex of sleek, modern high-rises interconnected with squat and sturdy nineteenth-century edifices located in the heart of Boston, University Hospital is the primary teaching hospital for uberprestigious University Medical School, and year after year is consistently ranked among the best hospitals in the world.

But the place means more to me than just a number on some magazine's "Best Of" list. Much more. Not a day goes by when I don't think about how special it is to be part of this place, or remember all of the years of soul-crushing academic labor it took for me to get here. Founded almost 250 years ago by the top doctors in colonial America, who themselves had been trained by the top doctors in Europe, University Hospital is steward of a grand tradition that stretches back generations: a mecca for cutting-edge medical innovation that's reliably churned out, in equal measure, Nobel Prize winners, medical-school deans, and surgeons general. Only the best of the best are chosen to train here.

And I'm one of them.

It certainly wasn't easy to get here.

I smile to myself and remember the very first speaker on my very first day of medical school: the dean. He was a burly cardiothoracic surgeon, a former Army Ranger stuffed into a three-piece suit, built like a tank and very imposing, especially to impressionable first-year med students. After making a few perfunctory welcoming comments, he walked out from behind the lectern, took off his suit jacket, carefully laid it over the back of a chair, and walked to the front of the podium. It was a slick move — folksy yet calculating, sparking an immediate sense of intimacy in a roomful of complete strangers. He then launched into an easygoing pep talk, full of earnest admonitions that your dad might have delivered over a mug of hot chocolate sitting at the kitchen table the night before you headed off to college.

He told us to relax; that we had made it; that our moms were already proud of us; that the competition was over; that it was time to stop trying to beat the grade curve and focus on becoming good doctors.

Right.

This to 120 hypercompetitive, anal-retentive, type A overachievers who had spent the last several years single-mindedly decimating any and all obstacles to gain the coveted seats they were now sitting in.

Who was he kidding? Half of the class was already taking notes. And who could blame us? We'd been competing against one another academically since practically before we could crawl. We were the ones who had survived the premed Darwinian free-for-all in college. We were the ones who had beaten the academic bell curve, who had successfully slipped into that thin sliver of grade Nirvana to the far right of the hump. That's a tough mentality to shake off. And one, I'm not ashamed to admit, I never have. It's what got me here.

Luis, the junior resident I'm currently working with, slouches into the seat across from me with a tray of food and grunts good morning, running his hand across his bald head, over his bloodshot eyes, and down his olive-colored face toward the rough, salt-and-pepper stubble dotting his chin. It's a striking, if not particularly handsome, face — thin and long, almost gaunt, and all sharp angles, with thick cords of muscle extending from his chin down his neck. He was on call working in the hospital for most of the weekend, and this morning he's been in the hospital since well before 6:00 A.M., checking on our patients.

I sip my coffee, considering my breakfast companion as he scratches some notes on a piece of paper he's laid out on the table in front of him. Luis Martínez is a few years behind me in our training program, but this is the first time I've worked with him closely on a daily basis. His smoothly shaved head, by the looks of it a defiant stand against a markedly receding hairline, looks good on him; the prominent rise of his naked skull somehow makes him appear more commanding and belies the lower rung on the professional food chain he currently occupies in University Hospital. Even now, clearly exhausted, with another full day of work looming ahead of him, his squared shoulders and prominent jawlines betray not a hint of weakness or capitulation. He oozes self-confidence and radiates unassailable authority, even around me, and even though I'm his direct supervisor. But not in a bad way. He's not arrogant, or egotistical. Just self-assured. It doesn't bother me.

As a junior resident, Luis's job is to handle the myriad practical issues involved in taking care of hospitalized patients: medication orders, nursing questions, diet changes, initial assessment of problems, discharge paperwork — all of the minute-to-minute, hour-to-hour details and minutiae that constantly arise when patients are staying in the hospital. It's essential stuff. But it's also a lot of grunt work. In medical parlance, we refer to it as scut, and to the interns and junior residents who take care of it as scut monkeys. Surgeons hate scut. But scut pretty much sucks no matter what kind of medicine you practice.

I don't have to do scut anymore. I did my time in the trenches, when I was a junior resident like Luis. Now my job is to oversee Luis, teach him what I know, and pretty much make sure he doesn't do anything stupid. I've worked with him for only about a week now. He seems like an okay guy. Taciturn and gruff, he runs a tight ship and, for the most part, keeps his thoughts to himself. We don't talk very much beyond work-type stuff. He's older than I am, several years at least. I heard he did some time in the military before he went to med school. Beyond that, I realize, I really don't know anything about him — where he's originally from, or where he went to school. I make a mental note to find out more.

But he definitely gets the job done, and gets it done well. Quite well. I don't worry about his doing anything stupid with the patients. He's also unfailingly polite and attentive to my directions; although I suspect that he secretly considers himself to be a much better doctor than I am, despite my greater experience. But that's no big deal. Supreme self-confidence isn't necessarily an unusual, or even unhealthy, attitude to have in medicine. A lot of doctors, at all levels of training and in all specialties, think they're better than the next guy. It gives you the confidence you need to get up in the morning and go to work. Besides, in the end, the most important thing is that Luis always follows the chain of command and does exactly what I tell him to do.

Most weekday mornings, Luis and I meet here in the cafeteria to discuss our patients and plan their treatments for the day. This morning, as with every morning, I listen attentively over my coffee, interjecting now and then with questions, suggestions, or instructions on how to best take care of the patients. Most mornings, once he finishes going down his list of patients, I'll usually give Luis some more work to do, then retreat to the operating room to enjoy myself.

This morning is no different. After he finishes his report, I tick off the list of tasks — the scut — I want him to complete on each of the patients. Increase Mr. Kellogg's IV fluids; he's dehydrated. Switch Mrs. Cardoza to oral pain medications. Have physical therapy work with Mr. James; he's been a slug since his surgery and won't get out of bed. Order a CT scan for Mr. Richards; he's been having persistent fevers and belly pain the last few days, and I'm worried he might have an abscess lurking somewhere in his abdomen. Complete the discharge paperwork for Ms. Tang.

With each of my directives, Luis nods and writes something on his sheet of paper.

"We have a med student starting with us on service this morning," he says when we're done, leaning back in his chair and rubbing his palm over the top of his head, like he's polishing a doorknob. "She rounded with me earlier. She's at a student orientation or something right now, but she's going to meet up with us here in a few minutes."

"How is she?"

"Smart. Definitely knows her way around the hospital."

"Oh yeah?" I ask, marginally interested. Med students are usually pretty clueless. And therefore useless. "What's her name?"

"Gigi. G-I-G-I. Gigi Maxwell. People say her first name should be more like, 'GG.' As in the letters G-G. Short for 'Golden Girl.' Because she's such a terrific student. The word on the street is that she's been knocking it out of the park on her other clinical rotations. Hard worker, great attitude, whip smart."

GG. "Nice break for you. I'm sure she can help you out with some of your scut."

"Yeah. Look." He glances around and then leans toward me over the table. "You're married, right, Steve?" he asks, sotto voce. I can barely hear him over the din around us. I nod, curious as to where he's going with this. "Good. Let me warn you up front anyway." He lowers his voice even further, so that I have to scoot forward to make him out. "She's also pretty cute. With a good-sized rack on her. It's hard not to notice. A bunch of the surgery residents have been trying their best to get in her pants."

"Is she letting them?"

41

"No. That's my point. Exactly the opposite. She filed a formal complaint against Connors last month for putting his hand on her ass in the OR."

"Connors." I guffaw. "The guy's a douche bag. Thinks with his prick. He's banged half the nurses in the hospital."

"Right." Luis leans back and drapes his elbows on the back of the chair. "I for one am interested in keeping my job. Thought you would be, too. Wanted you to know the situation."

"Thanks, Luis." I'm grateful for the heads-up. It's not like I'm going to be hitting on her or anything, attractive or not, but sexual harassment has been a pretty sensitive topic around here for a while, ever since a drunken neurosurgery professor groped a few female residents half his age at an out-of-town conference a few months ago. Surgery has always been a male-dominated field; and its men's locker-room sensibilities have proven remarkably resistant to twenty-first-century notions of gender equality. Especially at a traditional place like University.

Anyway, after the neurosurgeon-groping thing blew up in a very public, embarrassing, and litigious way, every surgeon in the hospital — residents and professors alike, male *and* female — has had to suffer through sensitivity training lectures and weekly e-mail blasts reminding us of the importance of *maintaining a nonhostile work environment.* In the current climate, saying the wrong thing about, doing the wrong thing to, or acting the wrong way in front of a female medical student, especially one under your direct supervision, can get you into serious trouble. Connors, the surgery resident Luis is referring to, apparently hadn't gotten the message.

I point to my wedding band and unsuccessfully attempt to stifle a yawn. "I'm good. But thanks, man. Just try to keep her out of my way, okay?"

"Sure." He tips his chin in a direction over my shoulder. "Here she comes now."

I spin around in my seat and follow his line of sight to the cafeteria entrance, where a tall girl with dark brown hair, wearing the standard-issue short white coat of a medical student, is surveying the room uncertainly. Luis catches her attention and waves her over.

You can usually spot the med students from about a mile away: Their short white coats and deer-in-the-headlights gazes make them stand out like sore thumbs. But as GG weaves through the human traffic of cafeteria rush hour, I can tell right away that she's different. She's wearing crisp green surgical scrubs under her short white coat. The purposefulness of each stride matches the intense expression on her face. This is a woman, it seems, who knows exactly where she's going and how she's going to get there.

She reaches our table and introduces herself to me. My need to assert surgeon-like authority in front of a med student overcomes my urge to do the gentlemanly thing, so I remain seated as I size her up. She's tall — very tall, almost as tall as I, and at six-one, I'm no slouch — with a long, svelte frame. Her hair flows down her back in thick, straight waves before gliding to a graceful stop just past her shoulders. She has eyes the color of dark chocolate and sharp features that abruptly soften around her cheeks and the edges of her slightly upturned nose. I have to admit that Luis was right: She's pretty. Not beautiful, like a model; her body is a little too thick, her features just a little too asymmetrical.

But she's definitely good-looking — attractive in an intelligent, down-to-earth, approachable kind of way. And, as she leans over the table to shake my hand, I can't help but notice that Luis's description of her physical attributes was right on the money.

Now I truly understand why Luis warned me — I might be happily married, but I'm not dead, and I labor to keep my eyes from lingering over the utilitarian, but provocative, dip of her scrub top.

There's something else about her that stands out almost immediately. Something that's harder for me to put my finger on. Something elusive. A . . . *stillness*. A calm and magnetic self-composure that underlies everything she does and says. It's in the way she moves confidently toward me, locking her eyes onto mine and shaking my hand, her attitude and motions utterly devoid of uncertainty — like Luis, but less commanding. It's also in her voice, which is light and amiable and soothing, like a radio DJ's.

As she shakes my hand, her face breaks into a radiant smile, the lines extending across her smooth features, like ripples from a pebble tossed into the middle of a deep, placid pool. Her grin is broad and eager and completely natural, lacking any trace of self-consciousness, almost like the smiles of my daughters. Her hand is soft, her movements fluid and controlled.

"Nice to meet you, GG," I say. "I understand you might be interested in going into urologic surgery."

"Actually, Dr. Mitchell, I've already pretty

much decided that it's for me," she says. "What you guys do for a living is terrific. Kidney surgery, prostate surgery — I think that stuff's awesome. This is my subinternship, so I'll be with you guys for the next six weeks." During their last two years of medical school, University med students spend two-to-four-week blocks with various departments in University Hospital to earn credit toward graduation. Subinterns are advanced students interested in taking on more advanced tasks.

"Great. I just hope Luis and I don't end up making you change your mind."

"I don't think so, Dr. Mitchell," she responds seriously. "I've heard great things about you. And Dr. Martínez. I'm really excited to be working with both of you."

Luis and I exchange a look.

Is she bullshitting us already?

And even if she is, do I care?

I decide to take the compliment at face value. For now. "Well, thanks. And please call me Steve. I'm just a resident — I don't deserve any respect."

She chuckles appreciatively. Luis smiles thinly.

"Okay, Steve. Seriously, though," GG says earnestly, "just let me know if there's anything I can do for you guys. I really want

46

to help out as much as possible."

"Be careful what you wish for. We're going to take you up on that."

"That's what I'm here for."

She unclips a well-worn, black leather case from her hip, and holds up a sleek smartphone.

"Really, just tell me what I can do for you, and I'll put it right in my extra brain here. I can put anything you want me to do in my daily schedule right now. I'll be printing out some spreadsheets once I get home tonight to help get everything organized. Nothing too fancy — just Excel."

Luis and I exchange another glance. *Is she for real?* But I have to admit that GG's eagerness is infectious. Normally, I might brush off someone like her as an annoying kiss-ass med student, but instead I smile. "That's okay, GG. Luis and I will talk to you about that later. We don't have a lot of time right now. I have to go to the OR."

Undaunted, she immediately snaps the phone back in place on her hip, like returning a gun to a holster. "No problem, Dr. Mitch . . . er, Steve."

"Luis's going to take care of you this morning, get you all settled in, and assign you some stuff to do. In general, we'll pretty much expect you to function at the level of an intern: help in surgery cases, gather lab results, do some scut. Oh, and you'll be going to the resident's outpatient clinic every Tuesday morning to see patients with Luis. Okay?" I stand up without waiting for an answer.

"Great!" she exclaims.

"Oh, hey. Steve?" Luis asks.

"Yeah." I look at my watch, my mind already in the operating room.

"I forgot to mention it to you earlier — my ERIN account is all screwed up. It blew up on me during morning rounds, and now I'm locked out of the system. Can I borrow your account this morning until the IT people can fix it?"

"Sure, man," I say absently. ERIN is University Hospital's electronic medical records system. All of our medical orders and records, including medication prescriptions, are done on the computer. Without his ERIN account, Luis is helpless: He won't be able to order medications for our patients, and GG can't help him since medical students aren't allowed to order medications because they're not doctors yet. Without Luis ordering medications for our patients this morning, the wheels might come off our carefully tuned bus, and I might end up looking bad in the eyes of my bosses. I can't have that. So I quickly jot down my account name and password on his spreadsheet.

"Thanks, Steve. The IT people said they should have it fixed by noon today."

I glance at GG. She smiles broadly and opens her mouth as if she's about to say something.

"See you, guys." I turn and walk away before she has a chance.

Our first patient of the day, Mr. Bernard, is a carpenter from coastal Maine. He's having his bladder removed because of cancer. I find him in the pre-op area, a large room with high ceilings next to the operating suites, where surgery patients sit in small cubicles on gurneys, waiting to undergo final evaluations before being wheeled into the OR. Doctors and nurses buzz around their patients, going through final checklists.

Mr. Bernard is already dressed in his standard-issue hospital gown. With all the amazing medical advances that have occurred since I started medical school — face transplants and HIV wonder drugs and complex surgeries performed with robots through incisions no bigger than keyholes — I've often wondered why somebody hasn't gotten around to designing a better hospital gown.

Really. They're the same everywhere I go. Flimsy and drafty and cold, sporting a hopelessly complex assortment of strings for tying it in place and characterized by the one reviled feature that remains the universal bane of all patients: a long open slit down the middle of the back running from neck to knees, corresponding to the vertical line at the exact center of the buttocks.

So there Mr. Bernard quietly sits, on a gurney in one of the cubicles with his butt crack hanging out the back of his gown, behind a thin plastic curtain that looks and feels exactly like a shower curtain at a roadside motel and is meant to afford some modicum of privacy here in Grand Central to people waiting patiently for their surgeries. Mr. Bernard is muscular and wiry, with a thick mop of dark hair flecked with gray, and squints a lot after the pre-op nurses take his wire-rimmed glasses for safekeeping. Like rings on a tree stump, his face is etched with the deep lines of many summers spent working outdoors.

We shake hands. His palm is sweaty and slick, and after I withdraw mine I have to resist the urge to wipe it off on my white coat. He's not married and, unlike most of the other patients currently in the pre-op area who are surrounded by family members, is alone ("My girlfriend will be here later." He shrugs without further explanation). We talk about the risks of the operation. I give him the usual reassurances: that this is a routine operation; that our safety record is excellent; that bad things almost never happen.

I like him instantly. He's amiable, sharp, and witty. He's also very precise and asks a lot of surprisingly insightful questions for a carpenter. He seems satisfied with my responses. He signs the remaining paperwork, including the consent form that gives us permission to perform the operation, without even looking at what's written on the paper.

"I trust you," he says simply. "After all, according to *U.S. News and World Report,* you guys are one of the best."

Once the anesthesia resident and I are done running through our routine pre-operative checklist, we wheel Mr. Bernard into the operating room. We help him move off the gurney and onto the operating table. During this process, his gown accidentally slips off because of some ill-tied strings, and before the nurses or myself can react, he's naked from the waist down.

"Whoops. Sorry, everyone." He laughs nervously. "Not much room for modesty around here, is there?"

"No, Mr. Bernard, I'm afraid there's not. No problem. Let me help you out there." I take a blanket out of a steel warmer tucked in a corner of the room. The blanket radiates a pleasant heat that reminds me of fresh laundry taken out of a dryer.

I bring the blanket over to Mr. Bernard, and, as I lay it across his abdomen, I'm startled to glimpse the words "DO NOT REMOVE" written in large, block letters in black ink on the shaft of his penis, running from up to down like a crossword puzzle.

"Uh, Mr. Bernard?" I say. "Don't take this the wrong way, but is that what I think it is written on your, you know . . ."

"Yeah." He chuckles with a sly grin. "It is. I'm glad you noticed it before you put me to sleep. I wanted to see your reaction."

"Can't say I've seen that one before, Mr. Bernard," I say, laughing. I relay the joke to the rest of the operating team, who laugh appreciatively.

"Just wanted to make sure you people were all awake this morning." He chuckles again.

He lifts his head from the pillow and peers keenly at me over the top of the warming blanket as I adjust his feet on the operating table.

"Hey, Dr. Mitchell. What's your first name, anyway?"

"Um . . . Steven. Steve."

"Steve." He repeats my name as if testing the way it sounds coming out of his mouth. "So, you said you're a resident?"

"Yes."

"A resident. And that's like, what . . . a doctor in training, right?"

"Yes."

"Well, Steve, did you get enough sleep last night? I read in *Parade* magazine once that most resident doctors are sleep-deprived and that doctors make more mistakes when they're sleep-deprived. I hope you got enough sleep last night. I need you firing on all cylinders, you know?"

He seems like a good guy, what with the DO NOT REMOVE penis joke and all; so even though I've gotten a full night's sleep, and am actually feeling pretty energized this morning, I decide, perhaps a little recklessly, to play with his mind a bit.

"Well, Mr. Bernard, it's not so much that I was up all last night and didn't get any sleep that's bothering me. I just wish I hadn't drunk all that cough syrup this morning." It's a line from an old movie.

Mr. Bernard frowns, intently studying my masked face, apparently trying to decide whether I'm serious or not. I immediately regret saying it. What had seemed to me an exceedingly clever joke doesn't seem so exceedingly clever anymore.

After a moment, Mr. Bernard decides I'm joking . . . I think. He laughs . . . sort of. It sounds more like a grunt.

Dr. Andrews walks into the room. "Good morning, Steve. How are you today?"

"I'm good, Bill, thanks," I say, relieved by the distraction. "We're ready to go when you are."

"Great." He leans over and whispers in my ear, "Which patient is this?"

I turn my head toward him and whisper back, "Mr. Bernard. Young guy. High-grade urothelial carcinoma, likely T3. Metastatic evaluation negative. Completed neoadjuvant chemo. History of hypertension but otherwise healthy. He's a carpenter."

He nods and walks up to Mr. Bernard's head. "Mr. Bernard, how are you today?"

"Hi there, Doc," Mr. Bernard slurs. The benzodiazepine tranquilizer the anesthesia resident has given him is beginning to drag him under. I take comfort in knowing that he probably won't remember the cough-syrup remark. Prospective amnesia, it's

54

called, a common side effect of benzodiaz-
epines.

"Ready to get this done?"

"Get what done?"

"Your surgery. We're going to remove your
bladder this morning."

"Why?"

"Because you have bladder cancer."

"Ohh, yeah. Right. Sounds like . . .
good . . . cough syrup . . ." His voice trails
off into a snore.

"Did he sign the operative consent form?"
Andrews asks me, one eyebrow arching
above the other over the straight blue line
of his surgical mask.

"Of course."

"Good." The raised eyebrow drops back
in position next to its brother. "I just need
to use the little boy's room. You okay to
start?"

"Sure, Bill."

As the door swings shut behind him, the
anesthesia resident says, "I didn't expect
the benzos to put him out like that. Usual
antibiotics? You guys like to give one gram
of Cefotetan for these cases, right?"

"Yeah. Cefotetan. Usual poison."

"No problem."

The anesthesia resident's attending appears shortly thereafter and, once they've

put Mr. Bernard all the way under and secured a breathing tube down his throat, I go out to the scrub sink to wash, then return to the room and, with the help of the scrub nurse, put on my sterile gown and gloves. The scrub nurse and I trade small talk about our weekends as the two of us set up the sterile field and place a catheter in Mr. Bernard's bladder.

"Knife, please," I say after we're ready. I hold my right hand out behind me, looking not at her but at Mr. Bernard's abdomen. She passes me the scalpel with practiced ease. I close my fingers around the metal handle, still warm from the steam sterilizer, savoring the feel of it in my hand, experiencing the anticipatory thrill that always jolts my brain immediately before I cut the skin.

I make a vertical incision in the center of Mr. Bernard's abdomen from just below his belly button to just above his penis, where the DO NOT REMOVE is still faintly visible through the sterile, brown iodine solution that now covers his skin as if someone had spilled a bottle of thick maple syrup all over him.

I slice through the skin and enter the bright yellow fat lying immediately underneath. The scalpel is sure and sharp. As I cut through the fat, which is packed full of small blood vessels, the bleeding starts, and my white gloves are immediately dappled with irregular splotches of bright red blood, which transform my hands into something resembling two moving Jackson Pollack canvases, working in sync to open Mr. Bernard's belly and expose its contents to the outside world. I cut down quickly through the layers of fat to his abdominal muscles.

"Knife down." I turn and lay the scalpel down carefully on the instrument tray behind me.

"Thank you," the scrub nurse replies, whisking the scalpel away.

There is a fundamental ethical principle that governs the practice of medicine. It sums up in one succinct phrase the basic rule all physicians are expected to follow when treating their patients, the one that the colonial-era founders of University Hospital felt compelled to incorporate into the hospital's official seal more than two hundred years ago.

Primum, non nocere.

I first heard it spoken during my first year of med school from one of my older professors who had a proclivity for bow ties and Grecian Formula. He spoke the words with great flourish, reverently lingering over each syllable, caressing the Latin pronunciation as lovingly as he would his children. He attributed the phrase to the Greek physician Hippocrates, the doctor whose ancient oath freshly minted doctors recite each year at medical-school graduations around the world.

Now, I'm no historian, but I remembered thinking at the time that Hippocrates was a Greek who had lived hundreds of years before the Roman Empire, and wondered if Latin really would have been his idiom of choice for solemn ethical declarations. In fact, I've since learned that it was actually Galen, a medieval doctor and translator of Hippocrates' writings, who was probably the one who coined the Latin variation.

But, whatever. Doctors like to say stuff in Latin because it makes us sound smart. And, anyway, the essence of Hippocrates' message is the same in any language.

Primum, non nocere.

First, do no harm.

Well, when a surgeon operates, he or she *is* doing harm. Sometimes massively so.

Surgery is a violent art. It's the act of healing through deliberate injury to the human body. Scalpels slice through healthy skin to allow access to the diseased organs hidden underneath. Otherwise robust muscles are unceremoniously pushed and pulled and shoved out of the way and held out of the surgeon's working space — the "operative field" — for hours at a time with blunt metallic instruments called retractors.

Normal blood vessels are burned and strangled with fine sterile threads called sutures and cut with scissors, innocent bystanders felled by the surgeon's relentless march through the healthy parts of the body that invariably stand between the outside world and the site of the patient's disease.

In a way, then, the very act of surgery itself is a violation of one of the most fundamental ethical principles in the practice of medicine. The most iconographic and essential tool of the surgeon — the scalpel — is in essence . . . what? Nothing more than a really sharp knife, a variation on one of the earliest tools a human being ever conceived of to hurt other human beings.

The surgeon wields the scalpel with the intent to heal. The violence wrought is controlled, calculated, and precise. But it's still violence, nevertheless — pure and simple and primeval.

Another tool we surgeons use to cause harm is the electrocautery. Nicknamed the "Bovie" after its inventor, James Bovie, the electrocautery is like an electric scalpel. To cauterize means to destroy living tissue with heat, cold, or chemicals. The Bovie uses the heat produced by an electric current to burn through tissue. It's a pen-shaped instrument, held in the dominant hand just as you would hold a pen, with a metal tip on the end that directs an electric current into the patient at the point where the tip touches the patient's body. The surgeon switches the current on by pushing a button on the pen. As the current passes from the pen and into the patient, it meets resistance, which generates heat, which burns the things the metal tip is touching: skin, fat, muscle, whatever.

As the tissue at the point of contact between the Bovie's metal tip and the patient vaporizes, it produces a wisp of bluish-tinged smoke that carries with it a singular odor.

The odor of burning human flesh.

I pick up the Bovie and cauterize the bleeding vessels. The heat from the Bovie cooks the fat, and I inhale the familiar smell.

God, I love operating.

I can't believe they pay me to do this.

I'd do it for nothing.

I can't imagine what I'd do with my life if I couldn't operate.

When most of the bleeding has stopped, I put the Bovie down, then spread Mr. Bernard's abdominal muscles apart with my fingers. They pull away easily from each other, and I immediately know that I'm in the right place — between the left and right bellies of the rectus abdominus muscles, at the midline of the abdominal wall, which is the easiest, surest way into the interior of the abdomen from here. Next, I take a pair of scissors from the nurse and cut through the rest of the gossamer-like tissue lying between Mr. Bernard's bladder and me. Now my hands are inside Mr. Bernard's abdomen, probing and sweeping and searching. His insides are warm and moist, closing around my hands as if I had put them into a vat of warm Jell-O.

I'm fast. Andrews must have gone to get coffee or something because by the time he comes back, I've set up the metallic retractors, and, with the nurse's help, I've taken out all the lymph nodes from Mr. Bernard's pelvis. I've cut through blood vessels and fat to properly expose the bladder and prostate gland for the next part of the operation: the important and more dangerous part, when Andrews and I together carve Mr. Bernard's bladder and prostate out of his body.

This is what it's all about. This is why I went to med school in the first place.

Operating is a total rush for me. I can't get enough of it. The feeling is indescribable; it's pure exhilaration.

A friend of mine in college used to like to say that pizza is a lot like sex: When it's good, it's great; and when it's bad, well . . . it's still pretty good. I feel the same way about operating. When things go well during an operation it's absolutely exhilarating; a simple, pure joy that defies description; a jolt of adrenaline that makes you feel like you're on top of the world.

And when things don't go so well during an operation, I think it's still pretty good.

I was never an athlete. Not a serious one, anyway. But some of the surgeons I work with who were big-time athletes in high school and college tell me that when they're operating well, it's the closest thing they've experienced outside elite competitive sports to reaching that elusive mental sphere known as "the Zone."

The Zone, these guys tell me, is a mental Nirvana in which time slows down, difficult motions and complex movements are effortlessly and flawlessly executed, and scoring twenty points in the big playoff game — or performing cardiac bypass surgery — seems as ridiculously easy as sitting on the couch with a bag of chips watching TV.

The problem is, you can't always be in the Zone. No matter what you do for a living, every so often you're going to have a bad day. A day when you just can't seem to catch a break, when it's one bad thing after another, and you're just trying to make it through to quitting time so you can crawl home, toss back a couple of stiff drinks, and hope to God that tomorrow's better.

Doctors are no different. Surgeons are no different. Every surgeon has off days, days he or she would prefer to forget, when nothing seems quite right. Some surgeons have more bad days than others, obviously. The good surgeons are generally the ones who can perform well even on their bad days. A bad day for a good surgeon usually isn't all that bad for the patient. The good surgeons take the bad days in stride, and the patient never sees the difference.

As for the bad surgeons . . . well, I can only imagine. Whenever things aren't going too well for him in the operating room, one of my professors (a fantastic surgeon) likes to sigh dramatically and remind me that somewhere in the world at that moment a really, really awful surgeon is having a really, really awful day.

And God help that awful surgeon's patients on that awful day.

Today, though, there's nothing bad. I feel great. I guess I'm in that Zone, operating well even for me. One of my professors has told me that I'm the most naturally gifted surgeon to have come through our training program in the last ten years. I just can sense things about the operation; where I'm supposed to go, what I'm supposed to do, the next move I'm supposed to make.

I mean, you can teach a monkey how to operate. But you can't teach a monkey to do the kinds of things that I can do. I guess I'm just naturally able to take things to the next level. Mr. Bernard would no doubt be surprised, and not a little bit uneasy, to know how much of his operation is being done by me, a trainee. But Andrews, younger and less confident with this operation than some of the older professors, lets me do parts of the operation that I know he would never let any of the other residents do. I practically take Mr. Bernard's bladder out all by myself, then build him a new one made out of small intestine.

The whole thing takes us about five hours. Toward the end, I notice GG slip into the room to watch the final parts of the procedure. Andrews doesn't like to be interrupted while he's operating. Once, a few years ago, I watched him tear into a third-year medical student for asking an innocent but ill-timed question during a particularly stressful part of a stressful operation. Andrews completely lost it, screaming obscenities at her until she finally ran crying from the room.

That kind of behavior, routine back when surgeons ruled as god-kings over their ORs, feared by all and questioned by none, is no longer tolerated by medical schools and hospitals. And with good reason: As soon as her tears had dried, the student filed a formal complaint, threatening a high-profile lawsuit against both the medical school and the hospital — as well as full disclosure to the local press — because Andrews had employed some particularly choice sexual turns of phrase during his hissy fit. I heard that the hospital coughed up a bunch of cash to keep the student quiet and that Andrews had to take some anger-management classes to keep his job.

Classes or not, Andrews's anger has never seemed particularly well managed to me. So I ignore GG, and she has the good sense to slip into a corner and keep quiet.

We finish the operation, the speed and ease of which have left Andrews in a good mood. "Nice job, Steve." He extends his hand, and we shake over the juicy red and yellow maw in the middle of Mr. Bernard's abdomen. "Great hands, as always."

"Thanks, Bill."

"You okay to close?" He's already taking off his sterile gown and gloves, anticipating — or, more likely, not even caring — what my answer's going to be.

"Yeah, no problem."

"Thanks. Call me if you need anything." Then he's out the door, whistling to himself, without having even noticed GG still standing in the corner.

I now need an extra pair of hands to help me sew Mr. Bernard's abdomen together.

"GG, you mind scrubbing in and helping me close?"

"Are you kidding? I'm already there." She rushes out the door and is back in the room as quickly as the scrub protocol will allow.

After putting on her gown and gloves, she slides up to the side of the table opposite me. "Steve," she asks eagerly, "can I throw a few stitches through fascia? They let me do it on my trauma-surgery rotation."

I hesitate. Normally, since it's the strongest layer of tissue that will be holding Mr. Bernard's abdomen together and his guts inside his body after this operation, I wouldn't let a med student sew the fascia closed. But I get a good vibe from GG. And, more important, I'm confident I can fix things if she starts to screw up.

"Okay. Give it a try. Are you right-handed?"

"Yes."

I hand her a needle driver and a set of forceps. The needle driver, which is shaped like a pair of pliers, grips in its serrated jaws a semicircular needle with a diameter the size of a silver dollar. The needle is attached to a bright blue suture as thick as a piece of uncooked spaghetti. The suture, analogous to the thread of a sewing needle, will be what holds Mr. Bernard's belly together until it heals. The suture will eventually dissolve, but only long after the healing process is complete.

"Okay. Start here." I point to a spot at the bottom of the incision. GG begins right where I'm pointing, confidently sweeping the needle through the thick white fascia, which has the consistency and strength of beef jerky.

She's good. She really is. She handles the needle driver and suture with a dexterity and speed I've rarely seen in a med student before.

"Nice technique. I don't normally let med students do this, so I hope you're enjoying the experience."

"Oh, yeah. Definitely. Thanks, Dr. Mitchell."

"No problem. And, again, call me Steve."

"Thanks, Steve. This is the best."

I watch her work her way down the length of the incision for a while. "Take wider bites, GG. Catch more fascia laterally. I don't want to have to reclose this guy in the middle of the night after he coughs, rips his stitches, and his guts spill out. It makes me look bad." She stops for a moment, unsure, needle poised in midair, her brow furrowed.

"Here. Like this." I take the back of her hand in my own and gently guide it through the correct motions a few times before letting go.

"Okay, Steve. Sorry." She adjusts her technique accordingly with an ease that even some junior residents with a good three years of training on them can't muster.

Jeez, she is *good.*

She murmurs something I can't hear.

"Sorry. I didn't catch that," I say, leaning toward her.

"Strong hands," she repeats softly. "You have strong hands." She shrugs and glances up shyly. "It seems like . . . I mean, I think it's important for a surgeon to have strong hands. Don't you?"

"Ummm" is all I can manage. My cheeks

burn, and I'm grateful for the surgical mask covering them. My eyes dart self-consciously toward the scrub nurse, but she's completely preoccupied with counting and sorting the surgical instruments.

I'm still trying to figure out how to respond to GG when the anesthesiology resident (I still can't remember his name) diverts my attention.

"Hey, Steve?" he calls.

"What's up?"

"I just rechecked the patient's chart, and, ah, it looks like he's allergic to penicillin."

"So?"

"We gave him Cefotetan at the beginning of the case."

Shit. About 5 to 10 percent of patients who are allergic to penicillin are also allergic to Cefotetan. Mr. Bernard shouldn't have gotten the Cefotetan. It's a violation of hospital protocol.

"Okay. How'd we miss that?"

"I'm not sure. I guess . . . I don't know. I didn't see it on the front of his chart."

Stupid anesthesia resident. In my opinion, it's his job, not mine, to pick up on that kind of stuff. But my bosses will still blame me. If the patient has a reaction to a drug he shouldn't have received, it's the kind of thing that will make me look bad. Underneath my mask, I bite my lip and hold my temper.

"What's the allergy?" I ask mildly.

"Hives."

"Hives. Okay."

"I'm going to give him 50 mg of diphen-hydramine. You want a steroid, too?"

I think it over for a moment before answering. "No. Wound-healing issues. He doesn't need it."

"Okay. Whatever you say."

"Is that going to be a problem?" GG asks me, her eyes wide with concern, two brown orbs suspended over the horizon of her surgical mask.

"Nah," I reassure her. "It's no big deal. He'll be fine. Besides, what we really need now is some good closing music." Andrews doesn't like to listen to music when he operates. I do. Since it's his patient, he gets to call the shots as long as he's in the operating room. But he's not in the operating room anymore. "What've we got? Anybody? Anything?"

"I've got some stuff," the anesthesia resident replies, scrolling down his iPOD menu. He rattles off some options, and we eventually compromise on Norah Jones, whose sweet, organic lilt wrestles with the metallic, artificial snap of the staple gun as

GG and I finish the operation by firing stainless-steel staples into Mr. Bernard's skin to hold the edges of the incision together.

God, I love operating.

Life is good.

The languid strains of "Don't Know Why" chase away my residual annoyance over Mr. Bernard's botched antibiotic.

And, at this point, I'm blissfully unaware of how that simple mistake marks the beginning of the end of Mr. Bernard.

The surgeons' lounge, a spacious room adjacent to the OR, is unusually quiet for early afternoon on a Monday. Two heart surgeons I recognize but don't know by name are engaged in a hushed, intense conversation on a black leather sofa situated in front of a flat screen TV tuned to CNN with the sound off. On the opposite side of the room, a surgery resident with two days' worth of stubble and wearing scrubs with three days' worth of wrinkles snores thunderously in a broken massage chair. Nobody notices me walk in, grab a can of Diet Coke and a package of peanut butter crackers from the free supply in the refrigerator, and drop heavily into a chair in front of one of several computer screens lined up on a large table.

I try to concentrate on checking some patient labs and verifying Mr. Bernard's medication orders, but GG's comment in the OR lingers in my thoughts.

Strong hands.

Was she actually flirting with me?

Flirting.

The word sends electric jolts rattling down previously abandoned highways of my spine, an ego-stoking rush I haven't experienced since long before I was married. But I probably totally misread the signals. It's been so many years, I can hardly remember what flirting feels like; and, in any event, it's not like girls were exactly throwing themselves at my feet before I met my wife. I've always thought of myself as the average-looking kind of guy you see in beer commercials, the ones improbably hanging out with hot women. Not ugly. Just, you know, pretty much average. Okay, so maybe a *little* above average. GG's comment might have been completely innocent.

Besides, why am I even having this conversation with myself? Even if GG was flirting with me, it's not like I'm going to do anything about it. Right?

Right?

I glance over my shoulder. The heart

surgeons, still whispering urgently with one another, have gotten up from the couch. Oblivious to all else, they move past the unconscious surgery resident in the massage chair and out the door.

No one else is around.

I turn back toward the computer and gently stroke the smooth, worn keys without depressing any of them. My mind wanders back to the countless late nights I spent in college with my fellow geeks, hunched in cheap, wooden dorm chairs in front of our computers, strung out on beer and Mountain Dew and Fritos, amusing ourselves by slipping in and out of supposedly secure systems with impunity. These days, distracted by the burden of more adult pursuits like work and fatherhood, I've grown a little soft, and my skills aren't quite as sharp as they once were.

But they're good enough.

Despite all of her formidable talents, Sally isn't the most organized of people. In fact, she's constantly writing reminders to herself on sticky notes and posting them all over the house: which, of course, usually ends up defeating their purpose, since who can possibly keep track of them? Most end up carpeting the front of our refrigerator, merging into a multicolored quilt of phone numbers and to-do lists, bits of which flutter and drop to the floor like autumn leaves every time someone opens the refrigerator door.

Back when Sally was still working in Human Resources at University, part of her job was to oversee the electronic personnel files of all of University's employees — a position which, she confided to me at the time, gave her access to sensitive data on just about everyone from the hospital CEO down to the guy who waxes the floors. So when I happened one day across Sally's University computer ID and password, scrawled on a bright purple note stuck to the side of our home computer, I just couldn't help myself: My hacker instincts immediately kicked in, and I surreptitiously, if not a little guiltily, copied them down. I didn't use them, of course. For the most part, the University IT guys were, and still are, a bunch of idiots. Their security is a joke. But on the off chance I ever got caught breaking into the system, Sally would have been fired; so instead, I tucked them away for safekeeping. Just in case.

And then, right after Sally quit her job, I signed in to the system using her account, before the University IT folks had shut off her access. The rest was laughably simple: I made a few minor adjustments to the account so that it couldn't be traced back to Sally; and then, just to be sure, arranged the access to automatically run through a commonly used computer at a nursing station located on one of the busiest patient care floors in the hospital. That way, if anyone ever became suspicious, they'd trace everything back to that one computer, which dozens of different people use every day.

I've had unfettered access to the personnel files, and a whole bunch of other confidential information that runs through the Human Resources Department, ever since. Disciplinary actions. Malpractice suits. Medical-board inquiries. Patient complaints.

I'm not a creepy guy. Really. I'm just jazzed by the fact that I've pulled one over on the powers that be. I think it appeals to my basic hacker sensibilities. Just knowing that I have instantaneous access to this kind of data anytime I want is enough. It's not like I troll around the system, digging up dirt on my colleagues, or anything. In fact, even though I know exactly where to look, I've never before pulled the personnel files on any of the people I work with.

Until now.

Strong hands.

My head buzzing, I steal one more peek at my insensate companion in the massage chair, crack my knuckles, sign in to the system, and access GG's file.

Born in Pasadena, California. Undergraduate degree from MIT in electrical engineering, with highest honors. Marshall Scholarship to study bioengineering and organizational systems at Oxford University in England. Honors in every single one of her classes thus far at University Medical School. Truly, an overachiever's overachiever.

My cell phone abruptly buzzes in its hip holster. I take it out and look at the screen. The caller ID reads "Home."

"Hi, sweetheart." I clench the phone to my ear with my shoulder as I quickly close GG's file.

"Hi, sweetie. What are you up to?"

I study my Diet Coke and peanut butter crackers. "Lunch. How about you?"

She sighs wearily. "Lunch was a disaster. Tantrums. Food throwing. I have no idea what's with them. I sat them in front of a video a little while ago just to regain my sanity." Her voice softens, regaining a comfortable intimacy that pushes any remnants of GG from my thoughts. "*Anyway . . .*

How are *you* feeling? Are you ready for the meeting?"

"I think so. It's in about an hour. I was just about to get changed."

"Are you going to ask him about the job?"

"After last Saturday night, I don't think I have a choice."

In the background, I hear Katie shriek, "Mine! Mine!"

"Good God," Sally growls. "We'll talk later. Good luck, okay? I love you."

"Love you, too."

I put my phone down just as a hand claps me hard on the shoulder from behind, hard enough to make me wince in pain.

"Hey, Slick, what's up? Chatting with the old ball and chain?"

I scoot around to face the owner of the hand, whose bulky frame towers over me.

"Hey, Larry. Wait, what are you doing here? Are you operating today? Was I supposed to help you?"

He laughs good-naturedly. "Easy, Slick. Always on top of things, aren't you? Don't worry. You didn't miss anything. I was just checking on some new laparoscopic equipment coming in. Pretty cool stuff. Wait until you get to play with it."

Larry is my primary mentor and far and away my favorite professor. He has close-cropped, jet-black hair and a homely, open, amiable face that's dotted with old acne scars. Even though he tops out at well over six feet, four inches, Larry is surprisingly quick — so quick, in fact, he was an all-American linebacker at a Division I college. In the OR, as anywhere, Larry radiates a vibrant, manic energy: darting around constantly, always moving, always talking. I've never seen him sit still. He can't stand inactivity. Inactivity to him means inefficiency and wasted time. "Momentum!" He likes to exclaim in the OR when things aren't moving fast enough for him, "We need more momentum!"

And, man, he is an *awesome* surgeon. One of the best I've ever seen. He makes getting through the toughest operations seem like spending a sunny day lounging around at the beach. I've never seen him break a sweat or lose his cool — and I've seen him in some pretty tough situations. Even the other faculty members quietly acknowledge how good he is: a big deal for surgeons, who are usually reluctant to subject their egos to the kind of bruising it takes to admit someone else might be better in the OR.

Someday, I want to be the kind of surgeon that Larry is. I want to command that kind of respect.

He frowns at me, concerned. "Hey, you okay, Slick? You look kind of . . . I don't know, wiped, or something. A little pale."

"Nah, I'm okay. I just haven't been out in the sun enough lately." After talking with Sally, I'm now a little wound up by the prospect of my upcoming meeting with Dr. Collier, which is probably why I've lost some of my color. But I would never admit that to Larry. I don't want him to think that I'm weak — physically *or* mentally.

"Good. Hey, Steve, I saw a sweet case this morning in clinic. A big right adrenal aldosteronoma."

The prospect of a highly unusual and interesting surgical procedure is enough to temporarily quiet the butterflies knocking around my stomach. "Oh yeah? An aldosteronoma? I don't think I've seen one of those."

"It's a pretty rare beast. Even with my referral pattern, I've only seen three others over the last few years."

"Laparoscopic adrenalectomy?"

"Yeah, baby."

"Do you know when you're going to do it?"

"She's on the schedule for next week."

"Awesome."

"Yeah. Hey, by the way, how's that job hunt going?"

"Okay. I think Northwest Hospital might be getting ready to make a firm offer."

"Good for you. They're a strong group. Great reputation. Any other options?"

"Not really. No other bites so far."

"Have you met with Dr. Collier yet?"

"Later this afternoon. Why?"

"Just let me know how it goes," he answers cryptically. He punches my shoulder and speeds away.

The snoring resident mutters to himself in his sleep and rolls toward the wall.

Bemused, I rub my aching shoulder and turn back to the computer.

There's one more person I need to check on in the personnel files.

Luis Martínez, it seems, took a less traditional route than GG, or myself, or most other residents I know, to becoming a doctor. From his hometown of Los Angeles, he went straight from high school into the Marine Corps. No details on what he did or where he was stationed while in the Marines, but he was honorably discharged after ten years. Undergraduate degree from the University of California, Berkeley, with a double major in biochemistry and philosophy.

Philosophy?

I snort.

That's interesting. He never struck me as the philosophy type.

Still. A pretty smart guy. Harvard Medical School. Surgical internship here at University Hospital. Medical license in good standing from the Commonwealth of Massachusetts.

And something else. Something I've never before seen in this system.

An encrypted folder marked "Confidential."

Huh.

I wonder what *that's* all about.

I have just enough time to realize that the folder's encryption algorithms are quite secure, and well beyond my ability to crack them, before a door opens behind me, and I hear voices.

I hurriedly sign out of the system, erase the computer's Internet browser history, and start plowing once more through Mr. Bernard's medication orders.

An hour later, I'm sitting in Dr. Collier's huge office wearing a clean shirt, tie, and starched white coat. We face each other in comfortable leather chairs surrounded by a paper-and-glass sea of diplomas, medical-board certificates, awards, and signed pictures of famous, grateful patients. Soft classical music drifts from hidden speakers.

He starts off with some small talk, asking me about my family and such, then asks how the junior residents and the students are doing. He's particularly interested in GG, on whom he's already heard favorable buzz. I let him know everyone's doing fine and that GG seems to be the real deal.

He grunts his approval, settles back in his chair, and examines his elegantly manicured nails.

"So, Steven . . . since our last talk, have you given any more thought as to what you'd like to do next year after you graduate from our program?"

"Well, sir, we really enjoy living in Boston. Sally's family is here. So we were hoping to stay in the area."

"Mmm. I understand that Northwest Hospital has been speaking with you about a position."

"Yes, they have."

"That's a fine group." He's still examining his nails.

"Yes, sir, they are."

"If you're going into community practice, you couldn't do much better."

"No."

"Steve, have you considered *not* going into community practice?"

My heart hammers away at my chest as I struggle to play it cool. *Is this the opening I was hoping for?*

"I don't . . . I'm not sure I understand, Dr. Collier."

Dr. Collier's attention shifts from his fingernails back to me. He leans forward in his chair. The Italian leather sighs. "That is, would you consider staying here with us? At this medical school, in our department? As a member of the faculty?"

Yes!

"Ummm . . . honestly, I didn't know you were looking, Dr. Collier."

"Well, Steven, we aren't. Officially. But it's like the great football coach once said: Even if I don't have an opening on my team right now, if I see talent, I make an opening on the team. Do you know what I'm saying?"

"I think so, sir."

"Give it some thought. You're a talented young man. You have the potential to do important work in our field — with the proper guidance and mentorship, of course, which we can provide for you. I think you would do very well here with us."

"Thank you, sir. That's very generous. I

would most definitely be interested in staying here at University."

"Good. Now," he says seriously, his eyes narrowing, "bear in mind that this opportunity — I hesitate to use the word 'offer' at this point — is completely dependent upon your job performance for the remainder of this year. Any consideration of your staying on at University will be contingent upon the continued satisfactory execution of your duties as chief resident. Deviations will prompt immediate reconsideration of this opportunity. Think of the rest of your chief year as an audition, of sorts. Is that clear?"

"Thank you. I understand, Dr. Collier."

"Very good. You know, Steven," he says expansively, leaning back and spreading his hands, "academic medicine is an extremely rewarding pursuit. Joining the faculty of this medical school, fresh from my own residency training here, was one of the best decisions I ever made."

He rises from his chair. I follow suit.

Interview over.

We shake hands. He sits back down at his desk, studying the papers laid out in neat rows on top of it, already absorbed in his next administrative task of the day.

I leave his office with my feet floating six

inches off the ground.

Before I've gone ten paces from the door to Dr. Collier's office, I'm calling Sally to relay the good news.

It's late when I finally get home that night. The house is quiet. There's a light on in the kitchen. When I go to turn it off, I find a clean wineglass, a card, a single red rose, an unlit candle, and a half-full decanter of red wine with an uncorked bottle on the kitchen table. I gasp when I read the label on the bottle: an extremely expensive pinot noir that we've been carefully storing in our basement for the last several years, since our trip to California wine country. That was back before the girls came along, when Sally was still working, and we had some extra money. These days, with two kids and only my meager resident's salary to live on, we wouldn't be able to afford it.

I open the card. "Congratulations!" it reads. "I'm so, so proud of you and love you so much!"

"Way to go, Professor," Sally says from behind me. She's standing in the kitchen doorway, wearing a white T-shirt and pajama bottoms. "I thought I heard you come in. I was upstairs in bed reading." She walks over and hugs me. "I'm so proud of you," she whispers in my ear.

"You're amazing. You know that? I don't think it would have happened without you. Your conversation at the cocktail party greased the wheels for me."

"I know."

"How do you do it?"

"What can I tell you? You have your strengths, Mr. Surgeon. And I have mine." She looks me squarely in the eyes, very serious. "You know I'd do anything for you, right? And the girls? You guys are my life."

"What makes you say that all of a sudden?"

"No reason. Just because. I love you."

"I love you, too." I kiss her on the cheek and point to the wine. "I can't believe you cracked this wine open. It's one of your all-time favorites."

"Have some," she says, pulling up a chair. "We need to celebrate."

I usually never drink on work nights, but . . . what the hell? The job isn't guaranteed, but it's pretty much in the bag, and what better time than the present to pat myself on the back a little? So I pour myself a generous amount.

"But where's your glass?"

"I don't have one."

"Why?"

She holds up a home-pregnancy test-kit box and grins. "Positive. Twice."

"Holy crap!" The glass almost slips from my grasp, and some of the wine sloshes over the side and dribbles down my fingers, but I hardly notice. "Really? Why didn't you just say so, Sally? Oh my God." I reach across the table and hug her, spilling more of the wine on my shirt. "Oh my God." I'm suddenly as excited as a little kid who's just heard the tune of an approaching ice-cream truck. We've been trying for only a few months. 'Bella took a lot longer, almost a year (much longer than Katie), so I wasn't holding my breath this time. "I . . . wow. *Awesome.*" The words stumble out of my mouth. "Number three. A boy. Do you think it's a boy?" I lay my hand across her stomach. "It's got to be a boy. I *totally* deserve a boy."

"You're getting a little ahead of yourself there, Dad," she says, laughing.

"Wow. Number three."

"Number three." She gestures to the wine. "Have some."

"Yeah. I think I need it. But . . . you want me to drink without you?"

"I want you to celebrate *with* me. For both of us. For the job *and* the new baby."

"To our son, then." She laughs, and I take

a sip. Nice. Mellow and smoky, the wine meanders down my throat and unfurls warm tendrils through my chest. Sally lights the candle and turns out the kitchen light. We hold hands and gaze out the window.

Our tiny house sits on a small hill in Braintree, with the kitchen facing west. Far away, toward the Blue Hills Reservation, a lightning storm silently wreaks havoc, rending the night sky in violent bursts of white and blue light. It looks like it's moving this way. An ominous breeze stirs the trees in our backyard.

But here, for now at least, sipping the wine with Sally, the kitchen lit only by the flickering light of the candle, it's quiet.

"Do you remember when we first had this wine?" I ask.

She smiles. "What a great trip."

"I think that's when we made Katie."

"That's *definitely* when we made Katie."

"What was the play we saw? In San Francisco?"

"*Cats.*"

"That's right. *Cats.*"

"How could you forget?"

"Probably because I can't stand cats. And the play was lame."

"Cynic. I thought it was great. That was the, um, third time I'd seen it."

"Is that the one with . . . ?" I snap my fingers. "You know. What's that famous song? The cheesy one."

" 'Memory.' "

"Right. I'm sure that's *exactly* what T. S. Eliot's vision was when he wrote those poems: an actor in a ridiculous cat costume belting out some cheesy ballad."

"Stop." She hits me jokingly on the arm. "Don't pretend you didn't have fun. And there was that one character you really liked. Um . . . Deuteronomy. Old Deuteronomy."

"Was that the, like, older, leader cat?" I finish off my glass and pour another.

"Yes. You said that his songs were the only ones you thought really sounded like T. S. Eliot's poetry."

"Good memory." I laugh. "I totally forgot about that. Deuteronomy . . ."

"So. Complete change of subject. I met a nice woman last week at book club. Her name's Nancy McIntosh. Do you know her husband, Dan? He's a resident at University."

"Dan McIntosh? Yeah, I know Dan. He's one of the general-surgery chiefs. He's okay. A little hard-core — you know, in a general-surgeon kind of way. But generally an okay guy."

"I like Nancy a lot, but she's a little intense, too."

"What do you mean?"

"Well, she invited us to a barbecue they're having at their house next month, so of course I immediately offered to bring my special homemade potato salad. You know, the one everyone always raves about. Right?"

"Sure."

"And she said — now, let me get this right — she said, 'No, thank you. I think potlucks are gauche.' So they're having it catered."

"Really? She actually used the word 'gauche'? In casual conversation?"

"Yeah. It took me a few seconds to re-member what the word meant, then a few more to realize that I'd just been insulted. So I guess we're gauche." We laugh together.

"So what does she do?"

"She's a lawyer. With three kids, but still working full-time. Anyway, despite the gauche thing, I get the sense we really click. We're also going to be having dinner with them. I just wanted to give you a heads-up, and see if you knew who her husband was."

She yawns, leans back in her chair, and stretches, pushing her arms up over her head. Her T-shirt rides up to reveal her belly button and lower abdomen, which has remained remarkably flat after two pregnancies.

I drain the rest of my glass, lean across the table, and kiss her on the lips — lightly at first, then more deeply. She responds in kind, then pulls back and smiles.

She blows out the candle, takes me by the hand, and wordlessly guides me up the stairs. I peek in at the girls as we pass by their room at the top of the landing: Katie in her small bed, hemmed in by the wall on one side and a guardrail on the other; and Annabelle in the crib across from her. Their mouths are slightly agape; their tranquil, unlined features bathed in the soft yellow hues of the nightlight.

Sally walks into our bedroom ahead of me. When she reaches the bed, she spins around to face me and slowly, provocatively, takes off her T-shirt. I close the door to our bedroom.

Maybe it's the wine, or today's double dose of good news and the promise it brings of great things to come, but our lovemaking tonight is much more erotic than it's been in quite a long time. She sighs and moans and writhes as I explore the familiar contours of her body. The thunderstorm hits right as things are reaching their peak, and I'm grateful for the rain hitting the roof, and the thunder, which shield Katie and Annabelle from the unusually passionate clamor of their parents just across the hall.

CHAPTER 3

Wednesday, July 22

The last week has gone off without a hitch, except for one glaring exception: Mr. Bernard, the jovial carpenter from Maine. As if in direct challenge to my conversation with Dr. Collier, Mr. Bernard's recovery hasn't gone as well as it should have. In fact, it's gone pretty damn poorly. It's his kidneys: For some reason, they've stopped working, and we can't figure out why. It seriously bugs me, this single blemish on my otherwise spotless record.

Today, instead of our usual gathering in the cafeteria, Luis, GG, and I attend morning report: a weekly meeting of all of the residents, nurses, and professors in our department with a rotating schedule of educational, scientific, and administrative lectures. Morning report, as with all of our departmental meetings, is always held in a lecture hall located in the center of the oldest section of University Hospital. The hall was originally built in the middle of the nineteenth century as an operating-room theater, but it's since been converted into an auditorium with stadium-style seats facing a large projection screen and a lectern placed off to one side. Everyone calls it the Dome, a reference to its high, curved ceiling. Ornate marble lines the floor, and the wood-paneled walls groan under the collective weight of scores of fancy oil paintings and old black-and-white photos of the generations of redoubtable surgeons who paved the way before us, all stern, white males, their stale visages peering out over small bronze placards bearing the fading letters of their mostly forgotten names.

Luis, GG, and I find seats in the back of the room, near the projection booth. Today's talk is a dull treatise on billing procedures presented by some managerial University Hospital type with a shiny bald spot, nasal voice, bow tie, and cheap suit. Most of my fellow residents nod off, but I spend the entire time brooding about Mr. Bernard's kidney condition.

At the end of the lecture, Dr. Collier thanks the presenter and reminds the residents and medical students that, for those of us who recently volunteered to be participants in a University Medical School research study of a new experimental drug, the first round of dosages are going to be administered immediately after the meeting in the hallway outside the conference room.

I duly recall that I volunteered to be one of the human guinea pigs for this study, so after Dr. Collier formally dismisses us, I shuffle with the rest of the exiting crowd through the doorway and out into the hallway, where I line up behind some of the other residents in front of a folding table on which are placed a series of hypodermic needles, each labeled with a series of apparently random numbers and letters. Two guys wearing white coats and ties — one younger, the other older — stand behind the table.

Younger Guy looks bleary-eyed and tired. Older Guy, clearly a senior professor, is beaming rather greedily at us in a creepy kind of way.

A chair sits to one side of the table. As each subject sits down in the chair and rolls up their sleeve, they give their names to Younger Guy, who matches the name to a printed list, selects one of the hypodermic needles, then administers a shot.

Luis and GG fall in line behind me in front of the table.

"Is Mr. Bernard better today?" I ask Luis

hopefully.

"No," he replies. "I'm afraid he's worse. He threw up this morning, and his urine output dropped again overnight. He really looks like shit, Steve."

"Creatinine?"

"It's 4.5."

"Shit. That's up from 3.1 yesterday."

"Yeah."

I've reached the front of the line. I give my name, sit down, and dutifully roll up my sleeve. Younger Guy nods, checks his list, and chooses a syringe labeled *10032*. He vigorously rubs my shoulder with an alcohol swab. It's cool, and my skin tingles.

"Renal ultrasound?"

"Normal."

"Drain output — *Ouch!* Son of a *bitch.* What *is* that stuff?"

"We don't know," Younger Guy says, withdrawing the needle from my shoulder and applying a Band-Aid.

"What?"

"What my colleague means to say," Older Guy offers, smiling broadly and rocking back and forth on the balls of his feet, hands clasped behind his back, "is that you may be getting the placebo, or you may be getting the active drug. We don't know which. You're part of a double-blind, randomized

Phase II study."

"And the active drug is . . ."

"A melatonin derivative. It doesn't have a name yet. Very exciting stuff. Works to modify the body's response to sleep deprivation and disrupted sleep cycles. We think it helps allow people to function more effectively on less sleep. Sleep-deprived young people like you — overworked residents and senior medical students — are the perfect test subjects."

"Why not just let us sleep more?"

He beams at me and rocks back and forth on his feet.

"Okay," I say, rubbing my sore arm as I switch places with Luis. "So why can't we just take a pill?"

"Bioavailability issues," Younger Guy replies, selecting a syringe marked *10033*. "We can only administer it IM or IV. For now, it's IM. We're working on the oral formulation."

"And why did I agree to be part of this study again?"

"Probably because we're paying you a lot of money."

"Fair enough." I turn back to my junior resident. "So. Luis. Drain output?"

"Zilch." Luis doesn't bat an eye as the researcher jabs the needle into his shoulder and injects the contents of the syringe into his beefy deltoid muscle. "I don't think he's leaking urine from the reconstruction."

"Is he dry?"

"Maybe. It's tough to tell. Intravascularly, he's down. But he's net positive."

"Shit. Okay, so his acute renal failure is worsening. Why? We've ruled out most of the surgical causes. What do you think's going on? I need some answers." At this rate, Mr. Bernard's going to need dialysis soon.

Luis screws up his face as he rises from the chair. "I honestly don't know. Should we get renal on board?"

"Yeah. Good idea. Get a renal consult first thing this morning."

Luis jots down a notation on his worksheet.

"For you, *10034*," Younger Guy says. I watch glumly as GG sits down and receives her shot without protest, placidly staring off into the distance, as still as a statue.

Kidney failure.

Shit, I think to myself, absently massaging my sore shoulder.

I *hate* kidney failure.

CHAPTER 4

Friday, July 24

I'm changing out of my scrubs in the OR locker room, getting ready to head out after a long day. By now, our team has settled into a well-oiled routine. Luis continues to do a great job. And as for GG . . . well, GG is a bona fide superstar. Enthusiastic and effusive, her knowledge and skills are years beyond her level. She makes other University Medical School students — some of the best in the country — look like complete slackers.

But she's more than just a great med student: She's a machine. Absolutely fanatical. I've never seen anyone, med student or doctor, with such an all-consuming passion for medicine. Starting IVs, drawing blood, writing orders, checking lab and radiology results, helping out with operations — she's seemingly everywhere at once; always in a good mood, always with a serene smile on her face. Every morning, she's the first one through the hospital door; every night, she's the last one to pack up and head home. That is, when she even bothers to go home. Most nights, she'll stay in the hospital to help out the resident on call, catching a few hours of broken sleep in one of the doctor sleeping rooms.

Since her comment to me in the OR, she hasn't said anything even remotely flirtatious. But, every so often, I catch her looking at me just a beat too long; and once, sitting in the cafeteria opposite her, I could have sworn she deliberately rubbed her leg against mine: up one side, then down the other. It was probably just my imagination; but in my own mind, at least, it's enough to make me uncomfortable.

Meanwhile, after running a bunch of tests, the kidney specialists announced yesterday (rather pompously, I thought) that Mr. Bernard's kidney failure was caused by a rare condition called allergic interstitial nephritis — brought on, unfortunately, by the antibiotic he accidentally received during his operation. That one stupid medication, Cefotetan, set in motion the molecular chain of events leading to his present state. The kidney guys told us that it's only a temporary problem and that his kidneys should recover completely. Eventually. Luckily, he won't be needing dialysis.

But compounding Mr. Bernard's problems, and my own frustration, is that he's now also suffering from a condition called ileus. Ileus is what happens when the intestinal muscles shut down, like gears freezing up in a machine. Soon after his kidneys had started to fail, Mr. Bernard's abdomen became swollen and tense, simultaneously expanding like a balloon and tightening like a drum in grotesque disproportion to the rest of his body, like he had swallowed a basketball. Then he started puking his guts out.

There's very little we can actually *do* to make ileus better. It's frustrating as hell. The treatment for it is practically medieval. First, we keep the patient from eating or drinking, a treatment euphemistically referred to as *bowel rest.* Then we snake a plastic tube through the patient's nose, down the esophagus, and into the stomach. Which pretty much sucks — for both the patient and the nurse or doctor putting down the tube. Then we wait for the intestines to start working again.

So now, with a plastic tube stuck down his nose, and a thick IV line plugged into his chest to pump liquid nutrition directly into his veins, Mr. Bernard sits in bed, patiently waiting for his kidneys and intestines to start working again. Meanwhile, as the days have dragged on, Dr. Andrews has been getting increasingly pissed off, looking for someone to blame. I'm at the top of the list. So, my job prospects on the line, I've been quick to deflect Andrews's ire every chance I get toward the anesthesiologist who gave Mr. Bernard the antibiotic in the OR. I don't think it's working.

I decide to pay Mr. Bernard a quick visit before leaving the hospital for the night.

By design, luck, or both, Mr. Bernard has locked himself into a prime piece of hospital real estate: a highly coveted private room, perched atop one of the newest wings of the hospital, lined with bay windows that command a sweeping view of the downtown and waterfront. I usually find him these days sitting in a chair in front of the windows, gazing at the cityscape shimmering in the thick summer heat, watching the rest of the world continue on without him.

Which is where he is tonight. He manages a smile as I walk through the door, as he always does, but it seems a bit frayed. In fact, he looks rotten. He beckons to an empty chair next to his and asks me what I'm doing still in the hospital.

"Working," I respond tiredly, settling reluctantly in the chair. I don't want to stay too long.

"Things going okay, Steve?" Despite the way he must be feeling, his expression and tone express a genuine concern.

I like Mr. Bernard. I like him a lot. But I don't like it when patients call me by my first name. It's weird. It places us on a level of familiarity that just doesn't seem quite right, especially after I've had my hands inside their abdomens, pulling on their intestines. I don't correct Mr. Bernard, of course. That would just be rude.

"Just a little busy."

"Why aren't you going home? It's Friday. I've seen you here every night late for the past week. Why don't you go home? What about your rug rats?"

"Well, I've got a lot of responsibilities."

"Oh." His eyes narrow fractionally. "I get it. A lot of responsibilities. I guess I wouldn't understand something like that."

"That's not what I meant, Mr. Bernard."

"Yeah, I know. And I've told you a hundred times, Steve, call me Stu. Mr. Bernard's my father. I swear, you doctor types are way too freakin' uptight."

He shakes his head and adjusts himself in the chair with a grunt and a wince, then

103

folds his hands neatly on his lap. They're craftsmen's hands, worn and callused, but also graceful and dexterous-looking. Whenever we talk, whether he's sitting in the chair or lying in bed, he usually has them folded self-consciously in his lap, like he's guarding his livelihood. I guess the way he makes his living isn't too different from the way I make mine, after all: with his hands.

"Don't have a family myself," he says. "Marriage and kids and all that. It's not my style. Got a lady friend who lives with me. Been together a long time, my lady friend and me. She took some time off to be here for the surgery. Do you remember her?"

I do — a thick, sturdy woman with a bronze face as weathered as the paint on an old New England shore house and wispy blond hair beaten senseless by God-knows-how-many years of sun and salt. I remember talking to her in the waiting room after his surgery. She smelled like fresh sawdust. I smile and nod.

"She had to go back home for work. It's tourist season, you know, and she's been pretty busy at her bar." His thick Yankee accent transforms "bar" into "bahhh." "She calls me every day, though. I think she's, ya know, getting a little lonely for some lovin'." He winks at me, then smirks. His eyes dart down to his groin, and for a moment I think he's going to grab himself to emphasize the point he's making, but he doesn't. I grin back. "Good thing it's still attached, after what you did to me. Funny how I don't remember anything from the operating room. You sure you people really saw what I wrote on my dick?"

"Absolutely." We've been over this several times already. As I had guessed would happen, he's completely forgotten our conversation from right before his operation, when I spotted the DO NOT REMOVE written on his penis. "It's those drugs we gave you. They made you forget."

"I wish I remembered the looks on your faces," he says wistfully. He turns toward the window, his craggy face as inscrutable as a granite wall.

"I know how it is, though, Steve," he rumbles. "I used to be busy all the time, like you. Too busy to sweat the little things. My lady friend and me, we talked a lot about traveling. Going to Florida. We've never been to Florida. I'd like to see alligators. You know, go to one of them alligator farms? Where them crazy guys actually wrestle those big bastards? We got plenty of money saved up. Never really had the time to get down there. Figured there'd always be time. But you know what happened then?" He faces me again, a rueful smile playing about his lips.

"What?"

"Then one day somebody told me I had cancer." He pauses. "Someday, Steve, somebody might tell you that you have cancer."

He turns away. We peer at the city in silence. The only sound is the mechanical whir of the IV machine, like the gears of an old-fashioned grandfather clock, spinning fitfully as it pumps life-sustaining fluids into Mr. Bernard's veins.

After a while he asks, "Do you believe in God, Steve?" God comes out as "Gahd."

The question catches me completely off guard. I've never had a patient ask me that before. "Ummm . . . well, honestly, I don't think about it that much . . ."

"Do you go to church? Or temple, or something like that?"

"Uhhh, on Christmas, I guess. Sometimes." My cheeks burn a little, and I'm thankful he's still looking out the window.

"Do you ever think about death, Steve? I mean, your death?" He dismisses me with a wave of his hand before I can reply. "Nahh, of course you don't. Young as you are. You're surrounded by dying people every day, and I bet you don't give it a second thought." He tilts his head incrementally to one side. "Not that I blame you. I didn't used to, either."

"Huh." After thirteen years of college, med school, and advanced medical training, I can't think of anything more intelligent to say.

He's quiet again for a long time. Then, just as I think the conversation has ended, he says, "I'm not afraid, you know."

I slide back into my chair, from which I had started to rise. "Excuse me?"

"Of death," he replies matter-of-factly. "I'm not afraid of death. I figure it's like Socrates said: Death is a blessing no matter what happens after you die."

He scoots his torso around, wincing and holding his belly with both hands. "You know what I mean, right, Steve? About what Socrates said?"

I know what Socrates said. I've read *The Apology.* I'm just a little surprised to learn that Mr. Bernard knows what Socrates said. I open my mouth, then close it, unsure of how to respond.

"What, with all that school you doctors have to go through and all, you never bothered to learn about Socrates and what he had to say about death?"

"I know what he said," I answer, with just

a hint of indignation.

He grins at me playfully. "I'm sure you do. A well-educated doctor like yourself. And don't go looking at me like that, Steve."

"Like what?"

"Like with that 'how in the hell would a dumb-ass-working-stiff-high-school-dropout-like-this-jerk-know-anything-about-Socrates look on your face. Plain as day. Jesus, Steve. Don't ever try to play poker. You'll get your freakin' ass kicked. Anyways, so the way I figure, it's like this: Death is a win-win situation. Either it's paradise or sleep. So there's nothing to be afraid of. I've treated people good, and I believe in God, so if there's an afterlife, I'll go to paradise or Heaven or whatever, and like Socrates said, I'll hang out and see cool people who died before me. Like Jerry Garcia. Man, I'd love to hang with Jerry."

He winks. "But, if there's no life after death . . . well then, the way I figure it, I'll be in the deepest, most peaceful sleep ever, and won't know any better anyway. That isn't such a bad deal, either." He looks down, grimaces, and pats his swollen belly. "Sure as hell would beat the crap out of this." His gaze wanders back to the window. "I just want to see them alligators first," he says quietly. "Just as soon as I get my ass out of this hospital and back into the world."

"We'll get you out there just as soon as we can."

"Yeah. Yeah, I know you will." He suddenly seems very tired. "How many kids you got again, Steve?"

"Two."

"How old are they?"

"One's five, the other's ten months. Two girls."

"Daughters. Daddy's girls. Very nice. So explain it to me again, Steve: What are you doing here talking to a chump like me, and you've got those two rug rats waiting for you, along with your pretty young wife, at home?"

"I . . . had some things to do. To finish up. I, uh, have this weekend off."

"Right. Some things to do. Always things to do." He reaches out his hand, lays it on my arm, and leans toward me. The movement has an underlying urgency to it, and I'm startled to see that his eyes are wet. "Remember, Steve: The moment we're born, we start dying. We spend our lives dying. Some of us just get there sooner. You never know when you might hop off the local and end up on the express to death. Think about it."

I pat his outstretched hand, the one lying

gently on my arm, and tell him not to worry, that he's going to make it, that we're going to get him out of the hospital soon, and that there's a good chance we cured his cancer.

He shakes his head wearily, like a teacher with a slow student who just doesn't get it, and gazes into my face sadly for several moments before taking his hand off my arm, leaning back in his chair, and focusing his attention back to the cityscape.

"I think I'm done talking to you now, Steve," he says quietly.

As I'm leaving, I stop at the door and study his determined, craggy profile.

He looks strong. Indestructible, even, despite his grotesquely swollen belly, which pokes out from the folds of his thin hospital gown, and the thick plastic IV lines that tunnel into the skin of his arms and dive underneath his clavicle bone, tethering him to the metal IV pole standing next to his chair like air hoses attached to a deep-sea diver.

Those IV lines might as well be chains securing him to the chair, because he's trapped here in the hospital, just as surely as if he were in jail.

All because of me.

I shut the door noiselessly behind me.

It's the last time I ever see Mr. Bernard alive.

CHAPTER 5

Monday, July 27

I'm back from my weekend off, digging with flourish into a plate of steaming, syrup-laden pancakes, having successfully purged my mind of both Mr. Bernard and my guilt during a trip to the Franklin Park Zoo with my family. Sitting across from Luis and GG in the cafeteria, recharged with precious sleep and downtime, I'm refreshed and totally psyched up, ready to start off a new week by hearing that Mr. Bernard has turned the corner. But then Luis tells me that Mr. Bernard's belly is still blown up to the size of a watermelon and that there are no signs that his intestines are starting to work yet. GG, sitting next to him, nods in agreement. My good mood abruptly turns foul, and my temper flares.

Goddammit, I fume to myself. *Why didn't this problem get fixed over the weekend? Do I need to take care of everything myself?*

112

"The other problem is that he's seriously hypokalemic," Luis continues. "And we're having a hard time keeping up with his repletion." GG nods again.

Shit. It's always something.

"Why is his blood potassium level so low?" I growl.

"I'm not sure, but he seems to be losing a lot of K in his urine." Luis uses the resident slang term for potassium — the letter *K* — which sounds pretty cool, even though its origin is anything but: K is the symbol for potassium in the periodic table of the elements. Talk about geek chic. "I'm thinking that he's peeing out K right now because of his renal failure. I think he's starting to diurese."

"Okay, well, just add some potassium to his TPN bag."

"His kidneys still aren't working that well," he responds coolly. "His creatinine today is" — he scans the computer printout lying on the table next to his food tray — "3.5. His GFR's still less than 20. He's getting better, but slowly. With his renal function in flux, there's a decent chance that, with a constant potassium infusion from his TPN, he'll get hyperkalemic."

Hyperkalemic. That means too much potassium in the blood. Luis is afraid that Mr.

Bernard's weakened kidneys won't be able to process and filter the potassium that we give him and that it will begin to accumulate in his blood. It's a valid concern. Too much potassium in the blood can cause serious heart problems and even death.

But I'm skeptical. And thoroughly annoyed. I think Mr. Bernard's kidneys, which have been getting better, are up to the task.

Stubborn, Sally's voice whispers in my brain. I shove it aside.

"I doubt it," I counter. "If he's really losing that much K in his urine. Just go easy on the amount of K you put in the TPN bag. And keep checking levels. I'd much rather give him a steady amount of K and keep his blood levels stable rather than responding to low levels ad hoc. It makes us look bad. Like we don't know what we're doing."

"But . . ."

"Just fix it, Luis," I cut in angrily. I've no patience this morning for debating with my junior resident. Particularly in front of GG.

Luis's eyes narrow, and the corner of his mouth twitches. It's the first time I've seen him show any emotion and, for a beat, I think he's going to challenge me. But then he says, "Okay. Fine. I'll put some K in the TPN bag. But just a little. I really don't think this is a good idea, Steve."

"I really don't care what you think, Luis. Just fucking fix it already. Please. This patient should have been home last week. It's making us look bad." And I can't afford to look bad. Not if I want that professorship.

Besides — he needs to go to an alligator farm with his lady friend.

We run through the rest of the patients on Luis's list. There are no other major issues. I polish off my cup of coffee and head up to the OR. Sullen and bored, worried about Mr. Bernard, and pissed that we haven't been able to fix him yet, I participate without any real enthusiasm in the first two surgeries of the day, which are both dull.

But the third operation, scheduled after lunch, is cool, and my outlook brightens in anticipation as the start time approaches. It's the case Larry told me about last week: an adrenal gland tumor. The patient is a woman who needs to have her right adrenal gland taken out. Although the tumor is not malignant, it's been secreting a hormone into her bloodstream that has increased her blood pressure, made her retain water, and caused her to have severe headaches. The hormone is called aldosterone, so the tumor is called an aldosteronoma. Aldosteronomas are very rare and very interesting. Cutting them out of people is surgery at its purest and best: All we have to do is take out her adrenal gland, and the tumor with it, and she's completely cured. Clean, simple, and to the point.

I find the patient, Mrs. Samuelson, in the pre-op area, surrounded by her family. Friendly and effusive, she frets about how young, pale, and thin I look. She's chubby, with freshly scrubbed skin and thick gray hair that she wears in a long braid. The braid makes her look much younger. Her laugh is quick and easy and reminds me of wind chimes twisting in a light breeze.

She's from a small farming town. She's lived there all of her life, venturing out now only because she has to for this operation. It's easy to picture her in a busy kitchen, surrounded by her family, just as they surround her here in the pre-op area. Her three daughters look and sound exactly like her. They fuss and fret nervously, smoothing out the sheets of her gurney and adjusting her pillows.

Standing two paces from the gurney, looking thoroughly uncomfortable, is her husband. He has rough, callused palms, a pack of Marlboros tucked in the front pocket of his flannel shirt, stoic features, and not much to say. Standing next to him are two equally stoic sons-in-law, each with their own callused palms, flannel shirts, and packs of Marlboros. They have even less to say. The third son-in-law, I'm told, is out in the waiting room with the patient's new grandson, no doubt similarly dressed and stocked with Marlboros.

While she's being readied by the OR staff, there's a little bit of a fuss when Mrs. Samuelson refuses to remove her wedding band — it's OR policy for patients to remove all jewelry. But she finally relents, twisting it off her finger and handing it gingerly and, with great reluctance, to her husband.

After I'm done meeting the family, I walk over to the OR to check out our room. I like to do that before every operation, like a pilot inspecting the outside of a plane before takeoff, or a driver kicking the tires of a car. The scrub nurse is there, laying out instruments for the case. So is Larry, who's sitting on a stool and typing on a laptop perched on his knees, bristling with manic energy.

"Hey, Slick, what up?" He grins, puts his laptop aside, jumps up, and greets me with a fist bump.

"You ready to operate today, or what, Slick?"

"Always, Larry, always."

"Strong. Let's look at her scan."

Mrs. Samuelson's CT scan is projected on a large hi-def screen in a corner. Larry and I study it together. The right adrenal gland, the site of Mrs. Samuelson's tumor, sits on top of the right kidney, underneath the liver, and next to a big vein called the inferior vena cava, which we call the IVC for short. The IVC is the largest vein in the human body and looks like a bright white circle on the CT scan. The tumor is an ugly, misshapen sphere that pushes up against and slightly deforms the IVC.

"Looks like the tumor's lying a little medial," I say. "Right up against the IVC. Tiger country, huh?"

"Yes. Yes, it is." Larry rubs his chin, lost in thought, like a general surveying a field map before a battle, composing his plan of attack. He stands perfectly still. The manic vibe dissipates, and he suddenly looks and sounds very serious, every bit the Professor of Surgery. I've seen him do this before when he's worried about a patient, or — as with this case — planning out a particularly challenging operation.

"It looks pretty well circumscribed, so hopefully we'll be able to peel it away from both the IVC and the liver. But I agree: That medial dissection might end up being a bitch. It's really tough to see exactly where the right adrenal vein is — here, maybe?" He taps the screen with his finger. Identifying the adrenal vein, and preventing it from bleeding, will be an important part of the operation. "I'm not sure. We'll find out once we're in there."

"Do you think we'll have to convert to open?" I ask. I'm wondering if we'll have to make a big incision in Mrs. Samuelson in order to finish the operation.

"No, I don't think so. I think we can stay laparoscopic."

He glances furtively over his shoulder at the female nurse unpacking surgical instruments on the other side of the room, then leans toward me, and whispers, "Converting from laparoscopic to open is for pussies who don't know how to operate laparoscopically. You're not a pussy, are you, Slick?"

I chuckle. "Not the last time I checked, Larry."

"Good," he booms. The mania has returned. "That's what I like to hear. I'm glad you're going to be assisting me today, Slick. I need your skills. I hope you came ready to play." He claps my shoulder, hard.

"Larry, I always come ready to play." I try

my best to sound manly and not wince from the sharp pain now shooting up my shoulder.

The anesthesiology resident, a petite redhead named Susan, brings Mrs. Samuelson into the room with the anesthesia attending. They put Mrs. Samuelson to sleep, then deftly slip a breathing tube into her throat and hook it up to the ventilator that will breathe for her during the operation.

Now it's our turn. Larry and I gently lift Mrs. Samuelson onto her left side and secure her into position with padded foam straps. Once Larry and I are scrubbed and the sterile field is set up, we stick a needle through the skin of her belly button and start inflating her abdomen like a balloon. Literally — a machine pumps carbon dioxide through the needle and into her abdomen. The gas fills the enclosed space that lies between her abdominal organs and overlying muscles. Her plump belly quickly swells to several times its normal size, separating her abdominal wall from the internal organs lying underneath. We then make three small incisions with the scalpel across her abdomen, through which we insert a fiber-optic video camera and several thin surgical instruments.

When patients recover after surgery,

they're mostly healing from the damage done to them during the surgery itself, not from the disease that prompted the surgery in the first place. The goal of minimally invasive surgery is to speed up recovery by doing as little damage as possible. In traditional surgery, we make big incisions so we can stick our hands inside patients to operate. In minimally invasive surgery, we make small incisions through which we insert long, thin surgical instruments shaped like oversized chopsticks. Minimally invasive surgery is a much more precise way of operating than traditional surgery. I think of it as high-tech robbery, stealing valuable objects out of patients without touching anything else, making clean getaways from the insides of their bodies as if we'd never been there. It's also a lot like playing video games: Because we can't directly see the tips of our instruments, which are inside the patient, we instead stare at a video monitor mounted over our heads, using the images transmitted by a camera placed through one of the incisions to guide our movements.

Some researchers believe that my generation, the first truly video generation, has been naturally trained to do this kind of surgery from childhood. I've been cranking on joysticks ever since I could crawl, and there's no doubt in my mind that my gaming skills have crossed over to my surgical skills. Larry recognizes this, too. As we begin, he stands next to me, holding the video camera, intently watching the video screen, letting me do most of the work. Larry is partial to Led Zeppelin, so as I start poking around Mrs. Samuelson's abdomen with the oversized chopsticks, "Kashmir" from *Zeppelin 3* thrums from the speakers of Larry's iPod. Luis, interested in learning about this operation, soon joins us, taking control of the video camera from Larry so that he can follow my movements like a cameraman for an NFL game.

We find the tumor right away: a big, bright yellow ball pushing its way out from underneath the liver, just above the kidney. It looks completely out of place among the normal organs in Mrs. Samuelson's abdomen, a suspicious stranger skulking around an otherwise good neighborhood. Using the electrocautery, I begin to gently peel normal tissue away from the tumor and cut it away from the organs sitting next to it.

Today is a good day.

I'm in the Zone, baby. Definitely. I'm in that place where I know I can do no wrong. It feels great. Better than great. It's absolutely exhilarating. My hands seem to know where to go, to have taken on a sentience all their own, to consider multiple moves, then act without my even thinking. It's like I'm standing there, staring at the screen, a spectator in the room, watching my own hands operate. I barely have to think as I steer my instruments through her abdomen. What a rush.

Mrs. Samuelson has what we surgeons like to call a *virgin belly*. This means that she's never had an abdominal operation before and that her internal anatomy is absolutely pristine, just like a textbook, undistorted by scar tissue caused by prior hands probing inside her in search of appendixes or gall-bladders or uteruses to remove.

Larry stands next to me with his arms folded, at turns coach and cheerleader. He otherwise doesn't help. He doesn't need to. I make steady progress and, chipping away at the tumor like a sculptor working a piece of marble, carefully cut the attachments holding it in place inside her body, one by one. After an hour of meticulous work, I've released most of those attachments, and now the only major portion still anchoring the tumor to the rest of Mrs. Samuelson's body is the one that's sticking to the IVC. It's the same part Larry was worried might be tougher than the rest to cut out. It's also the part where, more likely than not, the main blood supply of the tumor is located.

Larry tells me to stop. He darts over to the video monitor on the other side of the table. He squints at the image, pressing his face up to within inches of the monitor, tilting his head — first one way, and then the other — before nodding approvingly.

"Okay, okay. Good, Slick, good. You're doing a great job. Keep going along that plane there" — he points to a spot on the screen — "but now I want you to start marching this way" — he draws an arrow in the air in front of the screen with his gloved finger to indicate direction — "*carefully*. We're not sure where the adrenal vein is yet. Okay?"

"Okay, boss. No problem." I'm sure it won't be.

Larry returns to my side of the table, and I start operating in the direction he indicated. But a few minutes later, Larry gets a call from one of the other ORs. The chairman of general surgery has unexpectedly run into trouble and needs some help. Immediately. And he wants Larry personally for the job.

This kind of thing happens a fair amount. Larry's so good that, whenever another surgeon at University gets in the weeds during a difficult operation, Larry's often the one they call for a hand.

Although I'm sure there's a part of Larry's ego that secretly loves it, and revels in being the go-to guy for some of the most important surgeons in the hospital, for the most part today he's annoyed. The patient is in an OR located in a different area of the hospital, and he'll lose several minutes just walking back and forth, not to mention however long it takes him to solve the other surgeon's problem. But this isn't a request, really — it's an order. So he sighs heavily and steps away from the table, ripping off his sterile gown and gloves while muttering obscenities.

"Okay, Slick," he says. "I need you to fly solo for a while. It should only take a few minutes. I'll be close by if anything happens. Keep going along that tissue plane I showed you. But once you get to the medial aspect of the tumor, where the adrenal vein is, stop and wait for me. I think it's going to be a really tough dissection in through there, and we may run into some serious bleeding. I don't want you trying it by yourself."

Fair enough. "No problem, Larry."

"I'll be right back." He leaves the room.

I turn to the video screen and stare at the

tumor: big, fat, and a grotesque shade of puke yellow.

It glares back defiantly, as if taunting me.

Well, what are you waiting for, Slick? Are you scared now that Daddy's not here anymore to hold your hand?

I think about my next move. In my left hand, I'm holding a pair of forceps: essentially a pair of metal pincers, like pliers, used to grasp and hold on to things. That's fine. But I need something for my right hand, which is empty.

"Sucker, please."

The scrub nurse hands me the sucker. I slide it through the plastic port and into Mrs. Samuelson's body. Its magnified tip appears on the video screen next to the forceps. The purpose of the sucker is exactly what it sounds like. The technical term is *vacuum suction device*. But everybody I know calls it a sucker, which is pretty descriptive, since it sucks blood and other bodily fluids away from the operative field so that surgeons can see what they're doing. Since being able to see what you're doing is one of the more obvious components of a successful operation, it's an immensely important surgical instrument, but it tends to be underrated because it's not as glamorous or sexy as the other ones. But I also like to use the sucker to dissect things during an operation, a habit I picked up from Larry. Now I put the sucker to good use, gently sweeping the tumor off the other tissue as I slowly but steadily march along the path Larry marked for me.

Sweep, sweep, sweep. Using the sucker, I delicately brush the tumor away from the tissue that's holding it in place. Things continue to go very well, and I begin to wonder what Larry was talking about. After all, this part of the dissection isn't so bad. Certainly not as bad as he thought it was going to be. My confidence swells, and I pick up the pace, swinging the sucker in ever-more-aggressive arcs that increase the speed of the operation and take me closer toward the area around the as-yet-unseen IVC and adrenal vein.

The area Larry told me not to work on by myself.

That last thought gives me pause. I stop to survey my handiwork. I'm now very close to the most dangerous part of the operation, and I really should stop and wait at this point for Larry to come back. I've never done anything like this before. But a large portion of the tumor, previously trapped in place, has peeled away in response to my work, curling away from the healthy tissue

127

to which it was previously clinging. I imagine that separated edge of tumor flapping in an imaginary breeze, begging me to keep going, to keep taking it off, to march ahead and finish the operation.

In my head, the tumor starts mocking me again.

You ain't no pussy, are you, Slick?

I decide to keep going. A little more progress before Larry gets back in the room won't hurt anything. Besides, I know what I'm doing.

Luis isn't so sure. "Steve. Shouldn't you stop and wait for Dr. Lassiter to come back?"

"No. We're okay. We've got some great momentum going with the dissection, and the exposure is perfect. If we stop now, we're going to lose our momentum *and* our exposure. I'm sure of it. That's a good teaching point for you, Luis: If you've got momentum going during an operation, try not to lose it. Besides, do you know what surgeons say about asking permission to do something?"

"No, what?"

" 'It's better to beg forgiveness than ask permission.' Remember that."

" 'Better to beg forgiveness than ask permission.' Roger that."

Sweep, sweep, sweep. I keep teasing the tumor away from the healthy tissue with gentle sweeps of the sucker. It's coming off perfectly now, as easily as peeling a self-adhesive postage stamp or sticker off the backing once you've worked off that stubborn first corner. Just a little bit more, and I'll have the tumor out before Larry's even back in the room.

"It's tough sometimes being so good," I say, sighing. Luis guffaws, jerking the camera. The image on the video monitor momentarily bounces up and down. The motion reveals a hint of blue at the bottom of the screen.

"Hey," I say, my excitement growing, "is that the IVC? Luis, zoom in on that blue patch." He does. It's the IVC. It's perfect, exactly the location where I want to be.

I rule.

"Yep. That's the IVC all right. Excellent. So if we push on it up in this direction . . ." I push upward on the tumor with the sucker. In response, the tumor slides smoothly away from the IVC. "We should be home free."

I push again in the same direction, and then again, and then again. Each push separates the tumor from the IVC a bit more. The tumor starts to move up and

129

away from the IVC in exactly the way I predicted.

Then, suddenly, it stops.

I push some more, but the tumor won't budge.

"Hmmm. It seems to be really socked in right here," I narrate to the rest of the room. Surgeons do that sometimes to help them think. "There must be some desmoplasia from the tumor making it stick a little bit. No big deal. I'll just have to push a little harder right about . . . here."

I move the sucker to a different spot on the tumor and push again.

Nothing.

"Maybe try the scissors here?" Luis asks.

"No . . . I think I'd rather stick with blunt dissection for now. I wouldn't want to stick the scissors directly into the IVC. The tumor's just putting up a little bit more of a fight now. No big deal. I'll get it."

I pick another spot on the tumor and push against it again with the sucker, a little harder this time, with steady and firm pressure, trying to coax it off the IVC just a little bit more.

It gives a little.

Bingo.

The tumor is stubborn, but so am I.

I push again.

The tumor gives a bit more, and suddenly I can feel that it's almost there, that there's just one more small spot that's still holding it to the IVC, just one more point to release before I'm home free and the hardest part of the operation is over. I can feel it. I know it. So I keep pushing up on the tumor. Up, up, up.

The edges at the sticky spot separate. The tumor starts to peel away again.

Yes! I imagine Larry walking back into the OR, checking out my progress, duly impressed at my having done such a difficult dissection all by myself, slapping me on the back, recognizing Slick's skills.

Almost there . . .

The tumor stops peeling. Again I push a little harder, up and up with steady, firm pressure, confident now that the sticky spot will give the same way it did before.

Suddenly, sickeningly, it does give.

It gives the way a stuck window that's been shut all winter gives during spring cleaning, after you've pushed against it with all of your might for several minutes, grunting and gasping and wheezing in the dust, until it slams upward against the top of the frame with a loud crash.

The resistance, *all* of the resistance, disappears.

My hand holding the sucker jerks forward. Bright red fluid jets upward like a geyser. *Blood.*

Before I have time to react, the jetting blood envelops everything on the screen. Tumor, kidney, liver, IVC, my instruments — all disappear underneath a bright red sheet of blood. It's as if a thick red curtain has dropped over the entire operating field. I can't see a thing. Everything is gone, lost in a disorienting, monotonous field of redness.

I feel my stomach drop through the floor. *Fuck.*

Sweat instantaneously materializes over every square centimeter of my body, my heart starts hammering away at the inside of my chest, and my breath feels like it's been knocked out of my body by a two-by-four.

"Oh, *shit,*" Luis gasps.

Behind me, I hear the scrub nurse sharply suck in her breath.

I frantically sweep the sucker back and forth, trying to part the red curtain and figure out what's going on, to figure out where the bleeding is coming from so I can put a stop to it before Mrs. Samuelson bleeds to death.

But nothing happens. The screen remains

a perfect, unblemished scarlet. There is only the red. There is nothing else. I can't see anything. And because I can't see anything, I can't do anything. I'm absolutely helpless.

Oh, God, please no. Please no. Oh God. Oh God.

My hands begin to shake so badly I can barely hold the instruments — which doesn't seem to matter too much at this point since I can't see the instruments anyway with all the blood in the way. I grab the camera from Luis and jerk it around, hoping to find a clear spot, but see nothing.

The bleeding, where's the bleeding coming from?

The steady, rhythmic beep of the cardiac monitor speeds up, jolted out of its earlier, complacent cadence by Mrs. Samuelson's heart, which has started beating faster in response to the blood now squirting ferociously into her abdomen.

"Anesthesia? I'm having some trouble here." I try to sound calm. I know I don't.

In response to the increased tempo of the cardiac monitor, Susan has already tossed her textbook aside and is standing up, her body tensed, perfectly motionless except for her eyes, which dart between her cardiac monitors and the video screen.

"I'm having a little trouble. We've got

some bleeding. Pretty brisk. Probably from the IVC, maybe something else, too. I can't tell where for sure. I think we're having some serious volume loss here."

Serious volume loss is euphemistic surgeon talk for *bleeding like a stuck pig.*

"Please call your attending now!" I call, still focused on the unchanged red image on the video screen, all the while sweeping the camera around with my left hand and futilely moving the sucker back and forth with my right. "And make sure she's got an active type and cross!"

Susan starts working furiously, simultaneously grabbing the telephone with one hand and one of the patient's IV lines with the other.

I try one more feeble pass with the sucker, groping this way and that, hoping that I'll get lucky, that I'll find the source of the bleeding, that everything will turn out okay, willing with every neuron in my brain for the blood to go away but at the same time knowing that there's not a chance on God's green earth that it will.

Nothing happens, of course. The absolute redness of the screen doesn't change one iota. Presumably, Mrs. Samuelson's blood continues to gush from the big hole I'm sure I've made in the biggest vein in her body and there's nothing I can do about it.

She's bleeding to death right before my eyes.

Raw, primal panic slams over me with the force of a sledgehammer. I freeze, staring at the video monitor in disbelief, paralyzed by what's happening, still holding the camera and sucker but doing nothing.

The blood, inscrutable and indifferent, stares back. I suddenly wish I were somewhere, anywhere but here. I feel as if I've plunged over my head into a frigid, roiling, black ocean, and I'm completely disoriented and don't know which way to swim to get to the surface.

All I want to do at this moment is drop everything and run home and hide in a closet and hope all this crap just goes away and everything goes back to the way it was before the bleeding started.

Shit, shit, shit. It's all my fault.

"Steve!" Luis is frantically tugging at the sleeve of my gown.

My fault.

"Holy shit, Steve!" Luis screams.

My fault, my fault, my fault.

"Do something! Let's convert! Holy shit!" He's practically yanking my arm off now in an attempt to get my attention.

Convert.

"Convert!"

Convert?

Right. Convert.

I've got to convert.

Right now.

Luis has managed to pull me back into reality, to jerk me to the surface of that dark ocean, by reminding me that the only option we have at this point is to pull out all of our laparoscopic instruments and make as big an incision as possible in Mrs. Samuelson's side so we can stick our hands inside her body and control the bleeding the old-fashioned way. To convert as quickly as we can from a minimally invasive surgical procedure to a maximally invasive one.

It's the only shot we have at saving her life.

"Call Dr. Lassiter. Now — 911!" I yell to no one in particular over Zeppelin, which is still playing in the background. "Give me a scalpel. We're going to convert. And turn off that goddamn music!"

I quickly open all the laparoscopic valves to let the carbon dioxide out of Mrs. Samuelson's belly. It escapes with an angry hiss, and her abdomen deflates like a popped balloon.

Luis and I start ripping the sterile sheets off so we can make a bigger incision in the skin. But the adhesive strips that hold the sheets to her body cling to our gloves and quickly become tangled like pieces of Scotch tape that stick to your fingers when you're trying to break them off from the dispensing role. Luis and I curse and fumble, losing precious seconds and even more precious blood, as we try to peel them off our gloves.

The cardiac monitor is really going now. Mrs. Samuelson's heart rate, which had been perking along at a nice, normal 70 beats per minute a moment ago, is up to 180. The individual, discrete beeps that signify each separate heartbeat are beginning to merge into a single, high-pitched, plaintive whine.

That's a really bad sign.

More ominous still, Mrs. Samuelson's abdomen is rapidly expanding again, filling up now not with carbon dioxide but with the blood that's supposed to be pumping through her arteries and veins but is instead now gushing ineffectually into her belly.

What a fucking flail.

"Her pressure's dropping," Susan calls out loudly. Too loudly. She sounds even more scared than I feel. "She's down to 60 systolic." The anesthesia attending arrives a second later and immediately takes control, forcing fluid and medications into Mrs. Samuelson's bloodstream to keep her blood pressure up while he calmly calls for emergency blood.

But all that barely registers because Luis and I have finally managed to get the sterile sheets off and expose enough of Mrs. Samuelson's skin to make a bigger incision. I seize the scalpel from the nurse and, in spite of my hand, which trembles like a leaf in a hurricane, manage to quickly carve a large incision that reaches first across her rib cage, then down her abdomen toward her belly button.

As I slide the blade down the length of her body, the scalpel in my hand and the sight of her skin parting like an opening mouth give me new resolve. I clutch the scalpel like a life preserver, dumping my will into its steel. I've got to do something, anything . . . and this is the only thing I can do.

I slice through Mrs. Samuelson's flank and abdominal muscles and enter the area immediately surrounding her kidney. A river of blood suddenly gushes up and washes over the sides of the incision and onto the floor like water from an overflowing dam. I'm not wearing the protective, waterproof shoe covers that I'm supposed to slip over my regular street shoes, and I can feel the warm blood spill over my sneakers, soak through my socks, and gather in sticky collections between my toes.

I place my sucker in the middle of the red torrent streaming out of her abdomen, but I might as well be trying to vacuum up a lake with a Dustbuster.

"I need another sucker. Now!"

Somebody thrusts one in my hands. I give it to Luis, and he plunges it into the middle of the blood, and, together, our two suckers make an obscene slurping sound as we try to keep up with the furious current.

But it's not enough. I still can't see anything. I move my sucker around with one hand while I reach around inside Mrs. Samuelson's abdomen with the other, desperately trying to find the anatomic landmarks that will guide me to where I think the bleeding is coming from.

I've never seen this happen before. I'm not really sure what to do. Worse yet, her intestines keep getting in the way, coiling through and over my hands like a nest of greased, wriggling snakes, obscuring my view. I try to move them out of the way, but they immediately slip right back through my fingers. It's like I'm trying to see down to the bottom of a bowl full of red-colored noodle soup using only my fingers.

As I struggle, I start to feel the panic close in around me again. The questions shoot rapid-fire through my brain, but I have no answers.

What do I do? How do I get my bearings? Where do I put my hands? How do I stop the bleeding? How do I keep her from dying right in front of me?

At that moment, Larry rushes in, tying his surgical mask.

"What's going on?" he rasps. His breath is coming in short, sharp gasps, the same as mine. His eyes widen as he absorbs the bloody scene playing out before him.

Thank God.

"I think we've got an IVC injury," I bark. "I've converted, but I can't find where the hole is. I can't see anything with all the blood."

"Goddammit! Gloves, now! Steve, get out of my way!"

In an instant his gown and gloves are on, and he's at the table shoving me to one side with his muscular frame. He hasn't bothered to scrub. It's a significant breach of sterile protocol, but protocol is pretty much out the window at the moment. As I dart around to the other side of the table next to Luis, Lassiter plunges both hands into Mrs. Sam-

140

uelson's abdomen up to his elbows.

"Suck!"

Luis and I comply, following Larry's darting hands with the suckers as he gently but quickly coils up the intestines.

"Towels, rolled! And a big Rich. Now, now, now!"

The scrub nurse hands him several rolled-up towels. He adroitly pushes the intestines to one side, places the towels and a large metal retractor over them, and then thrusts the handle of the retractor into Luis's hand. I peek inside Mrs. Samuelson. Except for the blood, the path through her body to the IVC and kidney is now clear. The intestines are completely out of the way, held from our path by the towels and the retractor.

"Now, suck!" Larry shouts. "Suck, goddammit! I can't see a fucking thing."

Luis and I do our best to keep up with him, holding our suckers underneath the bubbling, gurgling red pool, as Larry gropes around inside Mrs. Samuelson, his hands shifting this way and that underneath the roiling surface of the bloody pool. After a few moments he pauses and looks up at the ceiling, hands motionless. Over his hands, the surface of the blood shifts, swirls, and gurgles into the tips of the suckers.

141

"Sponge stick!"

He seizes the sponge stick — which looks like a long, thin pair of pliers gripping a soft white bandage in its jaws — from the nurse's outstretched hand and carefully positions it with the bandage pointing down below the surface of the blood and the handle sticking up in the air.

"Steve, take this. Push down as hard as you can." I grab the handle and push with all my might.

"Another sponge stick!" He repeats the gesture, positioning the second sponge stick a hand's length away from the first.

"Steve!" He shakes the handle of the second sponge stick, my cue to grab it. I hand my sucker over to Luis and comply.

"Harder, Steve! Push harder, goddammit!" I do. The blood is flowing more slowly now. Whatever Larry is doing seems to be working.

"Keep sucking, Luis!"

Slowly now, as our suckers wheeze and cough, the blood begins to clear from the operative field.

It's working. Whatever Larry's doing, it's working. The blood slowly empties from her abdomen like water draining from a bathtub. Her organs — the liver, intestines, kidney — gradually reappear, like islands emerging from a red lake. Normal anatomic landmarks take shape.

"There it is." Larry's voice is starting to regain some of its normal equanimity. "There's a big-ass tear in the IVC, all right. And a partial avulsion of the renal hilum. *Fuck.* The renal artery's holding on by a fucking thread. We're going to have to take her entire kidney to get the bleeding under control. Satinksy!"

I peer into Mrs. Samuelson's belly. The damage is even worse than I had imagined. There's an ugly, jagged gash in the middle of the IVC, as wide as my pinky and half as long, starting where her adrenal vein used to be and extending down the long axis of her body toward her feet. The renal artery and vein, which take blood to and from the kidney, are partially torn, and the kidney now dangles limply from its blood supply, like a broken tree branch that's been snapped by a strong windstorm.

As I'd suspected, I've ripped the adrenal vein right off the IVC, exactly the kind of mistake Larry had wanted to avoid. I realize now that the tips of the sponge sticks I'm still gripping in my hands are pushing against the IVC on either side of the huge gash, forming pressure points that temporarily impede the blood flow, like feet stepping on a garden hose. I never would have thought of doing that.

Larry takes the Satinsky clamp, an instrument vaguely resembling a backyard barbecue tong with a bent handle, and closes it across the gash in the IVC. He then takes a second clamp and closes it across the ends of the torn renal artery and vein.

The bleeding stops.

Larry's shoulders stoop a little, and he looks up wearily from the operative field to address Susan and her attending, who continue to work furiously at the anesthesia end of the table. "Okay, Anesthesia, we've got control of the bleeding. How's she looking up there, Carlos?"

The anesthesia attending looks at his monitors and grimly shakes his head. "Not good. We're looking at maybe a four-liter blood loss, plus or minus, over a very short period of time." So that means Mrs. Samuelson has lost about 70 percent of all the blood in her body. Thanks to me. "It's been tough to keep up with that kind of resuscitation requirement. I'm giving her packed red cells as fast as I can, but she's still tachy and hypotensive. I'm also seeing some diffuse ST elevations. I think she might be having an MI from all that acute volume loss." In other words, the anesthesiologist is telling us that she's probably having a heart attack because there's not enough blood in her arteries to feed her oxygen-starved heart.

Larry sighs heavily and mutters "Goddammit" so softly that only Luis and I can hear him. He then says more loudly, "How about her coags? What about the coags?"

"Coagulation parameters are okay, I think. For now. Her pre-op INR, PT, and PTT were all normal. I've got repeat parameters pending, and she's getting platelets and FFP right now. How is she down there? Oozy at all?"

"No, not really. Okay. I'm going to finish up and get the hell out of Dodge so we can get her off the table as fast as possible. Carlos, you do whatever you need to up there. Okay, man? Just let me know if there's anything I can do."

"Will do."

Larry goes to work repairing the damage I've done. I don't know what to say, so I start with the obvious. "Larry, I'm so sorry."

"Not now, Steve."

"But . . ."

"I said not now." His voice is calm, but low and menacing. I've never heard him talk that way before.

He sews the hole in the IVC closed with

sure, experienced movements, then quickly finishes taking out both the tumor-filled adrenal gland and her otherwise normal kidney, which can now no longer stay in her body because I've completely disrupted its blood supply. He speaks little, and then only to issue a succinct order to Luis or me as we assist him, or to ask the anesthesiologist how Mrs. Samuelson is doing. Otherwise, he doesn't acknowledge my presence or anything that's happened until we're stapling the skin incision closed.

"Steve, goddammit, I told you not to try that dissection on your own," he growls. He doesn't look up from what he's doing. "Why the fuck didn't you wait for me?"

"I'm sorry. I thought I could handle it —"

"You thought wrong," he interrupts. He shakes his head in disgust. "Jesus *fucking* Christ. Simultaneous avulsion of the right adrenal vein and renal hilum, with a corresponding tear in the IVC. Can't say I've ever seen that one before. How the fuck did you manage to tear both the renal vein *and* the artery? Congratulations, Steve: You just invented a completely new surgical complication. Jesus *fucking* Christ."

He's quiet again until the skin of her large incision — much, much larger than it should have been, I reflect glumly — is completely closed, and we're stepping away from the table. Luis is taping the dressing to her skin as Larry and I peel off our blood-soaked operating gowns and drop them wearily into a trash can marked red for biohazards.

"Steve . . ." he starts to say, but then shakes his head. "No, never mind. I can't talk to you right now. I really can't. I can't even fucking look at you." He stalks toward the door, calling over his shoulder, "I'm going to go talk to her family now and try to explain to them what the fuck happened and hope to Christ they don't end up suing the crap out of me. Just get her settled into the SICU."

At this point, he stops and spins around to glare into my eyes — the first time he's looked at me full in the face since this all happened — and stab at me in the air with his index finger. "And call me immediately, I mean *fucking immediately,* if there are any more problems. Do you understand?"

"Yes."

The OR door bangs closed after him.

I tell Luis to go finish up any work he has to do with the other patients, then head home for the day. He leaves without saying a word. I wonder what he's thinking.

The OR nurses, Susan, the anesthesia attending, and I carefully lift Mrs. Samuelson off the operating table and onto a special bed. Her long white ponytail spills out from underneath her scrub cap and curls down around the breathing tube that sticks through her swollen, cracked lips. She's too sick to breathe on her own. Her face is as puffy as a heavyweight fighter who's taken a twelve-round beating, the result of all the intravenous fluid and blood we gave her during the operation.

We wheel her out of the OR and out into the hallway leading to the SICU. Her family is already there, lining the hallway on both sides, probably alerted to our imminent transit by Larry. They form a gauntlet of seven anxious, drawn faces through which we have to run to get to the SICU. They watch in shocked silence as we slowly and ponderously wheel Mrs. Samuelson down the hall in her big bed, awkwardly dragging all of her life-support monitors and intravenous lines along with us. Susan manually pushes air into Mrs. Samuelson's lungs by squeezing a bright green plastic bag attached to her breathing tube.

In the middle of the hall, we stop briefly to let her family look at her. They close in and form a tight semicircle around the foot of the bed. One of the daughters cups a hand over her mouth and bursts into tears, wailing. With surprising tenderness, her stoic husband drapes an arm across her shoulders, and she buries her head in his chest.

Mr. Samuelson's eyes are moist. "How long before we can be with her, Doc?" he asks quietly. I explain that the doctors and nurses in the SICU need about forty-five minutes to get her settled in. He nods. "All right, sir. We'll wait right here."

We continue down the hall, struggling with Mrs. Samuelson's bed, which handles like a monstrously heavy shopping cart with broken wheels, until we finally pass through a set of automatic double doors into the SICU. The SICU is a large, circular room ringed by multiple glass-walled cubicles, each of which houses a critically ill patient. The cubicles line the outer wall of the room, forming a continuous circle broken only by two doors: the main entrance, through which we just passed, and a smaller, nondescript, employees-only door tucked between two of the patient cubicles on the far side of the room, exactly opposite the main entrance and accessible only with our coded University Hospital badges. Most of us refer to it simply as the back door. In the center of the room, from which all of the patient cubicles are visible, like the hub of a wheel, is a nurses' station with computer workstations, cardiac monitors, desks, and wheeled chairs.

We pause in front of the security guard and unit secretary seated at the nurses' station facing the front door.

"Which bed?" I ask wearily. "We're coming from OR two." The unit secretary directs us to an empty cubicle. Susan and I secure the bed in it as several nurses appear seemingly from nowhere. They quickly gather around Mrs. Samuelson, checking her vital signs and heart rhythm while hooking her up to a ventilator, chatting amiably about happy hours at local bars. They never miss a beat, expertly calling out vital signs and running diagnostics on the life-support machines even as they compare margarita specials.

I give a report to a harried-looking SICU doctor and then double back through the main doors and out into the hallway. There, I practically stumble over Mrs. Samuelson's family, who are clustered just outside.

Dammit.

I forgot they were there. I should have snuck out through the back door.

Mrs. Samuelson's family looks at me expectantly, silently pleading for more news, any news, I can offer.

Where do I begin?

What do I tell them?

The truth? That I single-handedly almost killed one of the most important people in their lives? Ripped the biggest vein in her body to shreds because I thought I knew what I was doing? Turned an otherwise fairly routine surgical procedure into a complete disaster?

"I'm so sorry," I manage to stammer. "Things were going well, but it was a really big tumor and then, well, we ran into some trouble . . ." I pause, groping for the right words.

Mr. Samuelson steps forward and clears his throat. "We understand, Doc." His tone is surprisingly paternal, like *he's* the one trying to make *me* feel better. "Don't beat yourself up too much. The other doc, your boss, already told us everything. Things happen. We understand. You folks are doing everything you can, and we appreciate it. We surely do. We're just so glad she's in such good hands. Other hospitals, she might not have made it. But here, well, you folks are the best. We're sure you folks are going to get her through this, with the Lord's help."

The rest of the family nods in agreement. "God is good," one of them murmurs. Even the daughter who had been wailing a few minutes ago out in the hallway is bobbing her head up and down emphatically, her cheeks flushed and wet. Her red eyes, glistening with hope and misplaced trust, are fixed on me. She sucks in her breath in short bursts as she chokes back her sobs.

"She's strong. She'll make it," I say. I have no idea if that's true or not. I don't know if she really is *strong* — whatever the hell *that* means — and she most certainly might not make it. She might die. She might die tonight, for all I know. But I can't think of anything else to say, and I've learned that it's usually the kind of stuff that families always want to hear from doctors in situations like this one.

She's strong. She's a fighter. She's going to make it.

Mr. Samuelson smiles. He actually smiles. "Yes. You've got that right, Doc. She's a strong woman. She surely is. She always has been. She's fought herself out of tighter spots than this one. Hasn't she, girls?"

All three daughters smile and murmur their agreement, wiping the tears from their eyes.

Suddenly, all I want to do is get away from these people as quickly as I possibly can. I smile weakly, shake hands with Mr. Samuelson, each of the daughters — the one with the tear-soaked cheeks keeps repeating, "Thank you, thank you so much, Doctor, thank you" — and the sons-in-law, and walk away.

That's when it hits me.

My stomach flips over, and a wall of saliva inundates the inside of my mouth. I grit my teeth and manage to dart around a corner where Mrs. Samuelson's family can't see me before stumbling into a bathroom. I lurch into the stall nearest the door just in time.

I drop to my knees and clutch the sides of the toilet, emptying the contents of my stomach into the bowl, heaving again and again; and suddenly I'm not a thirtysomething surgeon anymore at one of the best hospitals in the world, but a clueless eighteen-year-old kid again, squatting on the cold, indifferent tile of my college-dorm bathroom, regretting one too many plastic party cups full of foamy, frat-party beer.

I go on like that for a long time, intermittently puking and panting. Minutes, hours . . . I've no idea how long I'm there, retching and miserable on the floor in front of the toilet. Somewhere in the middle of it all my pager goes off, and I think I simultaneously hear a voice on the hospital's overhead public announcement system, as if through a tunnel, but I could not care less. My known universe has shrunk to the size of that porcelain bowl.

When I'm finally done, I flush the toilet and push myself up, using the sides of the stall for purchase. My stomach muscles, atrophied by years of an exercise-free lifestyle, scream as I inch my way up to a stand. My legs are trembling, but I manage to let go of the sides of the stall without falling. I try to swallow the vile taste lingering in my mouth, but I can't; the back of my throat is raw from the stomach acids that washed up along with my lunch. I stagger to the sink and turn on the water, dousing my head, letting the cool stream rush over my face and into my mouth. It's late now, and the rest of the bathroom has, mercifully, remained empty.

Oh, God. This sucks. This really, really sucks.

My pager goes off again. Somehow, the shrill chirp sounds more incessant this time. I'd forgotten it had gone off earlier.

I pull it off my belt and read the text message.

. . . 911 . . . Mr. Bernard coding . . . 911 . . . Mr. Bernard coding . . . 911.

Simultaneously, I hear the disembodied,

154

dispassionate voice of the hospital's overhead announcement system call, very clearly now. "Code Blue, Johnson Building, twelfth floor. Code Blue, Johnson Building, twelfth floor."

Code Blue.

Cardiac arrest.

Johnson 12 is Mr. Bernard's floor.

You have GOT to be kidding me.

I run to Mr. Bernard's room on shaky legs.

It's a total flail.

The second one of the day.

Mr. Bernard's room is on the other side of University Hospital and, because of my late start and crappy physical condition, by the time I get there, the code team has already been working on him for a while.

People are running around the room, shouting. It's the controlled chaos of a code, with nurses, medical technicians, and doctors weaving around one another like a crazy, hyped-up square dance. And in the middle of it all, the center around which this medical maelstrom is directed, is Mr. Bernard, lying on his bed, motionless and completely naked.

At the head of the bed is an anesthesia resident, rhythmically squeezing air into Mr. Bernard's lungs with a big green balloon attached to a plastic breathing tube that snakes through his mouth and down to his lungs. The balloon is called an Ambu bag. Each time the resident squeezes the Ambu bag, it makes a wheezing sound — *weeha* — as it blows oxygen through the tube and into his lungs, exactly like a giant bellows.

At the center of the bed, GG is working on Mr. Bernard's lifeless body, doing chest compressions, pushing down on his sternum with grim diligence. Mr. Bernard's torso bounces down and up — *down, up, down, up* — as GG pushes and releases, pushes and releases. Meanwhile, from the top of the bed, the anesthesia resident isn't even trying to conceal the fact that he's staring straight down GG's scrub top. In the middle of a fucking code.

An intern at the foot of the bed, a member of the code team, calls, "Hold compressions!" and GG and the anesthesia resident stop and back away. The medical resident squints at a portable cardiac monitor set up on a chair next to him. I can't see the screen from where I'm standing.

A second intern from the code team is clutching a pair of defibrillation paddles — for some strange reason, the old-fashioned kind that you hold in your hands rather than the newer ones that you simply stick on the patient's chest with adhesive labels. He yells, "One, I'm clear! Two, you're clear! Three, everybody clear!" with the eagerness of someone who's obviously never gotten to defibrillate someone before. After everyone else backs away, the resident steps forward and, with a flourish, slaps the paddles on Mr. Bernard's chest and depresses the buttons. Mr. Bernard's body convulses weakly. It's never as much as you see in the movies or on TV, but his lackluster response to the 200 J of electricity pouring into his body is discouraging.

"No rhythm, continue CPR," the intern at the foot of the bed calls. Defibrillator Resident backs away, paddles in hands. The anesthesia resident starts squeezing the Ambu bag again — *weeha, weeha, weeha.* GG steps forward and starts pushing on Mr. Bernard's chest — *down, up, down, up.*

Mr. Bernard's not going to make it. I can tell right away by the way he looks.

Mr. Bernard is going to die tonight.

In fact, he's pretty much dead already.

The medical resident overseeing the code is a mellow-looking guy with sandy brown, sleep-tousled hair. Standing quietly in a corner, gazing intently at the interns, he's wearing a wrinkled University Hospital scrub top over a white T-shirt, tan Gap slacks, and white sneakers. I introduce myself and ask him what happened.

He hands me an EKG strip, his gaze fixed on the code team and Mr. Bernard. "This is what we got just before he went into torsades, then pulseless v-fib arrest."

With my finger, I trace the dark, sharp peaks and valleys of Mr. Bernard's heart rhythm running across the pink-and-white-colored strip of EKG paper.

"Hyperkalemia?"

"Yes."

"Is that why he arrested?"

"Probably. The last K we got back was 8.1."

Mr. Bernard's heart stopped beating because he has too much potassium in his blood.

"And you guys treated him for it?"

"Sure."

"You tried the usual stuff? Calcium gluconate, insulin, glucose?"

"Yeah. Of course. Nothing worked. By the time they called us, he was too far gone to be able to do much about it. Way too gone." He stifles a yawn, then looks at me as if something has just occurred to him. "Hey, any reason you guys would have given him potassium today? This patient doesn't have a history of kidney disease, but I noticed he has a recent history of acute renal failure. In this situation, at the top of my differential for acute hyperkalemia would be an exogenous source of potassium overwhelming renal filtration in the setting of low GFR."

So he thinks Mr. Bernard's been over-dosed with potassium.

"Have you guys given him any potassium recently? You know, in his medications or IV fluids? I reviewed his medication history over the last few days, but didn't see anything that popped out at me."

I'm about to say no, of course not, why would I ever give a patient with kidney problems a dose of potassium, when I spot a half-empty TPN bag hanging on an IV pole next to Mr. Bernard's bed.

The TPN bag reminds me of the conversation I had with Luis and GG in the cafeteria this morning.

When I told them to put potassium in Mr. Bernard's TPN solution.

Despite Luis's concern that Mr. Bernard's kidneys might not be able to handle that much potassium all at once and that he would end up hyperkalemic.

Fuck.

For the second time today, my stomach drops through the floor, and I feel like I'm going to start throwing up again.

I look at the EKG again, then at Mr. Bernard's lifeless body as GG rhythmically pushes on his sternum — *down, up, down, up* — keeping time with the anesthesia resident forcing oxygen into Mr. Bernard's otherwise motionless lungs with the bright green Ambu bag — *weeha, weeha, weeha.* The activity in the room has slowed, most everyone now recognizing the futility of their efforts. Those not directly involved with resuscitating Mr. Bernard have either fallen back to the periphery of the room to watch expectantly or quietly wandered out the door and back to their usual jobs.

GG trades positions with a burly male nurse, who attacks Mr. Bernard's chest with macho gusto, at one point jerking down a little too hard with one of his chest compressions. There's a loud crack, like the sound of an enormous stick of celery being snapped in half, and Mr. Bernard's sternum breaks cleanly down the middle, his chest collapsing like a deflated accordion. A few *oooohs* escape from the remaining crowd.

Defibrillator Resident tries shocking him again. Mr. Bernard barely twitches. They might as well be trying to electrocute a rock.

"Well . . . we did put some K in his TPN," I admit reluctantly, as much to myself as to the medical resident, whose head now swivels from the code to me. "His serum levels had been running a little low, and we were trying to replete him." I'm staring now at the half-empty TPN bag, and the medical resident follows my gaze. "He's been hypokalemic lately, so we figured we'd just replete him by putting potassium in the TPN solution. We didn't give him that much — just enough to get his blood levels back up. At least, that's what we had calculated."

Actually, I have no idea if Luis really calculated out the proper amount of potassium based on Mr. Bernard's renal function or not. I hope he did. I suspect he just made an educated guess. That's what we usually do. It's normally not a problem.

"Really." The medicine guy hesitates, his face expressionless as he considers this new bit of information and stares at the half-empty TPN bag. Then he shrugs, and says, "Well, you can't be too sure that the TPN was the source of the K. Or at least the only source. I mean, if like you say, you didn't put that much K in the bag, and that you really calculated it based on his most recent GFR." He turns back toward me. "How much did you put in it?"

I haven't the faintest idea how much potassium Luis put in the bag. "Umm . . .

I'd have to go back and check our notes. See how we crunched the numbers again. We've had a lot of stuff going on today."

"Right. Sure. It probably wasn't that much." The medicine guy's voice is flat. His expression is blank. But the unspoken message I catch from his bloodshot eyes is pretty clear. *Stupid surgeon. Putting potassium in the TPN bag of a patient with acute renal failure. What an idiot.*

The medicine guy's reaction isn't surprising. I'm sure he thinks he's the smartest guy in the room. Medicine guys are the types of people who love memorizing obscure diagnoses and worthless facts, schooling themselves with bits and pieces of medical arcana that make them sound smarter. They love to know stuff like the species of scorpion that can cause pancreas inflammation — a handy piece of medical trivia that might help you out in case you ever happen to be stung by a scorpion while camping in certain areas of rural Mexico. (Or maybe not, since if you're unlucky enough to develop pancreas inflammation from a scorpion sting while camping in certain areas of rural Mexico, you're probably pretty much screwed no matter what you do.)

And most medicine guys are convinced

that, as a group, surgeons are brainless Neanderthals who cut first and ask questions later. Surgeons, for their part, think that medicine guys are overeducated wimps who talk a good game but never do anything about it. ("Intellectual masturbation" sniffed a general surgeon I know as we walked past a bunch of medicine guys on rounds one time, who were earnestly discussing some obscure disease outside a patient's room.)

Still, I'd better get used to the kind of withering look the medicine guy is giving me right now. I have a feeling it's going to be happening to me a lot after tonight.

"Look," the medicine guy says after an awkward pause. "The patient's not responding at all, and we've been going at it now for almost twenty minutes, mostly because I wanted to let my junior residents and interns practice running a code. But I'm getting ready to call it. Is that okay with you?" He stifles another yawn and checks his watch.

I nod, numbly. He's right.

"You'll take care of all the death-certificate paperwork, right? That's your responsibility, you know. It's not my job. My attending will back me up on that."

His reluctance is understandable. Death

certificates are a pain in the ass to fill out.

"I'll take care of it."

"Good." He gives the order to stop the resuscitation, formally pronounces the time of death, wishes me luck, and disappears.

Just like that, everyone stops, packs up their stuff, and clears out of the room: doctors, nurses, medical technicians. I step to one side as one of the nurses rumbles past me with the crash cart, loaded with the defibrillator and emergency medications.

Nobody looks back.

The junior residents and interns who ran the code clap each other on the back and compare notes as they saunter out the door.

Defibrillator Resident is euphoric. "Did you see me shock that guy?"

"That was *awesome,*" his companion replies enthusiastically. "Nice job. And you got to use the old manual defibrillator paddles! Old-school! Wow, what a rush. Too bad he didn't make it . . ."

Then, abruptly, it's just me, GG, and Mr. Bernard.

I slowly walk to the side of Mr. Bernard's bed. The floor of the room looks like something out of a crack den, littered with empty syringes and medicine vials and used IV bags. I pick my way carefully through the debris. GG follows me and stands by my side. Together, we gaze down at Mr. Bernard.

He doesn't look peaceful. The dead are supposed to look peaceful, but Mr. Bernard appears anything but. His head is tilted back at an unnatural angle, with his defiant chin pointed toward the ceiling, and his mouth is wide open, as if he's trying to scream around the breathing tube still lodged in his throat; and all of his limbs are tensed, as if he's trying to jump off the bed but can't, his muscle proteins beginning to lock up in the early stages of rigor mortis. Ugly, dark streaks crisscross the ashen skin of his thin chest: electric burn marks, tattooed by the defibrillator. His sternum, snapped by the overzealous chest compressions, is caved in like a pothole on a city street and contrasts sharply with the steep convexity of his massively swollen belly.

I thank GG for her help. She looks like crap: utterly spent, with flushed cheeks and beads of sweat running down her face, hair tousled, her chest still heaving up and down from the effort of the code. Most people don't realize how physically demanding it is to perform chest compressions. I'm sure her arms and shoulders are going to be sore as hell tomorrow. Her exhaustion seems as much emotional as physical: There are big dark circles under her eyes, and she looks very, very sad. Still, underneath the sadness, something else, too, stirs. I can see it in her eyes. A manic energy; something close to exhilaration, even.

Strange. But I've seen that reaction before. Hell, I've *felt* it before: that rush you get while trying to snatch a life back from death's clutches, win *or* lose. It's like those medicine interns just now, high-fiving each other, jazzed about the defibrillator. It was probably GG's first time at a code, and you remember your first code the way you remember other big events in your life, like your first kiss. It's that intense.

I tell her to go home and get some sleep. Instead of protesting, as she normally would, insisting that she stay and help, she just mumbles thanks and shuffles away.

Now it's just me and Mr. Bernard.

I stare at him for a long time.

I think of the DO NOT REMOVE scrawled on his penis.

I think of alligator farms.

I think of unfinished business.

I wonder whether right now he's in the deepest sleep ever or chatting with Jerry Garcia.

"All finished, Doc? I need to take him downstairs." A big man stands indifferently at the door, his huge hands on his hips, cracking gum. He's wearing a dirty white lab coat with the word "Pathology" embroidered across the left pocket in cursive. There's a metal gurney parked in the corridor behind him. He's waiting to take Mr. Bernard to the basement.

To the morgue.

Jesus, that was fast.

The nurses must have called him a long time ago, while the code was still running but its outcome appeared inevitable. I can't really blame them. Nobody likes having a dead body hanging around a busy hospital floor.

I nod numbly and glance at Mr. Bernard one last time as the man starts cramming the metal gurney and his own massive frame through the doorway. Then I remember that I still don't know how much potassium Luis actually put in the TPN solution. I pick my way through the debris over to the IV pole and read the label stuck to the front of the half-empty TPN bag hanging next to the bed.

Potassium chloride: 20 mEq.

In one liter of fluid.

Only 20 mEq of potassium, in this volume of fluid, is hardly any potassium at all. Practically nothing. I guess Luis had, just like he said he would, erred on the side of caution by putting only a little bit of potassium in the TPN solution.

Strange, though. Just 20 mEq of potassium shouldn't have been enough to cause hyperkalemia. But, then, I've seen weirder things happen in the hospital. I push the question from my mind. Right now, I've got more important things to worry about.

I leave the room as the guy from Pathology starts heaving Mr. Bernard (Mr. Bernard's *body,* I correct myself) onto the metal gurney, then walk down the hall to the nurses' station, where a mountain of paperwork — incident reports, death-certificate applications, medical charting, adverse-event notes — awaits me. It's always that way after a patient dies.

But the first thing I have to do is call Mr. Bernard's lady friend — his designated contact, it turns out; Mr. Bernard didn't report any immediate family on his admission paperwork — and let her know what happened. I pull the phone number from Mr. Bernard's chart and dial it. I'm immediately routed to her voice mail and wonder what the protocol is here.

What should I do? Leave a message telling her what happened?

Hi, it's Dr. Mitchell from University Hospital.

*Just wanted to call and let you know that I,
like, killed your boyfriend tonight. I gave him
too much potassium. Yeah. That's right.
Potassium. You know. It's the same stuff that
comes in bananas. It stopped his heart cold.
Potassium does that. In fact, it's what the state
uses to kill condemned prisoners by lethal
injection. It's supposed to be a pretty humane
way to go. Anyway, sorry about that. Give me
a call back when you get a chance. Thanks.*

I leave a message saying that something
serious has happened to Mr. Bernard and
that she needs to call the hospital answering
service immediately.

I then call Andrews at home. By now it's
pretty late. The call wakes him up. I decide
to tell him the whole story: renal failure,
TPN, potassium, hyperkalemia, cardiac arrest. Everything. Better, I figure, to just
come clean up front.

Andrews is understandably pissed and
screams at me for several minutes, ranting
so loudly at some points that I have to hold
the receiver away from my ear to keep his
raspy shouts from shredding my eardrum.
He finishes by promising me that I *haven't
heard the end of this* before the line goes
dead.

I take a deep breath and start in on the
paperwork.

It takes me a few hours to finish. I stop only once, to watch as Pathology Man wheels Mr. Bernard's body, draped in a white sheet stenciled with University Hospital's logo, past the nurses' station and toward the service elevators at the end of the hall.

A patient walking the hall for exercise, a gaunt, older woman wrapped in a frayed pink bathrobe, listlessly pushing her IV pole in front of her, stops in her tracks and stares as Mr. Bernard's body rolls by her on the gurney. She watches until the elevator doors close, snapping shut like a curtain falling at the end of a particularly grim play. She shakes her head, then resumes her walk with much more vigor and determination, leaning hard into her IV pole with renewed purpose.

By the time I'm done with the paperwork, it's very late, way too late to make it worth my while to go home. I call Sally to let her know that I won't be home tonight (but don't tell her what happened), then trudge wearily to a far-flung corner of the hospital, where the surgery-resident rooms are located, on the third floor of one of the hospital's oldest sections: a hundred-year-old forgotten bit of squat stone masonry poking sturdily and defiantly between the sleek, modern towers clawing skyward around it.

I enter the electronic combination of the gleaming modern door lock (apparently the only twenty-first-century update University Hospital has allowed for in this section of the building), which has been seared into my brain by countless prior nights spent in the hospital, open the door, and squeeze into the call room. I use the term "room" loosely, since it's essentially a large walk-in closet crammed with a narrow, metal-framed bunk bed, an old sink, and a telephone perched on a rickety nightstand next to the bed.

Like an old photograph that's slowly fading away, the call room seems drained of color and blurry at the edges. A tired fluorescent lamp hangs from the ceiling. The bulb sputters and gasps every few seconds, struggling to cast a semisteady, if anemic, stream of light. An ancient ventilation grate set in the wall above the bed blows a thin stream of cool air into the room. The rest of the walls, pockmarked in several places where the plaster has come loose from the underlying concrete, are otherwise completely bare except for a single mounted poster: a black-and-white picture of a kitten clinging to a clothesline with a caption reading "Hang in there, baby!" It's as much a part of the room as the bed and sink and window: Rows of screws pin it to the wall; its surface is faded and dusty; and someone long ago poked holes in the pupils of the kitten's eyes, which somehow makes it look more lifelike.

While I can only guess at the hanger's original intent, I know that the only thing that's been keeping that stupid kitten attached to that wall, at least since I've been at University, is a perverse sense of shared irony among the current crop of residents. Personally, I've wanted to tear it down for years. The damn thing gives me the creeps. I feel like the kitten's eyes never leave me for as long as I'm in the room. Besides, I can't stand cats.

A single open window covered by metallic bars, each one as thick around as my forearm, faces out onto one of the dingy side streets that ring the outer wall of the hospital. Outside, under the sickly orange glow of a streetlamp, I hear a drunk screaming in colorful yet surprisingly accurate anatomic detail about some of the things he'd like to do with the Queen of England and her various body cavities. With a grunt, I yank the heavy window closed, and the street drunk's ranting abruptly ceases. In contrast to the newer wings of University Hospital — with their paper-thin walls that transmit even the quietest conversations from one room to the next with perfect clarity — the thick, century-old cement of this part of the hospital is remarkably soundproof. The room is like a bunker.

Through the half-open door behind me, I hear a noise in the hallway. It sounds like a woman giggling. I peek out through the crack between the door edge and the frame. Standing outside one of the other call rooms on the side of the hallway opposite mine is Dan McIntosh, the general-surgery chief resident Sally mentioned to me while we were drinking wine in the kitchen. He's married to — what was her name? Natalie? No. Nancy. Sally's new lawyer friend who invited us to a barbecue and thinks that pot-lucks are gauche.

Anyway, Sally's friend Nancy is married to Dan; and Dan is now standing across from my room in the hallway with a cute, dewy, fresh-out-of-nursing-school brunette nurse I've seen around the hospital.

They don't see me. Which isn't too surprising, really, considering that Dan is key-ing a combination into the electronic lock in the panel located next to the door handle with his left hand while deftly slipping his right down the front of the brunette nurse's scrub pants. She closes her eyes and moans, arching her back and wrapping her left leg around his waist. The electronic combination clears with a mechanical click. Dan pushes the door open with his elbow, and the two of them tumble into the darkness beyond without closing the door behind them. I hear the rustling of fabric, a gasp, and then dewy brunette nurse begins to enthusiastically and rhythmically affirm Dan's prowess. I can't tell if she's saying "Dan" or "yes"; either way, the sentiment is pretty clear. But then the door slams shut, and silence suddenly envelops the hallway.

I shut my own door softly, turn off the light, and crawl into bed, the ancient metal springs groaning in protest. Light from the streetlamp outside plays across the room, and in the semidarkness I can see the kitten on the wall, watching me.

God, I hate that cat.

I think of GG, sleeping a few hundred feet away in one of the medical-student call rooms. My right hand steals to the ring finger of my left, and I self-consciously twist my wedding band, reminding myself of how much I love my wife.

When sleep finally overtakes me, it's not a good sleep.

CHAPTER 6

Tuesday, July 28

I wake up a few hours later, feeling like someone has viciously bashed my head in with a baseball bat. The phrase "waking up" applies only in a marginal kind of way since, despite how exhausted I am, I can't tell if I really slept at all. Guilt, anxiety, fear, and self-pity have taken turns poking at my brain all night long with a sharp stick.

With a groan, I fall out of bed, splash water over my face, and brush my teeth using a course toothbrush and cheap toothpaste from one of the toiletry kits the hospital provides for patients. It feels like running a Brillo pad through my mouth.

It's very early, much earlier than I usually arrive in the hospital. Without really thinking about it, I decide to skip my normal cafeteria routine and instead take the elevators upstairs, where I know Luis and GG will be meeting to round on our patients.

175

I find them at one of the nursing stations, gathering patient data and getting ready to start rounds. Luis doesn't mention anything about yesterday. Neither does GG. Both of them avoid direct eye contact with me. We exchange awkward greetings.

At first I'm in charge, but that arrangement quickly falls apart as I fumble my way through the first few patients, calling them by the wrong names, giving them incorrect diagnoses, and hesitating over even the most basic medical decisions. My brain is like cotton, insubstantial and weightless.

Luis and GG, sensing my complete worthlessness, diplomatically brush me aside. I let them, allowing myself to fade into the background and become just an observer. Luis and GG run the rest of rounds like they normally would in my absence, ignoring me completely as the three of us walk from one room to the next. I watch as they examine the patients and make plans for the day. They don't bother to ask me my opinions or what I think they should do. I'm merely a spectator.

At one point, we pass Mr. Bernard's room. I stop and linger briefly outside the open door as the rest of the group continues on to see the next patient. The remnants of last night's chaos are completely gone. The newly waxed floor sparkles. The furniture is neatly arranged. The bed is sitting in its usual spot by the window, and another patient — a young woman — is already in it, sleeping peacefully between crisp-looking sheets. Fresh bags of normal saline and other fluids hang on the IV pole next to her bed.

It's as if Mr. Bernard never existed.

After speeding through several more patients, Luis pauses to check the typed list he carries in his hand.

"Okay," he says with satisfaction, making a notation on the paper with his pen. "That's everyone." He hesitates, looks at me uncertainly, and adds, "Except for Mrs. Samuelson."

"Let's go," I say quietly.

We walk to the SICU and gather around Mrs. Samuelson's bed. Luis and GG examine the various plastic tubes and wires that connect Mrs. Samuelson to the array of life-support machines that cram her cubicle, while I log on to the computer next to the bed.

Things are looking pretty grim. I dig my front teeth into my lower lip and feel my stomach churn as I study her anemic life signs and read the electronic notes of the doctors and nurses who took care of her overnight. Their clinical observations are peppered with ominous-sounding phrases like "maximum pressor support initiated, concerned by worsening coagulopathy" and "end-of-life issues discussed with patient's family."

Mrs. Samuelson now clings to life by the most tenuous of threads, events having gone from bad to worse. Shortly after I dropped her off in the SICU, it became apparent that she had suffered a massive heart attack during the operation. What's left of her weakened, stunned heart struggles feebly to pump blood to the rest of her body. Her blood pressure is dangerously low and requires massive doses of medications to maintain it at a life-sustaining level. She also has a bleeding disorder, called disseminated intravascular coagulation (DIC for short), which is causing her to bleed internally. She's been getting blood transfusions all night, and still her blood counts keep falling.

Gnawing furiously on my lip, I step away from the computer, move to the side of the bed, and look down at Mrs. Samuelson. Her hair braid juts out from underneath a dense tangle of wires connecting her body to the various life-support machines that jam the cubicle. Her hair looks surprisingly fresh and neat — perhaps attended to by one of her daughters last night. It stands in stark organic contrast to all the harsh hardware she's hooked up to and surrounded by; indeed, it's the most human thing about the room.

I grip the metal handrail that lines the perimeter of the bed with both hands and squeeze. Hard.

There's absolutely nothing I can do for her now except hope that she gets better. I feel helpless, just as helpless as I was yesterday in the OR and last night when I watched Mr. Bernard die.

I hate it so much, this helplessness.

God, how I hate it.

I stare at the braid and squeeze the hand-rail. Luis walks up behind me and places his hand lightly on my shoulder.

"Steve. Anything else, man? I've got to get going. I've got things to do before I scrub on my cases this morning."

I look down stupidly at my hands, which remain wrapped around the handrail of Mrs. Samuelson's bed. Both sets of knuckles are bone white. I let go. The blood rushing back to my fingers makes them tingle. I open and close my hands a few times and rub them together to make the tingling go away.

"Are you all right, Steve?" Luis is staring at me. So is GG.

"Yeah. Yeah. I'm okay." I blink and rub my eyes, which burn as if someone has propped open the lids, dumped hot sand into them, then stirred the sand around with their thumbs. "Late night. I didn't get much sleep. I'm just a little wiped. No big deal."

"Sure," Luis says neutrally. "Anything else?"

"No. There's really nothing for us to do here except let the SICU guys do their jobs and wait for her to get better."

"Right." He runs his hand over the top of his shaved head. "Look, Steve — the OR schedule is pretty light this morning." He coughs. "They're all small cases. GG and I can cover them. Why don't you just take it easy?" He rubs the top of his head again and tugs on his ear. His expression remains as aloof and unreadable as ever.

I'm grateful for the gesture and the opportunity for the much-needed rest it will provide.

"Yeah," I reply. "Okay. Thanks. I mean . . . yeah, that's what you guys should do this morning." I stand up straighter and try to act a little bit more like I'm the one still in charge. "That's what I want you guys to do this morning. Cover the cases. I've got

180

paperwork to catch up on. Call me if you guys have any problems."

"Sure, Steve."

I leave the two of them there in the SICU and head down to the cafeteria, where I grab a doughnut and some coffee. I then walk to the small office I share with the other two chief residents. Luckily, I have the office to myself. One of my colleagues is on a medical mission to Africa for the rest of the summer, and the other is assigned to our sister hospital across town. I drop heavily into the chair at my plain wooden desk to finish some paperwork on the computer.

I once read that some species of shark must constantly keep swimming forward or they die. The forward motion allows them to move water over their gills, which allows them to extract oxygen from the water to survive. If they stop swimming forward, they can't extract oxygen from the water, and they drown.

So it is with being a sleep-deprived resident: As long as you keep moving forward, the sleep deprivation won't catch up with you, and you survive. I've stopped moving forward. The paperwork piled high on my desk and stretched across my computer screen is dense and boring. Anxiety over

Mrs. Samuelson or not, yesterday's events are finally starting to catch up with me.

I put my head down on the firm, battered wood of the desk and am asleep within seconds.

A few hours later, the fallout from yesterday starts raining down.

It's my pager that wakes me up. The shrill scream is like an ambulance siren in the small office. I jerk my head up off the desk and out of a pool of saliva that's accumulated underneath my cheek. The part of my cheek not submerged in spit throbs with pain from where a spiral notebook was sandwiched between it and the hard surface of the desk. I wipe off my cheek with my palm, and a stabbing pain shoots through the back of my neck as all of the muscles there conspire in unison to involuntarily contract.

I look at the text page. It's from Dr. Collier's secretary, summoning me to an immediate, emergency meeting with him in his office.

Shit.

Here it comes.

I make a feeble effort to straighten out my hopelessly wrinkled white coat, run my fingers over my stubble-covered chin and through my oily, unkempt hair, and grimace into a small mirror fixed to the wall. My eyes are like two overripe tomatoes that have burst. Several red semicircles run in a neat row across the middle of my right cheek, a calling card from my spiral-notebook pillow.

But here's no time to clean myself up now.

I hurry to Dr. Collier's office. His summons doesn't surprise me. Nor does the tone of our meeting, which hovers light-years away from the last one. What a difference one night and two patients — one dead, the other halfway there — make.

This time, no small talk. This time, no posh leather chairs. This time, no job "opportunity."

This time, I sit trapped in the deep recesses of a low-lying couch in a dark corner of the office, its soft cushions enveloping me like quicksand and pulling me toward the floor. A familiar show tune plays softly overhead from the hidden speakers. "Memories," I note sourly. From *Cats*.

Dr. Collier shuts off the music and steps out from behind his desk. He takes a seat a few feet away, directly opposite me, in a captain's chair, the black wood of which is polished to a high sheen. He seems to tower twenty feet over me as I sink downward, my butt settling inches above the plush carpeting, my knees reaching up toward my chin. The attendings and residents in our department, most of whom have found themselves sitting in this exact same position at one time or another, refer to this experience as "couch time."

Dr. Collier is wearing his white coat, surgical scrubs, and a hard expression. His shoes are off, and his feet, clad in argyle socks, are planted firmly on the floor. Two crisp manila files sit on his lap. He doesn't waste any time.

"Bad day, Steven. Bad day. Frankly, I couldn't be more disappointed in you." His tone is glacial.

"Yes, sir."

"Our department has had an excellent safety record for years, and now you've managed to single-handedly turn that around in the space of a single afternoon. Things happen, Steven, but really, this is unacceptable. You of all people should know better."

"Yes, sir."

"Now, directly because of your actions yesterday, this department has one dead patient, one critically ill patient, and two potential lawsuits on its hands. On top of that, two of my attending surgeons — highly

respected professors at this institution —
are fit to be tied. And with good reason,
considering what you've done to their
patients. One of them is already demanding
that I fire you immediately."

I swallow hard.

Larry? Andrews? Which one? Andrews can
be a real prick. God, I hope not Larry. He
was pretty pissed, though.

"Yes, sir."

"Now I have to figure out what I'm going
to do with you. First, let's talk about this
radical cystectomy patient who arrested on
the floor."

He opens the first manila folder, gracefully touches the tip of his index finger to
his tongue, and starts flipping through the
contents. "I've read your event note in his
chart and reviewed the medication and TPN
orders."

He looks up. "I don't think you should
have put potassium in the TPN solution. I
think it was stupid. I think that it showed
poor judgment. I'm convinced that it was
the potassium that killed him. As far as I'm
concerned, instead of giving this unfortunate man potassium, you might just as well
have shoved him down an open elevator
shaft from the top floor of the hospital. You
would have achieved the same result."

I cringe and stare at the plush carpet underneath his feet.

"Not to mention the fact that, as I understand it, this particular patient's demise was initiated by his receiving an antibiotic in the operating room to which he was allergic, in direct violation of this hospital's perioperative patient-safety protocols. Is this true?"

"Well, the anesthesiology resident —"

"Is this true?" he interjects sharply.

"Yes, sir."

"Fine. Now, since this is a mortality apparently related to a medication error, the hospital is going to do a formal investigation into the cause of death, overseen by the Hospital Safety Committee in coordination with Risk Management."

Risk Management. The hospital lawyers.

"The family consented this morning to an autopsy, and as per hospital protocol, the TPN solution was saved and submitted to an independent lab for formal analysis."

The family? What family? Mr. Bernard never talked about his family, just his girlfriend. But Dr. Collier's continued verbal body blows distract me from turning that thought over some more in my head.

"Since there is no obvious evidence of overt negligence on your part, just stupidity, the Safety Committee will not be formally investigating you — at least not yet, anyway — just interviewing you to get your version of the events leading up to this sentinel event. I expect you to give them your full cooperation. I want you to remember that the Safety Committee is not your enemy. Its members will simply be ascertaining what happened. You will, of course, comport yourself in a professional manner at all times and answer their questions with absolute candor. Do you understand?"

"Yes, sir."

"Mmhmmm. All right, then. So there we have the cystectomy patient. Now, with respect to the adrenalectomy patient." He closes the first folder and opens the second, again dexterously moistening his index finger. "Dr. Lassiter tells me that he specifically instructed you not to perform the adrenal-vein dissection by yourself because of the risk of injuring the IVC — which is exactly what ended up happening. Is that true? Did he really tell you not to perform the dissection until he returned to the OR?" His eyes bore through me like steel drills through Kleenex.

"Yes."

"Why, then, did you proceed with the dissection?"

"Well, things seemed to be going okay, so

I guess I just kept going. I really thought I could handle it by myself, without Lar—without Dr. Lassiter in the room."

Dr. Collier sighs, closes his eyes, and gently massages the side of his face for a few moments with his right hand, the index and middle fingers moving in slow, circular arcs over his right temple. He stops massaging and, without opening his eyes, shakes his head, his fingers still pressed against his temple. I notice that his eyelids are as deeply tanned as the rest of his body.

"Steven, Steven. I know you're good with your hands, and confidence in the operating room is not just an admirable trait — it's a necessary one for any good surgeon. But a truly great surgeon knows his limitations."

He drops his hand and opens his eyes. The hardness of his gaze has softened a bit around the edges. "Not only were you thoroughly incapable of performing that dissection on your own, you were completely unprepared to handle the catastrophic results of your actions. Your surgical skills simply were not up to the challenge, and as hard as that may have been to admit to yourself, you should have realized that you had reached the extent of your skills and asked for help. Do you understand what I'm saying?"

"Yes, sir."

"I hope so. Or your surgical career will be extremely short-lived. There is nothing wrong with asking for help when you need it." He snaps the second file closed. "But you're young, so for now I'll give you the benefit of the doubt and chalk your actions yesterday up to your lack of experience."

He leans back in the chair, crosses his legs, and tents all ten fingers by pressing the opposing tips together, right against left. His eyebrows draw together.

"You know, Steven, we all make mistakes. Especially as young surgeons. And we learn from those mistakes. It's what surgeons do. That's how we all improve, both individually and as a field. We're constantly improving, constantly challenging ourselves, constantly pushing ourselves ahead for the benefit of our patients. Things don't always quite work out the way we hope and plan. As my own chairman used to say to me back when I was a young surgeon, 'Robert, good judgment comes from experience, and experience comes from bad judgment.' " He arches his eyebrows. "You certainly showed some bad judgment yesterday, Steven. I hope you learned something from the experience."

"Yes, sir."

"It's a shame that these two unfortunate patients had to become part of your personal learning curve. Especially since these are the kinds of adverse variables that affect our department's rankings in *U.S. News and World Report.* Mortality data are very important to maintaining our extremely high position on that list, Steven. The events of yesterday are the sort of" — he pauses and momentarily purses his lips before continuing — "*discrepancies* in patient care that can cause us to slip in those rankings. Patients pay attention to that sort of thing these days, Steven — magazine lists and hospital rankings. They shop around and do their research. Patients are not going to want to come to University Hospital and let us care for them if we have a mortality rate significantly higher than that of our competitors. Do I make myself clear?"

"Yes, sir."

He stares at me then, silent and thoughtful, for what seems a very long time. Not angry at this point, really — just disappointed, as if I'm his sixteen-year-old son, and I've banged up the family car, or raided the liquor cabinet with my buddies, or flamed out on my report card. I already feel bad enough about what I did to those patients; Dr. Collier is now making me feel as if I've let down my dad, in the worst possible way.

Finally, he asks, "How is the adrenalectomy patient doing today?"

"She's currently intubated and in the SICU. She had an MI from all the volume loss. She's also coagulopathic."

"Mmhmmm." He nods gravely. "I hope she survives."

"I hope so, too, sir."

"Mmhmmm." He nods once more before smoothly rising from his chair.

Meeting over. With some difficulty, I manage to extricate myself from the cushiony depths of the couch. Dr. Collier walks me to the office door and opens it.

"That's all for now, Steven. Please keep me updated on this patient's progress. Also know that I'll be keeping a direct line of communication open with the Safety Committee. Again, I expect your full cooperation in their investigation."

"Yes, sir. I understand." I walk through the door and start to speed away, grateful to be off that couch and out of that office.

"And remember," Dr. Collier calls to me from his open doorway. I freeze and look back at him.

"I'll be keeping an eye on you, Steven. We all will."

He motions to his secretary to follow him into his office. She immediately jumps to attention and scurries into his office, clutching a notepad of legal yellow paper and a pen. The door closes after them.

God, please let her get better. Please don't let her die.

Please, God. Let her get better.

CHAPTER 7

Wednesday, July 29 to Friday, August 7

But Mrs. Samuelson doesn't get better.

In fact, she gets worse.

Much worse.

Everything gets worse. One day blurs into the next while Mrs. Samuelson clings to life in the SICU, and the Safety Committee begins its formal inquiry. Work sucks. Each day, I slog through my stuff, going through the motions, starting out each morning with a lead weight in my stomach that just grows bigger and heavier as the day wears on, like a bucket that gets heavier the more you fill it with water.

It seems like everyone in the department treats me differently. Just as Dr. Collier had promised, everyone seems to be watching me. Maybe I'm just being paranoid, of course. But you're not being paranoid if everyone *really is* out to get you. Right? I can't shake the feeling that everyone *really is* out to get me.

Andrews screams at me without provocation at least once per day, reminding me how stupid I am and how he will never let me touch any of his patients ever again. I'm also periodically summoned to Dr. Collier's office, slouching uncomfortably in the couch as Dr. Collier sits regally in his captain's chair, listening impassively to my updates on Mrs. Samuelson's condition. I hold out the small hope that the job offer we discussed a few weeks ago to join the faculty will come up again, but it never does.

What hurts more — far more — is Larry's reaction. He stops talking to me. Completely. He won't take my calls, ignores me during our departmental conferences, and speaks directly to Luis about his patients, including Mrs. Samuelson. When I show up a few times in the OR to help out with his surgeries, he barely acknowledges my presence and wordlessly performs each operation himself with me standing off to the side, watching. So I stop showing up to his operations, sending Luis to take my place. Depressed and increasingly worried about my future job prospects, I type out a formal letter of apology for what happened and leave it with Larry's secretary. I don't receive a response.

Other things are less obvious but no less painful. Although nobody comes right out and says it, I suspect that I'm a favorite topic of conversation among the other residents. Doctors are just as prone to gossip, Machiavellian infighting, and office politics as those in any other profession. In fact, in some ways doctors can be even worse: driven type A's who are always looking over their shoulders, forever wary of a smarter, more successful, or more devious colleague; ready to pounce on the chance to exploit others' misfortunes and professional miscalculations to press their own advantage.

I've never been particularly close to any of the other residents in our training program, and I think my fall from grace has provided them an opportunity to take me down a few pegs, generating a barrage of small indignities that dog me all day long at work: mostly things like low-toned conversations between residents that abruptly end as I walk within earshot; followed by their knowing smirks as they clap me on the back and smugly ask me how things are going.

And as for operating, well . . . it's bad. Bad in a way that I never could have imagined.

Because the joy is gone.

Part of it is that I don't think the professors trust me anymore. Since the word has gotten out about what I did to Mrs. Samuelson, some professors who previously let me do their most complex operations will now barely let me touch their patients. When they do let me operate, they second-guess, scrutinize, and criticize every single move I make.

But it's more than that. Something worse — much worse — has robbed me of my love of the operating room.

I'm afraid.

Afraid of operating.

Afraid of doing something bad to another patient, of inadvertently ripping apart another organ, of having to face another family like Mrs. Samuelson's. The fear paralyzes me in the OR. I can't pull the trigger anymore. Even during the simplest, most straightforward operations, I keep freezing up. Before, I never hesitated, never doubted myself. Ever. This fear is completely unfamiliar and makes me feel . . . emasculated. Angry.

Intensifying my misery is that fact that, through all of this, I don't really have anyone I can talk to. I would normally go to Larry, but he's too pissed at me. There's Luis, I suppose, who remains cordial and respectful; he moves through our daily routines as if nothing ever happened. But I'm much too embarrassed to talk about it with him, especially because, in both cases, he tried to stop me from being so stupid: first, by trying to talk me out of giving Mr. Bernard potassium; and second, by urging me to wait for Larry to come back to the OR before forging ahead with Mrs. Samuelson's surgery. So Luis is out.

Sally means well but just doesn't understand. When I first tell her about what's happened with Mr. Bernard and Mrs. Samuelson, she's sympathetic and deeply concerned. But she's not a surgeon, so how can she truly empathize with what it feels like to make the kinds of mistakes I've made? Besides, she didn't know Mr. Bernard the way that I did. She wasn't there for our final conversation, in his hospital room; doesn't realize what I robbed him of, doesn't know that, because of me, he'll never again spend time with his lady friend, or see an alligator farm in Florida. And she's never seen the pale, drawn faces of Mrs. Samuelson's husband and daughters; never heard them sobbing, or watched them pray over her bedside.

Besides, I feel incredibly ashamed that I might have completely blown my chances at staying at University Hospital, and guilty about having let her down. So I withdraw, both emotionally and physically. I keep the guilt and the fear and the frustration corked up and I start spending less time at home.

Instead, I pass hours at night sitting alone at my computer in my cramped cubicle in my office, wishing I had done things differently, burning a hole through my stomach worrying that the Safety Committee is going to recommend that the hospital fire me. Meanwhile, as Mrs. Samuelson hangs on by her fingernails, I pore over her vital signs, studying every minor change in her lab results, praying for her to get better. I obsess about her operation, replaying the series of events in my head again and again and again, thinking about what went wrong.

Because of my self-imposed exile in the hospital, I end up spending a lot more time with the only other person who's in the hospital as much as I am.

GG.

GG — ever eager, admiring, and calm — is always there at my side.

She never mentions Mr. Bernard, or what happened with Mrs. Samuelson; never stops complimenting me on my skills or medical decision making, never once throttles back from her relentless work schedule or apparent determination to prove to the rest of us that she is the greatest medical student in the history of medical students. We work together, eat our meals together, and, when I'm not hiding in my office feeling sorry for myself, hang out together in the residents' lounge, talking for hours.

Soon I'm seeing more of her than I am of Sally, Katie, and Annabelle. I tell her about my life, and she, in turn, confides in me about hers: her childhood in Southern California, the daughter of two Cal Tech professors who nurtured a passion for all things scientific; the pressure to achieve in such an academically high-powered family; her first place in the Westinghouse National Science Fair competition in high school; her years at MIT; her recent research in a heart laboratory at University Medical School.

So, in a weird way, as I sort through the emotional debris left in the aftermath of Mr. Bernard and Mrs. Samuelson, GG quickly becomes more my friend and confidante than any of the most important people in my life.

CHAPTER 8

Saturday, August 8

In the morning, I round on the patients with GG. It's just the two of us because Luis has the weekend off. I occasionally have to round like this on weekends, when Luis isn't working, and I like to strike out early in order to get done as quickly as possible. Patients are less likely to ask you annoying questions (and hence slow you down) when you've just roused them from sleep at some god-awful hour of the morning.

So it's still dark outside when we start. Things are quiet. All of the patients are doing well. GG and I flit from one room to the next, examining abdomens, checking bandages, removing bladder catheters, and reassuring groggy patients blinking the sleep from their eyes that they're doing just fine. We move smoothly and efficiently.

Toward the end of rounds, however, one of our more verbose patients traps me in her room with an endless series of questions. Luis and GG have dubbed her "Chatty Kathy." She's an immense, flatulent mother of two with orange-brown, tanning-booth-toasted skin, curly, bright red hair, and a high, childish voice. She likes to keep a rust-colored, red-haired teddy bear with her in the bed. The bear looks disturbingly like her.

The most exasperating thing about her is that I don't even understand why she's in the hospital. She has a bladder infection, but as far as I can tell, we're not doing anything for her that couldn't be done at home. I think she just likes it here in the hospital, and her attending, an affable and absentminded older professor, is too nice a guy to kick her out.

Anyway, this morning, Chatty Kathy keeps repeating the same questions over and over, clutching her teddy bear while absently brushing out its red hair. There's no end in sight, and I'm finding it increasingly difficult to stifle my exasperation or suppress a growing desire to reach across the bed, bury my fingers in the flabby flesh of her neck, and throttle her.

I'm just starting to wonder if I'm ever going to be able to get myself out of her room when the piercing tone of my pager interrupts Chatty Kathy's discourse mid-sentence. I read the text message: U R NEEDED IN HALLWAY STAT. I glance around and realize that GG is no longer there — she must have slipped out of the room, unnoticed by either Chatty Kathy or myself, and paged me from out in the hall-way.

Brilliant. It's exactly the cue I need to escape.

I frown with appropriate doctorly concern, gesture toward the pager screen, and tell Chatty Kathy that I'm very, *very* sorry, but there's an emergency with one of my other patients, and I have to leave right away. She thrusts out her lower lip like a pouting child as I flee the room.

GG is waiting for me at a discreet distance down the hall, leaning against the wall, smirking, with her arms folded.

"Thanks," I say once Chatty Kathy's door swings shut behind me.

"No problem." Her smirk widens into a broad smile. She looks really good this morning. Her hair is pulled back in a ponytail, away from her face, which accentuates her dark, placid eyes; and instead of a scrub top, she's wearing a formfitting, white, short-sleeve shirt. "Let's keep moving. We just need to see Mrs. Samuelson, then we're done."

We make our way to the SICU, taking care to use the back door so that we don't run into Mrs. Samuelson's family out in the waiting room. She looks a little better this morning; a few of her medications have been discontinued, a few of the plastic tubes connecting her to the machines have been taken out. I hold out a small measure of hope that she still might survive. After seeing Mrs. Samuelson, we head downstairs to the cafeteria.

Sally, the girls, and her parents drove down to Sally's sister's place in Providence this morning, and won't be back until tonight. Without a reason to go home, I linger over breakfast with GG, trying not to think about the fact that part of me is glad to have an excuse to spend more time with her; and to ignore the way her T-shirt lingers over the curves of her body; and to not notice the very pleasant feminine smell (some kind of shampoo?) wafting across the table.

Eventually, the conversation peters out, and we each become lost in our own thoughts. I stare at my empty plate, pondering Mrs. Samuelson's latest vital signs.

"Steve, do you mind if I ask you something about Mr. Bernard?" She looks pained.

Neither she nor Luis has ever spoken to me directly about what happened to Mr. Bernard.

Surprised, I take a stab at feigned indifference by shrugging and shaking my head.

"I heard that you've been meeting with the hospital Safety Committee investigating his . . . you know."

"His death. Yeah."

"How's it going?"

"Working with the Committee? Okay, I guess."

Working with the Safety Committee isn't an entirely accurate way of describing the way I feel about the whole experience. *Interrogated by* is more like it. I've met with the Committee three times now, a glum panel of senior medical-school professors, hospital administrators, chief nurses, and hospital lawyers. Both times I felt as if a German guy wearing a brown trench coat and a fedora was questioning me under hot lights.

What made you decide to order the potassium? Did you think it was indicated in this clinical situation? Did you ever suspect that hyperkalemia might have been a problem? Talk! What do you know? Where are the plans? Your papers are not in order!

The only friendly face on the Committee is an orthopedic-surgery resident named Jason Kobayashi. Jason has been a good friend of mine for years, since we were students at University Medical School together. We met in gross anatomy class, and subsequently bonded together for hours at a time over a dead body. Although we haven't hung out much lately, we used to go out regularly for beers, until both of us started having kids at roughly the same time.

During the meetings, Jason looks as serious and somber as the rest of them but somehow manages to also come off as marginally sympathetic. And he never asks me tough questions.

But he's also been extremely careful to keep his distance. I sense that he doesn't want the other members of the Committee to know that we're friends. I play along during the meetings, pretending I don't know him; and I haven't tried to contact him otherwise. I guess I just have to trust that he'll help me as best he can.

At any rate, the Committee itself seems to be moving with unusual speed. Dr. Collier originally told me that this kind of investigation can drag on for months; but as I was leaving my last interrogation, I overheard the chairman say to another member that he wanted to get a formal report on the hospital CEO's desk within a few weeks. I don't know if the Committee's fast pace is a good thing or a bad thing. I suspect that it's a bad thing: After all, aren't the speediest trials the ones that invariably end with the defendants lined up against a wall or dangling from a rope?

So, all in all, I'd have to say that my experience with the Safety Committee has, like the rest of my life lately, totally sucked.

I don't tell GG any of this. I simply shrug, and say, "It's okay, I guess. They're waiting right now on the final autopsy results. The Committee doesn't tell me much; they just ask me a lot of questions about what happened." My suspicion is that the Committee is keeping me in the dark because my actions — my *mistakes* — are an integral part of their investigation.

"Can I help you somehow? After all, I was there for the code, right? I'm really interested in improving patient safety: preventing medication errors, medical mistakes, that kind of thing."

"That's great. But I don't think you can help." I watch over her shoulder as an older man and woman push a younger, gaunt woman past our table in a wheelchair. The woman is tethered to an IV pole on wheels. She has a scarf tied around her head. A cancer patient.

"Mr. Bernard was the first patient I saw die. I was . . . the first one to find him."

"Uh-huh."

"I guess you've probably seen a lot of people die by now."

"Some."

"It wasn't . . . it wasn't what I expected."

"What did you expect?"

"I guess I, well . . . I'm not sure. It was like he was alive and then . . . not alive. That was it. There was nothing more to it. I expected something else."

"Like what?"

"Like, umm . . . I don't know. Something more dramatic."

"Like a signal, or a sign? Something poetic? Watching the soul shuffle loose the mortal coil? Glimpsing the ghost as it escaped the machine?"

"Maybe. You know, people always talk about the light going out of someone's eyes when they die. I'm not sure what that means. What do you think, Steve?"

"I usually don't. Not about this stuff."

"Yeah, well, there wasn't anything poetic or mystical about Mr. Bernard's death. He just . . . died. It was stupid. I don't know how I missed that potassium."

"You know, you really shouldn't feel badly about what happened, GG. It's not your fault. It's mine. I'm the one who gave the order. Besides, you shouldn't have to worry about stuff like that — don't take this personally, but you're just a med student."

"It's just . . . I mean, for Mr. Bernard to make it through major surgery, only to die from a preventable mistake. It's just so . . . I'm sorry you have to go through this."

She reaches over and gently touches my bare forearm. The brief contact is enough to send the hairs on the back of my neck standing on end and my heart racing. Underneath the table, she shifts her legs and moves one up against mine, lightly at first, so that it could almost be an accident, but then more firmly and with definite purpose, stroking my calf with her foot. She leans forward, her immense brown eyes — so serene, so assured — fixed on my face. Involuntarily, my own eyes flicker a beat too long over the revealing neckline of her T-shirt.

She notices me noticing her, and a knowing smile plays about her lips.

I finally come to my senses and, with more reluctance than I care to admit, pull my leg away, cough, and become very interested in the cancer patient over her shoulder. GG settles back in her seat and returns to her bagel.

The moment is over.

Silence descends as she nibbles on her bagel, and I sip my coffee while gazing over her shoulder at the cancer patient.

"It's kind of weird, though. You wouldn't have thought we gave him enough potassium to cause the arrhythmia," GG says thoughtfully.

"What?" The cancer patient is eating a doughnut now, smiling weakly as her companions urge her on with each bite.

"It's just . . . you know, we really didn't give him all that much potassium. It just seems like it shouldn't have caused any problems."

I put down my coffee and stare at her, surprised, the awkward exchange of a few minutes ago completely forgotten. Lately, during my hours of solitary brooding, I've circled back to that same thought myself several times, which first occurred to me the night Mr. Bernard died: the idea that we didn't order enough potassium to have killed him. I've been hesitant to pursue it, because I haven't wanted to falsely raise my hopes that there's a way out of this mess that doesn't involve my accepting complete responsibility. Besides, the Safety Committee's relentless questioning has kept me off-balance.

"What makes you say that?"

She shrugs. "Did you know it takes 100 mEq of potassium chloride in 50 cc of normal saline to kill an average adult? Given all at once as an IV bolus?"

"Really? That much?" I ask, with genuine interest.

"Yeah. The Chief Medical Examiner for Boston told us that during one of our pathophysiology lectures. I know Mr. Bernard's kidneys were still recovering. But still — we gave him way less than 2 mEq per cc. And we spread it out over several hours of infusing time."

"Huh." I gaze over her shoulder at the cancer patient. She wipes chocolate frosting mixed with sprinkles off her lips and says something I can't hear. Her companions laugh heartily in response. "So then let's talk hypothetically for a second. Mr. Bernard clearly died of hyperkalemia. But if we didn't give him enough potassium, where did it all come from? What could have made his serum K go up? Something in his other medications? Potassium in one of the carrier fluids? Rhabdomyolosis? But, then, why would he have gotten rhabdo? All of those seem pretty unlikely."

"What if he was accidentally given potassium by someone else, like the pharmacy?"

"Maybe. But I would think, I would *hope,* the pharmacy would have safety measures in place to prevent that kind of thing from happening. Or at least it should."

The cancer patient finishes her doughnut. She looks tired but triumphant.

My conversation with GG stokes my curiosity. Is it really possible that we didn't give enough potassium to Mr. Bernard to have killed him? I send GG home (though doubt she's really going to leave) and, armed with a fresh cup of coffee, hunker down in my office. Over the next several hours, I examine all of Mr. Bernard's blood-potassium levels and kidney-function test results in the days leading up to his death, which are still stored in the computer. Back when I was a medical student, I completed some advanced course work in nephrology, so I have experience with the kinds of calculations I need to make. I'm a little rusty at first, but after a while I'm able to chart out all of his blood-potassium levels and compare them to how well his kidneys were working in the hours leading up to his death.

The answer I finally arrive at, as the sun filtering through the windows softens into midafternoon, is clear: even accounting for Mr. Bernard's renal failure, the amount of potassium we put in the TPN couldn't have made his blood levels go up so high, so fast.

In other words, based on my (admittedly crude) calculations, we couldn't have killed him.

I check my equations twice more to be sure, then lean back in my chair and chew on the tip of my pen, trying to contain the nascent excitement squirming in my chest. Part of my brain — the reasonable, cautious one — reminds me that it probably isn't the best idea in the world to latch onto my amateur postmortem analysis. I mean, how could I have missed something so obvious, so straightforward, so right-in-front-of-my-face the whole time? Could it really be this easy? Numbers that don't quite match up? Something even a medical student thought of? And what about the Safety Committee? Shouldn't they have stumbled onto this by now? Why haven't they mentioned it?

I heave a sigh and concede that this conclusion is probably too good to be true; and my initial excitement dies a quick, reluctant death.

But my curiosity does not.

So I call my friend Richard, a young professor at University Medical School who specializes in kidney diseases. He owes me a couple of favors, not the least of which is that I introduced him to his fiancée, a fact about which I subtly remind him near the beginning of our conversation. I explain what I need and, even though it's the weekend, he agrees to meet up with me.

We rendezvous at a Starbucks on Harvard Street about an hour later. I spring for a couple of lattes. We find a quiet table in the back and, after some perfunctory chitchat, I show him my equations, arrayed carefully on several sheets of paper. Using some apps on his smartphone, Richard reviews them line by line, asking me pointed questions about how I crunched the numbers. Fortunately, for some reason, he doesn't ask me why I want to know what I want to know, or grill me over the exact circumstances surrounding Mr. Bernard's demise.

He works quickly, practically at light speed compared to my stumbling pace earlier in the day; next to him, I'm like a kindergartner wielding crayons, and he's finished before my latte is even halfway gone. He makes a few corrections here and there, moves some decimal points around, and pokes a couple of small holes in my assumptions.

But, for the most part, Richard completely agrees — there's no way Mr. Bernard's blood potassium could have climbed as quickly as it did based solely on the amount of potassium that Luis and I ordered for him. He slides my papers back toward me across the table and finally takes a sip of the latte.

I don't know if it's the latte, his answer, or both, but my hands tremble markedly as I pick the papers up and place them carefully in my shoulder bag. Richard watches me with polite concern and asks me if there's anything else I need. I tell him no and thank him for his help. He gives me a hard look, opens his mouth as if to say something, then snaps it shut. He shakes my hand and pushes himself away from the table.

As I watch him leave, the cautious part of my brain again tries to have its say.

It can't be that easy!

But my ego, emboldened now, up off the mat and ready for some payback, quickly shouts that part of my brain down. It latches greedily onto this new development.

Of course it could be that easy.

A sudden surge of desperate manic energy roars through me, like swollen river rapids through a narrow mountain gorge, filling me with a euphoric sense of hope that, after the persistent gloom of the last two weeks, is practically intoxicating. My head spins. I want to pump my fists in the air and scream like one of those body-painted idiots at a football game.

Why? Because I'm giddy with the tantalizing prospect of absolution. After all, if I didn't give Mr. Bernard enough potassium to kill him, it must have come from somewhere else.

It wasn't my fault.

The questions now rush at my addled brain like baseballs firing toward me in an automated batting cage. *What made the potassium go up so high, so quickly? Where did all that potassium in his blood come from? If we didn't give him too much potassium, then who did? And how? And what about the Safety Committee?*

The Safety Committee.

Shit.

I completely forgot about the Safety Committee.

See? I told you, cautious brain smirks.

Shut up, ego replies.

I sit for a moment, thinking. If I was able to figure this out, there's no way the Safety Committee wasn't.

I pull out my cell and call Jason, my friend on the Committee. He answers right away. He's friendly at first, but cools quickly as I reveal the underlying purpose of my call. Before he can hang up I quickly explain the discrepancy in the potassium levels and ask him if the Committee has found anything similar in its investigation.

The other end of the line is quiet for several long beats. My first thought is that the call dropped.

"Jason? Hello? Can you hear me?"

He makes a sound that's somewhere between a grunt and a sigh. In my mind's eye, I can picture him on the other end of the line as he thinks things over, his broad, handsome face scrunched up in concentration as he holds the cell phone next to his ear with one thick, muscular hand while absently and repeatedly running the fingers of the other through his thick, jet-black hair — a nervous tic that always surfaced in med school when he was answering a difficult question in class or poring over a particularly challenging problem in a textbook. He has absolutely nothing to gain and potentially a whole lot to lose by telling me anything. If I were in his position, I probably wouldn't say a thing.

"Yeah, I'm here, dude. Look, Steve," he says haltingly. "I'm really not supposed to talk to you about this. Technically, I'm not supposed to talk to you *at all*. If the Committee found out, I'd get into a lot of trouble. Real trouble."

"I know, Jason. It's just that things have been kind of rough for me lately, and I thought you could . . . that it wouldn't hurt anybody to give me a little more information."

"Yeah. Yeah. I know, man. I'm sure it sucks for you right now. Well . . . I guess it's okay to let you know, at this point." I suck in my breath and clutch the phone harder. "You can't repeat to anyone what I'm about to tell you, Steve, okay? Really, man. I'm serious about this. You really can't. For real. I would get into a lot of fucking trouble. I had to sign a nondisclosure agreement. It's serious business. If it ever got out I talked to you, I'd be in a world of hurt. We both would."

"I understand." I swallow hard, trying to imagine how much more hurtful my current world can possibly become.

"Okay, so, the Committee met again yesterday. We're pretty much done, Steve. And I think you should know that the reason why we're moving so fast is that, apparently, your patient was quite a VIP. Or at least the son of one. His father is some reclusive billionaire who's given tens of millions to University Hospital. Anonymously. He keeps a very low profile, but has some serious fucking clout. So the hospital CEO and medical-school dean are really putting the screws to us to take care of this quickly and quietly."

Mr. Bernard? The son of a billionaire? He never told me he even had a family. I wonder what his backstory was. Maybe he didn't want his family to worry about him while he was in the hospital. Maybe he was too proud to ask for help when he was sick. Maybe he was a prodigal son — a prodigal son who'll now never have an opportunity to return home.

"Steve? You still there, man?"

"Yeah, yeah. It's just . . . he never talked about his father. The patient, I mean."

"Sure. Okay. Whatever. So, the autopsy confirmed that your patient most likely died from a catastrophic cardiac arrhythmia secondary to hyperkalemia. No surprises there. All the tissue assays were consistent with that diagnosis, and the rest of the autopsy findings were unremarkable. His medications checked out, too. But there was one thing that really jumped out."

I swallow. Hard. "Which was what?"

"The total parenteral nutrition — TPN — solution, which was the presumed source of the potassium that killed your patient."

"What do you mean?" I clench my fist.

He lowers his voice. "The concentration

of potassium in the TPN was at least a hundred times greater than the amount you had ordered for him. Possibly more."

"Really." I unclench my fist.

"Yeah. Really. We've checked it four times now at three different labs."

"So . . ."

"So you're right. The numbers don't jibe. It was the massive amount of potassium in the TPN solution that killed your patient. There was enough in there to have killed a horse. But you didn't order that potassium. It all came from somewhere else." He pauses. "I'm impressed you came up with that on your own."

I feel like dancing around the room. "Thanks, Jason," I say, forcing myself to sound calm. "It's something that's been on my mind a lot lately."

"I can only imagine. But . . . there's something else I think you should know."

The discomfiture in his voice makes my palms start sweating. Suddenly, I don't feel like dancing anymore.

"What?"

There's a long pause, long enough for me to again think that the call dropped.

"Jason? Are you still there? Hello?"

"Yeah, dude, I'm still here. I told you this

much, so I guess it can't hurt to tell you the rest."

"Tell me what?"

"I just don't want you to be blindsided when the official report comes out."

"Blindsided by *what*, Jason?"

"By the rest of the report. By what it's going to say about the extra potassium in your patient's TPN bag. Where it came from."

"Okaaaaay. So, where did it come from?"

He quickly explains that hospital pharmacists prepare each individual TPN bag based on the doctor's orders. A pharmacist checks the orders, withdraws the exact amount of each ingredient from the pharmacy's computer-controlled storehouse, then combines all the ingredients into a single, sterile solution with the help of a semiautomated assembly line. The Committee believes that the pharmacist who prepared Mr. Bernard's TPN solution may have accidentally put in too much potassium.

Great, I reply. So it was the pharmacist's fault.

Except, Jason continues, the computer-controlled storehouse is like a big ATM machine. The pharmacist keys in the exact amount of each ingredient desired — of potassium, sodium, whatever — and gets back only that amount from the storehouse.

The computer keeps a strict digital record of each transaction, allowing the pharmacy to keep track of how much is coming in and how much is going out. According to the computer record, the pharmacist who prepared Mr. Bernard's TPN that day withdrew from the computer-controlled storehouse the exact amount of potassium that had been ordered.

"Okay, so . . . where did all that extra potassium come from then?"

"We'll never know for certain. What we think happened is that the pharmacy computer made a mistake and gave out too much potassium. The pharmacist never realized it, and the computer never recorded it. Just between you and me, it wouldn't be the first time something like this has happened. There was a near miss very similar to your case several months ago — a patient almost received a lethal dose of magnesium because the system gave out ten times the requested amount. The pharmacy dispensing system is old. Everything needs to be replaced."

"Are you going to go looking for that extra potassium? Audit the system?"

"No. There's no point. The extra bit of potassium that killed your patient is a drop in the ocean compared to what comes through this hospital every day. There's no way we could ever definitively track it all down. More important, hospital leadership is not . . . overly anxious to draw any more attention to this whole thing. Safety issues. Bad press. The hospital is simply going to overhaul the entire pharmacy system."

"Okay. Good for the hospital. What has any of this got to do with me? I wasn't the one who put the extra potassium in the bag."

"No, but . . . here's the thing. The Committee is concerned that you have a pattern of ordering a lot of potassium for patients who don't really need it. They think that you — uh, that you demonstrated poor clinical judgment that created an unsafe situation."

"What the hell does that mean?"

"Well, the Committee went back and audited all of your medication orders over the last six months. It's very easy to do these days. In fact, you can do it yourself. You probably already know how. ERIN tracks every order made by every doctor in the hospital. According to ERIN, in the weeks leading up to that patient's death, you ordered IV potassium for a bunch of patients who didn't need it."

"*What?* What are you talking about?"

"Steve. Look. I'm just telling you the way it is. I saw the orders myself. During the first part of July, you ordered IV potassium for fifteen patients with completely normal potassium levels: fifteen patients, none of whom had any business getting IV potassium. They were small doses, and nobody got hurt, but the Committee was extremely concerned about the pattern."

I have no idea what he's talking about.

"I have no idea what the hell you're talking about, Jason. Not a clue."

"Look. Everyone just wants this whole thing to go away. Quietly. The word on the street is that the lawyers have already cut a deal. The patient's dad — the rich guy — is anxious to avoid publicity of any kind, and he's already accepted the results of our investigation — and, uh . . . your, uh, role in his death."

My role in his death.

"So what does this mean for me?"

"The final conclusion of the Committee will be that your poor clinical judgment substantially contributed to this patient's death." His voice has become clipped and formal, like he's reading the official report to me over the phone. "First, you allowed this patient to receive the wrong antibiotic in the operating room. The antibiotic caused the renal failure. Second, and more important, you put potassium in the TPN solution. Putting potassium in the TPN was a mistake, a mistake consistent with your prior erratic ordering pattern. The recommendation of the Committee will therefore be that you undergo remedial medical training. The hospital will temporarily suspend your operating privileges while you take some courses in the med school on electrolyte management and patient safety. For the duration of the suspension, you won't be able to operate."

"What? Screw that. I'll be nothing more than a fucking med student again," I say loudly. A well-dressed, middle-aged couple at the table next to mine glances sourly at me before continuing their conversation.

"Steve," he says patiently, "if you do what they tell you, everything will eventually turn out okay. A slap on the wrist. They'll put a disciplinary letter in your confidential personnel file, and you'll be fully reinstated within a few weeks, once you've finished the remedial coursework. That's it. That's as far as it will go. You bend over and take it up the ass for a while, then it'll be like it never happened."

"And if I don't? If I refuse to cooperate?"

"They're going to kick you out of your

residency program. They're going to fire you."

It's like someone's punched me in the face. My head reels; I grab the side of the table with my free hand to keep myself steady. I feel like I'm going to puke, and I mark the fastest way to the bathroom as a precaution. But then my initial shock is swept away by a rising tide of indignation and embarrassment. My vision steadies; my stomach settles.

"I can't believe this, Jason. This is bullshit. This is complete bullshit."

I'm practically shouting into my cell phone now. The couple at the next table has stopped talking and is glaring at me with open hostility. A few other patrons surreptitiously size me up over the tops of their laptops and lattes. "I . . . okay, yeah, I let the guy get the Cefotetan in the operating room. It was stupid. I admit it. But I did not order potassium on any other patients. I swear to God I didn't. I'm going to fight this."

"Don't shoot the messenger, okay? I'm really going out on a limb here by giving you all of this information. And I tried, man. I tried to get them to go easier on you. But those potassium orders you wrote . . ."

"I didn't write those fucking orders!"

"Look, I know it sucks —"

"You don't know shit!"

"Fine," he huffs. "But before you get all worked up, *Doctor,* you might want to take a look at those potassium orders yourself."

He hangs up.

"That's exactly what I'll do!" I scream into the now-dead connection before flinging my phone on the table. The middle-aged couple casts one final, baleful scowl at me as they head outside, and as the rest of the seats in the general vicinity discreetly empty. The acne-laden baristas confer anxiously behind the counter, no doubt trying to decide which one of them is going to ask me to leave.

But I don't care. I know exactly how to audit my own electronic medical orders. I pull my laptop out of my bag and boot it up. My fingers flying furiously over the keyboard, I remotely access ERIN, key in my account ID and password, and pull up the medication-ordering system. Spitting invectives at Jason, I quickly locate all of the medication orders I've written since June. The data scroll rapidly across the screen as I work my way through June and July.

And suddenly, there they are.

Potassium orders.

A whole series of them. Starting in the

middle of July. Stopping the day before Mr. Bernard died.

I blink, and my jaw goes slack. I can't believe what I'm seeing.

Holy shit. You have *got* to be kidding me.

Fifteen patients with normal potassium blood levels.

Fifteen orders for IV potassium.

All made by me.

Date: July 16. Patient: HS. Medication: Potassium Chloride. Dose: 30 mEq IV.

Date: July 17. Patient: LP. Medication: Potassium Chloride. Dose: 20 mEq IV.

Date: July 17. Patient: GN. Medication: Potassium Chloride. Dose: 20 mEq IV.

And so on.

All told, according to the computer, in just under ten days, I ordered a total of 300 mEq of intravenous potassium — a whopping amount of potassium by any measure — all in separate, small doses for fifteen patients with normal potassium levels. All for patients who didn't need potassium.

I lean back in my chair, stunned, my jaw slack.

How the hell could this have happened? Could I have ordered that much potassium without realizing it? Not likely. I could never have written fifteen separate orders like that and just forgotten about it. I'm busy, but

I'm not that busy. Besides, it's Luis who writes most of the medication orders for our patients.

Computer glitch? Maybe. But that would have had to be one major fucking glitch.

An absurd suspicion occurs to me: Could somebody have hacked the system and faked the orders? Deliberately set me up? Made me look bad just to draw attention away from the hospital's flawed pharmacy dispensing system?

My pager goes off, derailing my train of thought.

Now what?

Steve, it reads, *have patient with multiple GSW 2 pelvis. OR 6. ASAP. Thx. Dan, gen surg.*

GSW 2 pelvis. Gunshot wound to the pelvis. A trauma. I have to get back to University Hospital right away.

By the time one of the baristas has finally worked up the nerve to approach me, anxiously wringing her hands, I've already shut down my laptop and packed it away in my shoulder bag.

"Never mind." I brush past her brusquely. "I was just leaving."

Thirty minutes later, I'm in a fresh set of scrubs and walking into OR 6, which is humming with activity. To my surprise, GG is already there. I don't know how she heard about this patient, but she's sitting at a table in a corner of the room at a computer, energetically filling out electronic paperwork. I nod appreciatively at her, and she pauses long enough to give me a thumbs-up.

At the center of the room, a couple of general-surgery guys are hovering around a small man lying on the operating table. One of them is Dan — the chief resident, married to Sally's friend — the same one I saw banging the brunette nurse in the call room a few weeks ago.

As I move closer to the operating table, I realize that the patient lying on top of it is not a man but a young kid, barely a teenager. He's completely naked except for a bunched-up, bloodied hospital gown that covers his genitalia like a fig leaf on an old Greek statue.

He's already asleep, his smooth, pubescent features obscured by the plastic endotracheal tube secured in his mouth. His eyes are taped closed, a single strip placed vertically over each eyelid. The tape, a common practice in the OR to protect the eyes from drying out during operations, always makes me think of ancient Greek funerals, when family members placed coins over the eyes of the departed so they could pay the ferryman Charon to cross the river Styx into Hades, the land of the dead. It's a creepy analogy, I know. So I don't exactly go around sharing it with people at work.

Dan approaches me, his handsome face and straight blond hair obscured by his surgical mask and cap. We exchange pleasantries.

"So." He jerks his thumb toward the kid on the operating table. "Sorry to bother you. Thanks for coming up so quickly."

"No problem. What's up?"

"Healthy fourteen-year-old black male with multiple GSWs to the abdomen and pelvis. The usual bullshit: Said he was standing on a street corner, minding his own business, when some guys he didn't know just came up to him and shot him for no good reason. Anyway, he's been hemodynamically stable, but the CT showed multiple bowel injuries, so we're exploring him. A few of the bullets also hit his, uh, his . . ." He gestures vaguely toward the bunched-up gown covering the kid's genitals, then coughs.

"Penis? Testicles?"

"Yeah, his penis." He coughs again. "And testicles. I think. It's a fucking mess down there, and we were more worried about his abdomen, so I didn't take a very good look."

"Okay." I put on a pair of gloves and walk over to the table. Bullet-entry wounds can look deceptively unimpressive. Three are scattered across this patient's lower abdomen: irregular puncture marks in the skin, each one no bigger across than my fingernail. I gingerly pull off the bloodied hospital gown covering his groin and let it fall to the floor.

Here, in the area previously covered by the gown, the wounds are a lot more obvious. One of the more seasoned scrub nurses, laying out instruments on a table behind me, stops to peek over my shoulder and whistles. GG, who's joined me at my side, gasps.

One of the bullets has entered the skin near the base of the kid's penis and torn a path like a gopher through moist soil down nearly the entire length on the left side, exiting near the tip through a large, ragged hole located right next to the catheter that's draining urine from his bladder. Another bullet (or the same one, maybe, but it's hard to tell with all the dried blood and shredded skin; in any case, the question is pretty much academic) has ripped through the left side of his scrotum. A bloody, pulpy mess

— the remains of the left testicle — pokes out of the torn skin. Through the same gaping hole in the skin, I catch a glimpse of the right testicle, which looks okay.

I'm abruptly struck with an image from an old World War II movie I saw once. It's a scene in which a GI gets one of his balls blown off by a land mine, and his grizzled, been-there-done-that sergeant tosses the emancipated testicle away over his shoulder and assures the poor guy that his other testicle is just fine and that everything's going to be okay because *that's why God gave us two, soldier.*

I tell Dan that the kid's going to need some work and to call me when his team finishes fixing the intestines. GG affirms she's going to stay and help. I call Dr. Jones, the professor who's on call, and then Sally (just back from Providence) to let her know that I likely will just sleep in the hospital tonight. GG and I then head to the cafeteria to grab some dinner. With time to kill, and the potassium weighing heavily on my mind, I take her into my confidence, telling her all about my conversations earlier that day with my friend the kidney doctor and Jason. She listens intently, wide-eyed, hanging on my every word, vowing to help me solve the mystery of where the potassium came from.

GG and I meet up with Dr. Jones in the OR a few hours later, after Dan's team is done. Jones is really pissed about having to come to the hospital tonight, something about leaving in the middle of his daughter's engagement dinner. Very old-school and very cranky, he keeps mumbling stuff like "Why can't these people just shoot each other in the head and save us the trouble?" and "Well, the sooner we fix him up, the sooner he can go back to selling drugs and shooting his friends."

By the time we're done, I'm firmly decided to stay overnight in the hospital. I dispatch GG to the medical-student sleeping rooms and trudge to my dingy call room, where I'm greeted once again by its dusty kitten denizen on the poster hanging on the pockmarked wall. The room is eerily quiet — no drunks or amorous couples tonight — just the occasional speeding car or distant police siren echoing along the deserted city streets below my window.

I lie down on the bed. The kitten dangling from the clothesline regards me from its spot on the wall, its furry outline and the black circles of its punched-out eyes both visible through the orange-hued darkness.

Hang in there, baby!

The urge to rip the fucking thing from the

wall almost overpowers me. Gritting my teeth, I roll over; which at first isn't much better because then I have the insane sense that the smug little bastard is *watching* me. But, eventually, the feeling goes away, and I'm fading off to sleep when the metallic click of the electronic door lock jolts me awake.

The last few weeks have left my nerves as frayed as those of the PTSD-stricken vets I've taken care of over at the VA Hospital across town. Adrenaline surging, I'm out of bed in an instant, flipping on the light switch and squinting through the flickering light at the lithe, tall figure darkening the doorframe.

It's GG.

She slips into the room, the door closing softly behind her.

How does she know the combination to the electronic lock?

Wordlessly, she unhooks her omnipresent smartphone from its hip holster and places it gingerly on the bedstand. She turns to face me, her lips slightly parted; her thick brown hair falls languidly over the right half of her face, partly covering her right eye, but she doesn't brush it away, which, of course, makes her look really sexy.

She wraps her arms around me and starts

kissing my neck.

I don't resist, but I don't respond, either. I just stand there, my arms hanging limply at my sides, feeling her soft, warm lips press lightly against my skin.

Oh my God, that feels good.

"GG, I don't think . . ."

Her hands steal to the drawstrings of my scrubs, exploring the thick folds of cloth with an urgent dexterity. Her breathing quickens, hot on my neck.

"My wife . . ."

She's loosened the drawstrings and is reaching inside my pants. I somehow manage to suppress the groan rising from my throat.

"I have a family . . ."

And then she whispers in my ear the four words that I don't want to hear.

And yet want her to say more than anything in the world right now.

"Nobody has to know."

An oddly detached part of my brain — the cautious one again, I reason dimly — realizes with remarkable clarity that I'm disinhibited by sleep deprivation and chronic stress, which is a mental state not unlike being drunk. It tries desperately to pull me back from the brink of this looming chasm by reminding me that nothing good can possibly come of this whole thing.

But something brittle inside me snaps. All of the strain of the past several weeks swirls together in an intoxicating kaleidoscope of images that overwhelms my fragile emotional state and throws reason out the window. The Cefotetan. Mr. Bernard. Mrs. Samuelson. The Safety Committee. The potassium orders. My inability to reach out to Sally. Watching my career evaporate before my eyes.

The attractive med student who now has her hands down my pants.

All at once, this maelstrom of emotions and stress overruns the teetering defenses that have thus far stood between fidelity and GG's unabashed advances.

I press my body against hers and kiss her hard on the lips. She responds eagerly, and I lose myself in her.

In retrospect, the one thing that surprises me the most about our encounter is how wild she gets. A feral, GG she-id surfaces, replacing the calm, reserved persona I thought I knew so well. I mean, she *really* gets into it, moaning and screaming and passionately calling out my name. She even digs her nails into my back and butt hard enough to draw blood. I've never had such rough sex before, but I can't say it doesn't turn me on even more, especially after years of pleasant, but overall pretty vanilla, sex with Sally. I wonder, in spite of the relatively soundproof walls of the call room, if her screaming is going to wake the whole hospital.

Both times.

Afterward, lying in the narrow bed together, drawing circles around my belly button with her finger, she coos, "So, do I get that 'A' now, or what?"

"Yeah, I think you earned it." I laugh, a little uneasily.

"What do I have to do for extra credit?"

"I'll try to come up with some, uh, extra assignments for you."

"Anything you want. I'll do anything you want me to."

Joking around or not, that last line creeps me out — especially since a strange, pouting quality has crept into her voice, almost like a little girl, that I've never heard before. It suddenly dawns on me that the naked woman curled around me is not my wife. My stomach does a guilty flip.

"What are you thinking about?" she asks after a few minutes of silence.

"Nothing."

"Liar."

"I guess . . . I guess I just never planned on something like this happening."

She props herself up on one elbow. "It's okay, Steve. I'm not looking for anything serious. I like you. And I just want to have a little fun with a guy I like."

I stare at the ceiling and say nothing.

"Don't pretend like you don't want me, Steve. I know you do."

"That's not the issue. Or maybe it is. I don't know. I'm just . . . very confused."

She smiles impishly. "Maybe I can straighten things out for you." She bends down and starts kissing my stomach. Then she methodically starts working her way south.

And, much to my chagrin, and shame, two times becomes three.

CHAPTER 9

Sunday, August 9

I wake with a start. Bright sunlight pours into the room in defiance of the single dirty window and spills across my eyes. I groan and roll over onto my back. The very first thing I see is the kitten on the wall, studying me indifferently from across the room. I groan again.

I hate that cat.

Her smell lingers everywhere: the pillows; the sheets; even on me. But GG is nowhere to be found. Neither are my clothes; and their absence fuels my embarrassment and shame. I stare at the ceiling, the surface as blemished as the face of a teenager, my stomach churning with guilt. I've done some pretty stupid things in my life, but nothing has ever come close to this. I'm like a remorseful drunk the night after a wild party, only worse: I've broken my wedding vows, violated Sally's trust, and jeopardized the most important relationship in my life. Plus, unlike a drunk, I remember every-thing.

And for what?

Cheap sex in a hospital call room.

With a woman who could now, if it ever suited her, if ever she felt spurned, if ever she got pissed off at me, in a heartbeat turn my ass in to University Hospital for sexual harassment.

How could I have done this to Sally?

To Katie and Annabelle?

I close my eyes. I remember that night several weeks ago, when Sally and I sat in the kitchen, sipping our precious pinot noir by candlelight.

Congratulations, Professor!

I'm so proud of you!

I recall how tranquil Katie and Annabelle appeared that night, asleep, serene in their youthful ignorance, oblivious to all of the bad things going on in the world beyond their room. Then my imagination picks up the ball and runs with it, flash-forwarding to their teenage years, when they're old enough to first realize what a shitty father they have; and in my mind they stare at me, silent and accusatory; and I can see the sad-ness, the disappointment, the *resentment* in their eyes.

I pound the bed with my fists.

Fuck!

They can never know about this. None of them.

This *never* happened.

I yank myself out of bed. A brief search of the room reveals my clothes crumpled in a heap in one of the corners. As I'm dressing, GG calls me on my cell to tell me that she's already in the SICU, checking labs on the only two patients we really need to see this morning: Mrs. Samuelson and the kid from last night with the gunshot wound.

The sound of her voice — cool, detached, clinical — is like a punch in the gut. I feel like I'm going to puke. I don't know how I'm going to face her this morning.

I don't know how I'm going to face *anyone* this morning.

But I splash cold water on my face and meet GG in the SICU at Mrs. Samuelson's bedside. GG is nothing but business as she rattles off Mrs. Samuelson's blood-test results and current vitals; and as I watch her, I find it hard to reconcile this GG with the uninhibitedly amorous one of a few short hours ago. As for Mrs. Samuelson, well, she's pretty much status quo — she's not getting any better, but at least she's not getting any worse.

When we walk over to the gunshot kid's cubicle, I realize that we still don't know his real name. He's listed in the hospital census as Male X. Last night was a bad night for the end of the alphabet: according to the hospital census, Male X is located right next to another trauma patient named Male Y, and just across the hall from Male Z.

Male X is asleep.

Good.

I'm hungry and tired and consumed by guilt. I feel . . . dirty. I have an urgent desire to get out of this hospital and home to my family. So my entire purpose in life at this moment, the entire focus of my existence, is to slip in and slip out of Male X's room without actually having to talk to him.

I press my finger to my lips and motion GG to step back while I move forward to inspect our handiwork. I carefully pull the covers down from the lower half of his body to check the surgical dressings. At one point, he jerks restlessly in his sleep. I freeze, waiting to see what will happen, but he doesn't wake up, so I carefully finish my exam.

Relieved, I start to move away from the bed.

That's when he opens his eyes, reaches

out, and feebly tugs at the base of my white coat.

I groan inwardly. The motion reminds me of the way Katie pulls at my pant leg when she's trying to get my attention.

Katie.

I *really* need to get home to my family this morning.

I look at him, and he looks at me. His eyes are a little glazed over from the narcotics and the sedatives, but lucid enough for me to know that he's probably going to remember our conversation. He's wearing nasal cannula — clear plastic oxygen tubes that clip underneath the nostrils, beloved by soap operas and TV medical dramas. They hiss gently, like two docile snakes.

I muster my best doctorly smile. "Hi, I'm Dr. Mitchell. You're okay. You were shot last night, and we had to operate, but everything went well. Your operation's over now. You're in the intensive care unit of the hospital. Everything's going to be just fine."

He says something I can't hear. I lean over and ask him to repeat it.

He swallows, licks his lips, blinks, and says, "Doc, do I gots the bag?"

Damn. I guess he hasn't talked with any of the trauma surgeons. He wants to know if he has a colostomy bag. He does. The trauma team had to give him one because one of the bullets shredded his colon.

I don't want to be the one to have to tell him. I glance around, hoping to catch a glimpse of someone to whom I can pass responsibility for telling this fourteen-year-old kid that the contents of his intestinal tract now empty into a plastic bag attached to a big, man-made hole in his abdominal wall.

I try to punt. "You really need to talk to the other surgeons."

He blinks. "Do I gots the bag?"

I glance over my shoulder. *Shit.* Nobody here but us urologists. Where the hell is the trauma-surgery team this morning?

I put my hand on his shoulder, lean over him, and say in a low, even voice, "Yeah, guy, you have the bag. One of the bullets hit your large intestine and ripped it up pretty good. That bag on your belly will keep you from getting sick and give you time to heal." I'm careful to hold eye contact with him. He deserves that much.

He shakes his head and closes his eyes. He doesn't cry, exactly; but his entire body shudders once, twice, three times. For several seconds he keeps his eyes squeezed shut, and when he opens them again, they're glistening with a fine patina of moisture. He turns his head away from me, puts his thumb in his mouth, and fixes his eyes on the wall.

The kid's reaction stirs in me a need to reassure him that everything's going to turn out okay. So I tell him that the trauma surgeons will be able to hook his intestines back up the way nature made them once he's had some time to heal. That he's lucky he won't be in a wheelchair for the rest of his life. That he's lucky to be alive.

And I realize, in the telling, that I haven't been doing enough of this with my patients lately. Of sitting down with them and just being a doctor.

But it doesn't really matter. He doesn't hear a word of it.

"Yeah, a'ight." He stares at the wall and sucks his thumb, an urban man-child who, before last night, had a completely intact intestinal tract, two testicles, and no reason to think that that state of affairs would ever change. He couldn't care less about what I'm saying, his attention no doubt now completely focused on the plastic bag taped to his belly that will start slowly filling up with shit once his intestines start working again.

I take my hand off his shoulder and leave

without telling him that he only has one testicle.

Better to wait on that for another time.

GG is waiting for me outside the cubicle. She's leaning against the wall with an amused expression, arms crossed.

"What was *that* all about?" she asks as she falls in step next to me.

"What do you mean?"

"You. All of that compassion for our teenage friend with the acute lead poisoning. It's not like you."

"It just . . . I don't know. It seemed like the right thing to do."

"I guess," she says indifferently.

We head together toward the elevators, my remorse mounting with each step, my brain scrambling to determine an expedient exit strategy from this walk of shame.

"Buy you a cup of coffee?" she asks brightly.

Not the exit strategy I had in mind.

"Ummm . . . I really need to get home this morning, GG."

"Come on," she coaxes playfully as the elevator doors open. "Just one cup. You don't even have to drink the whole thing."

I follow her onto the elevator, relieved to see that the other passengers — a group of chattering nursing students — will prevent us from being alone. It kills me to admit it, but she looks good this morning. Unlike me, she's puts some thought into her appearance by taking a shower and putting on a fresh pair of scrubs. Her hair is thick and lustrous. And if she's feeling sleep-deprived, it certainly doesn't show on her face, which is unlined and fresh.

By the time we've reached the first floor, I've relented. I'm not exactly sure why.

After we've grabbed our coffees and found a seat in the mostly empty cafeteria, she says, "So about last night — when can we do it again?"

I nervously finger the sides of my coffee cup. "GG, I, uh —"

"I bet it took your mind off that whole potassium thing."

"Yeah. Definitely. Look, I, uh . . . Last night . . . it was great, but —"

"But what?" She tilts her head to one side, studying my face. "Oh, okay. I get it. Look. I already told you, Steve: I don't want anything serious. I don't need the hassle. I'm way too focused on my career for that kind of distraction. Nobody has to get hurt."

Except Sally.

I stare morosely into my coffee without responding.

"Honestly." She rolls her eyes. "I don't

think I've ever seen a guy get so bummed out over getting laid. Tell you what. Go home. Do whatever it is you feel you have to do. And when you work through this, I'm here, okay? Or I'm not. No pressure. Think of me as a friend with benefits."

She stands up, crisply straightens out her scrubs, and snatches her coffee, all business again. "I'm going to head upstairs and enter Male X's orders into the computer. The ones we talked about."

"Umm, okay."

"Then I'll sign out to Toby. He's the resident who's cross-covering. Okay?"

"Sure. Thanks."

"You're done for today, right? Alan, the chief resident over at St. Mary's, is cross-covering?"

"Yeah." I'd almost forgotten I have the rest of the day off. I'm going to a barbecue with Sally and the girls.

Quality family time with the family I betrayed last night.

Then, down deep in my brain, underneath the roiling combination of guilt and fatigue, something jars lose.

Something about what GG just said bothers me, and I frown in concentration, trying to figure out what it is.

I'm going to head upstairs and enter Male

X's orders into the computer.

Eyeing my expression, GG asks, "Was there something else?"

I bet it took your mind off that whole potassium thing.

"No. Everything's . . . fine."

"Okay. See you on Monday, Steve." She flashes an uncertain smile and starts walking toward the cafeteria exit.

I stare at the table, trying to put a mental finger on what's bothering me, to make a connection I can't quite explain. It's like I have the final piece of a puzzle, but I don't know what the puzzle is supposed to look like when it's finished.

Male X's orders. The potassium thing.

Then, in a flash, it's there. The pieces fall into place.

"GG?"

She stops midstride, a few paces from the table, and wheels around with an expectant look on her face.

"What did you mean just now when you said you were going to enter Male X's orders?"

"The ones we talked about earlier. I was just going to enter them into ERIN so that Toby doesn't have to worry about it. No big deal. Routine stuff."

She starts to walk away again.

249

The hairs on the back of my neck spring up, and my heart beats a little faster.

"But how?"

This time she takes a few steps back toward the table and shakes her head with an indulgent smile.

"What do you mean?"

"How are you going to enter the medication orders? Med students can't do that. You can't enter and sign patient orders. You're not allowed to."

"I know I'm not allowed to. That's why I've been using your account and password to enter medication orders into ERIN since the middle of July."

A frigid hand grips my stomach.

"What?"

"Your ERIN account and password. I've been using them. Didn't you realize that? You gave them to Luis the first day I met you. I was there, too. I wrote them down."

I remember that morning. The hand grips my stomach a little more tightly.

"GG, those potassium orders I was telling you about yesterday. Is it possible that you might have had something to do with them? Or could you have given my password to someone else? I'm not looking to get anyone in trouble. I just need to know."

GG furrows her brow and lowers herself

warily back into the seat opposite me. I nervously finger the sides of my coffee cup, my conscience withering under the force of her wounded gaze, wondering if I've made a serious mistake. The last thing I need right now is for her to get pissed off at me — it's an extra variable in the infidelity equation I don't think I can handle.

Then, just as I decide that I've screwed up, and begin to open my mouth to apologize, the most inconceivable thing happens.

GG's lips curl into a smile.

A terrible smile.

An empty smile.

A smile that lacks even the faintest hint of humanity or compassion.

I've seen a smile just like it. Once. Back when I was an intern assigned to the ER, when the police dragged in a violent, acutely psychotic patient. He was handcuffed and pissed as hell, kicking and screaming and spitting obscenities, threatening to kill every last one of us with his bare hands. Maybe he could have, given the chance.

Anyway, after medicating him, we soon discovered he was a psychopath with a sadistic taste for capturing, then slowly torturing to death, cats and dogs in his quiet, upscale, urban neighborhood. Tipped off by a suspicious neighbor, the police had discovered in his basement a bizarre and elaborate medieval torture chamber for small animals, as well as an industrial-sized freezer stuffed full of their dismembered bodies. Whether he would have eventually graduated to humans is anyone's guess.

More than anything, I remember the way that patient smiled at us as he recounted — in a bizarre, singsong lilt — the singularly cruel things he had done to those cats and dogs.

His smile looked exactly like GG's.

Cold. Empty. Disconnected.

The frigid hand that's clamped around my stomach tautens into a vise. My mouth suddenly feels parched, like every bit of moisture has been sucked out of it by a vacuum cleaner; my palms, in contrast, are slick with sweat. I lick my lips and run my hands up and down my pant legs in a futile attempt to dry them off.

"I was wondering when you were finally going to start to figure this out, Steve," she says silkily, folding her hands together on the table in front of her. "It sure took you long enough."

"What are you talking about?"

"Are you asking me if I used your pass-word to order potassium for patients who didn't need it?" Her tone is breezy and conversational, as if we were discussing the weather; her face is a mask of tranquility, as placid as the surface of a mountain lake.

"Well, I . . ."

GG shakes her head in a way that is oddly patronizing, as if our roles were reversed, and she was a chief resident with nearly ten years of advanced medical training, and I was a relatively clueless medical student. Although it's becoming frighteningly clear that GG isn't anywhere near as clueless as your average medical student.

"Just answer the question, Steve," she says, like a kindergarten teacher patiently prodding one of her pupils toward the correct answer. "Are you asking me if I ordered IV potassium for patients who didn't need potassium by using your password?"

"Well, y-yes," I stammer. "I guess I am."

"Yes. For fifteen patients."

Now the cold hand wrapped around my stomach is clenched so tightly, I can barely breathe.

"Why?" I rasp.

"To collect enough potassium to kill Mr. Bernard, of course."

Reality seems to warp as my mind struggles to embrace this bizarre revelation. The room tilts, and I hear a roaring in my ears; my peripheral vision fades, and all I see now is GG, calmly regarding me as if from the end of a long, dark tunnel, and I worry that I might actually pass out.

This isn't happening. This can't possibly be happening right now.

But then the feeling like I'm going to faint passes; the world around us rights itself, the tunnel disappears, and the roaring in my ears fades. For one fleeting moment, I think it's all some sick joke at Mr. Bernard's expense. I even consider laughing.

But then I notice GG's eyes. I mean, *really* notice her eyes. Staring into them, I can sense an impenetrable blackness hidden beneath the surfaces, like cold, inky waters lying deep under a calm ocean. They blaze with a twisted energy. Ambition. Determination. Madness. They're all in there, tussling, jockeying for position.

The GG who followed me around like a faithful puppy for the past several weeks — the eager, enthusiastic med student and, as of a few short hours ago, passionate lover — is completely gone. She's been replaced by something more primal — a creature that, I'm strangely certain, is entirely capable of having killed Mr. Bernard.

I open my mouth to speak, but all that comes out is an inarticulate grunt, like I've been sucker punched in the stomach.

She throws back her head and laughs; the sound, which once reminded me of the pleasant cadence of wind chimes, now runs up and down my spine like ice-cold fingers.

She immediately places a hand over her mouth, seemingly embarrassed by her response. "I'm sorry, Steve. I didn't mean to laugh. But you should see the look on your face right now. You look like a fish."

"Why?" I croak. "Why did you kill Mr. Bernard?"

"To serve a greater good," she says mildly.

"To serve . . . what?"

"A greater good. But more on that in a second." She leans forward eagerly. "First, don't you want to know how I did it?"

She seems genuinely excited. I get the impression she's been waiting a long time to tell somebody whatever it is she's about to tell me. Not that it makes me any more enthusiastic to hear it.

She continues without waiting for a response. "You've probably noticed, Steve, that a lot of people like me. Professors. Residents. Nurses. Especially the nurses. I've spent a lot of time here in the hospital, working with the nurses. Learning their routines. Helping them with their work. I've fixed IV pumps, drawn blood, placed catheters, even changed bedpans. It's gotten me into their good graces, and a lot of them now pretty much trust me with anything. Like giving medications."

She sips from her coffee and grimaces. "Coffee's strong today. Anyway, it all ended up being so easy, really. I ordered the IV potassium using your ERIN account, then went to my favorite nurses — the ones I'd really been softening up — and offered to administer it to the patients for them. They'd pull the IV bag from the electronic medication dispenser, log it into the system, hand it to me, and go back to doing the twenty other things they were trying to do at the same time. They never gave me or my poor little bag of potassium a second thought.

"And why not? They'd seen me give IV medications to patients hundreds of times. Not one of them — *not a single one* — even bothered to check to see if the patient actually *needed* potassium, much less confirm that I'd actually given it. That's how much they trusted me. Besides, I never asked for very much potassium at one time, so why should they have cared?

"Then, instead of giving the potassium to the patient, I pocketed the bag, brought it home, and stuck it in the fridge. A little bit here, a little bit there . . . it didn't take long for me to build up a pretty good stockpile of medical-grade potassium." She points her index finger directly at me. "All ordered under your name, Doctor. Of course, I had to distill off some of the saline to achieve just the right lethal concentration. But that wasn't too hard."

She smiles benignly, and her gaze settles on a faraway spot somewhere over the top of my head. Her eyes glaze over, like she's having an out-of-body experience.

"I don't really remember exactly what I told him," she says serenely. "As I pushed all that potassium through the central line. I probably reassured him, told him I was giving him some medication to help his ileus. I don't know. It doesn't really matter."

She blinks, hard, and her eyes return to me. "Anyway, once I was done, I waited in a chair next to his bed. It didn't take long for him to die. Three, five minutes maybe. Very anticlimactic. He just closed his eyes, and that was it. After he had stopped breathing, I waited a while just to be sure, injected some extra potassium into the TPN bag to set up the accidental overdose story, pocketed the empty bags, then hit the code button and started chest compressions. The rest you already know. I got rid of the empty potassium bags, all fifteen of them, after I left the hospital later."

I recall that look on her face, right after Mr. Bernard's code. The exhilaration that lingered in her eyes. At the time, I shrugged it off.

How wrong I was.

She enjoyed it. Watching him die.

I find my voice. "Why are you telling me all this?"

"From the beginning, I assumed that you would eventually work through a lot of this on your own. After all, there were some pretty obvious loose ends. In fact, you disappointed me. I thought you'd figure it out more quickly." She sips from her coffee. "I wanted to move you in a certain direction. Get you to confide in me. It's all been part of my plan."

Plan? What the hell is she talking about?

"But aren't you worried I'm going to tell someone?"

"You're not going to tell anyone, Steve."

"Why?"

"Because you have absolutely no proof. You're the one who ordered potassium for patients who didn't need it. If you tell people you gave me your computer password, and that I ordered the potassium in your name, I'll deny it. Besides, giving out your password to med students violates a whole bunch of rules and laws. You could get fired.

"And anyway, who would ever believe you? What are you going to tell people? That some psychotic med student is running around the hospital killing patients? Come *on.* Listen to the way that sounds. People would think you were crazy."

She takes out her smartphone, touches the screen, and hands it to me. "All the same, though, I'm not the kind of person who likes to take chances."

The video images playing out on the screen are clear and irrefutable. Perfectly positioned on the bedside table of the call room, her smart phone captured every vivid detail of our intimate rendezvous of last night with what looks to be some kind of slick, wide-angle lens camera app. Even the kitten on the clothesline is clearly visible in the background. All dated and time-stamped with a running clock in a corner of the screen.

"Here," she says, reaching over and turning up the volume. "You don't want to miss the best part."

First there's her screaming, which I'm startled to realize doesn't sound nearly as sexy on the video as it did last night. In fact, it's tough to tell whether she's enjoying the experience or yelping in pain. But what follows is even worse.

So, do I get that 'A' now, or what?

Yeah, I think you earned it.

What do I have to do for extra credit?

I'll try to come up with some, uh, extra assignments for you.

Cold sweat erupts across my forehead.

"I know," she says. "The dean of the medical school, and the hospital lawyers, would hate to deal with another high-profile sexual harassment case." She pauses, then adds softly, "And then, of course, there's Sally."

"Don't say her name." It's like listening to rough fingernails scrape across a blackboard, hearing Sally's name coming out of her mouth.

"Suit yourself. But, after last night, a little late for righteous indignation on your part. Don't you think?"

I ignore her and stare at the phone. I'm seized by an impulse to run away with it.

But GG is one step ahead. "I've already downloaded the video, obviously. And selectively edited it for content."

The words "utterly defeated" don't even begin to describe the way I'm feeling right now. I resignedly place the phone in her outstretched palm.

"Why me?" I ask. My voice sounds tiny

and insignificant.

She regards me with something approaching sympathy.

"Opportunity, Steve," she says, not unkindly. "Pure and simple. Before I'd met you, I'd already decided that I was going to kill a patient using potassium. I was waiting for the right opportunity. I needed the right combination of factors to allow me to accomplish my goal. Unfortunately for you, you unwittingly provided me with them." She ticks them off on her fingers, one by one. "Access to your ERIN account. Mr. Bernard's Cefotetan-induced renal failure. The potassium order in the TPN. Your mishap in the OR with Mrs. Samuelson, which distracted you and Luis long enough for me to inject the potassium.

"So now you know the how. Which brings us to the other important question: the why. Why did I kill Mr. Bernard?" She licks her lips. "Do you want to know?"

I nod. It takes a surprising amount of effort. My head feels as heavy as lead.

"To serve a greater purpose."

"Which is?" I ask dully.

"To make hospitals safer."

What?

"Each year in this country nearly one hundred thousand patients die in hospitals

261

from medical mistakes. Needlessly. That's the equivalent of a jumbo jet crashing every single day for a year with everyone on board dying. It's inelegant. Perverse."

"Perverse. Inelegant." Interesting word choices for her in this particular situation. "Okay — so, what has that got to do with Mr. Bernard?"

"We engineer systems that keep jumbo jets from crashing. Why can't we do the same with hospitals? Mr. Bernard is the first step. You told me yourself: The potassium overdose forced University Hospital into reengineering a dangerously outdated pharmacy system. Think how many more deaths Mr. Bernard's sacrifice will prevent."

The absurdity of this conversation is growing exponentially by the second. "Let me get this straight — you killed Mr. Bernard and made it look like an accident to . . . make University Hospital safer for patients?"

"Absolutely. And not just University Hospital. All hospitals, eventually. The Safety Committee loves my ideas."

I blink, hard, at the mention of the committee.

"Don't look so surprised," she says. "I've been involved with it since my first year of med school." She leans forward, her face shining with excitement. "I'm going to change things. Change the world."

I'm about to answer when one of our senior professors, a gregarious, beefy man with a bright red face offset by a shock of snow-white hair, appears at our table holding a doughnut. GG literally jumps out of her seat to greet him. I remain seated, too anesthetized by what's been happening to think of doing much else.

The professor vigorously pumps GG's hand, his eyes twinkling with grandfatherly affection.

"I've seen a lot of good medical students in my day, Steve," he beams, directing his considerable girth in my direction and winking. "A lot. And GG here is one of the best, if not *the* best."

GG blushes. She actually *blushes.* Blushes! Right on cue. *Amazing.*

"Thank you, sir," GG murmurs bashfully. "Coming from you, that really means a lot to me."

"It had better," he booms. "Keep an eye on this one, Steve. She's going to be famous one day."

I mumble a halfhearted response into my coffee.

GG sits back down and, smiling vacantly, watches the professor amble away.

"Think about it," she says thoughtfully, once he's out of sight. "People can go through their entire lives without needing a lawyer. Or an accountant. Or a stockbroker. But everybody, *everybody*, needs a doctor. That's power, Steve. *That's* how you change the world."

She stares over my shoulder again, un-blinking, as if in a trance. The peaceful, dreamlike look on her face is eerie. Having finally shared her story with someone else, she looks perversely satiated, and I half expect her to reach into her pocket for a cigarette.

"No," I sputter with as much resolve as I can muster. "You're wrong. I didn't become a doctor to have power. I just want to help people."

She looks momentarily surprised. And then she laughs.

"You don't care about making people feel better. You became a surgeon because you love surgery. For you, the patients are a means to an end. They're a drug that fuels the high you get from operating. In the end, it's still all about the power. It's all about you. You and I really aren't so different."

Maybe as some kind of mental safety feature — like an automatic reflex of my brain that unconsciously kicks in to shield my psyche from these bizarre body blows and keep me from completely losing my hold on reality — my medical training takes over, and I find myself remembering back to my psychiatry lectures on psychopaths and start ticking off the list of characteristics.

They're pathologically deceitful.

Check.

They show complete lack of remorse for their actions.

Check.

They demonstrate a reckless disregard for the safety of themselves or others.

One big (and rather ironic, given her twisted career goals) check.

I don't bother to run the whole list, since she's already three for three for the first three criteria that pop into my head.

GG is watching me shrewdly. "I know what you're thinking. You're thinking that I'm a psychopath. Such an ugly word. And so simplistic. Okay, sure, I might fall somewhere along the antisocial-personality-disorder spectrum. But I want to *fix* things. I'm one of the good guys."

"I doubt Mr. Bernard would agree."

"If he knew what his death had achieved, he'd be grateful for being a part of it."

"Grateful!" She really *is* crazy. "This can't

be happening. This *cannot* be happening." I close my eyes and put my head in my hands. Ten minutes ago, I thought my life couldn't get any worse. But now I find myself pining for the relatively simple, straightforward dilemmas posed by an extramarital affair and a few bad career moves.

She leans across the table, pushes our coffee cups aside, and grasps both my hands in hers. I jerk my head up and recoil. She maintains a gentle but firm hold on my hands. I check our surroundings. The cafeteria is almost completely empty. Aside from an exhausted-looking nurse hunched over a newspaper and a janitor emptying a trash bin, we're completely alone. Neither one of them is paying any attention to us.

She tilts her head in toward mine and speaks in a low, soothing voice. "Shhh. It's okay. Shhh. You and I are more alike than you might think." Her breath is warm on my face and smells like peppermint mixed with French roast coffee. "When I first met you, I saw you as nothing more than a means to an end. But then you started to grow on me. I wasn't lying last night when I told you that I liked you. Your ability to focus — to concentrate on an operation without worrying about what might happen to the patient — is amazing. It's . . . a turn-on, actually. I wish I'd been there to see you take on Mrs. Samuelson's tumor. You almost pulled it off on your own."

She strokes my hands. "You know, we'd make a great team. Help me with the next part of my project. I can help your career. Not to mention the . . . fringe benefits." She slips one of her shoes off and begins to run her foot up the inside of my leg.

I regain some semblance of my senses and shove her away, a bit more roughly than I'd intended. "No!"

The commotion attracts the attention of the tired nurse, who gives us a curious once-over with her red-rimmed eyes before returning to her paper.

GG nonchalantly leans back, shrugs, and carefully straightens out her ponytail.

"Too bad." She rests her hand on her right chin, places her right elbow on the table, and gazes at me tranquilly. Several uncomfortable minutes tick by.

Help me with the next part of my project.

"What did you mean?" I finally ask. "About helping you? With your project?"

"Hmmmm?" she responds dreamily without taking her eyes off me.

"You asked me if I wanted to help you with your project."

"Yes."

"What did you mean? What project?"

"Why do you care? You already told me you weren't interested." She starts stroking her ponytail. Her mouth unfurls into a sly grin.

"What did you mean?" I persist.

She looks up at the ceiling, grinning.

"Yes. Why not?" she says to the ceiling. "Let's make things more interesting. Mr. Bernard was way too easy. I need a challenge. So why not?"

Her eyes drift back down to me. "Mr. Bernard was a start. But there are more problems in University Hospital. And Mr. Bernard has taught me how to fix them. Another patient is going to die. Like Mr. Bernard, it will be from a completely preventable medical mistake." She pauses. "I dare you to try to stop me, Steve."

I frown. "I don't understand."

"Think of it as a game."

"A *game*?"

"You predict who's going to die, then prevent them from dying. If you win, the patient lives, and there won't be any more accidental patient deaths involving me."

"And if I lose?"

"The patient dies." She smirks and strokes her ponytail. "And then you and I pick up again where we left off last night. Until I say it's over between us."

I laugh, in spite of all this craziness. "Right. Or else?"

"Or I show that video to Sally."

I wince.

"Steve." She pretends to pout. "Don't you realize how many guys around here want to sleep with me? And I've picked *you*."

Hooray for me. "And if I don't want to . . . *play*?"

"Another patient dies. Followed by more." She stretches her arms, like a cat unwinding from sleep. "Anyway. I promise that the patient won't die until the last week of my rotation. Right before the next Morbidity and Mortality conference."

I count the days in my head. "That's two weeks away."

"Exactly. Plenty of time for you to work things out. And then, right after Morbidity and Mortality conference, we'll meet face-to-face to discuss the results. In the Dome. Fair enough?" She stands up without waiting for an answer. "I need to get going. Oh, and I don't think I should go upstairs and put those orders in ERIN. As you pointed out, med students can't enter medication orders."

She bends down and places her lips to my ear. Her ponytail tickles my neck.

"One last thing," she whispers seductively. "About our *game*. It's for you. Only you. Asking for help will earn you a penalty."

"A penalty? What kind of penalty?"

But she's already gone, sauntering toward the exit with that unshakable confidence of hers.

I stare into my half-empty coffee cup, considering my options.

It doesn't take too long. I don't have any.

GG's right, of course. Nobody would ever believe me. How could they? I'm not sure I believe it myself. I have no evidence and even less credibility. Even if I were crazy enough to try to tell someone, they'd think I was making up some ridiculous story about a med student just to save my own skin.

And, of course, there's that video . . .

As for her dare — well, let's face it, the only reason why GG even bothered to throw down a gauntlet is that she knows I won't pick it up. The thought of playing her game, of trying to prevent her from killing again, seems even more ludicrous than telling other people about what's been going on.

I can't tell anyone that she killed Mr. Bernard.

I can't stop her from killing again.

Ergo, I'm screwed.

She's a great med student all right, I grimly reflect as my cell phone hums with a text from Sally, reminding me about the barbecue this afternoon.

I think nobody really realizes just how good GG really is.

"Here, Steve. Left! Left here!" Sally commands.

I jerk the van over for a hard left.

"Again! Do it again!" Katie screams happily from the backseat.

"Where the" — Sally glances back at the girls — "H-E-L-L is your brain, anyway?"

"Sorry," I mumble. "I was thinking about — something else."

"No kidding," she says sardonically. "You've been thinking about something else a lot lately. Not that I've had much of an opportunity to notice. You're hardly ever home anymore. Is there something going on I should know about? Other than that sick patient?"

I swallow hard.

If she only knew . . .

"No. Just, you know. I'm trying to keep the bosses happy."

"Oh? I didn't know that keeping the bosses happy meant you had to abandon your family."

"I'm sorry if I've been distracted. I had . . . a really bad week. I don't want to talk about it. Is that okay?"

"It just seems — I don't know. It just seems that you don't want to talk about much of anything lately. Is it *really* that bad at work? I thought you already had the job."

"I, uh, do. It's just that there's a lot of pressure on me still to perform. Even more than before, if anything."

She turns toward me and places a hand on my shoulder. "Look, Steve. I understand that what happened in the OR with that lady is really bothering you. But what's done is done. You've got to move on. Please. For me. And the girls."

I would move on. Except now, after this morning, Mrs. Samuelson is the very least of my worries. But I can't tell Sally that. "You're — right, sweetie. I'm sorry. It *has* been on my mind a lot lately. And it's not fair to you guys. I'll do better. I promise." I pat her hand, and she squeezes my shoulder. "So — who's going to be at the barbecue?"

She brushes a stray strand of hair from her plain but beautiful face. "Nancy told me that lots of different people from the hospital are coming with their kids. Mostly surgery residents. Should be fun."

With that last turn we wind deeper into

the suburbs and climb higher up the socio-economic ladder. Town homes and economical ranchers give way to staid colonials that glower at the shiny young upstarts in their midst: sparkling McMansions, many clustered together in gated neighborhoods with soothing names like "Bridgewater" and "Greenleaf." Sally directs me into one of these gated communities. We drive through the open gate, past an empty guardhouse, and down the broad main street of the development.

"There," Sally says, pointing to one of the houses, which sports a shiny collection of balloons tied to an ornate wooden mailbox out front.

"Wow," I observe as we drive past the balloons, following the gentle curve of the cul-de-sac. "Pretty nice. And in Weston, to boot." Set well back from the cul-de-sac at the end of a long driveway, the house is large and imposing, practically the size of an English country estate.

"Family money. Her family."

Cars crowd the front of the house and driveway, an armada of minivans, SUVs, and family station wagons occupying every inch of cement around the circle, stretching along both sides of the cul-de-sac's short stem and spilling out onto the main street. I troll along the rows of cars, looking to claim my own section of the curb.

"You weren't kidding. This is a pretty big deal."

"Well, from what I know about her, Nancy doesn't do anything halfway."

"No, I guess she doesn't."

After I finally find a spot, we walk with the kids along the cul-de-sac and up the huge expanse of driveway, past a large white catering truck, and up to the front door. Taped to the door is a sign, printed on a high-resolution printer, with a photo of three young blond children: two girls and a boy. The children are smiling in a blank, Teutonic, automaton kind of way.

We dutifully follow the instructions on the sign and walk into the foyer, Katie shuffling in front of us. The foyer is refreshingly cool and dark, in stark contrast to the brightness and oppressive humidity lying just outside the door. It reminds me of escaping into movie theaters for a summer matinee when I was a kid.

As my eyes adjust to the darkness, I see that the inside of the house is just as new and nice as the outside. It smells like a museum. I wonder how we're going to keep Katie from breaking anything.

As if in open defiance of my anxiety, a

group of screaming children bursts into the foyer from one of the adjoining rooms, almost knocking into us. They ricochet about the foyer like silver balls in an old pinball machine, shouting and laughing. Katie wraps herself around my leg, looking apprehensive. I extricate myself from her and kneel, whereupon she throws her arms around my neck.

"It's okay, sweetheart. You can play with them. Look how much fun they're having." Her gaze shifts from me, to the kids, then back to me. Determination replaces the trepidation on her face. She lets go of my neck, jumps up and down in place a few times as if warming up, and launches herself into the melee. The group moves en masse out of the foyer, out a sliding glass door, and into the backyard beyond, absorbing the odd stray child along the way, an inexorable, giggling tide.

I survey the situation in the opposite direction, where Sally has already walked into a living room. Men and women, mostly our age, stand around talking, many bouncing small babies in their arms. Some of them look familiar, faces seen in passing in the corridors of University Hospital, but I don't know any of them personally. They acknowledge me with expressions that convey the same vague recognition and continue with their conversations.

Sally joins a circle of other moms and starts chatting. Bella is tucked in the crook of one arm, eating her foot with one hand and clutching a cracker with the other, her face a Zen mask of contentment. Sally sways from side to side, talking and nodding and smiling, effortlessly transferring weight from one foot to another with unconscious maternal grace.

I really don't want to join the group or their conversation. I catch Sally's eye from where I'm standing in the doorway. She absently waves me off, hardly turning from her conversation.

This unusual (and likely brief) double reprieve from parental sentry duty makes me realize how hungry I am. With everything that's been going on, I haven't eaten for over fifteen hours. The general surgeons have an old adage about how to make it successfully through a busy night on call in the hospital when you're a resident.

Eat when you can, sleep when you can, and never, ever fuck with the pancreas.

I've always liked this axiom, which is more or less specific to general surgeons. The pancreas is an important, irritable organ that sits in the middle of the abdomen, tucked between the spleen and the liver. Bloated with its own self-importance, the pancreas is essentially a big bag of caustic digestive enzymes that is, among other things, responsible for regulating blood-sugar levels. A fickle, spiteful mistress, it can spit those digestive enzymes out at sur-rounding organs at the slightest provocation and make people sick as dogs. Hence the admonishment to treat it well.

In any event, now that I have the op-portunity, I'm ready to eat.

So I wander through the house, indiffer-ent to the chatting young parents and shout-ing kids, until I finally stumble upon the kitchen, a gleaming array of serious Williams-Sonoma hardware. A knot of women I don't know stands in one corner next to a coffee service, talking and sipping from mugs decorated with Impressionist paintings. They don't seem to notice me. They're discussing their children's bedtimes and the difficulties involved in coaxing reluctant toddlers to go to bed. I overhear one of the women say, "Well, I must be very lucky, because let me tell you: My children beg to go to bed. Absolutely beg." The other women smile politely but look doubtful.

Meanwhile, I look around for food. There are glasses and silverware and napkins and place settings and the coffee service. But no food. In a kitchen. Whatever.

Before I can dwell on this fact, though, I'm distracted by a large dry board hanging from and completely dominating an entire wall over a large, wooden kitchen table. I walk over to study it. It's about five feet wide and four feet tall and divided into four large rows and several columns. In the first column on the left side of the board, under the heading "Names" written by hand with erasable black marker in the top row, are three names — Connor, Emma, and Hannah — each hand-printed in neat letters with black marker.

No, neat isn't the word to describe that lettering. The penmanship is absolutely flawless. How can a human being possibly write with such mechanical precision?

Each name takes up its own row in the first column. The rest of the columns stretch across the width of the board like a computer spreadsheet, each headed by a single entry in the top row printed in that same scarily precise hand: music class, soccer practice, karate class, Chinese class, yoga class (yoga for kids?), something called the Math-Magicians Club . . . The list stretches from one end of the board to the other, an impressive collection of after-school activities representing, as best I can tell, the sum total of all human endeavor.

"What do you think? That's our master schedule," a clipped female voice says from behind me.

I jump and turn to face its source: a rail-thin woman, pretty in a patrician kind of way. Her face is pale but not unhealthy-looking; Jane Austen might have described it as *alabaster* or *ivory*. She's wearing a crisp white cotton shirt with the word "HARVARD" printed in discreet crimson letters over the left breast. Her shirt isn't so much tucked into as fused with her stylish tan shorts, the two joined together in a seamless, wrinkle-free union. Her attractive legs are as pale as her face but look positively charcoal compared to the flawless white brilliance of her sneakers. She wears her long, straight, blond hair in a tight ponytail, which pulls her entire face back toward her ears, her prominent cheekbones supporting the rigid skin like tent poles. The ponytail reminds me of GG.

"Oh, I'm sorry, I startled you." Her taut smile draws her face even tighter, the way a surgical glove molds itself over your hand when you pull it toward your wrist, the elastic material stretching itself over your fingers. I worry that her cheekbones might rip right through the skin. She offers me her hand. The gesture is effortlessly graceful. "Hi, I'm Nancy. You're Steve, right? Sally's husband?"

"Yes." I take her hand and she squeezes back lightly. It's like shaking hands with tissue paper. I feel her bones, light and delicate as a bird's, slide just underneath the skin.

Her face relaxes as she draws her hand away with prim precision. "I just ran into the kitchen to pull my next round of appetizers out of the oven. Even with the caterers, I like to do a few things on my own."

She produces an oven mitt, from where exactly I can't tell, and rummages through the oven. She takes out a baking sheet covered with neat lines of flaky pastries, puts the sheet on top of the stove, and with the oven mitt and a spatula starts placing them on a serving tray. Meanwhile, my mind scrambles back to Sally's prior briefings about our host today, which return to me in fits and starts. Nancy, Sally's friend from book club . . . her husband is Dan, the general-surgery resident I operated with last night.

She spins back toward me, offering a tray of steaming flaky pastries. "Here. Help yourself. Please."

I take one of the pastries off the tray. It's hot, so I bounce it lightly from one hand to another, blowing on it.

"Ooops! Careful. They're hot."

"Thanks." I take a bite. "Wow. That's really good." It really is.

The taut smile appears again, and the professional side of my brain idly wonders how often she smiles and how the skin over her cheekbones can take that kind of repeated tensile punishment and still look normal.

"Thanks. Only twenty percent calories from fat and very low-carb." She places the tray on top of the stove.

I wave toward the board with the remains of the appetizer. "Your, er, scheduling board is very impressive."

She beams at the board as if watching one of her children cross the finish line first at the Olympics. "Yes. Well. Just a little organizational habit I picked up at Harvard Law. Dan and I met at a graduate school mixer while he was at Harvard Med."

"Oh, right. Right. I think Dan mentioned that to me." Dan and I have had maybe two extended conversations over the last two years, neither of which involved our wives or where we went to med school.

"You have to be organized in my line of work."

"Which is?"

"District attorney. I like to catch bad guys."

My stomach flips over. I can think of one bad guy I would love for her to catch. "Oh, really? That sounds very —"

"I could have been a doctor," she continues without pause. "In fact, I even took some of the premed classes my freshman year at Stanford. But it just wasn't for me." She wrinkles her nose like she's sucking on a lemon. "Honestly, I don't know how you people made it through organic chemistry."

"Well, I —"

"But I love being a lawyer. Really. Very gratifying. It's hard at times not being home full-time with the children, like Sally, and it's hard to get 'me time.' " She draws quotation marks in the air with the index and middle fingers of each hand while saying "me time." "There are only so many hours in a day."

I nod blankly. I don't think she notices.

"The two girls are blossoming. Thriving, really. By the time she turned five, Emma was already reading at a second-grade level. Hannah, well, she just *loves* music and numbers. Only seven and already a genius on the piano."

She frowns. "The only one of them that's been giving me any problem at all is Connor. Emma knew all of her state capitals by heart by the time she was three and a half. But Connor? He's almost four and I can't get him past Annapolis. Oh well."

She sighs and looks thoughtfully at the scheduling board. She's finished arranging the crab things on the serving tray. "I'm thinking that if we hire a part-time tutor before prekindergarten classes start, we're still on track to squeak him into one of the lesser Ivies. Or maybe Duke. He's going to have to really want it, though. He'll probably end up being our little athlete. He's very coordinated. . . ."

I begin to consider socially acceptable exit strategies. I'm still hungry, but I worry that taking another crab thing will somehow seem impolite. I need to get out of here and find some food. Besides, given the events of the last few hours, I don't know how much longer I can credibly feign interest in the brutal selectivity of private preschools. So, marshaling one last look of sympathy and shared parental concern, I manage to interrupt her dissertation on the statistical correlations between kindergarten success and lifetime earning potential by telling her I need to check on Katie.

"It was a pleasure meeting you!" she chirps. "Feel free to help yourself to anything. Our caterer is out back manning the grill. *Nuestra casa, su casa!* We'll talk more later. I really want to get to know you. I've heard so much about you from Sally."

I step out the back door of the kitchen, blinking in the bright sunlight. The football-field-sized backyard is, if anything, nicer than the inside of the house. I head to a table loaded with appetizers and side dishes and dive into it, gorging myself on cheese and crackers while carrying out a cursory conversation between bites with a radiology resident I know only vaguely. His interest in the food is as fervent as my own, so I don't need to concentrate very hard on the conversation, and as we're talking, GG materializes in my mind's eye, calmly stroking her ponytail, smiling a vulpine smile, her chocolate eyes brimming with unsettling mirth.

Mr. Bernard was a start.

I shovel a handful of potato chips in my mouth and blink hard.

But the image won't go away.

You're free to stand back and watch someone else die a needless death.

I abruptly leave the table and my radiology acquaintance behind (who's still eating, though more efficiently now that he doesn't have to maintain a pretense of talking to someone) and grab a burger from a sweaty catering chef manning a large steel grill loaded with a butcher shop's worth of inventory. By the time I've taken five steps from the grill, I've wolfed it down.

I pause in front of a red Igloo cooler full of ice and beer, awkwardly licking the burger grease from my fingers.

Mr. Bernard was a start.

There are so many different reasons why I shouldn't have a beer right now.

I'm not a big drinker.

It's the middle of the day.

I'm sleep-deprived, stressed, angry, and depressed.

Fuck it. Absurdly, I look furtively around, like a guilty teenager sneaking a drink from the family liquor cabinet, as if someone would possibly care. I grab one, then hesitate only momentarily before snatching a second. I pop the lid off both of them with a bottle opener dangling from a chain attached to the cooler.

. . . watch someone else die a needless death.

I'm halfway done with the first beer by the time I've walked across the length of the patio to the edge of the bright green lawn, which is maintained with geometric precision. I don't know much about beer, but what I'm drinking tastes really strong; it's got a funky-looking label with a stylized picture of Paul Revere on it, so it's probably some kind of local microbrew. An India Pale Ale. Aren't those supposed to have higher alcohol content, or something? Whatever it is, I can feel it rocketing straight to my head.

I survey the vast green expanse of the backyard. In one corner of the lawn sits one of those big, brightly colored, air-filled moonwalks enclosed with black netting, which are pretty much de rigueur these days for children's parties. The electric hum of the air pump mixes with the laughing and screaming of several children, who bounce up and down happily in the middle of its inflated floor. Small shoes lie scattered on the grass outside the netted entrance, through which a collection of parents help children in and out while policing the ones inside and unsuccessfully attempting to maintain adult conversations with each other.

I choose a strategic vantage point at the edge of the patio to keep an eye on Katie, who's running around with some of the other kids on the lawn, and drink my beer.

"Cute kids," a familiar voice says from

right next to me. "Is one of them yours?"

"Luis," I exclaim. I didn't notice him standing there. Or did he just walk up now? If so, the guy moves like a cat.

"You don't have to look so shocked, Steve. I do have a life outside the hospital, you know."

"It's just — I didn't know you and Dan were friends."

"He and I went to med school together. He was my senior adviser." He takes a pull from a can of diet soda, staring at me closely.

Based on my quick perusal of Luis's University Hospital personnel file and my recent conversation with Dan's wife, I put two and two together. "Ah. Right. Haaaah-hhhvahd." I finish my first beer, toss the empty into a nearby trash can, and start in on the second. Already, my head is swimming.

"What?"

"Harvard. You guys went to Harvard."

"Yeah. So. One of the kids. Yours?"

I take a healthy swallow from the fresh beer bottle and point to Katie, "My daughter. She's five. Going on fifteen." Luis guffaws politely at the tired joke. "Do you have kids?"

"No," he says curtly, turning away. He

doesn't offer any additional information.

By now, Katie has joined a group of children clustered around a plastic horseshoe set on the far side of the yard. A man who looks like one of the fathers flits about in the middle of them.

In spite of my mood — a potent mix of guilt and anger and anxiety made even more potent with the addition of alcohol — I smile to myself when I realize who the man is: Jason Kobayashi, my friend from med school on the Safety Committee. His shoulder-length black hair is swept rakishly back from his chiseled features, and a thin gold chain dangles from his thick neck. His clothes — tank top, shorts, a baseball cap turned backward, and flip-flops — accentuate his impressive build: muscular and cut, like a classic Greek statue, or a drawing from an anatomy textbook.

Jason is explaining to his son how best to toss the plastic horseshoes to beat the other little kids. His testosterone-laden voice drifts across the yard, strong and deep and earnest and peppered with frequent "dudes." He has an easy laugh. A few of the parents of the other children involved in the game look on from a slight distance, their expressions ranging from bemusement to mild annoyance, but none of them intervenes.

"Who's the frat boy?" Luis says, pointing to Jason with his can of diet soda. "He looks familiar."

"Jason Kobayashi. He's one of the ortho chiefs."

"An orthopedic surgeon. Why am I not surprised." It's a statement of fact, not a question. Luis's tone is flat and laconic, but without malice.

True or not, stereotypes among doctors are a lot like those in the high-school cafeteria, with many of the usual high-school suspects replaced by various medical specialists: pathologists (nerds), psychiatrists (oddballs), internists (know-it-all teacher's pets), and pediatricians (spirit captains).

Orthopedic surgeons are the jocks of the medical world.

"So — which varsity sport in college guaranteed him his spot in med school?"

"That's not fair, Luis," I respond, annoyed. "I've worked a lot with Jason. He's a good guy and a great doc. Very smart."

"I never said he wasn't."

I gulp my beer and Luis sips his diet soda as we both watch Jason instruct his son on the finer points of outperforming the other six-year-olds with the plastic horseshoes.

"So, which one?" Luis asks.

"Wrestling. At Princeton."

"Uh-huh."

As if sensing that he's the focus of our discussion, Jason turns toward us. My insides give a little unpleasant tug, since the last time Jason and I spoke was when he leaked the Safety Committee report to me, and I screamed at him in frustration.

But he just smiles, his prominent deltoid muscle rippling beneath his tank top as he raises his arm in greeting.

"Steve, dude, what's up?" he calls genially.

"Not too much, Jason. How about you?" I answer.

"It's all good, brah'. No worries." He pauses, grinning affably, and inclines his head to one side. "Good to see you out here enjoying the sun." He flashes the hang-loose gesture, glances quizzically at Luis, then focuses his attention back on the horse-shoes.

Luis and I watch together silently for a few more moments. "So. Steve. I'm glad I ran into you. I've been wanting to talk to you. About Mr. Bernard."

"Why?" I drain the rest of my beer and walk unsteadily over to the cooler to grab another.

He waits until I return to the edge of the patio before responding, evenly, "How you and I didn't put enough potassium in that bag to kill him."

The freshly opened IPA halts halfway to my lips. "What do you mean?"

"You're not stupid, Steve. You must have realized it by now."

"What if I have?"

"Well, don't you think it's strange? Where did all of that potassium come from? We didn't order it."

"I don't know." I raise the beer the remaining distance to my lips and take a big swallow. "What do you care, anyway? You didn't get screwed to the wall the way I did."

He looks annoyed. "The hell I didn't. I'm the one who actually put the order for the potassium into the computer. Remember? It's my name on the medical record. I'm the one officially listed as having ordered potassium. Because of that, Collier raked me over the fucking coals. I was interviewed by the Safety Committee — same as you. And I got a letter of reprimand added to my file."

"But . . . the potassium was my idea. You tried to talk me out of it." I never realized that the Safety Committee had dragged him into this as well.

He shrugs. "It didn't make a difference. You ignored me and, against my better judgment, I did exactly what you told me to.

Collier had a fucking fit — screamed at me for ten minutes for writing the order even though I disagreed with you."

"Collier doesn't scream." I stubbornly fold my arms and watch as Katie runs from the horseshoes to the moonwalk.

"You know what I mean. Besides, getting in trouble didn't bother me nearly as much as the fact that a patient of mine died. For no good reason. I want to know how I could have kept that from happening. I want to know what I could have done better." He pauses before adding, with a touch of reproach, "Don't you?"

I turn away from Katie just long enough to cast him a sour look. *How can he possibly understand? There's nothing we could have done better.*

He's quiet for a moment as the happy screams of the kids wash over us from across the lawn. "So. Where did all of that potassium come from?"

"How should I know?"

"I thought you of all people would care. Don't you? Doesn't it bother you that one of our patients died, and we took the fall for it? It damn well bothers me. A patient died on my fucking watch, and I want to know why."

"Of *course* I care," I say, closing my eyes

and rubbing my temples. The ground feels unsteady under my feet. This really *is* strong stuff.

"You're not acting like it." I open my eyes. Luis is studying me shrewdly, and it strikes me how short and wiry but immensely strong he looks, like a gymnast, or a wrestler. His body and mannerisms convey a carefully disciplined and powerful physical energy. Even now, as he leans casually against a wooden post, it's like he's a coiled spring. His eyes have a hard look to them. He's older, I know, but those eyes seem *a lot* older. Like he's seen a lot of shit in his time. I wonder why I never noticed that before.

I examine the side of my empty beer bottle and start to carefully peel the label off one of the corners.

What exactly am I thinking?

I'm not sure, really.

"I heard you were in the Marines. Is that true?"

His face darkens. "What the hell does that have to do with anything?"

I swallow hard. I'm not really sure where I'm going with this. "Well, were you?"

"Yes. So?"

"What did you do? In the Marines?"

He turns away and gazes at the children

in the moonwalk. "Things I try to forget."

I pick at the label on the bottle, watching Luis out of the corner of my eye. Maybe it's the beer. The stress. The desperate need to turn to somebody, anybody, now that I'm boxed into a corner.

Luis seems as good a person as any. He has the same problem I do, after all — blamed for something he didn't do. In a way, he's also been used by GG, set up by her to make Mr. Bernard's death look like an accident. In fact, he just might be the only other person in the world capable of understanding.

"You know something. Don't you?" Luis is staring at me again. "Something you're not telling me?"

I shrug noncommittally and pick at the beer label. *But can I trust him?* He seems like a good, stand-up guy and all, but I still hardly know him. And what about that folder marked "Confidential" I found in his University Hospital personnel file? What the hell is *that* all about?

"Steve," he says earnestly, putting a hand on my shoulder. It's a surprisingly gentle gesture. "Really. Please tell me. What is it? This whole thing has been bugging the crap out of me. I don't mind being humbled every once in a while. Hell, being humbled is good for you. I learned that in the Corps. It helps me keep things in perspective. But being interviewed by the Safety Committee was *fucking humiliating,* man."

Yes. It was.

I pick at the label, thinking.

He seems genuine. But, let's face it, it's an insane story. I barely believe it myself. And what's to keep him from blabbing about it? What if he listens to what I have to say, then decides to tell Dr. Collier that I've completely lost it? That I'm accusing the star medical student of *murdering a patient*?

Worse — what if he tells GG?

His expression conveys curiosity, mixed with a sincerity that lends an unexpected hint of vulnerability to the ex-Marine who to me has always seemed so distant and hard.

"Confidential" the encrypted folder in his personnel file read.

I make a decision. One that will change my life forever.

"I know where the potassium came from," I hear myself say.

This is crazy.

"What?" He shifts his weight and regards me curiously.

"The potassium. I know where the potassium came from."

"Okay." He crosses his arms. "Try me. From where?"

And suddenly I'm telling him. Everything. At first, I just mean to give him a few snippets, carefully edited pieces that play down the absurdity of my predicament. But then, my tongue loosened by the IPA, it all comes tumbling out in a steady stream of consciousness, my mouth speaking before my brain even knows that it's forming the words. It's like somebody else is doing the talking for me.

Luis listens attentively, leaning in close, his face emotionless and unreadable, bland even, as I quickly relate all of the events of the past forty-eight hours. He reacts only once: when I get to the part about having sex with GG, he blinks long and hard and offers a noncommittal grunt.

It takes less time than I would have thought. Or maybe it's just my inebriated perception of time. In any event, when I'm finished, I don't know whether to feel relieved to get it off my chest or horrified by my impulsiveness. I try to stop the shaking in my hands with a big swallow of beer.

For his part, Luis simply nods, uncrosses his arms, runs a hand over his smooth scalp, finishes his soda, and says, "Okay."

"*Okay?* That's all you have to say?"

"At the moment." He places the empty soda can on a nearby table. "Yes."

"B-but!" I sputter, "Don't you —"

"Not now," he mutters. "Here comes Dan."

Dan McIntosh — the general-surgery resident married to Nancy the lawyer, the same one who called me last night from the OR to help with the gunshot wound and who I saw screwing around with a nurse outside the call rooms — is indeed ambling toward us across the lawn, holding a beer and greeting guests along the way. Dan is handsome in a bland kind of way. He's like a preppy high-school bully from a 1980s teen movie, an impression accentuated today by his unfortunate choice of wardrobe: an untucked pink Izod shirt with the collar turned up, turquoise-colored shorts, topsiders without socks, and mirrored aviator sunglasses. He's fit but not bulky, with straight blond hair combed over in a neat part and sharp, all-American features lifted directly from fraternity row or the varsity locker room.

He flashes a toothy smile that stretches beneath his mirrored glasses in a configuration reminiscent of the Cheshire cat. A smaller, distorted version of myself regards me from each separate lens of the glasses.

Dan is the type of guy who walks around with a perpetual self-satisfied smirk on his face. I've always kind of liked him though. A lot of general surgeons like Dan have attitude. I don't really hold it against them. They are what they are. It takes balls to cut people open for a living, and I think the size of the balls required to get the job done right is in direct proportion to the chances of killing the person you're cutting open. General surgeons routinely do some of the biggest, riskiest operations on some of the sickest people around. So attitude? No big deal, in my book.

"Steve. Luis. How're you guys doing? Thanks so much for coming." Dan's back is ramrod straight, broad shoulders square, chest puffed out.

"Hey, Dan." I take his extended hand. His grip is strong, and I surrender to a juvenile urge to exert a manly squeeze in return. Or what I hope in my intoxicated state passes as manly. The awkward pause that follows, with him grinning his Cheshire-cat grin, makes me realize that he's waiting for me to say something. "Uh, thanks for having us over." I cough. "This is a great party. The kids are having a blast, especially with the jumpie." I wave my hand toward the moon-walk, in which a bunch of kids are bouncing around like popcorn popping in a tub. A corner of my mind hazily notes that Katie is no longer with them and wonders if I should track her down.

She's fine. Whatever.

"No problem, no problem," Dan says silkily. "It's all about the kids. Kids love jumpies." His head is already swiveling toward Luis, and the distorted, dual images of me in his sunglasses are replaced by reflections of Luis. "What's up, man?"

For the first time since I've known him, Luis breaks into a genuine, unguarded smile. He and Dan exchange an affectionate and bearish man hug, replete with several thunderous back swats.

"Just talking with my boy here," Luis says casually.

"Ha! Your boy. Well, *your boy* and I were up late last night in the OR patching up a gangbanger whose dick ended up on the wrong side of a .38 Special. A newly minted member of the gun-and-knife club who's half the man he used to be." He throws his head back and laughs and claps me on the shoulder. At the same time, something flits across Luis's face, like a dark cloud racing across the sun on a summer day. It's gone almost as soon as it appears.

Dan doesn't notice. "Apparently, some of

his buddies came looking for him late this morning hoping to finish off whatever it was they had started out on the street. Did you hear that?" I shake my head. "Yeah." He nods sagely. "I wasn't there, either, but I heard that Security kept things from getting out of hand." Because of a continuous stream of patients like Male X, the University Hospital Security team is like its own police force: armed to the teeth, well trained, and intimidating as hell. "It's a good thing they keep the SICU locked down so tightly," he continues. "Between the nurses and the Security guy at the front desk, nobody so much as sneezes in there without someone's say-so."

"Hey, speaking of things going wrong," Luis says conversationally. "I heard you guys had a big flail back in May. Something about a patient's dying because of a major medical mistake? A patient-safety thing?"

Despite the heat of the day, and the alcohol percolating through my system, I suddenly feel very cold and struggle to maintain a straight face.

What's Luis doing?

Dan grimaces. "It was ugly. A total fucking flail, bro'."

"Really?"

Dan's wife Nancy, she of the scheduling

board and tight white skin, appears with Sally, who is drinking Perrier from a glass bottle. Nancy and Luis hug, and I introduce Sally to Dan and Luis. Sally explains that Annabelle and Katie are now inside under the watchful eye of Nancy and Dan's nanny.

"What are you guys talking about?" Nancy asks.

"That patient who died in May. Did I tell you about him? No? Well, we were rounding one morning when we found one of our patients completely unresponsive. We tried to resuscitate him, but it was no good."

"So what happened?" Luis prompts.

"The central line. One of the unused ports was uncapped. It was completely open to the air for at least an hour. Maybe more."

Luis grunts. At the same time, I suck air into my mouth while gritting my teeth, which produces a loud and protracted hiss — *much* louder than I anticipated or intended. Sally glares at the half-empty beer bottle I'm still clutching. The others stare politely. I cough and self-consciously place the bottle on a nearby patio table . . . and promptly knock it over as I clumsily, drunkenly, draw my hand away. I try to pin it down and right it as it rattles noisily over the top of the glass table, but I only make things worse, and it's about to roll off the edge of table and smash on the concrete when Luis adroitly snatches it and throws it in a garbage can.

"Pulmonary air embolus?" Luis asks, wiping the beer off his hands with a napkin. Dan nods.

"What's an air bolus?" Sally asks.

"Air *embolus*," Dan gently corrects, smoothly launching into an impromptu lecture. "An embolus is something that blocks a blood vessel. If you think of blood vessels in the body, arteries and veins, as pipes, and blood as water flowing through those pipes, an embolus is like a big hairball clogging a pipe. An air embolus is a clog made out of air. So just like when water backs up in a clogged pipe, and overflows the toilet or kitchen sink, the blood backs up behind the air bubble and bad things start to happen."

"What kinds of bad things?"

"It depends on where the blockage is. Most of the time, it's something called a pulmonary embolus, when the flow of blood from the heart to the lungs is blocked."

"How can air get into the blood?"

"The bends. If a diver comes up too fast, nitrogen in the bloodstream that's been compressed by the pressure of being deep underwater suddenly expands and forms air bubbles. Or, in this case, it was a central line going into the patient's internal jugular vein." He taps the right side of his neck. "We put large catheters in big veins a lot, especially in the ICU. It's real important to keep air from getting inside them. In this case, somebody left the cap unplugged, which means that there was a direct connection between the patient's bloodstream and the air in the room."

"Was the patient upright?" Luis asks.

"Yeah. He was sitting in a chair."

"Makes sense. Each time he inhaled, negative pressure formed between his chest and the atmosphere. It would have sucked air through the catheter and into the internal jugular vein like a big vacuum cleaner."

This lecture's getting old. "So what happened?" I ask Dan impatiently.

"We ran the code and everything, but the patient never really had a chance. He was already dead when we found him." He shrugs. "What's really been killing me is the paperwork. Have you guys heard of the Safety Committee?"

I scratch my ear and look the other way. Luis silently straps on a poker face.

"Yeah, well, be grateful. What a bunch of freakin' Nazis. They had me fill out a ton of reports, then grilled me until they were convinced I had nothing to do with what happened. Anyway, it's been a pretty big deal. I heard the family was already talking major lawsuit and that University just anted up right away."

"I don't doubt it," says Nancy in a crisp, lawyerly voice. "It's the smart move. University wouldn't have had a chance with a jury. Not to mention all the negative coverage in the media. Who left the cap off the line?"

"Nobody's talking." His eyes are unreadable behind the glasses. "Maybe a nurse." He shrugs. "We all make mistakes." But something about his shrug conveys a tacit *except me.*

Nancy politely excuses herself, hugging and air kissing Sally before floating off to greet other guests. Dan and Luis start talking baseball, good-naturedly ribbing each other about the Dodgers and Red Sox, respectively.

Sally grabs my elbow. Her fingers dig into my skin as she leans over and hisses in my ear that it's time for us to go. We say our good-byes. Dan smiles his shark smile and crushes my hand in his. Luis, betraying no acknowledgment of our prior conversation, offhandedly tells me he'll see me in the cafeteria tomorrow morning.

Sally and I collect Annabelle and Katie

from the nanny and walk out to the car. Sally maintains her composure for the girl's sake, but I can tell from the subtle accents in her body language that she is *pissed*. "So," she quietly fumes, as we settle the kids into their seats. "Did you have a good time hanging out with your drinking buddies?"

"I had — a bad week," I return lamely.

"And the mature and appropriate response is, of course, to get drunk in the middle of the day. In front of everybody. Leaving me to keep an eye on the girls. What were you thinking, Steve?"

"I'm sorry. I'm really sorry."

Her face is as dark and forbidding as a line of thunderheads on an August afternoon as she secures Annabelle into her car seat. "Nancy and Dan invited us over here for a dinner party next Saturday. So I sure hope next week goes better for you." She secures the last strap in place with a decisive click, slams the door closed, and climbs into the driver's seat.

The mood in the car on the ride home is silent and dreary. Sally grips the wheel, clenching and unclenching her fingers, staring intently at the road. Katie and Annabelle are uncharacteristically quiet, perhaps sensing the tense atmosphere.

I gaze out through the open car window.

The air blowing in is warm and comfortable, laced with the earthy scent of summer foliage. Afternoon sunlight plays through bright green leaves. The pleasant scenery stands in mocking contrast to both the bleak ambiance inside the car and the wreckage of my life.

Confiding in Luis was definitely a roll of the dice, and I don't know quite what to make of his reaction to my story earlier. How tomorrow will play out at work, with me and GG and Luis all thrown together under this new and utterly bizarre set of circumstances, is anyone's guess. And then there's the whole matter of that confidential file in his personnel folder. What the hell is that all about?

I try to figure out my next step. But my beer high is wearing off, and fatigue creeps through me, like a late-day fog moving inland from the ocean, probing and spreading vines of mist across the coast. Biochemically speaking, alcohol is a depressant, which is why people can so quickly yo-yo from life of the party to passed out senseless on the floor. I'm quickly heading for the passed-out-senseless-on-the-floor phase.

And it's more than just the alcohol. I'm tired. Bone tired. Every limb in my body aches. The human brain and body can only

306

take so much punishment at a time. It's a physiologic fact. My brain and body, racked by stress, are running on fumes and are starting to shut down.

When we get home, I help Sally unload the girls from the car and get them settled inside. By now, I'm so mentally and physically exhausted that I'm barely able to help Sally feed the girls, bathe them, and get them in their pajamas before I stagger to our bedroom, kick off my shoes, sprawl across the bed with my clothes on, and give myself over to a dreamless sleep.

CHAPTER 10

Monday, August 10

I decide that I can't handle my usual breakfast meeting in the cafeteria with Luis and GG. It would be too much weirdness all at once, trying to keep up some pretense that things are somehow still normal after the events of the last seventy-two hours — particularly in front of the only other two people in the world who know they're not.

Besides, although I'm relatively well rested this morning, my mind sharper than it has been in weeks after nearly twelve hours of unbroken sleep, I also feel like someone has driven a large metal spike through the center of my skull — a painful calling card from yesterday's beer binge.

I call Luis early, tell him I'm not going to meet with them this morning, and instruct him to just handle everything himself this morning for the patients. He grunts his acknowledgment and hangs up.

Luis. Alone in the OR changing room, brooding, I shake my head as I pop a couple of Advil, deposit my street clothes into my locker, and change into scrubs.

How could I have been so stupid? How could I have just told him everything like that on a drunken whim? What did I possibly hope to accomplish? He must think I'm hopelessly delusional.

And why not? It's a perfectly reasonable assumption. If our positions were reversed, and he confided to me that a star medical student was actually a ruthless murderer of patients trying to advance her career, I'd think he was, medically speaking, out of his *fucking* mind. Or maybe making some kind of sick joke.

I slam the locker door closed.

I feel like a complete ass. The only question now is what Luis will do with the information. Will he tell everyone I've gone off the deep end? Or report it to Dr. Collier as some kind of weird paranoid behavior? I honestly wouldn't blame him if he did. In fact, going to Dr. Collier might work out nicely for him. Earnestly confiding to the boss that he's really worried about my mental health might help absolve him of his role in the potassium incident. Unfortunately, it would also erase any shred of credibility I have left and send my career into a complete tailspin.

Or would he tell GG?

That last thought gives me pause.

I've never really stopped to consider their relationship. GG and Luis have worked together a lot, undoubtedly sharing meals and long hours in the hospital the way she and I did. Has she played Luis the way she's played me, I wonder?

And what did GG say to me on Saturday?

Asking for help will earn you a penalty.

What the hell did she mean by that? I suppress a shudder and decide not to dwell on it, at least for now. What's done is done. I'll just have to see how things develop and make it up as I go along.

Later that morning, as Jason predicted, the Safety Committee issues its final report on Mr. Bernard's death. Quietly, of course. There aren't any public announcements, only a stern lecture from Dr. Collier, who, waving a copy of the report in front of my face as I'm sitting on his couch that afternoon between surgeries, informs me that, effective immediately, I'll be "standing down" from the operating room for the next several weeks. I'm forbidden from operating on patients in University Hospital. I'll also be temporarily removed from my position as Luis's boss and won't be routinely rounding on our patients.

In place of my usual duties, Dr. Collier tells me, I'll be temporarily reassigned to the outpatient clinic (replacing Luis, in fact) while I take the Safety Committee-mandated remedial coursework through an online system directed by University Medical School. Perversely, it'll be like a vacation — because the Safety Committee is restricting my activity, and clinic is only one day per week, and the course work will only be a few hours per day, I'm going to have a lot of time on my hands. The most I've had in years.

Dr. Collier makes it absolutely clear that any reluctance on my part to participate in any part of this plan will result in the immediate termination of my employment at University — a black mark beyond black marks. My surgical career would be over.

What else can I do but bend over, grab my ankles, and take it? Some illogical part of me, a hopelessly optimistic ember, burning God knows where deep in my consciousness, thinks I can still ride this whole thing out if I play my cards right. The trouble is, I really don't have any cards right now. And even if I did, I wouldn't have the faintest idea how to play them.

After my meeting with Dr. Collier, I trudge listlessly upstairs to my locker to change out of my scrubs. I spin the combination, tug the lock open, and open the door.

A folded piece of paper drops out of the locker and floats to the floor.

Curious, I pick it up and read the four, neat, hand-printed lines.

The Old Crow.
Financial District.
7 PM tonight.
Tell no one.

What the hell?

I look around the locker room, but it's empty except for me.

I pause just inside the threshold of the Old Crow and survey the dimly lit room, squinting into the semidarkness. The bar is small, with an upscale-pub kind of vibe, and is pretty packed — a white-collar, post-work crowd by the looks of it, intermixed with some college kids. A Red Sox game is playing on several flat-screen TVs.

After several minutes, I finally spot him sitting on a barstool next to a high table in a far-flung corner of the room opposite the entrance. His back is to a wall, and he's facing me. A Red Sox baseball cap partly obscures his face. I note that half the guys in the place are wearing Red Sox caps; and, for some odd reason, even though he didn't wave or otherwise overtly acknowledge my presence, I get the impression that the only reason why I'm able to pick him out from the crowd is because he allowed me to.

I weave my way through the throngs of tightly clustered twenty- and thirtysomethings and approach the table, on which sits a half-eaten plate of french fries and a glass of soda.

"Hi."

Luis inclines his chin incrementally. "You're late."

"Do you mind if I sit down?"

His gaze remains fixed on the door through which I just walked. "I wasn't sure you'd come."

"I almost didn't." I had stared at that piece of paper for maybe thirty minutes, reading and rereading it, before finally making my decision. "I wanted to hear what you had to say." I pull a barstool up to the table.

"Did you tell anyone where you were going tonight?"

"No."

"Even your wife?"

"Nobody knows I'm here. Except you."

"Have you told anyone else about GG and the potassium and Mr. Bernard?"

"No."

"Were you followed?"

"No. I mean, I don't know, Luis," I snap. "Look. I got the message in my locker. So I'm here. Aren't you being a little paranoid about this whole thing?"

He snorts and diverts his attention away from the front door just long enough to shoot me a disdainful look.

"GG murdered a patient right under our noses at one of the most prestigious hospitals in the world," he growls. "*Our* hospital. She's got you by the balls and, from what you told me, seems to be loving every minute of it. Personally, I don't think I'm being paranoid enough."

I flush and consider the underlying significance of this statement as he eats a french fry and takes a sip of the soda. "So . . . you believe me?"

"Yes."

"Really. Why?"

He pushes a sleek, silver-colored metallic object the size and shape of a man's wallet across the table toward me. "I found this duct-taped to the underside of your car this afternoon. In the hospital parking lot."

"How do you know what my car looks like? Or where it was parked?"

"Do you know what it is?"

"No." I pick the silver thing up.

"A GPS tracking device. The nicer ones retail for about $175 on the Internet."

My throat suddenly feels as if it's been grabbed by a meaty pair of hands, and I struggle to draw a thin, reedy breath, as if trying to sip air through a straw. "What?"

"A GPS tracker. Did you put it there?"

"No."

"Did your wife?"

"No! Of course not."

"Well, someone's interested in following you. My bet is GG."

I stare at the device in my hand.

Son of a *bitch.*

"You know, Steve," Luis says matter-of-factly, reaching over and gently taking the tracker from me before placing it in his pocket. "I have to admit that yesterday I was a little . . . uh, doubtful when you first told me. I mean, a med student, a really good one, who's actually a psychopath murdering patients to advance her own career? On the face of it, most people would say you're either lying or need to be institutionalized." He shrugs and chews on a fry. "But truth can be stranger than fiction. I've seen some pretty weird shit. And the sheer audacity of it makes it all the more credible — because, who would ever suspect her of being capable of such a thing? Of anyone's being capable?"

He wipes his mouth with a napkin. "But the facts all fit. She was there when you gave me your ERIN password that morning in the cafeteria. She watched me write it down. I didn't think it was a big deal at the time, your giving me your password — I mean, what the hell, we all do it. She was also there when you gave the order for the potassium. And she was the first one in the room when Mr. Bernard coded. Even before the code team."

He pops another fry in his mouth, wipes his hand on the napkin, and drops it on the table in front of him. "I watched her today. Carefully. There's no doubt in my mind she did it. Back in the day, when I was still in the Corps, I would have spotted her sooner."

"What do you mean?"

He purses his lips. "Let's just say that studying people was part of my job. I ran across quite a few characters like GG in my time. All over the world. Psychopaths. Murderers. People that I hoped to Christ I would never see the likes of again."

I think again of the encrypted folder

marked "Confidential" in his University Hospital personnel file. The more I get to know Luis, the more I wonder what's in there. "People like who?"

"It doesn't matter." The corner of his mouth twitches. "I'm not allowed to talk about it. I don't want to talk about it." He shoves the plate of fries away. "What matters is that she's given you a little under two weeks, and two weeks isn't a hell of a lot of time to act. We have to jump on this now if we're going to catch her."

"Catch her? What do you mean? I don't understand."

He leans toward me, his voice low and barely audible over the wash of conversation, splashes of laughter, and intermittent cheers and groans around us as people take in the game. His eyes dart from me to the front door and back again. "I mean I want to help you. What do you think? Was she serious? Is she really going to kill someone else the way she said she would?"

I dare you to try to stop me, Steve.

I remember the look in her eyes: the cold, calculating, remorseless resolve.

Let's make things more interesting.

Mr. Bernard was way too easy. I need a challenge.

"Yes. I think she was completely serious. I

think she's going to kill again. I think she wants me to try to stop her just for the sport of it and that she's going to play by that bizarre set of rules she laid down."

"In that case, she's presented us with a golden opportunity."

"To do what?"

"Beat her at her own game. Between the two of us, I'm convinced that we can outsmart her. Not only prevent her from murdering her next victim but gather the evidence we need to trap her. Catch her in the act, basically. But we need to work together. I propose a . . . partnership."

"What kind of partnership?"

"She won't suspect me. So I'll follow her. Study her routines. Figure out what she's been up to. Get to know her patterns. Meanwhile, you pretend to play her game. Get inside her head. Try to anticipate her next move. Identify her future victim." He leans back. "What do you think?"

"How do we keep her from getting suspicious?"

Deep lines etch themselves across his brow. "She probably thinks you're broken. Because you've had your balls served to you on a silver platter." He glances at me thoughtfully. "Are you? Broken?"

"No." I sound a lot more confident than I feel.

"Good. We can use that to our advantage. If she thinks you're well and truly beaten, she might let her guard down. There's a good chance her ego might blind her." He pulls the baseball cap down a little more tightly over his face and looks up briefly at one of the TVs as jeers ring throughout the bar, presumably over some injustice visited upon the Sox. "Dr. Collier told me that he's pulled you out of the OR for the next few weeks."

"Yes."

"I'm sorry." He sounds sympathetic. "I really am, Steve. That sucks. I'm supposed to temporarily take over running the hospital service."

"Yeah. And I'm supposed to run your Tuesday outpatient clinic."

Luis looks pensive. "With GG."

"What?"

"She goes to clinic on Tuesday mornings. Remember? We talked about it in the cafeteria, during her first day of the rotation. She's been there every Tuesday this month, helping me out. Doing a hell of a job. Not surprisingly."

Crap. I'd completely forgotten about that. I sigh, squeeze my eyes shut, and rub my eyelids with my fingers. Just me and GG, working for hours together. Awkward, to say the least. The thought makes me queasy. Not from fear. I'm beyond fear, at this point. I mean, what the hell else can she do to me?

When I open my eyes, Luis is staring at me. "A prime opportunity for you to collect some intel."

"What?"

"Intel. Intelligence. Information on her."

"Oh. Yeah. I guess." I scratch at a mark on the table.

He folds his arms and looks at me appraisingly for several long seconds. "So. What do you say? Are we working together on this?"

I wring my hands together and squirm in my seat. "I'm not so sure, Luis. I — I need some time to think."

The corner of his mouth twitches. "You don't have any time. If you didn't want me to help you, then why did you bother to tell me about her in the first place?"

Because I was drunk and stupid.

"I — maybe I was just looking to confide in someone who I thought would understand."

He scowls. "Bullshit. I'm not your priest, Steve. She's going to kill again. And she's going to do it soon. With or without you,

I'm going to stop her." He reaches for his wallet and begins to rise from the stool.

"Wait." I grab his arm. "Let's do it." Like a lot of things emerging from my mouth lately, the words are out there before I've consciously decided to say them.

"Okay, then," he says, folding his arms and settling back down on the stool. "But first, I want a guarantee that you're going to do exactly what I tell you, when I tell you. If we do this together, we do it my way. No questions asked."

What choice do I have now? "Fine." I grit my teeth and, without thinking about it, extend my hand over the table.

His gaze flickers over my outstretched palm with thinly veiled contempt. "Are you kidding me? This isn't some fucking contract negotiation, Steve."

I flush at the rebuke, withdraw my hand, and ball it up in my lap, digging my fingernails hard into my palms. "So, now what?"

"Have you thought about other ways she might kill people and make it look like an accident?"

I have, actually. How could I not have, if only out of morbid curiosity? I clear my throat, relieved to be able to finally add something useful to the discussion. "Well, I think there are two points we need to keep in mind. First, I think she's going to use a method she hasn't used before. She made that clear to me on Saturday. Second, she's going to do something that she believes, in her own twisted way, will benefit future patients."

He strokes his chin and nods thoughtfully. "So what do you think?

"The potassium overdose was a perfect modus operandi. Quick, lethal, relatively easy to pull off, and difficult — if not impossible — to trace back to her. I'm not surprised she used it first."

"Agreed. So what else is there?"

"Well, there's a pulmonary air embolus. Like the one Dan told us about at the barbecue yesterday. A central venous line is a ripe target."

He grunts, and the corner of his mouth twitches. Otherwise, he remains still as a statue. "Go on."

"Except a determined killer wouldn't leave anything to chance by simply uncapping a central line. What I would do is inject several hundred cc's of air directly into the subclavian, internal jugular, or femoral vein. That amount of air rushing into the pulmonary artery all at once would stop the victim's heart almost instantaneously. Just like the potassium — easy, quick, lethal, and difficult to trace.

"But I think also unlikely, at least in this case. According to Dan, that patient's death in May triggered a hospital investigation. GG would know that."

"What if she was the one who caused the embolus?"

I shift uneasily on the stool, which isn't very comfortable and is pressing up against my tailbone. "That went through my mind, too. What if Mr. Bernard wasn't her first victim?"

"Exactly."

"But either way, even if she *did* kill that other patient, it wouldn't benefit her to do it again. She's not going to waste her time on something that's already happened recently. She's going to come up with something new. Otherwise, it's not worth her while. So I think we can cross air embolism off our short list for now."

He pauses for a fraction of a second. "Agreed. What else?"

"Insulin overdose. She could crash the blood sugar in a diabetic patient. Lethal within minutes. But more difficult to accomplish. How would she give the patient the insulin without anyone's knowing it? And once the seizures start, the hospital code team is going to respond quickly, and one of the first things they'll do is check blood sugar and give an amp of glucose.

"In addition to insulin, there are all kinds of potentially fatal medications. You and I have both changed our ERIN passwords, but we have to assume that she's resourceful enough to find her way back into the medication-ordering system."

"Agreed." Luis has turned away from the door and is now scrutinizing me closely. His eyes are devoid of all emotion; his expression is like a blank sheet of paper. I'm again reminded of a large jungle predator — watching, listening, waiting.

"Medications lead to a host of possibilities. A big IV dose of epinephrine — say, a couple of milligrams — would induce a massive non-Q wave myocardial infarction. A huge bolus of morphine, obviously, would stop someone's respirations cold. Overdoses of anticoagulants like heparin or Coumadin could precipitate devastating bleeding. Especially in a postop patient. All creative and harmful — but none with ironclad guarantees of lethality. MIs can be treated, morphine and other narcotics countered with naloxone, anticoagulants reversed.

"You could inject a lethal bacterium directly into a patient's bloodstream. I read recently about several patients who died in a hospital because their TPN fluid was infected with *Serratia marcescens*. VRE or MRSA might work also. But you'd have to isolate and obtain the bacterium. And, of course, there's always the possibility that somebody would identify the infection and treat it effectively before the patient died. Not very practical.

"Then there's acute radiation poisoning. Several hospitals have gotten into trouble when their patients were injured or killed by CT scanners mistakenly set to dangerously high radiation levels. Theoretically, you could rig one of the diagnostic CT scanners or radiation oncology-treatment machines to deliver a lethal dose of radiation. That would require some major recalibration of the hardware and the software, though, and that would be *really* tough to pull off. It's a little far-fetched. Besides, death would be slow and painful. And, again, by no means guaranteed."

Luis's mouth twitches, like a cat flicking its tail. "Agreed. Anything else?"

"Not right now. I'll keep working on it."

"That's a pretty good start," he says, sounding impressed. "You have some good ones in there that I never would have thought of." He snorts. "It's amazing that there are so many different ways to die in a hospital that have nothing to do with being sick. Here. Before I forget. This is for you." He discreetly passes me a cell phone underneath the table.

"I already have a phone," I say, examining the cheap display.

"It's a disposable. Prepaid. In cash. The account's untraceable."

"What do I use it for?"

"To communicate with me. Only texting. Never, *ever* any calls. And I'll be the one doing the texting — from the disposable cell phone I'll be using. Keep it on you at all times. Don't ever lose it. Even though the account is untraceable, the number's not, and if someone gets ahold of either of our cell phones, the other can be tracked through calls sent and received. Take this."

"What's this?" The sheet of paper he hands me has two columns printed on it: one column contains six rows, numbered one through six; the second column contains a single street address corresponding to each number.

"Code. I want you to memorize the number in the first column with its corresponding address in the second."

"Memorize?"

"Yes. Right now."

"How does this code work?" I peer at the

numbers.

"I'll text you the number in the first column, followed by a specific time — in four-digit, twenty-four-hour military time. We'll meet at the corresponding location at the stated time."

"So," I say, picking the number five from the first column on the paper, "if you text to me the number five . . . followed by, uh, one-nine-zero-zero, we meet at —" I squint at the paper, examining the address printed in the second column next to the number five. "At 125 Chestnut Street. At 7:00 P.M."

"Roger that."

"And you want me to memorize these codes. Now."

"Roger that."

"Why?"

"Basic counterintelligence. If it's in your brain, nobody can get to the information unless you tell them."

Swearing under my breath, I memorize the codes. He has me recite them back to him, twice, before taking back the piece of paper, stuffing it in his pocket, and dropping some cash on the table. "I'll be in touch within the next few days. Just stick to a regular routine. Do what Collier says. Fade into the background."

"How should I, you know, act around

her?"

He strokes his chin thoughtfully. "De-pressed. Beaten. Like you want no part of her *or* her game. Like all you want to do is pretend nothing ever happened and that you're desperate to just go back to the way things were. In the meantime, keep working on her most likely strategy. Beginning tomorrow morning in clinic."

"How do I do that?"

"I'll leave that to you." He shrugs. "What-ever you come up with, remember that she likes to get to clinic early. Usually by seven thirty. And don't tell *anyone* about this. Not even your wife."

I nod numbly. I have plenty of reasons to keep Sally in the dark for now.

"After I'm gone," he instructs, "wait at least fifteen minutes, then leave through the front door." He jumps off the stool, lithe as a panther, and moves quickly toward an inconspicuous door in the wall immediately next to us marked by an EXIT sign. I hadn't noticed it before, but I note that nobody has come in or out of it the entire time we've been here.

"Hey. Luis."

He stops under the EXIT sign, his field of vision evenly split between the front en-trance of the bar and me.

"What did you do in the Marines?"

He flashes a crooked grin.

"Force Recon. Intelligence. Ooo-rah."

He slips out the back door and is gone.

I stare dumbly at the disposable cell phone in my hand.

Now what the hell do I do?

Try to anticipate her next move, Luis had said.

Great. And how the hell am I supposed to do *that*?

Think, the rational half of my mind, the persistent friend I've been snubbing a lot lately, urges. *What are you good at?*

I chew on my lower lip, staring into space, as the Sox pull ahead and the increasingly raucous evening crowd presses in around me. Luis's designated fifteen-minute wait time bleeds into twenty, then thirty.

My mind lingers over the fact that I'll be working with GG in clinic tomorrow morning. *A good opportunity to collect some intel,* Luis had said. But how?

And then I get an idea.

I dutifully exit through the front door and, before heading home, drive to a small computer store in Cambridge. It's been a while since I last shopped here, but I immediately recognize the clerk behind the counter: a guy with perpetually half-closed

329

eyelids, greasy blond, waist-length hair, and a nose ring. He's wearing an untucked, faded Pink Floyd T-shirt. His potbelly bulges over the beltline of his jeans. We trade some obligatory but friendly small talk before I tell him what I need.

"Keystroke logger? Sure, man. I've got just the thing. Top-of-the-line." He heads into a back room and emerges with two items: a software CD and a small, gray, rectangular object about the size of a car key. He places them on the counter between us.

I pick up the CD. "Easy to install," he says. "Works on just about any operating system around. *Totally* undetectable by anti-spyware or countersurveillance security programs. And it'll automatically sort and then forward the keystroke data to an encrypted Web account accessible only to you." He grins. He's missing one of his incisors. It looks like a hole in a white picket fence. "The trick, of course, is loading the software onto the target without getting caught."

"It always is," I reply absently. "And this?" I hold up the smaller object. "A portable one, I'm guessing? With a USB interface?"

"Yep. It's got an eight-megabyte memory core built directly into the casing. It instantaneously downloads and stores the keystrokes — again, in an encrypted format. Might come in handy in a pinch, man."

"Pricey."

He shrugs. "You get what you pay for. These'll never let you down, man." He moistens his lips with a brief flick of his tongue. It reminds me of a lizard. His eyes gleam under the half-closed lids. "So. Which'll it be?"

"Both."

"Right on, man." He grins. He may look like he just spilled out of a Grateful Dead concert from the seventies, but deep down, he's pure capitalist.

On the drive home, I glance down from time to time at my purchases lying on the passenger seat next to me, my palms slick on the steering wheel, my guts twisted into a ponderous Gordian knot as a single, gnawing thought worms itself deep into my brain, like a splinter.

What the hell am I getting myself into?

CHAPTER 11

Tuesday, August 11, 7:01 A.M.
I grit my teeth and speed through the empty clinic waiting room. I was too nervous to eat anything for breakfast, and my stomach acids feel like they're burning a hole through my stomach wall. Clinic doesn't start until eight, but I need to load the software onto the clinic computer before GG comes in, and Luis had pointed out that she always gets there by seven thirty. Unfortunately, the automated electronic doors leading into the clinic don't unlock themselves until seven, so I haven't been able to enter the area until now.

It's going to take me about thirty minutes, plus or minus, to load the keystroke software, so I'm going to be cutting it *awfully* close. In other situations, I might have been able to load the program onto the clinic computers remotely, from a different computer. But because of the University Hospi-

332

tal security lockouts, I need to download it directly using the software CD.

I don't know which stresses me out more: trying to download the software before GG arrives, or the mere prospect of spending the entire morning with her. I'm not scared of her, or anything. Not anymore. It's more like performance anxiety. I still haven't decided how I'm going to act. *Depressed,* Luis has said. *Beaten.* I'd lain awake half the night trying to figure out what a *beaten* guy would say and do in this situation.

Not to mention that the thought of being in the same room with her makes my skin crawl. By now, I'm way over the shock I experienced Sunday morning. Helplessness and fear have taken a 180-degree turn into repugnance and anger. The way she manipulated me makes me feel . . . *used.* I hate being played. I hate not being in control. I love control. It's one of the reasons I became a surgeon. So it *really* pisses me off, what GG's done to me, boxing me into a corner like this. I want control again.

Not to mention a little payback.

I pass by the nurses' station and the patient examination rooms and head to a small room in the back of the clinic with two computers — a glorified closet where the residents and med students sit. Since these are the only two computers in the clinic GG and I are allowed to use continuously (the others are earmarked for the professors or located in the patient exam rooms), I know that GG will be on one or both of them throughout the morning. I take a seat at the first computer and reach into my white coat pocket for the CD. The cheap cell phone Luis gave me is sitting on top of it. Because it's hard for me to squeeze my hand past the phone, I draw the phone out first and absentmindedly rest it on the table next to the computers before taking out the CD and slipping it into the drive of the first computer.

The University Hospital IT folks have diligently installed, no doubt at great time and expense, several security measures to prevent someone from doing exactly what I'm about to do: place unauthorized software onto one of University's computers. It's not terribly difficult for me to get around the security lockouts, but it's tedious, and by the time I've finished loading the keystroke logger onto the first computer and erasing my digital tracks, it's seven fifteen. I hastily eject the disk, drop it into the second computer, and begin to repeat the process. By now, sweat is dripping off my forehead, and I have to periodically take my fingers off the keyboard to wipe it out of my eyes.

I glance at my watch — 7:29.

I hear a door open at the front of the clinic.

Oh shit. If she walks in now, I'm screwed.

Distracted by the noise, I make a mistake while inputting a command and have to repeat a step.

Shit!

Whirring and clicking and wheezing, the computer accepts my command and lurches into the final stages of the download.

Come on.

Footsteps — women's shoes, by the sound of them — are echoing down the hall, coming this way.

Still downloading.

Come on.

The steps are right outside the room now.

Come on!

The computer finally signals its acquiescence. The keystroke logger is completely loaded.

I frantically eject the software CD and slide it into my pocket. Now both of the computers she'll be using today are primed.

Just in time.

"You're here early, Steve." She's standing in the doorway to the room.

Here we go.

"So are you," I say evenly, turning away from the computer and summoning will-power I never knew I had to sound as calm as possible.

"I like to be early," GG says, gracefully alighting in the seat next to mine. She's holding a cup of coffee. Underneath her short white coat, she's wearing a white blouse and black, knee-length skirt. Very proper and businesslike. She smiles. Her teeth are straight and white. Not too white, like a TV anchor's, but appealing in an understated kind of way. I never noticed that before. I have a decidedly undoctorlike urge to rip each of them out with a pair of pliers. *How could I ever have been attracted to this woman?* "What's *your* story this morning, Steve?"

"I've got a lot of extra time on my hands these days." I'm surprised by how much genuine bitterness seeps into my voice. *Maybe this acting thing won't be as hard as I thought.*

She hears it, too, and nods sympathetically. "So I heard. Sorry. I know how much you love to operate." She squints and leans forward. "Why are you sweating, Steve?"

"Oh. Yeah." I dab at my forehead. "I guess

I am. Whatever. The humidity's killing me today."

"Hmm." She takes a sip of coffee and looks thoughtful. Her eyes light on the phone Luis gave me, which is still sitting where I'd left it, on the table between the two computers.

Shit. Idiot! Why hadn't I put it away?

I manage not to react as she picks it up.

"Yours?" she asks.

"Just an old phone of mine," I mumble. "Deactivated. I found it in my locker. Forgot I had it. I'm taking it home to Katie. I thought she might like it as a toy." I casually hold out my hand toward her, palm up.

But she continues to stare at the phone, twisting it this way and that, a vague half smile on her lips. I feel a fresh crop of sweat spring up. *Has she seen Luis carrying his phone? Mine and his are identical, after all. Is she on to us already?*

Finally, after what seems like hours, she places the phone in my palm. "Of course. How sweet. What a devoted dad you are."

She stares intently at me over her coffee cup as I stick the phone back in my white coat pocket. "So," she says. "Here we are."

I drop my gaze to my lap and grunt.

"This isn't going to be too weird for you or anything, is it, Steve? Working with me?"

She sighs. "Because I, like, hate weirdness."

"You hate . . ." I shake my head, incredulous. How can she act so *normal*? "What is it you want from me, GG?"

"To play my game."

"You're crazy."

"How's it going? Any ideas yet?"

"You are well and truly out of your *fucking mind.*"

"I guess that's a 'no.' " She reaches out and touches my hand. "How about me? Have you thought about *me*?"

I recoil from her touch, as if a tarantula had tried to crawl up my arm. "Look." I concentrate on my anger, using it as a focal point for my charade, letting it guide what I'm saying. "I don't want to talk about *your game.* And the other night — as far as I'm concerned, it never happened."

"So that's it? You're just going to give up?"

"Give up what? I never wanted this. Any of this."

"You wanted me. And I can't believe that you're just going to sit back and let another patient die. When that happens, knowing what you know now —"

"Shut up. Just *shut up.*" I glare at her, perhaps a little too boldly, but by now I'm pretty worked up. "You really are a fucking *whack job,* GG. You know that?" I've never talked to anyone like this before in my life. It's a little unsettling, to so blithely give my id free rein. But also weirdly invigorating. It feels good to be asserting myself again with her. Very surgeonesque. "This might be some kind of twisted game to you. But it's my *life*. And I want it back. I'm done. You and I are through. So kill patients. Save patients. Whatever. *Just leave me the fuck alone.*"

I don't think I've ever used the word "fuck" so many times all at once, and *God,* it feels *fucking* good.

For her part, if she's startled or unnerved or pissed off by my tirade, she sure doesn't show it. Eyes expressionless, she studies me with cool indifference, like — ironically enough — a psychiatrist sizing up a patient on a couch in her office.

There's a pregnant pause, and for a moment, just a moment, I wonder if maybe I went too far. She opens her mouth, like she's about to reply, but a burst of laughter from outside the room interrupts, followed by snatches of genial chatter and the clatter of approaching footsteps. The clinic staff has arrived. And the moment is over.

I swivel in my chair toward my computer and log on to the electronic patient schedule for the day, breathing hard, my heart hammering away in my chest. "You asked if this was too weird for me," I say quietly, my eyes fixed on my computer screen. "Weird doesn't even begin to cover it. But I'm a professional, goddammit. A surgeon. And we have patients to see this morning. That's what I care about. If I have to work with you, fine. If I have to see patients with you in order to get the job done, okay. I'll get the job done. But if you bring up *any* of that other crap around me again, you might as well be having a conversation with a wall. Understand?"

She leans over and whispers in my ear, "You are *so* sexy when you're mad." Then she licks my earlobe.

"What the fuck!" I exclaim, wiping off my ear with my sleeve and self-consciously glancing out the door.

With a slight smile on her face, she calmly starts pecking away at the keyboard of the other computer. I glare at her, but she ignores me, so I guess she has nothing else to say. For the next twenty minutes, we sit there next to each other, not speaking, each of us typing away on our computers, the clicking of the keys sounding like rain intermittently falling on a tin roof. I watch her out of the corner of my eye, trying unsuccessfully to see what she's up to, acting casual but hardly daring to breathe, hoping that the keystroke logger is working.

Our first patient arrives at exactly 8:00 A.M.

Residents' Clinic is full of the patients the more important, senior doctors don't have the time or inclination to see. They're the patients without high-end health-insurance plans, or platinum Visa cards the receptionist up front can run through her scanner, or deep pockets for donating to University Medical School research projects or new wings for University Hospital.

Quite the opposite, actually. My bosses like to refer to these patients as "great teaching cases." Some are Hispanic migrants who stay behind in the city while relatives work organic farms or construction sites out in the exurbs; others are homeless HIV-positive drug addicts sent over from the hospital free AIDS clinic; or prisoners from the city jail clad in bright orange jumpsuits, their metallic wrist and ankle shackles clanging together as they hop awkwardly down the hall to the exam room flanked by burly armed guards; or mentally handicapped adults with the intellectual capacities of toddlers, carted in from group homes and accompanied by state-appointed wards with powers of attorney who wipe the drool off their chins and fuss over them like anxious parents; or ancient residents of nearby nursing homes, tucked in wheelchairs and sucking on portable oxygen tanks through clear-plastic masks that they clutch in their shriveled hands like talismans to ward off death.

In short, these are the patients we're allowed to practice medicine on before we actually go out into the world and practice medicine.

There's an attending who's nominally in charge of us and might even pop his head in every once in a while if you ask him to. But that's a rare event. The clinic is, for the most part, run by the residents and medical students, and we're pretty much left to our own devices.

After examining patients separately, GG and I convene in the tiny residents' room, scouring lab results on the computers and developing a plan of care for her patients. Whatever's going through that bizarre mind of hers, whatever alien roadways her thoughts are traveling down after our earlier confrontation, she assumes a demeanor of studied yet casual professionalism so convincing it's like the events of last weekend and earlier this morning never occurred. She carefully recites each patient's history, physical-exam findings, and proposed plan of care — medication orders, lab tests, X-rays. We then see each of her patients together and, as always, her assessments are spot-on.

She'd make a magnificent doctor, I think to myself, almost wistfully. Too bad she's just as likely to kill her patients as heal them.

It's not too busy today, which is a little unusual for Residents' Clinic. It leaves us with a little extra time in between patient visits. During these intervals, I'm careful to leave GG alone in the resident room as I chat with the clinic nurses and secretly pray that the keystroke logger is working.

The hours pass quickly and uneventfully; eventually morning makes way for afternoon, and GG leaves to attend to other duties. I want to check the keystroke logger, but things immediately pick up after she's gone, and I don't have time. The patients become an unremitting tide that spills and flows out of the waiting room and into the hallway outside. They sit in extra chairs the staff and I hastily set up in the corridor, some even sit on the floor. I work furiously, cataloging symptoms, performing exams, dispensing pills. I don't even have time for bathroom breaks.

At the end of the afternoon, utterly spent, I finish up with what I hope is my last patient of the day and trudge wearily to the nurses' station, where our chief nurse is waiting for me. She and I are the only two staff left; everyone else has left for the day.

"Am I done? Please let me be done. Am I done?"

"Not quite. You've got one more. Mr. Abernathy is waiting for you." The tone of her voice is as sour as the look on her face.

With good reason. "Mr. Abernathy? You're killing me, Jane. You mean he's still alive?" I met Mr. Abernathy back when I was an intern. I haven't seen him for a few years, since I usually don't work in clinic anymore. "What are you doing, letting him come in at the end of the day like this?"

"Don't ask me. And don't blame me. Wendy up at the front desk put him on the schedule at the last minute. Apparently, he walked in without an appointment and asked to see you. You specifically, *Doctor.*" She slaps me in the chest with his old paper patient chart, the one that existed before we switched over to the computerized system. I manage to grab it just before the stack of sheets inside, thick as a phonebook, tumbles to the floor. "He heard you were back in clinic. He's always had a special place in his heart just for you, Steve. He's missed you. He's been talking about you ever since you left clinic, asking where you are."

"Great. Well, I guess I won't be going home anytime soon."

"Oh, no you don't. I can't leave until you're done, so don't you dare stay late with him. I've got to pick up my kids from day care by five thirty."

"I'll do my best."

"I don't want your best, Steve. I want you *done.*"

"Which room is he in?"

"Five."

I walk over to exam room five and pause outside the closed door, my hand resting on the doorknob. I glance back at Jane and wince. She points at her watch, then at the exam-room door, then emphatically stamps her foot.

Mr. Abernathy.

Shit.

I sigh, hunch my shoulders as if I'm about to walk outside into a driving snowstorm, turn the knob, and push open the door.

He's just as I remember him.

He's waiting for me, tensed and ready to pounce, sitting perfectly erect in a chair opposite the door, back straight, both feet on the floor, his lanky, gaunt frame unbent by his ninety-odd years, his gray eyes bright and cold and hard as granite. His nose, broken God knows how long ago or how many times, juts off at an odd angle from his long and skeletal face. His tired skin hangs limply from his jaw and neck, reaching toward the floor like the saggy paunch of an elephant at the zoo; age spots and scars dot the generous expanse of bald palate stretching between the few remaining tufts of wispy white hair. Even though it's ninety degrees and as humid as a tropical jungle outside, he's wearing thick brown corduroy pants and a frayed long-sleeve flannel shirt buttoned all the way up. A city bus pass nestled in a clear plastic carrier dangles from a strap around his neck.

His eyes narrow as I walk through the door, and he scowls. I've never really seen him do much of anything else in terms of facial expressions, but the one he greets me with today is particularly unpleasant.

"Hi, Mr. Abernathy. How are you?"

"Screw you, Doctor. You know how long I've been waiting?"

"Good to see you too again, sir." I drop heavily onto a rolling stool opposite his chair.

"Don't you get smart with me, sonny." He vigorously shakes a long, wraithlike finger at me. "I killed Japs in the Pacific for smart-mouthed little shits like you. I watched my platoon buddies get blown to all hell on Iwo Jima. I took a bullet in the belly thirty-five years before you were even born. So don't you go getting smart with me. You and your goddamned smart mouth." Then follows an impressive string of expletives, sprinkled intermittently with the words "Iwo Jima," and punctuated liberally by bony flourishes of his extended index finger.

I wait, with a mixture of resignation and self-pity, for him to finish. Some days it's Guadalcanal, others Okinawa. Today it's Iwo Jima.

Eventually he stops midsentence, retracts his finger, folds his arms, looks down at his lap, mumbles something I can't hear (nor really want to), then looks up again at me expectantly.

"What can I do for you today, Mr. Abernathy?"

"You can start by goddamn telling me what kind of goddamn pills your quack friends gave me the last time I was here."

I check the clinic notes on the computer screen sitting on the table in front of me, which is currently displaying Mr. Abernathy's electronic patient information. "Ahh, that would be finasteride, sir," I say, scanning Luis's note from the previous week's visit. A very reasonable choice, in my opinion. "It's a pill to shrink your prostate and hopefully keep you from getting up ten times a night to pee."

"Those goddamn pills gave me the shits."

"Hmmm. I haven't heard of that particular side effect before, Mr. Abernathy."

"Well, then, you've goddamned heard it now. I've been squatting on the goddamned shitter all day and all night since I started those goddamned things last week. And they haven't made me piss any better."

I grind my teeth together.

"Those pills take at least three months to start working, Mr. Abernathy. And even then, they're not going to help you pass your water as well as the last pill we gave you — the one that you didn't want to take anymore. Besides, you don't even know if it's the finasteride that's giving you the intestine problem. It's probably something else, like a stomach bug. Have you talked to your family doctor?"

"Yeah, I called her."

"What did she say?"

"She told me to talk to you."

"Of course she did."

"Besides, I know it's those goddamned pills, 'cause when I missed a day, I stopped shitting. I'm not waiting three months.

Especially with these shits the way they are. I want you to do something now. Can't you give me something else?"

"Well, I can give you the pill that we tried before this one. The one you decided to stop taking."

"Which one was that?"

"It's called tamsulosin."

"Is that the one that made my eyes all blurry?"

"No, that was the pill you tried before the tamsulosin. You told us that the tamsulosin made you sweat."

"Oh yeah. That goddamned sweating. Almost forgot about that. I was soaking my goddamned sheets for three weeks. Ya got something else then, Doc?"

I sigh. "We've already tried just about everything else, Mr. Abernathy. The only thing I can offer you now is the surgery." I don't bother to remind him that we've been recommending surgery for his condition for the last several years.

"Ohhh, no. No you don't." He starts shaking his finger at me again. "I've already told you goddamned quacks — you ain't gonna cut on me. I ain't goin' under no knife. Not for my prostrate. Not for anything."

"It's a very minor procedure, Mr. Abernathy. Low-risk."

"I ain't goin' under no goddamned knife!"

And so it goes for the next half hour. Eventually, I somehow manage to convince Mr. Abernathy to keep taking his pill. For me it's a Pyrrhic victory, thirty minutes of my life I'll never get back, and I'm certain he'll be back next week with a whole new set of complaints. Mr. Abernathy grunts his good-bye as he shuffles away, and Jane races out the door to pick up her kids from day care, leaving me all alone in the clinic.

I hurry to one of the examination rooms, close the door, pull out my laptop, and remotely log into the encrypted keystroke logger account. My hands shake with anticipation, and I have to concentrate to keep from hitting the wrong keys. Once I've accessed the account, strings of neatly arranged code immediately appear on the screen.

Yes! The keystroke logger secretly recorded everything GG typed into the computer over the course of the morning. I've dug up an absolute gold mine of juicy data: e-mail address with her account login and password; bank account login with password; credit-card number — for someone so smart, GG seems to be no more computer savvy, or wary, then the average Internet-surfing American. Not that she necessarily should be. The University main-frame is reasonably secure. To *outside* threats.

Allowing myself a slight smile, I sign into GG's e-mail account and rapidly sort through her messages over the past month, which are striking in their general lack of social connectivity. She seems to have very little correspondence with friends or family — not unusual for a psychopath. Most of the messages pertain to school and her classwork. Certainly nothing related to planning a murder. It's not much. But at least it's a start.

Satisfied, I'm about to snap my laptop closed when something else in the code catches my attention.

It's a link to another Web site, with a corresponding login and password.

Curious, I follow the trail to its source.

And just about fall out of my chair.

GG apparently links her smartphone and home computer to a centralized server; a service that backs up data and enables users to access it, with a login and password, from any computer linked to the Internet. The Web site I've just entered is her account on the server: which, from what I can tell, she uses as a repository for all of her smartphone and computer files. *Including the videos.*

It doesn't take me long to find our sex tape, the one she made that night in the call room. It takes me even less time to determine that there are only two existing copies: the one on the server and the original one on her phone.

Grinning, I reach for the delete command . . .

. . . and pause, my finger hovering over the keyboard.

Shit.

If I delete the file, she'll be on to me, and she still has the original copy on her phone. Unless I find a way to hack or physically steal her smartphone, I'm still screwed.

But that's okay. You and I have just gotten started, GG.

I sign out of the system, close my laptop, and savor my small victory.

Game on, GG. Game on.

CHAPTER 12

Wednesday, August 12

Mrs. Samuelson's bloodstream now teems with a fungus caused by a contaminated IV catheter. Despite the antibiotics, it has fed and multiplied and spread like wildfire through dry brush, setting in motion a terrible process called sepsis.

Sepsis is what happens when the body's immune system short-circuits. Normally, the immune system fights infections through a complex mechanism overseen by white blood cells and proteins. Like soldiers in a microscopic army, the white blood cells and proteins talk to each other through an elegant communication network as they fight off the infection. As with all battles, there's usually some peripheral damage. Fevers, muscle aches, runny noses, nausea, headaches — these are symptoms called into service in the fight against the infection; a scorched-earth approach representing the body's way of transforming itself into an inhospitable environment for the invaders.

But with sepsis, the communication network short-circuits, and the immune system goes haywire. The collateral damage becomes catastrophic: a massive shock-and-awe campaign that indiscriminately destroys healthy as well as unhealthy tissue. The medical term is "multi system organ failure" — an underwhelming phrase that, like most medical terminology, describes little of the human suffering that accompanies it.

When the infection first started spreading, Mrs. Samuelson's blood pressure dropped precipitously, and she required ever-greater amounts of powerful IV medications to keep it at life-sustaining levels. She swelled up like the Michelin Man, her bloated, fluid-filled body pressing outward against her frail skin, stretching it taut like the surface of a drum. The contours of her body gradually faded; her knees and ankles and elbows disappeared; her face bulged; her fingers grew to the size of sausages.

Then, one by one, like a line of toppling dominoes, her major organs began to give up the ghost.

Her lungs went first, flooding with fluids as she began to drown in her own secretions. The oxygen levels in her blood plummeted. In response, the SICU doctors cranked up the pressure setting on the ventilator, squeezing air into Mrs. Samuelson with ever-greater force. But the lungs are fragile organs, and Mrs. Samuelson's creaked and moaned under the incessant pounding of the ventilator, threatening to rupture like overfilled balloons.

Her one remaining kidney went next. Oxygen-deprived and exhausted, it shut itself down and refused to filter blood. Her body stopped making urine. The toxic substances the kidneys normally remove from the body piled up to dangerously high levels in her blood. So the SICU doctors rammed a huge dialysis catheter into a large blood vessel in her neck, which now intermittently sucks the blood out of her body and runs it through a larger dialyzing machine positioned next to her bed. The machine removes all of the waste products before dumping the filtered blood back into her body.

Meanwhile, Mr. Samuelson sits there every day with his three daughters, patiently keeping vigil in the SICU waiting room (the sons-in-law have long since disappeared) or at the bedside during the few hours allotted to visitors, their hands frequently linked in prayer, all of them serene in their conviction that Mrs. Samuelson will wake up anytime now. Mr. Samuelson keeps her wedding band, the one she was so reluctant to take off before the operation, in his front shirt pocket. He's taken to rolling it absently in his thick, nicotine-stained fingers as he keeps vigil by her bedside.

"Circling the drain," one of the anesthesia residents working in the SICU says to me that evening as I'm sitting in Mrs. Samuelson's room. She's squinting at the computer monitor next to Mrs. Samuelson's bed, studying her latest test results.

"What?" I look up from my laptop.

"Her." She points at Mrs. Samuelson with her pen. "Circling the drain. If she doesn't clear this infection soon, she's not going to make it." She taps out a quick note on the computer and moves on to the next patient without glancing back.

Despite my temporary banishment from the OR, I'm free to come and go as I please in the SICU. I don't know exactly why I'm sitting at her bedside. Is it for her sake? Or mine? To make myself feel better? To assuage my guilt? To exert some measure of control in an otherwise completely uncontrollable situation? I'm not really sure. Certainly, it's not for the human interaction, or for the satisfaction of developing a stronger doctor-patient relationship. I'm in the same room with Mrs. Samuelson, but not really. She's removed, distant, separated from me by the impressive array of technology keeping her alive, cut off from the rest of humanity like an astronaut or deep-sea diver.

The nurses, many of whom have known me for years, leave me alone as they go about their nightly business: adjusting medication drips, repositioning patients, monitoring ventilators, recording vital signs. A few stop their work long enough to say hi. Earlier, I watched as one of them wordlessly rolled a cart carrying a creaky TV monitor and DVD player into the cubicle next to Mrs. Samuelson's, turned the monitor toward the cubicle's comatose denizen, and switched on an old concert video of Shania Twain. Weird.

I twist my head slowly around: first to the left, then to the right. The kink in my neck unknots itself with a loud and satisfying pop. I absently rub my sore shoulder, where I received another injection this morning for the research study, and look back down at the screen of the laptop perched on my knees. I click on a file. Several documents, the products of my research thus far on

GG's background, appear. With my banishment from the OR, I've had a lot of extra time to do research this week.

I open all of the files. One of the larger documents contains everything I've collected on her state of mind: mainly snippets from research articles and textbooks. As best I can tell, GG is a "semipsychopath": Ruthlessly self-centered, she possesses many — but not all — of the traits necessary for being classified a full-blown psychopath. Clearly, she's highly functional, capable, and shrewd, someone able to project a veneer of reassuring sanity to everyone around her.

There's even, I begrudgingly recognize, a certain method to her madness, a pitiless resolve to achieve success, no matter the cost. In fact, as I read again through all of the materials, I realize how blurred the line can often be between psychopaths and the rest of us; and I wonder how many other highly successful people there are like her in the world — political leaders, Wall Street traders, lawyers, even other doctors — who secretly, or maybe not so secretly, harbor psychopathic traits.

Her background, gleaned by way of (surreptitiously performed) background checks, social media pages, and GG's own computer files, isn't all that remarkable. A lot of people mistakenly think that psychopaths are made, not born: all of them the products of broken homes or predatory priests or some other kind of brutal childhood trauma that molded them, like innocent lumps of clay, into pitiless monsters.

But that's a misconception. The truth, experts will tell you, is more complicated. And a lot more boring. Most psychopaths come from completely normal families and totally unremarkable upbringings. Sure, there are a few who certainly caught bad breaks as kids. But for most, there's no smoking gun, no sentinel event in their lives to which deviant behavior can be traced, no discernible *reason* why they should be psychopaths.

So it is with GG. I can't find anything that might have even remotely provoked her murderous obsession with patient safety. She's the middle of three successful kids, with an older brother who graduated from Yale Law and is now a corporate attorney, and a younger sister studying biochemistry at UCLA. She has no trace of a criminal record, not even so much as a speeding ticket; hell, not even a *parking* ticket, from what I can tell. Granted, that's a little unusual for a garden-variety psychopath: By the time most are GG's age, they'll have left more of a trail of social misery in their wakes, beginning in childhood. Behavior problems. Poor grades. Run-ins with the law. Trouble holding down a job. A string of failed relationships.

GG, apparently, is a brilliant, higher-functioning psychopath who has managed to play it close to the vest. Granted, she seems to be a bit of a loner, with few friends, acquaintances, or activities outside the hospital, which at least partly explains her work ethic. But certainly not someone you'd otherwise worry is suddenly going to snap and shoot up a school bus full of kids or anything.

While all of this psych stuff hasn't really helped me predict her next victim, it has driven home one very important point for me, which if it wasn't completely clear before, certainly is now: Nothing I can say or do will ever turn her away from her current objective. GG is what she is. I can't reason with her to stop killing people. I can't appeal to the better part of her nature because there isn't any. It's either play along with her game, or beat her at it.

I click on her résumé next, which by now I've practically memorized. As I scroll through it, her singular achievements once again parade before me: the innumerable academic awards; the engineering degree from MIT with highest honors; a black belt in tae kwon do — where the hell did she find time for *that*?

More recently, she's done a lot of research on a type of heart device called an implantable cardiac defibrillator (or ICD for short), on which she's published several scientific papers in very prestigious medical journals. It's not unusual for med students of GG's intelligence and motivation to publish scientific research under the guidance of more senior scientists. In fact, I even published a few back when I was a med student.

From what I know about ICDs, it makes sense that GG would be interested in them, given her engineering background. An ICD is a miniature device surgically implanted directly into the heart muscles of patients with certain heart problems. The job of an ICD is to automatically deploy a miniature electric shock to the heart in case it enters into a life-threatening arrhythmia. But GG's research papers, all of which I've gathered and read, then read again, are dense, technical, and — as far as I can tell — offer no real clues. And neither do the files she downloaded from her smartphone and computer onto the server I hacked.

I sigh and close the file.

That's when Luis's cell phone, set on vibrate, starts jerking around in my front pocket. It startles me; it's the first time it's rung. I fish it out and peer at the screen. Just as Luis promised, a series of five numbers appears: the number two, followed by a space, followed by the numbers 2-0-0-0. I concentrate for a moment, retrieving the address from my memory: 100 Charles Street was the address that corresponded to the number two on the sheet he handed me Monday night at the Old Crow. So, according to the code, Luis wants to meet me at 100 Charles Street at 7:30 P.M. — a mere thirty minutes from now. I hastily gather up my things and leave.

As I'm walking through the parking garage, a strange sensation seizes hold of me, like I'm being watched. I stop and spin around 360 degrees. Nothing. I'm completely alone. I shrug the feeling off and head for my car.

Twenty-nine minutes later, I'm walking into another bar, this one just off the lobby of an upscale hotel near Boston Commons. The inside is dark and adorned with swanky fixtures and well-heeled patrons sipping stylish cocktails. Just like the last time we met, I have a hard time spotting him at first.

"What is it about you and bars?" I settle

onto a thick, plush chair across from Luis. He's facing the door I came in through — as best as I can tell, the only one into and out of the place. I can barely make out his face, which is shrouded almost completely in shadow. He's drinking mineral water. "Shouldn't we be meeting, I don't know, in an abandoned garage or burned-out factory or something?"

"Hollywood bullshit." Luis scowls, and his downturned jawline emerges from the semidarkness. "The last thing we want to do is draw attention by trekking to some out-of-the-way, isolated shit hole. That'd be sure to raise red flags. Best to meet in crowded, public places."

A waitress materializes to take our order. In keeping with the décor of the place, she's drop-dead gorgeous: green eyes, dark brown skin, and glossy black hair. Luis orders another mineral water. He and the waitress look at me expectantly. "Gin and tonic."

"So. What have you got?" he asks, as he and I watch the waitress glide away on her long legs.

I tell him about the keystroke logger, and clinic, and what I've learned about GG.

"Good for you, man," he says, as the waitress delivers our drinks, then waits until she leaves before continuing. "Nicely done."

He frowns. "Although I'm not so sure about being so angry with her, Steve. Maybe not such a good idea. I'd have tamped it down a little. Not yelled at her so much. You don't want to provoke her."

"Into doing what?"

"I don't know," he says, thoughtfully rubbing the top of his head. "Remember — she's a psychopath. We really don't know *what* she's capable of."

"She seems to have bought into it."

"Maybe." He sounds unconvinced. "Okay, well, what's done is done. So. What do we know so far?" He ticks the points off on his fingers. "She's smart. She's an electrical engineer with first-rate technical training and an interest in medical hardware. She's obsessed with patient safety. She's been working with the Safety Committee since she was a first-year med student. Clerical stuff, mostly, it seems. But I don't know for sure."

"You mean, her work may be more than just clerical?"

"Exactly. We can only speculate as to how she was able to manipulate things behind the scenes with Mr. Bernard's investigation. I imagine she did everything she could to make you the fall guy. Anyway. A good place to start may be medical hardware and patient safety."

"I'll see what I can come up with." I take another sip of my drink. "What about you? Any progress?"

"Some," he answers evasively. "I think I've discovered something important. I'm chasing down a pretty good lead right now that could be the key to bringing her down. Once and for all."

"Really? What? Let's hear it."

"Not yet."

"Why?"

"Compartmentalization. Basic rule of intel. The idea is to keep vital information separate — compartmentalized — in case one or both of us is somehow compromised by the hostile. You, obviously, are in much more danger of being compromised than I am. She won't be able to extract information from you if I don't give it to you."

He lifts his wrist and glances at his watch, which is reversed, so that it's facing in the same direction as his palm. It's one of those fancy diver's watches. "I have to go. Same drill as last time. After I'm gone, wait at least fifteen minutes before you leave."

"Okay."

He hands me a twenty. "This should cover the cost of my water." He smirks. "Barely. Wait until you see the price of that gin.

You're going to have a heart attack."

I tuck the twenty in my pocket. "When will I hear from you again?"

"Soon." To my surprise, he heads not for the entrance I walked through but in the opposite direction, toward the bar. He and the bartender exchange friendly nods as he steals through an unmarked door behind the bar — an entrance to the kitchen, by the looks of it — that's partially obscured by liquor and wine bottles.

I slowly empty my gin for fifteen minutes, then pay a bill that, as Luis implied, will likely cut into my kids' college fund.

As I'm walking to my car, I'm overcome, again, by an odd sense that I'm being watched. I try to dismiss it as harmless paranoia brought on by spending too much time with Luis. But the feeling persists.

I spin to my right. Nothing.

I turn to my left.

And there she is.

Her back is to me. But I know it's her. I can make out her ponytail flipping jauntily up and down as she speeds away, around a corner of a building down the street.

What the hell? I'm too angry to be surprised, or to wonder how she followed me, or to worry if she spotted Luis and me talking in the bar. Who the hell does she think she is? Furious, I sprint down the block after her. I round the corner, grab her by the shoulder, and spin her roughly around.

"What the hell are you doing —"

I bite off the words and drop my hand from her shoulder.

The ponytailed teenage girl who gapes back at me, her face frozen in fear, shares GG's exact height, build, and hair color. But she's definitely not GG.

"Oh, I'm so sorry," I say, lamely, as she slowly backs away from me. "I thought you were someone else."

Her father, a burly, tattooed man who had been walking a few feet in front of her, is understandably somewhat less solicitous than I am, and as I'm driving home, my hands still shaking from the encounter, I count myself lucky to have escaped with an obscenity-laden diatribe and a mouthful of intact teeth.

For reasons I can't quite explain, I'm still uneasy about being followed and keep checking my rearview — which is absurd, really, because even if GG were behind me right now, how the hell would I know? I don't know what kind of car she drives or how I would pick it out from the light traffic flowing smoothly around me. Or even if she has a car. I think she mentioned to me once that she lives in the city, which means she wouldn't have much use for one. And what would I do even if I spotted her? The closest I've ever come to this kind of thing is watching a James Bond movie. It's not like I'm going to try to lose her, or anything. Or run her off the road into a ditch. Although I certainly wouldn't mind doing so.

I pull up to our house well after dark. The light is on in the kitchen, but first I tiptoe upstairs to the girls' room. Katie and Annabelle are asleep. They look beautiful, so still and perfect. Like some kind of painting in a museum. I kiss Katie on the forehead and stroke Annabelle on the cheek. Katie smacks her lips and sighs musically. Annabelle is unmoved by my affection and doesn't stir. Gazing down on them, gnawing on my lip, I think of what GG and I did in the call room last weekend, and a stabbing pain suddenly shoots down my left chest and arm. *Real* pain, not metaphorical. I mean, it really fucking *hurts,* like a hot knife stripping off my flesh.

I gasp and stagger toward the window, clutching my left pectoralis major muscle, speculating through a haze of agony that the muscles of the coronary artery, the main blood supply to my heart, are spasming shut, squeezing off the blood supply to my heart, a condition called Prinzmetal's angina.

Great. Now I'm having a heart attack.

And then, as quickly as it appeared, the pain is gone. Catching my breath, I brace myself against the windowsill and peek out through a corner of the closed window blinds in their room. The street below, in front of our house, is quiet.

Massaging my tingling left arm, I trudge downstairs and join Sally, who's waiting patiently for me at the kitchen table with a warmed-over dinner plate, fresh out of the microwave. I peck her on the cheek, drop wearily into a chair, and pick up a fork.

"Hi," I say mechanically.

"Hi." Her elbow rests on the kitchen table, and her chin is propped in her hand. She contemplates me with a mixture of concern and puzzlement, which starts to provoke the knifelike pain in my chest all over again, and I drop my eyes to my plate, so I don't have to look at her. The pain subsides.

The short length of table separating Sally and me in our cramped kitchen mocks the emotional gulf starting to stretch between us, at least from my perspective. *You know I'd do anything for you, right? And the girls? You guys are my life.* That's what she had told me at this very table a few weeks ago, offering me a bottle of her favorite wine even though she was pregnant and couldn't drink; back when we were savoring the simple pleasure of just being together.

With all of the time I've been spending at the hospital, Sally and I haven't spoken much since the BBQ a few days ago, when I temporarily retreated into those beer bottles. Barely even a few perfunctory words exchanged between us. For the past two nights, I've arrived home late, exhausted, too tired even to talk, grunting hello before slipping into bed. Each morning, I've been out of the house before she wakes up.

Which is, I reflect sadly, the way I prefer things right now.

Why? It's simple, really: I'm a coward. Although I've told Sally about Mr. Bernard's death and Mrs. Samuelson's condition, I haven't told her anything about the Safety Committee report, my banishment from the operating room, or the remedial training. I can't bring myself to do it. I'm too embarrassed about my temporary demotion, too ashamed of the fact that the job at University Hospital, the one she sweet-talked her way into helping me get, is pretty much out the window at this point.

And then, of course, there's the whole GG thing.

"Shame" is just a word. The actual experience of it, day in and day out, is something else entirely. My guilt is like a worm in an apple, twisting and feeding, burrowing into the soft substance of my conscience. I've tried to tell myself that it was just one moment of weakness, that I should get a free pass, that being set up by a murderous psychopath doesn't count.

But it does. Because I *let* it happen. Besides, I keep thinking about all of the things Sally's put up with over the years for us. For *me*. Defying her parents by not marrying a nice Korean boy from a good Korean family. Supporting us financially during my time in med school. Spending all of those nights and days at home alone while I was at the hospital during my internship and residency.

It's not like Sally's a saint. We've had our fights. Sure, there've been plenty of times that I've been pissed as hell at her, and she with me. She thinks I'm stubborn and willful. I think she's disorganized and judgmental. But, on the balance of things, I'd have to say I've gotten the better end of the deal in this whole marriage thing. She's popular, effusive, charismatic; me, not so much.

Which is, maybe, what scares me the most. Part of me (that damn smart part, again) *wants* to tell her. Knows that, ultimately, coming clean is the only way to make things right between us again. That she deserves to know the truth. But one terrifying thought, a by-product of a deep, dark recess in my psyche, holds me back: What if Sally doesn't need me as much as I need her? And she just walks away? With the girls?

No. That can't happen. I'd sooner rip my own heart out with a spoon as tell Sally about GG and risk losing my family. My only way out is to follow through with Luis's plan — to flip things around and trap GG in the same corner she has me in right now. That's the only way to sweep this thing under the rug forever. Only then can I be certain that Sally will never find out about this, and I can move on with my life.

"Tough day?"

"Yeah," I grunt, pushing my lasagna around my plate without any real interest in eating.

"We haven't had much of a chance to catch up lately."

"I'm getting hammered. It's been really busy." Which isn't a lie, I think, lifting my fork to my mouth. Technically.

"How's your lady doing? The one in the Intensive Care Unit?"

"Same."

"Is she getting better?"

"No."

"I'm sorry."

"Hmm."

She pauses, then says, "Don't forget. We're having dinner at the McIntoshes' house on Saturday. My mother will watch the girls."

"Okay."

"And remember that the girls and I are spending a week at Anita's place in Providence. I know we were just there with my parents, but my brother's going to be there with his kids, and we thought it would be nice to get all the cousins together. I mentioned it to you last week."

I forgot she was spending the week at her sister's. It's not unusual. She and her sister are very close, and she drives to Providence often with the girls. "Right. When are you leaving again?"

"Next Monday. We'll be back the following Sunday." She purses her lips. "Are you sure you're going to be okay here? All alone?"

I stare at my plate and shrug. "Sure."

"Do you think you might be able to get away for a night to come join us? The girls would love it."

"I'll see. Maybe."

She watches me eat for a while before

continuing. "I also thought it'd be nice for us to go out to dinner on Friday as a family. We haven't done that for a long time. I know work's been really busy, but can you manage to get home early? Say by six?"

"I think so. Yeah. Sure."

"Good." She folds her hands in front of her. "By the way. Andrea called me today. From University."

"Andrea. Andrea?" I put down my fork. "You mean . . . your old boss Andrea?"

"Yes."

"Why?

"It's not the first time. She calls me every once in a while to see how things are going. I call her every once in a while to keep a toe in the water with the career stuff. We had lunch one time last spring while my mom watched the girls."

"You've never mentioned that to me."

She shrugs. "It's never seemed important. I think she likes to think of herself as my mentor." She pauses before adding, "She's the CEO now. Of University Hospital."

"I know," I reply, a little testier than I'd intended. Of course I know that. I feel a little queasy, and the lasagna flips around in my stomach, like clothes in a dryer. How involved has this woman Andrea been with Mr. Bernard's case, I wonder? How much does she know about my punishment? Probably everything. To think that Sally's only one degree of separation away from independently knowing how bad things have been for me at work makes me uneasy. "So, why are you telling me this now?"

"Because she offered me a job."

"Oh. Huh." Why the job offer now? Is the timing coincidental? I don't know. All I can do at this point is try to act natural. I casually pick up my fork and start eating again. "Well, what did she say when you said no?"

"I didn't say no, Steve. I told her I'd think about it."

"What . . . really?" I put down my fork again. This I *really* didn't see coming. "I didn't . . . I mean, you want to go back to work?"

"I'm thinking about it, Steve." She twists her hands together. "Hospital administration is always something I've loved. And, well, I really miss it."

"What about the new baby?"

"Right. I've been thinking about that a lot. The baby's due next February. You'll be starting your new job at University next July, right?"

I nod and keep a straight face.

"Andrea is saying I could start part-time that fall," Sally says. "That would give me six months off after I have the baby. Katie will be starting preschool. My mom's offered to help out more and, with the extra money we'll have, we can easily afford some day care. Maybe even a nanny. Nancy McIntosh — she's a lawyer, you remember — is really encouraging me to do this. She loves splitting her time between career and kids, and does it really well. She's been giving me some terrific advice."

"Hmmm." Nancy. For some reason, her involvement in all of this really bothers me. Probably because *Nancy* really bothers me.

"Anyway, Andrea offered to take me out to dinner, in the city, next week after we get back from Providence. I was thinking maybe Thursday night? The same night you have Morbidity and Mortality conference? That way, I can take the train into the city, and you can drive us both home after we're done. What do you think?"

"Umm, sure," I mumble. "I guess."

"But . . . what?" Her eyes narrow. "What's wrong?"

"It's just . . . I guess I just need to, uh, process all of this, Sally. I didn't realize that you wanted to go back to work."

"Does that bother you?"

"No," I say quickly. But it *does* bother me. If only a little. I've become very comfortable with our current arrangement: I go to work; she stays home with the kids. Simple, straightforward, and convenient. Especially for me.

"Fine. Now. Do you want to tell me what *is* bothering you?"

"What do you mean?" I push the food around my plate, avoiding her eyes.

"Steve" — she sighs — "living with you is getting to be like living with a teenager. You sulk. You talk in one-word sentences. You're hardly ever home anymore." She reaches out and grasps my arm with both of her hands. "What can I do to make things better? Tell me. You just need to talk to me. Please."

"Look," I say, putting down my fork. "I know I've been a little . . . distracted. It's just — it's just been really bad for me at work. You — you wouldn't understand."

"Try me."

I shake my head. "I'm sorry. I can't."

"Why?" she asks suspiciously, pulling her hands back. "Where were you tonight? And why does your breath smell like booze?"

"I —" I pause, feeling the blood rushing to my cheeks. "Luis and I stopped at a bar after work. To talk about some work stuff." I pick up my fork again. "Really."

She stares at me for perhaps thirty seconds. "Okay," she says matter-of-factly, pushing herself away from the table. "Well. I'm going to bed. Turn out the lights when you're done." I hear the sound of her light footfall on the stairs, followed by our bedroom door's closing.

I steeple my fingers under my chin and linger alone in the kitchen, the rest of my food cooling, staring into the dark night outside the kitchen window.

CHAPTER 13

Thursday, August 13

My cell phone is ringing.

My real cell phone. Not the one Luis gave me.

Sitting on the nightstand next to my bed, inches from my ear, it yanks me from a deep sleep. I fumble for the phone on the nightstand next to the bed and squint at my bedside clock. 3:05 A.M.

Sally groans, rolls over, and pulls a pillow over her head. I take my cell and stumble across the room into our tiny walk-in closet. I close the closet door behind me, flip the phone open, and blink blearily at the screen. The caller ID is blocked. The soft light from the screen plays about the cramped confines of the closet, casting everything in an eerie green glow.

I'm wide-awake in an instant. My heart starts racing. This can't be anything good. Who would be calling me now?

I push the ANSWER key and prepare for the worst.

"Dr. Mitchell."

"Hello, Doctor? Are you there? Is that you? Doctor? Doctor? Hello? Goddammit! Can anybody hear me? Hello? Hello?"

I know that voice.

"Mr. . . . Abernathy? Is that you?"

"Yeah. It's me. I need to talk to you, Doc."

How the *hell* did he get my cell-phone number?

"You need to talk to me . . . now?"

"Yeah, about my prostrate. It's killing me.

"Your prostrate? I mean, your *prostate*?"

"Yeah. Goddamn thing's still got me up going to the bathroom all night."

Mr. Abernathy is calling me on my private cell phone.

At home.

At 3:00 A.M.

Because he wants to talk to me about his prostate.

I take a deep breath. "What is it that's bothering you?"

"I'm getting up every night to piss."

You've been getting up every fucking night to piss for the last twenty years, you evil old man. Why should tonight be any fucking different?

"Mr. Abernathy, are you still able to

380

urinate?" I ask, with what I consider to be remarkable calm under the present circumstances.

"Hell yes, Doctor! I can't stop! That's my goddamn problem. What kind of a goddamn question is that? Aren't you listening to what I got to say?"

I take another deep breath. "Do you have a fever?"

"No."

"Chills?"

"No."

"Any trouble breathing right now?"

"No."

"Chest pain?"

"No."

"Pain in your belly?"

"No."

"Are you getting up more tonight to piss . . . er, urinate, than you did last night?"

"No."

"Mr. Abernathy, is there any difference at all between the way you're feeling tonight — right at this very moment, talking to me right now — and the way you were feeling last night, or the night before that?"

He hesitates. "No."

"Mr. Abernathy, is this an emergency?"

He hesitates again, much longer this time. "Well . . . not exactly, I guess. It's just . . .

it's just that these other pills you gave me still aren't working. They're not helping me. You've got to do something about it, Doc. I'm still getting up all night to go to piss. It's killing me."

I tighten my grip on my cell. The phone's plastic casing groans ominously. "Okay, yeah, but is this maybe something we can talk about next week in my clinic, Mr. Abernathy? During the day? I can't really help you much right now over the phone."

Especially at three o'clock in the fucking morning, you fucking old bastard.

"Well . . . I guess if you think it's all right to wait until then. Like it's not an emergency, or nothing."

"No, I don't think this is an emergency, Mr. Abernathy. I think it's okay if we wait until next week to discuss your prostate problem. During the day."

"Okay, then. If you say so, and all. Good night, Doc."

"Good night, Mr. Abernathy."

Goddamn motherfucking motherfucker cocksucker!

I stab the DISCONNECT button with my thumb and throw the cell phone down to the floor as hard as I can. It bounces off the thin, cheap carpeting of the closet at a crazy angle, hits the wall with a thud, and breaks into several pieces. Cursing under my breath, I bend over to pick up the splintered electronic components; then, while standing back up, I bang the back of my head against a low-lying wooden shelf hard enough to see stars. I dig my front top teeth into my lower lip, deep enough to draw blood, to keep from waking up the whole neighborhood.

Rubbing my pounding head and tasting the warm, salty blood, I realize I forgot to ask Mr. Abernathy how he got my private cell-phone number. Probably from a naive hospital operator, who should have known better.

God*damn* the man.

I climb back into bed, but the combination of the adrenaline stirred up by Mr. Abernathy's call and my throbbing head make it difficult for me to go back to sleep. So I just lie there, trying to collect my thoughts, which swirl around aimlessly, like autumn leaves scattered by the wind.

One month ago, my life was just fine, thank you. I was blissfully unaware of psychopathic, blackmailing med students. The way ahead was clear. The plan simple and straightforward. My dream job was waiting for me. All I had to do was to work hard and keep my nose clean.

I turn and gaze at Sally, who has fallen back to sleep. I listen to her slow, steady breathing. I sense the warmth of her body next to me.

I reach out for her in the darkness. She mumbles something incoherent, recoils from my touch, and edges away from me, curling up into a tight ball on the far side of the bed.

I sigh, flip over on my back, fold my hands behind my head, and study the cracks in the ceiling, waiting for sleep.

I have to wait a long time.

CHAPTER 14

Friday, August 14

"Daddy! I drew this for you!" Katie holds up her kid-friendly paper place mat, a collection of generic mazes and puzzles, which is now almost completely covered by indecipherable crayon scribble.

"What is it?"

"It's you!"

"That's beautiful, Katie."

"Look, 'Bella!" She holds it up for her sister. Annabelle, half of her face covered with mashed potato, like a bushy white beard, signals her approval by banging her fists on her high-chair tray and squealing. Her shriek disappears into the communal clamor of the family-friendly franchise restaurant near our house. Katie starts drawing on a fresh place mat (the hostess was nice enough to give us a whole stack of them when we first sat down) as Sally reaches over and tries to dab the mashed potatoes from Annabelle's face with a napkin. It's a pretty futile gesture, as Annabelle cheerfully starts shoveling more mashed potatoes into her mouth, most of which end up smeared on her cheeks. Exasperated, Sally drops the napkin, picks up her fork, and flashes me a weary grin.

"Whatever," she says, digging into her salad. If our conversation the other night angered or upset her, she's certainly not showing it. Tonight, in fact, has been a really good night; the first good night we've had together as a family in a long time. Too long, I think ruefully. I smile back at Sally, take another bite of my burger, and run my tongue over the warm grease dribbling down my chin. It tastes really good.

Everything is good tonight.

I wipe the grease from my chin and fingers. With Katie and Annabelle temporarily occupied and content, now seems like a good time for a bathroom break.

"Okay if I go to the bathroom?" I ask.

"Sure," Sally says between bites of her salad. "Do you want me to order anything else for you while you're gone?"

"No, thanks. I'm good."

Strolling through the restaurant to the men's room, I start whistling to myself. After what I've been through lately, I find the normality of the place — the relentlessly cheery, toothsome teenage waiters with striped red-and-white shirts and suspenders; the traffic lights and neon signs adorning the wooden walls; the legion of strategically placed flat screen monitors tuned in to various sporting events — comforting. It reassures me that much of the world still functions the way I expect it to. Here, surrounded by my family and my fellow denizens of suburbia, oblivious to all but their potato skins slathered in cheese and bacon bits, I can almost forget about homicidal med students. At least for a little while.

Besides, the curly fries here are awesome.

After I'm done, as I'm walking back to our table, I notice that two women have joined Sally and the girls. The first, about our age, blond-haired and chubby, is chatting with Sally, standing next to the table as she bounces a baby, maybe six months old, in her arms. I recognize her as a stay-at-home mom who lives on our street. Her name escapes me, but I remember that her husband is a med student at University (I can't conjure up his name, either). The second is squatting on the floor with her back to me, engaged in an enthusiastic game of patty-cake with Katie as Annabelle looks raptly on.

I'm not too surprised. This kind of thing happens a lot when we're out and about in our neighborhood. Restaurants. The grocery store. The cleaners. Sally seems to know just about everyone in our little corner of suburban Boston. I sigh and plaster a mechanical smile on my face as I approach, hoping it doesn't take too long to get rid of them. All I want right now is to get back to my burger and curly fries and enjoy the rest of the evening with my family.

"Steve," Sally says. "You remember Ellie, right? Her husband Brian is a med student at University? They live five doors down from us. The house near the corner. And this is Ryan. Who's *getting to be such a big boy.*" Sally tickles Ryan under his chin, and he grins toothlessly at her. "Yes you are!"

Ellie and I exchange greetings.

"And this is . . ." Sally gestures to the other woman, who's finished her round of patty-cake with Katie and is now rising to greet me. "I'm sorry, your name again is?"

The woman is tall, almost as tall as I, and her long brown hair is pulled back with a ponytail. She smiles graciously at Sally.

"Gigi. Gigi Maxwell."

The pain in my chest, the same one that gripped me last night, is so sudden, so excruciating, that I nearly black out. The world tips dangerously, first to the left, then to the right, before finding the horizontal again. I clench my jaw and bite down as hard as I can. It starts to subside.

"Gigi. *That's* right. Sorry about that, Gigi. You told me that not thirty seconds ago, didn't you? It's my mind. Starting to go in my old age. Early-onset Alzheimer's, I guess." GG and Ellie chuckle appreciatively. "Steve, this is Gigi."

"Hi, Steve. Sally tells me that you're a resident at University, but I don't think we've met before. I'm a med student there." Smiling, she extends her hand. Her expression is warm and congenial and reveals not even a hint of recognition. It's a performance worthy of an Oscar.

I think my lips form into some kind of configuration vaguely reminiscent of a smile. But it's hard to tell because it feels like I'm having an out-of-body experience, as if I'm floating above myself, disconnected. I watch, absorbed, as my hand, seemingly under its own volition, reaches out to hers. I don't feel anything when we shake hands. I listen, curious, as someone else says, "Hi. No, I don't think we have. Nice to meet you."

"Brian's on call tonight in the hospital," Ellie says. "So I thought it'd be nice to get out for a change. Actually, it was GG's idea. She called me right before she came over and literally dragged me here. My first time out of the house in ages."

"I happened to be in the neighborhood," GG says, glancing first at Sally, then at me. Her eyes light on me a beat longer before moving back to Ellie.

"GG and I got to know each other when she and Brian were in the same study group, before Ryan was born," Ellie explains. "She's been nice enough to hang out with us even after we became boring parents who stay home all the time!"

"With a boy this cute, how could I not?" GG tickles Ryan in his belly. He giggles and reaches for her. She takes him from Ellie.

"Gigi's offered to do some babysitting for us, Steve," Sally says. "Isn't that terrific?"

"Yeah." My hands are cold and numb, and everyone's voices seem to be coming from far away. The pain in my chest begins to return.

"Even with my parents around," Sally confides to Ellie and GG, "you can never have too many babysitters." They nod sympathetically.

"Isn't that true?" Ellie says. "All of my friends with kids say you really can't."

After that, there's some more bland conversation about kids and babysitters before a hostess signals Ellie that their table's ready, but I don't really hear any of it. I just smile blankly and nod every once in a while and hope that the discomfort in my chest doesn't get any worse. Luckily, it doesn't.

As we all say our good-byes, GG shakes my hand and smiles again. I'm sure to everyone else at the table it's a pleasant enough smile. But to me, that smile conveys an unmistakable message.

I know where you live, Steve.

I know where your family lives.

Discreetly clutching at the tightness in my chest, my stomach balled into a tiny knot, I sit back down to my half-eaten burger and curly fries.

But I'm not hungry anymore. I stare at my plate.

Sally watches me silently for a moment, briefly furrows her brow, then turns her attention back to Katie and Annabelle.

CHAPTER 15

Saturday, August 15

"Don't forget," Sally says. "I'm leaving for Providence Monday morning with the girls."

"Hmmmm."

"Steve. Are you listening?"

Not really. Head down, I'm staring blankly at the pavement of Nancy and Dan's driveway in Weston as we hike to the front door from the car. Since last night's encounter with GG in the restaurant, when she took things to a whole new level, I've been a little preoccupied. "Sure. Tomorrow morning. Providence."

Sally, walking next to me, stops dead in her tracks, so abruptly that, in my distracted frame of mind, I don't even notice at first. I walk a few paces beyond her, hands in my pockets, before following suit and turning around to face her.

"Steve. Really. Are you okay? You've been like this since we got home from the restaurant last night. This is starting to get a little ridiculous. It's like I'm talking to myself."

"Yeah. Sure." I don't tell her how, after she had fallen asleep last night, I had checked all the doors and windows, twice, to make sure they were locked; or how many hours I had lain awake afterward, alone with the pounding of my blood in my ears, twitching at every creak in the walls and scrape of windblown branches against the windows; or how I had finally drifted into an uneasy sleep only after deciding that GG was most likely just messing around with my mind. After all, if she'd really wanted to do something horrible to my family, she would have already done so. Still, I'm glad that Sally, Katie, and Annabelle will be leaving town for a while. And, besides, my brain keeps circling around one thought: Why did she even bother to mess around with my mind in the first place?

"Why were you in the hospital all day?"

"I was working." Spurred on by the restaurant encounter, I had spent the day in my office, from early in the morning until late in the afternoon, trying to figure out GG's next move.

"On what? You're not on call this weekend."

"Ummm . . . a, uh, research project. For

Dr. Collier. I want to keep him happy."

Frowning, she shoots me a questioning look, then shakes her head before resuming her trek up the driveway.

I fall in step next to her. "What?"

"Nothing," she says neutrally, looking straight ahead.

Nancy and Dan greet us at the door. We're the first ones there. Nancy and Sally immediately start chatting like old friends. The two of them move off, leaving Dan and me standing alone rather uncomfortably in the hallway. We try some small talk, in the halting way of guys who don't really know each other that well but whose wives are already good friends. And then Dan hits on the universal guy conversation starter.

"Hey, wanna beer?" he asks.

"Sure."

He leads me to a spacious family room with an immense flat-screen TV mounted on a wall and a wet bar with granite counters. Seated on the plush carpet in front of the TV, optimally placed to catch the full glory of the surround-sound system, little head tilted upward toward the crystal-clear, high-definition images, is a boy of three or four, a miniature version of Dan. He's sporting bright red pajamas with a picture of Elmo over the left breast. His wet blond hair is combed over in a neat Aryan part.

"This is Connor. Our nanny is upstairs with the girls. Hey, buddy. How's it going?" He strokes Connor's head with genuine affection.

Connor ignores his father. His face is locked on the video screen in an expression of mindless fealty, little mouth slightly agape, blue eyes vacant, pudgy but square jaw slack.

Dan shrugs, grabs two beers from a refrigerator at the wet bar, and hands one to me. We walk out onto the spacious and screened-in back porch. A short while later, Jason, my friend the orthopedic surgeon, and his wife, Lisa, show up, followed, to my complete surprise, by Luis. I wonder if he was as clueless about tonight's guest list as I was. Luis's presence tonight is unexpectedly comforting and sweeps away some of my lingering unease from last night. I want desperately to talk to him about GG, but before I have a chance to corner him privately, the rest of the dinner party arrives: an epidemiologist with wire-rim glasses and long, carefully groomed, dark hair that cascades in neat waves down to the top of his shoulders (the kind of guy you might see banging away self-importantly on his laptop in Starbucks while flipping through a dog-eared copy of Sartre), followed by a very well dressed couple. Nancy introduces the male half of the couple as one of her Harvard classmates who now runs his own hedge fund or private-equity something or other. He's wearing a bright blue silk dress shirt with a French collar, untucked, elegant gray dress slacks, and loafers without socks. His companion is a pale and pretty model type with short blond hair who appears one celery stick short of clinical malnutrition. Her face is frozen in sulky boredom. She clearly isn't the sharpest tool in the shed and doesn't have much to say.

In stark contrast to her boyfriend, who has a lot to say, mostly about himself and what he does for a living. For a while, after we sit down to dinner, all we hear about are *longs* and *shorts* and *secular bear markets* and a lot of other things I don't understand. Nancy sits next to him at dinner, nodding enthusiastically as he weighs in on every conceivable financial topic and pompously explains exactly what's wrong with the economy and how he would fix it.

But it's difficult to hold court over a room full of doctors with obtuse financial discourses. And it's downright impossible to get a group of young doctors together without having them talk about . . . well, being young doctors. Fueled by several glasses of wine, Dan takes the lead tonight by relating the story of a young male patient with HIV and a severe case of anal herpes. It was the worst case, Dan claims, anyone on their surgical team had ever encountered, including the senior professors. None of the usual medications worked, and every bowel movement sent him into debilitating paroxysms of pain. Eventually, Dan's team concluded that the only way to definitively relieve the patient's pain was to perform a colostomy.

"That was six months ago," Dan says. "At first, the guy did great. But then he showed up last week at our clinic with a relapse of his herpes."

"Around his anus?" Luis asks.

Dan smirks and winks at Business Guy's blond companion. "No. That's the best part. Over his colostomy stoma. Spreading outward along his abdomen."

Jason makes a face. "No way. No *way*. Dude, please tell me that the herpes was somehow transmitted from his anus during his surgery. Please tell me that."

"No. A brand-new infection. Apparently, from what he told us, this guy's colostomy made him popular in his, uh, social circles.

His friends were lining up at parties to get a chance to, you know . . ." He gestures with his hand in a vaguely suggestive way. "Be *intimate* with the colostomy." A chorus of groans erupts around the table.

"That is SO nasty." Jason is gasping with laughter. "So nasty." He bangs the table with his hand, palm open, and the fine china plates rattle.

The doctors at the table laugh. The non-doctors turn various shades of green. After dabbing the corners of her delicate, pouty mouth with a napkin, Business Guy's companion bolts from the table without a word.

"I mean, can you believe it?" Dan continues, almost in tears. "The guy didn't think —" His voice abruptly trails off as he locks eyes with Nancy, who is hurling visual daggers down the length of the table. He coughs, then quickly adds, "Anyway, we're not sure what we're going to do with him now." He stares at the floor and takes a big sip of wine, squirming under Nancy's bellicose gaze.

The rest of us focus our attention on our dinner plates. The conversation abruptly ends; the only sounds are the scrapes of utensils against china. Although Sally gamely jumps into the void by initiating a discussion about a new movie that's out, dinner limps its way to the finish line with a decidedly subdued tone as a housekeeper materializes and clears away the dishes. Business Guy begs off, his slim lady friend in tow, as does the epidemiologist (who's name I still don't catch). Luis abruptly disappears, so I end up following Dan and Jason downstairs to the finished basement.

Sans wives and children, surrounded by the manliness of classic arcade machines, foosball, and a dartboard, the alcohol flows freely from a bar amply stocked with liquor and beer with expensive-sounding names. Dan fires up some classic music from the eighties and nineties, and within short order, he and Jason are pretty hammered. I pour myself a glass of scotch and sip from it, but I'm otherwise too distracted to join in their drunken debate as to the feminine merits of the various Disney Princesses. So I wander back upstairs, where I stumble upon Nancy, Sally, and Lisa in the living room. Nancy and Lisa are sharing a bottle of chardonnay; Sally is drinking water.

The air is thick with estrogen and talk of Jane Austen novels, so I beat a hasty retreat onto the cavernous, screened back porch, carrying my half-full glass of scotch. The lights are out, and as I move farther away from the door, I quickly become shrouded in darkness. It's a pitch-dark, moonless evening. The darkness vibrates with the steady drone of crickets.

"What's up?"

I jump so high I practically knock my head on a rotating ceiling fan.

"Jesus, Luis, you scared the shit out of me," I gasp, clutching at my chest like an old lady and squinting in the direction of his voice. "I thought you'd gone home."

"Sorry." I can make him out now, sitting at the end of the porch in an Adirondack chair — a dark ghost projected against a slightly denser black background. Pungent tendrils of cigar smoke scrape across the back of my throat, trailing a gravelly residue that reminds me of my grandfather's house when I was a kid. He takes a puff on the cigar in his hand, and his face briefly glows red, illuminated by the embers at the tip.

"Are you out here all by yourself?"

"Yes."

"Can I — uh, join you?"

"Sure." He waves to a chair next to him and offers me a cigar. With his help, I awkwardly prep and light it, take a few tentative puffs — and immediately start hacking my lungs up.

"Easy there, boss." He chuckles. "Not all

at once. Do it like Bill Clinton: Don't inhale."

"Got it," I sputter between coughs. "I didn't know you were going to be here tonight. It's a funny coincidence, seeing you here."

"Not really. I knew you were coming and wrangled an invitation out of Nancy."

"What?" I wheeze, surprised. "Why didn't you tell me? When I saw you last Wednesday?"

"Basic rule of intel: You didn't need to know. Mentioning it ahead of time wouldn't have made any difference. Right? And it saved you the trouble of having to decipher another one of my texts and meet me in some bar somewhere downtown."

"Yeah. Okay." I take a hesitant puff on the cigar. This time I manage to get through it without coughing.

"You were at University Hospital again today."

I don't bother to ask him how he knew that. "Yes."

"You've been there a lot lately."

"It's where I get my best thinking done."

"It's risky, is what it is. You're not supposed to be there. What if GG spots you, gets antsy, and starts acting up or something?"

I wince. "I don't think we need to worry about that anymore."

"What do you mean?"

I tell him about seeing her in the restaurant last night.

"It freaked me out a little, Luis," I admit. "I wasn't expecting her to crank it up a notch like that, to take it out of the hospital."

"Disconcerting." I can see his face now. My eyes must be adjusting to the darkness. His mouth twitches, and he rubs the top of his head. "An aggressive move. She's definitely sending you a message. The question is: What's she trying to tell you? I wonder if she's trying to goad you into some kind of action after your spat in clinic last week." He strokes his chin thoughtfully, and his eyes fix on some far-off spot. "We're going to have to move quickly, Steve. I don't like this. Not one bit." His eyes refocus, as if his mind has come back from someplace far away. "I have a plan. I'll be working in University Hospital from tomorrow morning until Monday. I'll put the final pieces in place while I'm there."

"What are you going to do?"

"A guy like me, doing the kind of work I used to do, has a lot of" — he takes a drag on his cigar — "*useful* professional connections with a lot of very interesting people. People with unusual skill sets valuable to the task at hand. People who don't ask questions. Suffice to say, I've called in some favors from some of these old acquaintances."

"Can you tell me what you have in mind?"

"No. Not now. Not yet. I need to make the arrangements first. Expect a call from me sometime on Monday morning. I'll explain everything — and I mean everything, Steve — then. Really. No bullshit. I'm going to need your help to make this work."

"What should I do in the meantime?"

"Well, it would still really help us if we knew which patient. That intel would increase our odds of success. Have you got anything more since the last time we spoke?"

"I think so. We have a lot of diabetics we take care of. I think a diabetic patient in the hospital would be a tempting target."

"Ahhhhh. You're thinking induced hypoglycemia."

"Exactly." Insulin, commonly used to treat diabetes, coaxes the body's cells to suck sugar out of the blood. But too much insulin, given all at once in one mighty dose, causes an immediate and catastrophic drop in blood-sugar levels that will, within minutes, induce seizures, loss of consciousness, and death.

"But how to give the insulin fast enough to beat the code team? Without the patient, the nurses, or the doctors realizing what's going on?"

"I asked myself the same question. And then it occurred to me: an insulin pump."

A grin slowly unfurls across Luis's face. "Of course."

An insulin pump is a motorized reservoir of insulin implanted under the skin of diabetic patients. The pump delivers carefully regulated, preprogrammed doses of insulin so that the patient doesn't need to keep injecting it.

"A motivated individual, with the right kind of technical expertise, could theoretically reprogram a pump for an overdose right under everyone's noses," I say. "And, in retrospect, it would look just like an accident."

"Nice. I like it. How would she reprogram the pump?"

"I haven't gotten that far yet. I'm working on that. I'm going to lock myself in my office tomorrow all day and see what I can come up with."

"Good man. But remember: Try to lie low.

We don't need GG getting a whiff of what we're up to."

"I will." I take a puff of the cigar. "Luis. What are our chances? Of beating her? Really."

He smiles, and his teeth gleam in the half-light of the porch. "I like them, Steve. I really do. If we move quickly. And guess right."

"What if we guess wrong?

"We won't. We can't."

We sit for several minutes, quiet as monks, listening to the crickets.

"So I hear you're from LA," I say, apropos of nothing. I wonder vaguely if small talk might help me discover what's lurking in that confidential file of his.

He blows a very respectable-looking smoke ring. "Yes."

"Which part? Like, a suburb?" I swirl the remaining scotch around in the glass.

His laugh is short and humorless, like a dog's bark. "East LA isn't exactly a suburb, Steve. Especially the part I'm from."

"Oh." I don't know that much about East LA, but I know enough to realize that, based on his reaction, Luis probably didn't grow up in the same kind of modest but comfortable middle-class neighborhood that I did. That's something I've never stopped to consider before. Smart and smooth, Harvard-educated, he doesn't . . . seem like he'd be from a place like East LA.

I must be broadcasting my thoughts on my face. "Surprised?" His voice is soft. Even a little dangerous. I've never heard him sound this way before. "Why? Am I not living up to your expectations? Of what an East LA boy should be?" And then he shrugs off his generic American accent as effortlessly as sliding out of a pair of flip-flops. "*¿Que onda, guero?*" he growls in a thick Latino accent. "Huh, 'mano? 'Choo want me to talk like thees, 'esse?" He dismisses me with a wave of his hand and slips seamlessly back into his normal inflection. "No offense, but you white boys from the suburbs are all the same. You see exactly what you expect to see. Even Dan. He's my friend, but the way he talked the other day about that patient of yours, the kid who got shot in the penis, made me want to puke."

"I worked hard to get where I am," I say defensively.

"I never said you didn't." He inhales, and his face lights up like a flame, all shifting patterns of shadow and scarlet, before the smoke from his exhalation obscures it. "Don't get me wrong, Steve. But when you were a kid, were you ever afraid — and I mean well and truly scared shitless — to go to school? And I'm not talking about some bitch-ass anxiety dream about not studying for the big test or showing up in your underwear."

I don't answer. I don't need to.

"Back home, do you know what they called the boys who managed to graduate from high school in my neighborhood?

"What?"

"Alive."

I squirm in my seat and take a sip of my scotch. I mean, how the hell do I respond to *that*?

His lean, olive face emerges from the darkness as he bends forward in his chair, peering at me intently. "So. That's my story. What's yours?"

"You don't know?" I ask, genuinely surprised. "I figured you would have had your . . . *people* figure that out for you by now."

"It wasn't relevant to the task at hand. I only went back as far as your college."

"Then how'd you know I'm from the suburbs?"

"It wasn't hard to guess."

I shrug. "Not much to tell. I grew up just outside of Philly, across the river in Jersey. My mom's a fifth-grade teacher. My dad works at the airport, as a ticketing agent for one of the big airlines. My older sister is married to a fireman — a really good guy. She stays at home with the kids. They live down the street from my parents."

"So you're the first in your family to become a doctor?"

"Are you kidding? Do you even need to ask?"

"I bet they're proud of you. Your parents."

"They hosted a block party the day I graduated from med school in my honor. A *block* party. Closed off the street. Diverted traffic and everything, thanks to a little help from my brother-in-law. What can I say? Parental pride is what two hundred thousand dollars' worth of student loans buys you these days." I rub my free hand, the one not holding the cigar, down my face, and wonder what my parents would think of my present predicament. I don't dwell on it for long since the thought of letting them down is something I can't even begin to wrap my head around; just the memory of the block party alone is starting to make my throat tighten. "You know, just a few months ago, the prospect of having to pay off that debt was, like, the biggest problem in our lives. Sally and I talked about it a lot. But now, well . . ." I stare out into the night.

For at least a full minute after my voice trails off, I can sense Luis just sitting there, completely still, puffing on his cigar and silently considering me.

"You're a lot tougher than you look, man," he finally says. "And stubborn as hell. You would've made a decent Marine." He reaches over and claps me on the shoulder. "Ooo-rah."

"Thanks." I smile back. High praise coming from him, but just for fun I add, "I think." He guffaws. I take a drag on my cigar. "Speaking of the Marines, why'd you first sign up, anyway? Did you always want to be a soldier?"

He exhales lazily, and the smoke stretches languid fingers up toward the slowly rotating ceiling fan. "Not exactly. The Corps was my way out."

"You mean . . . it paid for college and med school?"

He smiles, not unkindly. "Yeah, the Corps covered my education. But it meant much more. The Corps saved my soul." His eyes burn almost as brightly as his cigar tip. "Don't take this the wrong way, man, but the Corps means something, teaches things, that you'll never understand." He rubs his free hand, the one not holding the cigar, across the top of his head. "Let me put it this way. Why are you trying to stop GG?"

"Well, to save my family and career, I guess. To get her the way she's gotten me."

"Those motivations are . . . understandable. And completely justifiable." He inhales, then blows another ring. "You know, you've never asked me why I'm helping you. Why I'm willing to devote so much of my time and energy, hell, even risk my *own* career, to catch her."

I blink. He's absolutely right. I've never stopped to consider why exactly he's been so motivated to take GG down. "I guess I just figured that you were, well, pissed that she had used you, too. To kill Mr. Bernard."

"No. I mean, sure, I was pissed. Who wouldn't be? But it's not that simple. I'm helping you because it's the right thing to do." His voice is deep and forceful and betrays not a trace of irony. "The honorable thing. Because, as a Marine, I was taught to protect the weak. She's preying on the weak and the innocent. That's an *abomination,* Steve. It's my duty to stop her."

I twirl my glass around, scrutinizing the bottom of it. "The Marines also taught you how to kill. Right?"

He reflects on that for perhaps half a heartbeat. "Yes."

"Have you ever killed anyone?"

"Yes."

"Were you . . . good at it? Killing?"

"Yes." The corner of his mouth twitches.

"So, then — why'd you decide to become a doctor?"

"I discovered that I liked healing people better than killing them."

"Oh. Sounds like you had a . . . calling."

He grunts noncommittally. "Something like that."

The high-pitched laughter of the wives floats through an open window.

I drain the rest of my scotch. "Have you ever considered killing GG?"

"Yes," he answers impassively. "But I'm not going to."

"Why?"

"It wouldn't be the honorable thing to do." He stubs out his cigar in an ashtray with a finality that signals the end of that particular line of conversation. "So why'd you go to med school, Steve? A thirst to prove yourself? Or a fear of failure?"

Both. Neither. Who knows anymore? I think about how GG once told me how much I was like her.

You don't care about making people feel better, Steve.

For you, the patients are a means to an end. It's all about you.

"I used to tell myself it was about the patients, but now . . . now I don't remember," I say, my voice barely registering above a whisper.

Was it ever about the patients?

I shake my head very slightly and look down at the empty scotch glass cradled between my thighs. "I don't remember."

If the ensuing silence makes Luis uncomfortable, he doesn't tip his hand. "So," he says quietly, after a brief pause. "What period of literature did you study?"

"What?" The non sequitur catches me completely off guard.

"In college. What period was your literature degree in?"

"Ummm — Russian. Mostly nineteenth and twentieth century."

"Dostoyevsky. Solzhenitsyn. Good stuff. Do you speak Russian?"

"A little. I'm better at reading it."

"Me too. It's a beautiful language," he says, in perfectly accented Russian. I gape at him, incredulous. *Jesus, how many layers are there to you, Luis?* And then, switching back to English, he says, "But, myself, I've always been partial to science fiction. You ever read a guy named Philip K. Dick?"

"No."

"You should. He's great."

"What has that got to do with anything?"

"Nothing. Or everything. We'll see." He pushes himself gracefully out of the chair, all sinew and muscle, and stretches.

"You're leaving? *Now?*" There's still so much more I want to ask him.

"I have a few things I need to take care of. Besides, I'm on call tomorrow night, and I need to get some sleep. I never sleep very well in the hospital. That fucking kitten in the call room always messes with my mind."

I can't help but smile. "You, too? It's funny how none of us have ever taken it down."

"Makes you wonder what's behind it, doesn't it?" He's wearing a very strange, lopsided grin.

"I guess."

"You still have the phone I gave you?"

"Sure."

"Expect a text very soon." He moves toward the porch door.

"Luis?"

He stops and, without turning around, inclines his head to one side, his body silhouetted against the light shining from inside the house.

"I don't know how much longer I can keep doing this," I admit. "It's just — I'm, well, I feel like I'm in way over my head."

413

He nods once, very slowly, still facing away from me. "As the poet once said: If you aren't in over your head, how do you know how tall you are?"

"Which poet?" The quote sounds familiar, but I can't quite place it.

"You were the literature major. Look it up. And Steve?"

"Yeah."

He turns around and looks me directly in the eye. "Don't forget what we've talked about here tonight. You might find it useful. Someday."

Useful? Random musings about the Russian language and an obscure science fiction writer?

"Useful how?" But he's already gone. And I'm alone.

Until a few minutes later, when Jason flips on the overhead porch light, flops down in an empty chair next to me, and reports with no small amount of satisfaction that Dan is now upstairs sleeping things off, much to his wife's mortification ("Dude, those general surgeons are such fucking lightweights," he says with a laugh), and that our wives are still going strong in the living room, having cracked open a fresh bottle of wine.

"Your friend gave me one of these as he

414

was leaving," he says offhandedly, slipping a cigar into his mouth. "Interesting dude. Talk about the strong, silent type."

"You could say that."

"He told me you were out here and could use the company."

"Sure." My insides give a twist. There's something I need to get off my chest. "Jason."

"Yeah, brah."

"That day we talked on the phone —"

"Forget it, dude."

"But —"

"Forget it. Enough said." He expertly lights the cigar. "Speaking of which, how's the probation stuff going?"

"Taking it up the ass, just like you advised."

He laughs heartily. "Good man. Just like I told you — keep your head down, play ball, and this will all be over soon."

Right. One way, or another. "Hey, can I ask you something, Jason?"

"Sure, man."

"Why'd you become a doctor?"

"Easy. Because when I was a kid, I had cancer and almost died."

My jaw drops so far that my chin practically sits on my chest. "Cancer?"

"Yeah. Acute lymphoblastic leukemia.

When I was seven."

"Holy shit, Jason. You never told me that. In all the years I've known you."

Jason watches the fireflies drifting around outside the porch screen. "It's not something I like to talk about much."

"Was it bad?"

"Yes," he says unemotionally. "I almost died. Neutropenia from the chemo."

I imagine a seven-year-old version of Jason, sitting not in a comfortable Adirondack on a back porch enjoying a cigar but in an oversized hospital chair in a pediatric-oncology ward somewhere, attended by an array of plastic tubes. Feverish and confused, poisoned by the chemotherapy, sallow, sunken cheeks drawn tight over frail bones, his small hands gripping the arms of the chair as he pulls each breath as if it were his last with shallow, labored rasps.

"How did you end up on the Safety Committee?"

"A long story." It's clear by the tone in his voice that he's not going to tell it.

"What kinds of things does the Committee get involved with? Besides me?"

He chuckles. "Oh, lots of stuff. Most of which I'm not allowed to talk about. Quality of care, obviously. But we also deal with security issues. One of my jobs, believe it or not, is to liaise with University Hospital Security."

"Really?"

"Yeah. I've been around security my entire life. My dad owns a small security-consulting firm. I worked there during summers in high school and college."

"On what?"

"Oh, just about anything, really. Most of it pretty boring stuff. Not nearly as glamorous as it sounds. Data security. Fraud. Surveillance. That kind of thing."

The door to the inside of the house opens, and Nancy pokes her head out, sniffing the air suspiciously. She purses her prim lips when she spies the cigar in Jason's hand and the one still smoldering next to me in the ashtray. "Gentlemen, can we put our cigars out, please?" she says with a tight, cloying smirk. "The smell is practically impossible to clear from the patio upholstery." Jason and I mumble our apologies and dispose of the cigars. It's just as well, anyway: Between the scotch and the cigar, there's a rank taste in my mouth, and the nicotine from the cigar is making my heart beat like a rabbit's.

"What's her story?" I ask as the door slides shut behind her. "Kind of intense."

"Nancy is Nancy," he says neutrally.

"She's like a lawyer, or something?"

"Yep. A DA. A damn good one. *Harvard Law Review,* and all that crap. Hell-bent on rising to the top. Always looking for the big, glamorous cases. The ones with lots of publicity. I wouldn't be surprised if she runs for office one day."

"I don't like her." The scotch has hindered my already limited natural ability to mince words.

"Careful!" He laughs good-naturedly. "Your wife sure does."

"Yeah, I noticed." I lean my head back and look at the stars. "I noticed."

CHAPTER 16

Sunday, August 16

I'm out of the house before anyone else is up. I drive to the hospital, stop by the cafeteria for a bagel and a large coffee, and park myself in front of my computer in the otherwise deserted office. I crack my knuckles and pull up the same materials I've been staring at all week.

Okay, so now what?

I retread the same ground, going over and over the same material I've already gathered on her, looking for things I might have missed. After several hours, I'm paged by the hospital operator. When I call her, she immediately connects me to Mr. Abernathy, who still hasn't learned to appreciate the virtues of boundaries, because now that I've changed my cell-phone number, he's calling me through the hospital. For several minutes he gives me his usual profane earful, at one point accusing me of being a *goddamned quack doctor.* I'm too tired to get pissed, or to point out to him that there are more important things in the world than his bathroom habits. So I just listen quietly to his abusive rant until he's done, then tell him to call next Monday to make an appointment to see me in clinic. He seems satisfied and hangs up.

I put down the phone, rub my aching eyes, and check my watch. I'm hungry and tired; the large coffee cup, drained long ago, sits on the desk in front of me next to the computer. With one frustrated swipe, I knock it off the desk with the back of my hand.

Screw it.

I'm not getting anywhere. So I go for a walk to clear my head, heading in the direction of the ICU, with vague thoughts of seeing how Mrs. Samuelson is doing. The corridors, particularly in this area of the hospital, where many of the resident sleeping rooms and offices are located, are quiet and empty on a Sunday. I'm walking around a corner, lost in thought, oblivious to my surroundings, when I run headlong into somebody coming the other way. The collision scatters a bunch of papers the other person was holding onto the floor. We both automatically bend over to gather them up.

"Oh, jeez, I'm so sorry!" I say, picking up one of the papers — a medical journal — then rising. "Are you all right —"

I freeze. My outstretched hand, holding the journal, drops to my side.

It's GG.

She appears just as startled as I am.

"Steve. What are you doing here?" Something odd, completely out of place, flutters across her features, almost like she's — flustered, maybe? She blinks, gathers herself together, then points to the journal in my hand. "May I?"

As I wordlessly pass it back to her, I note that it's a prominent scientific publication focused on the heart called *Circulation*. Printed on the cover, I spot the words "Special Issue," "implantable cardiac defibrillator," "pacemaker," "complications," and "malfunction." I guess she hasn't lost her interest in studying mechanical heart devices.

"Thank you," she says, brusquely tucking the journal into the front pocket of her white coat. "So." She smooths out her clothes. "What are you doing here, Steve?"

"Working," I reply warily.

"Really? You're not supposed to be taking care of patients in the hospital this weekend." She smirks. "Shouldn't you be home with your wife and daughters?"

My temper, shortened by all those long hours in my office, flares. I ball my hands into tight fists. "Stay the fuck away from them, GG. Fine. You proved your point in the restaurant. You know where to find me. But they have nothing to do with you and me. Or your stupid game."

"Point?" she says innocently. "I don't know what you mean. I was out with my friend, she lives in your neighborhood, and we happened to run into you in a public place. What's the big deal?" She scans the empty hallway and takes a step toward me. "You mentioned the game. How's it going for you?"

"I told you last week. I don't want any part of you or your *insane* game, GG. I just want to be left alone. And if you're wondering what I'm doing here, it's no big mystery. I'm on my way over to see Mrs. Samuelson."

"The woman you almost killed. Sure. I can only imagine the guilt you're feeling. She's improving, you know. She might just make it." She sighs and looks disappointed. "Too bad. I was really hoping it would be more interesting this time. Your guilt over what you did to Mrs. Samuelson is going to be nothing compared to what you'll feel

422

after this next patient dies. And the one after that. I guarantee it."

"Whatever. Just leave me the hell alone. Okay?" I stride quickly away before I have a chance to say something stupid. The less I say around her, the better.

GG wasn't kidding. Amazingly enough, Mrs. Samuelson hasn't died yet. More amazing still, she's actually getting better. A lot better. Her recovery has been nothing short of remarkable. She's off dialysis, and her internal organs are waking up, one by one. The ICU team is talking about pulling out her breathing tube tomorrow. She still might leave the hospital alive.

I sit at Mrs. Samuelson's bedside, sifting through my thoughts, while Shania gyrates through her usual routines in the room next door. I'm not so sure about the insulin-pump approach anymore. The more I've delved into it, the more I've realized how many different variables and details are involved with trying to surreptitiously access the programming of an insulin pump. There are *so* many, in fact, that I'm beginning to doubt even GG could pull it off. But I still think medical devices are her most likely approach.

I sigh and watch Mrs. Samuelson's digital EKG tracing on her heart monitor. Her heart was damaged when she bled in the operating room but, like the rest of her body, has been recovering nicely.

The heart. The engine of the circulatory system. Poets and writers have spent generations plumbing its metaphorical complexity. But when you get down to it, it's really just a hollow sack of muscle and nerves; the fleshy, fragile motor that drives blood through the human body.

My gaze drifts over the electrodes connecting Mrs. Samuelson to the cardiac monitor, and I think of all the things doctors use to keep sick hearts beating properly: EKGs and powerful medications and high-tech electronic devices. My mind wanders idly over GG's heart research, and the medical-journal article she was carrying —

I grip the arms of my chair.

An engineering degree from MIT.

Research in a heart laboratory.

A medical journal focused on the safety of implantable heart devices.

Of course.

It was there in front of my face the entire time.

I race back to the office, jump in front of the computer, close my eyes for a moment, and take a deep breath, my hands poised over the keyboard.

And then I go.

God, it feels good. It's as if the keyboard is an extension of my fingers, and my fingers are directly fused to my brain. I'm at the peak of my form, like when I was in college wired on caffeine and the inexhaustible energy of youth, oblivious to all but the images floating in the soft glow of the screen, drowning gloriously in the digital ether as I dig up everything I can on ICDs: documents from the National Library of Medicine, Google Scholar, medical-device manufacturers, the FDA, even the same issue of the medical journal I saw in GG's hand.

The data that stream in front of me over the course of the afternoon leave little doubt in my mind that tampering with an ICD would be straightforward, difficult to trace, and deadly — just like the potassium overdose. The latest ICD models are sophisticated minicomputers with wireless radio receivers to allow cardiologists to download data for testing and recalibration. The software is laughably vulnerable and can be altered with something as simple as a pocket magnet, or even an iPod. A determined individual (or a not-so-determined individual, for that matter) could easily hack an ICD's programming remotely with a computer.

Why? Because no reasonable ICD manu-
facturer would build a security system
sophisticated enough to protect it from attack against someone like GG. Their threat
models never anticipated someone like her.
Who could imagine that someone would be
disturbed enough to deliberately mess with
a piece of medical machinery buried deep
in the heart muscle of another human being? Besides, encryptions are expensive, and
continuously running them would eat up
precious battery life on the device.

So, instead of sophisticated encryption
algorithms, the security of any given ICD
radio signal depends upon two key, easily
surmountable elements. First, like any
consumer-electronic device, each ICD has a
unique serial number, and each command
to any given ICD needs to be prefaced by
its serial number. But serial numbers are
not kept secret and can be readily obtained
from the patient's medical chart. Second,
ICDs have very limited radio range, and
inputting remote radio commands requires
relatively close physical proximity to the
patient — within a several-foot radius.

So, given that an ICD can easily be hacked
by any individual with access to the medical
chart and the opportunity to be close
enough to the patient to input commands,

the next issue is: what to tell an ICD to do after gaining access to its software system? One approach is to simply switch it off. But there's no guarantee that the patient will die once the ICD is turned off because the patient's heart would then have to spontaneously enter into what's called an arrhythmia — an abnormal heartbeat — in order for him or her to suffer immediate and irreparable harm.

Which leads me to an equally simple, but much more lethal, command.

Tell the ICD to shock the patient.

Cardiologists shock patients all the time under controlled conditions, remotely dumping up to 700 volts of juice directly into the heart via the ICD. The jolt is enough to induce arrhythmias, including something called ventricular fibrillation, or v-fib for short. V-fib is a condition in which the heart starts quivering ineffectually and can no longer pump blood to the rest of the body. Without treatment, it's fatal within minutes.

In some patients, cardiologists deliberately induce v-fib to make sure the ICD is working properly: If the ICD is working, it immediately senses the v-fib and shocks the heart back into a normal rhythm. If the ICD isn't working — doesn't detect the v-fib and/or deliver the second shock to stop it — the cardiologist steps in and immediately corrects the situation.

With the proper series of commands, a hacker could simultaneously induce v-fib and switch off the ICD's ability to stop it. And with something relatively straight-forward called a buffer-overflow attack, a hacker could gain deep-level access to the system in order to erase and reset the software logs. If it was done at night, to a sleeping and otherwise stable patient, during a work shift when up to four hours can elapse between nursing checks, a patient could be dead for hours before anyone realized it. There's even a chance that the initial shock would induce an immediate cardiac arrest. In either case, an autopsy would later show that the patient had died of a cardiac arrest caused by a malfunctioning ICD.

Brilliant.

I have the how. Now all I need is who. Who is she going to attack?

I lean back in my chair, massage the back of my neck with fingers numbed by thousands of keystrokes, and, glancing out the window, realize with a start that it's dark outside. I try to puzzle out the next logical step, to start picking out a likely victim, but

I hit a mental wall. My brain has been on afterburner for hours. I'm starting to come down from my high and feel my ripe old age of thirty-two. I decide to call it a night. Tomorrow, I can compare notes with Luis, and we can start identifying potential victims together.

Sally is up waiting for me when I get home, sitting on the couch in the living room. The house is quiet. She sets aside the book she had been reading and crosses her arms as I come in and wordlessly take a seat on the opposite end of the couch. She seems . . . small, somehow. Deflated. Resigned.

We sit there without saying anything, the two of us, separated by the space on the couch.

"Is this how it starts?" she asks calmly after several minutes.

"How what starts?"

"You know. Divorce. Do you think this is how it starts? Or at least, how it starts for us?"

Wow. I wasn't expecting this.

"You mean . . . you want to get a divorce?"

"No, Steve . . . Jesus, for such a smart guy, you can be so goddamn literal some-times. No, I don't want a divorce." She grabs a throw pillow and hugs it tightly to her chest. "At least, not yet."

She turns to face me.

"Are you screwing around?" she asks. "Is that what this is about? All the nights and weekends at the hospital, the sudden and complete lack of interest in me or the kids, coming home at all hours with alcohol on your breath, mysterious research projects . . . If you're screwing around, just tell me now, and we'll go on from there, okay? I'm not stupid, Steve. I know what goes on there. In the hospital. In those call rooms."

I wasn't expecting this, either. "No, I'm not screwing around." I'm careful to use the present tense, which means that I'm not lying. Technically.

"I don't believe you."

"Really, Sally. I'm not screwing around. Do I look like the kind of guy who can score a little action in the hospital whenever he wants to?"

The levity gambit doesn't work. In fact, it only makes her angry. "Don't do that, Steve," she fumes, drawing herself up and throwing the pillow aside. "Not now. Don't joke around. This is serious. If you're screwing around, I want to know. Right now."

"Sally. I'm not screwing around."

She purses her lips and shakes her head.

"Honest to God, Sally! I'm not."

"I don't believe you." She gets off the couch, walks over to the window, and gazes out into the front yard. Sally has never been very emotional. Instead, when she gets upset, her voice and demeanor assume a flat, calm quality. I think it's how she's able to really hold it together in a crisis.

You'd never know it now, but Katie was born almost two months premature, with severely underdeveloped lungs that weren't yet equipped for breathing on their own. She almost died. It was that bad.

Sitting next to her incubator in the Neonatal Intensive Care Unit, wearing the bright yellow smock all the parents had to wear, I was an emotional wreck, weak and scared and numb: ironically enough, completely incapable of any coherent interactions with Katie's doctors. But not Sally. Sally was the one who calmly listened to the neonatologists recite grim survival statistics as our newborn daughter walked the razor's edge between life and death for days. Sally was the one who prepared for the worst and made all of the decisions. She never lost it, not once — something which, as a surgeon, I've always respected the hell out of her for.

Luis told me last night that I'm a lot tougher than I look. Well, at five-foot-one and one hundred pounds, Sally's a lot tougher than *she* looks.

Anyway, the more upset Sally gets, the calmer she sounds. And right now, she sounds very, very calm. "I'm sorry. But I don't believe you."

"I don't know what else to say, Sally."

"Tell me what's bothering you, then. Tell me where you've been spending all of your time."

"I've already told you. In the hospital."

"But why?"

"I told you that, too. Doing research."

"We've got to fix this, Steve." She turns around and spreads her arms. "Before the baby comes, and I go back to work."

I frown, and say, "Are you sure you really want to go back to work? Now?"

She walks back to the couch and sits down next to me. "Is *that* what this is all about? My going back to work? I thought you said it didn't bother you."

"I don't know," I say, shrugging. "Maybe."

"Nancy told me this might be a problem," she says, sighing. "Dan has issues with her working, too. Even with the nanny."

Her again. "Nancy?" I growl.

"We've spent a lot of time together the past few weeks."

"And because of that I'm supposed to take

advice from her about my personal life?"

She draws her mouth into a tight line. "If you hadn't noticed, you haven't had much of a personal life lately."

"Yeah, well," I say grouchily, "if you'd like to know about screwing around, talk to Dan."

"What do you mean?"

"He's been banging every nurse in the hospital. I know. I saw him one night."

She blanches. "I don't believe you."

"It's true."

"Okay, fine. But even if it is, what does that have to do with us?"

"I don't like your talking to Nancy about our personal life."

"I don't care. And it's not like you have any say in the matter."

"I have plenty of say. It's my life, too."

"I have to talk to somebody. At least, somebody who can carry on a conversation about something more sophisticated than Elmo. And you haven't been around." She sighs, exasperated. "Look. Whether you like it or not, I'm going back to work. Andrea, at University, has officially offered me the job. And I'm going to take it. We're going out to dinner in the city a week from next Thursday to hammer out the details." She reaches over and takes my hand. "Please.

It's something I *need* to do, Steve. I've wanted this for a long time. Nancy only helped me realize that. But I can't do this without your help. It's not going to be easy. For either one of us."

"I know. I just — I need to get used to the idea." I squeeze her hand.

She studies my face. "You've really just been doing research? At University?"

"Yes," I say. It's true, at least lately, so I have no trouble looking her straight in the eye. "Really."

"Okay. Is it going to last much longer?"

"No. I don't think so."

"Good." She kisses me on the cheek. "Enough said, then." She stands up and yawns. "I want to get off to an early start tomorrow, so I'm heading to bed. Have you eaten?" I shake my head. The mention of food makes my stomach growl. She hears it and grins. "Sorry. I didn't fix you a plate."

Understandable, given the fact that she was ready to accuse me of adultery the moment I walked in the door tonight. "No problem."

"There's a frozen pizza in the freezer."

"Thanks."

"I'm guessing you'll be gone tomorrow morning when I wake up?"

"Tell you what. I'll go in a little later, so I

can help you get the kids ready and load the car up."

She smiles appreciatively. "Thanks. I'd like that. Turn off the lights when you're done." She walks upstairs as I head to the kitchen in search of frozen pizza.

CHAPTER 17

Monday, August 17

I'm walking through the main door of the hospital, eager to talk to Luis. I'm anxious to discuss my ICD idea. Plus, my conversation last night with Sally, and time spent with Katie and Annabelle this morning helping to get them ready for their drive to Providence, have fired me up with new purpose: The sooner I deal with GG, the sooner I can get the rest of my life back in order. Luis's cell phone is tucked securely in my pocket, and I take it out for perhaps the tenth time that morning to make sure it still has a full charge. I wonder when he'll call and what he has in mind.

That's when I see the crowd.

A press of people — some appearing subdued and somber, others simply curious — are gathered to one side of the cavernous main lobby. Several cops are milling around with University Hospital security officers, and a local news reporter is talking to one of the cops.

My stomach gives a little lurch.

"What's going on?" I ask a medical student who's alternately taking in the scene and thumbing the keys of her smart phone.

"Haven't you heard? They found one of the residents dead this morning." She glances up from her phone, and adds, conspiratorially, "Here. In the *hospital.*"

My breath catches in my throat.

"How?"

"Suicide. They think. He was in a call room. There was a note, I heard."

Luis's phone slips from my hand and clatters to the floor.

It couldn't be, I think frantically, dropping to one knee to scoop up the phone with shaking hands.

And then, as I straighten up, I spot Dr. Collier, ashen-faced, speaking earnestly in hushed tones to a woman dressed in heels and an immaculate gray power suit. She looks pained. It's Andrea, Sally's old boss. The CEO of University Hospital.

And I know.

But I ask anyway.

I have to.

"Do you know who?"

"Some guy with, like, a Spanish-sounding

437

name. I'm checking the University Hospital Web site to see if I can figure out who it was."

"Luis," I whisper, as the police clear a path through the crowd, through which a man and a woman, blank-faced and wearing bright yellow jackets with the word CORONER stenciled on the back, push a body bag on a gurney. The onlookers stir. A few are holding up cellphone video cameras. Somewhere, I hear a woman sobbing.

"His name was Luis."

After watching the police cart off Luis's corpse, the rest of the day flashes by in a series of disturbing images, like when you're sick in bed, and you're sleeping, but you keep having disjointed, fever-induced nightmares from which you intermittently emerge, semiconscious and soaked with sweat.

Around lunchtime, I attend a hastily called emergency meeting of our department, at which Dr. Collier, visibly shaken, his voice hushed and quavering, confirms to the faculty, residents, nurses, and administrative staff assembled in the Dome that Luis is indeed dead and that the initial information indicates it was most likely a suicide. He leads us in a moment of silence, and then reminds the stunned audience that, despite our shock and grief, our patients still need us, and that daily routines will continue uninterrupted. He announces which residents will be temporarily assuming Luis's hospital duties until a more permanent solution is reached. I note, with some bitterness, that my name is not among them. He pledges to provide further updates as more information becomes available.

Afterwards, in the hallway outside the conference room, my colleagues gather into tight groups, hugging one another and crying. I mingle with a few of them, briefly, before splitting off and collapsing against a nearby pillar. I rest my head against the cool marble, and close my eyes.

This sucks.

So what do I do now?

"I warned you not to ask for help, Steve," a familiar female voice whispers seductively in my ear. "I said there would be a penalty if you did."

I spin angrily on GG and, unnoticed by our distraught coworkers, guide her firmly by the elbow into a sheltered alcove off the main hallway. "So it *was* you," I hiss. "You killed him. It wasn't a suicide."

"I didn't say that," she replies with a coy smile that makes me want to grab her by the neck and throttle her.

"But why *kill* him, GG? What does Luis's death have to do with keeping patients safe? It doesn't make any sense. You said you were only interested in patient safety."

"I am," she explains patiently. "And his death is all about patient safety. Everyone knows that residents are overworked and fatigued; many are clinically depressed. In fact, the prevalence of drug and alcohol abuse among doctors and residents is much higher than in the general population. Depressed, substance-abusing doctors can, through no fault of their own, make mistakes that kill patients." She reaches over and casually brushes a piece of lint off my shoulder. "Oh, I'm sure the Safety Committee will be *very* interested in Luis's death, Steve. The Committee might even make recommendations for further reducing resident work hours and screening for depression. Poor Luis." She shakes her head in a mockery of sympathy. "He had a history of drug and alcohol problems. Did you know that?"

My cartoonish expression of surprise, complete with slack jaw and wide-set eyes, is all the answer she needs.

So that was what was in his confidential folder.

She blinks innocently. "I see that you didn't. Well, I guess his inner demons finally overtook him. Once an addict, always an addict. At least, that's what everyone is going to say."

"You *bitch,*" I snap, incensed by her smugness, inadvertently launching flecks of spit at her nose in irregular arcs. My fury over her complete disregard for Luis's life — *all* life — almost overcomes me, and it is all I can do to keep myself from smashing my fist into her face. And then another thought occurs to me. "You planned this from the beginning, didn't you? As part of your patient safety thing. You were going to kill Luis whether I talked to him or not."

Unmoved, and without taking her eyes off me, she placidly and methodically wipes the spit off her cheek with her shirtsleeve. "The important thing is that you *did* talk to him. Didn't you think I'd notice? Since when had the two of you ever spent *any* time together outside the hospital? Whatever it was the two of you were up to, all alone talking in that bar over by the Commons last Wednesday, it's over now. Yes, Steve. I was there. I even saw you grab that poor girl by the shoulder. Did you think she was me?" She giggles. "She did look a little bit like me, I guess. I honestly thought her father was going to kill you." Now her voice becomes low and menacing. "I warned you that there would be a penalty, Steve, for breaking the rules. Now, here's another one: I'm moving our timetable up. The next patient is going to die this week."

"What?" My anger deflates, like a popped balloon. "But . . . you said it wouldn't happen until next week."

"You broke the rules, so I'm altering them. Try to stop me." She shrugs. "Or not. It doesn't matter to me at this point. It's up to you." And then she levels an icy gaze at me that makes the hairs on the back of my neck stand up. "And you alone. No more violations, Steve. Don't give me a reason to link patient safety to Katie and Annabelle. Do you understand what I'm saying?"

Jesus.

If she was able to get to *Luis,* for God's sake — with all of his training, military experience, paranoia, and preparations — then how safe are Sally and the girls?

Seeing my expression, she smiles and leans in toward me.

"That's right, Steve," she whispers. "Be scared. Be very, very scared for your family."

I need to get away from her.

Right now.

I stumble out of the alcove and take off down the corridor, away from GG and the Dome, weaving in and out of the dense flow of midday human traffic. I don't know where I'm going and really don't care. I don't look back, but I can feel her eyes following me, and I can picture the smirk on her face.

As I turn a bend in the corridor, I pull out my phone and call Sally. It's a hollow gesture, I know — I mean, if GG was really determined to hurt them, there's no doubt in my mind that she'd track my family to Providence. But when Sally picks up, sounding surprised and a little touched that I would be checking in so soon after their departure, it nevertheless makes me feel better to hear that she and the girls made it to her sister's house just fine. The sound of her voice alone is comforting. We chat briefly about nothing in particular. I don't tell her about Luis, knowing that now is not the time to open up that particular can of worms. Some kind of dispute between Katie and Annabelle draws her attention; before hanging up, she promises to call tomorrow.

With nothing else to do, and Luis weighing heavily on my mind, I wander to the cafeteria. I sit at an empty table in a depopulated corner and call Jason — guessing, correctly, that he would be an informed and sympathetic source of information about Luis's death.

It quickly becomes clear by his pressured speech and anxious tone, so unlike his normally carefree persona, that Jason is well and truly freaked out over Luis's death. It's also obvious that, probably because of his position on the Safety Committee, Jason is up to speed on everything that University Hospital currently knows about the situation, the details of which he freely offers up in a manic, stream-of-consciousness soliloquy. I'm not really sure why. Maybe he just needs to unload on someone as a kind of mental therapy. In any event, I think he ends up telling me a bunch of shit he probably shouldn't.

Luis, Jason confirms, had a troubled past and a documented history of drug use. He had started out as a teenage gang leader and spent his late teens drifting into and out of prison, mostly for dealing and doing drugs. But around the age of twenty, Luis had managed to turn his life around: He had dried out, received his high school equivalency degree, joined the Marines, and earned a spot in one of their elite units.

Jason tells me that Luis had reportedly seen a lot of combat and served with distinction for many years in Iraq, Somalia, Afghanistan, and probably a bunch of other places that would never appear on his official record. He also had a documented history of PTSD, which was successfully treated prior to his beginning medical school.

The suicide note Luis allegedly left behind — neatly typed and folded in an envelope found next to his body — is apparently pretty convincing. In it, Luis admitted to doing drugs again, heavily, to cope with a resurgence of his PTSD and the stresses of residency. He professed self-loathing over his perceived lack of control and discipline, and expressed an inability to bear the shame of his weaknesses.

"Christ, Steve," Jason says, his voice shaking. "The cops think he pumped himself with enough meds to bring down a bull elephant. He put a central line in his own femoral vein to inject them, for Christ's sake. I mean, there's precedent for that kind of thing. There's a report of at least one anesthesiologist who accidentally killed himself injecting drugs into his own femoral vein. But — *Christ.* Luis? Who would have guessed? We just saw him the other night at Dan's house. It hits so close to home. Christ. He seemed perfectly fine."

That's because he was. "What drugs?"

"It'll take weeks to get the definitive results back. Between you and me? There were so many different kinds, he had to label all of his drug vials so that he could keep track of what was what. The cops found bottles marked as narcotics and benzos. Some lidocaine. Oh, and ketamine."

"Ketamine?" *That's an unusual choice.* "You mean the anesthetic also used as an animal tranquilizer?"

"One and the same. It's got hallucinogenic properties and pretty decent street value."

"Didn't anybody see or hear anything?"

"Nobody else used that call-room suite last night. One of the residents found him after he didn't show up for morning rounds or the operating room."

A virtuoso, brutal maneuver. GG engineered a perfect setup with a completely credible backstory: a doctor with a troubled past, unable to cope with the stresses of residency, who overdoses in a hospital call room. She played the former Force Recon Marine as if he were a puppet on strings.

Which, of course, raises some nagging questions. Like, how was she able to get to Luis? And what was he about to tell me this morning?

And, most important, if Luis couldn't beat

her — how can I? All on my own?

"I mean, *fuck,* Steve. You worked with him every day. Did you see this coming?"

"No," I answer honestly. "No. I didn't."

Jason keeps talking, but I'm no longer listening.

What else can't I see coming? I wonder.

What else does she have planned?

Mrs. Samuelson is asleep.

Not in a coma. Not unconscious. Not sedated. But in a real, honest-to-God state of deep slumber. The SICU doctors took the breathing tube out this morning. She's hoarse, but otherwise, remarkably, none the worse for the wear.

It's evening now, and I'm sitting next to Mrs. Samuelson's bed in the SICU. I don't remember how I got here. In fact, I don't remember much of what happened today after my conversation with Jason. I know I somehow ended up in my office, but I don't remember exactly what I did there. I think I might have napped, but I'm not sure. My waking and sleeping states feel like they're merging.

I should be happy, I guess, watching Mrs. Samuelson sleep. I should be as ecstatic as her family, grateful that she most likely is going to make it out of the hospital alive, despite my best efforts in the OR to bleed her to death.

But, instead, I'm scared.

Scared as much, maybe, as I've ever been at any point in my life.

My fear is like a nest of snakes in my stomach, their slick coils writhing and twisting as they slide over and across one another, again and again. It kind of feels like I want to puke, but I know that puking won't make the sick feeling in my stomach go away. My hands are cold. I keep rubbing them together, trying to warm them up, but the cold comes from the inside, so no amount of rubbing helps. My breathing is quick and shallow, and my heart pounds away in my chest.

I try to calm myself down by thinking about the physiology underlying these symptoms: the catecholamines, secreted by my adrenal glands, that are flooding my body and activating the same so-called fight-or-flight mechanism we share with our animal cousins inhabiting other branches of the evolutionary tree. But my basic instincts win out, and the fear remains.

I rest my face in my hand and knead my temples with my fingers.

I'm done. It's over. How can I possibly outmaneuver a psychotic med student who managed to take down a combat-hardened former Marine? All I can do now is keep my head down, wait for the next patient to die, and, once the dust has settled, try to pick up what's left of my career and marriage. And hope I can forget any of this ever happened.

But, deep down, I know that, if I do nothing, if I just allow the next patient to die, then I won't be able to leave any of this behind.

Ever.

Shania's relentlessly sunny lyrics drift in from the cubicle next door.

Oh, oh, oh . . . men's shirts, short skirts, oh, oh, oh . . .

"Hi, Dr. Mitchell. How are you tonight?" one of the nurses, just starting the evening shift, whispers as she enters the room.

"Hi, Carol," I murmur, picking my head up and folding my hands in my lap. "I'm okay. How are you?"

"Oh, okay, I guess. Same old, same old." She quietly starts adjusting some of Mrs. Samuelson's intravenous lines. A fortysomething, battle-scarred veteran of the SICU front lines, Carol is plump with frizzy black hair, pendulous breasts, and a pragmatic, no-nonsense approach to nursing gained from decades of experience caring for critically ill patients. "Mrs. Samuelson here isn't giving up without a fight."

"No, she's not."

"Tough lady."

"Yes, she is."

The best part about ah-bee-yin' a woman . . . is goin' out and havin' a good time . . .

"Carol?"

"Yes, Doctor?" she says absently, checking the ventilator settings.

"I've been meaning to ask . . . what's with the Shania Twain concert every night next door?"

She chuckles. "Oh. You mean Mr. Nelson over there. He's one of our permanent residents. No family. He's been here almost four months now. He had a massive stroke after his surgery, and he's been nonresponsive ever since. We can't get him off the ventilator, and every time we try to move him, his blood pressure bottoms out. Nobody knows why. So he just sits there, while the doctors and lawyers try to figure out what to do with him."

"So what about Shania?"

"Oh, right. Shania." She's finished with the ventilator and is now working on the array of tubes that still attend Mrs. Samuelson. "So, anyway, this one time, one of the other girls is a Shania fan, so she brings in that video, just for fun, and puts it on for him. From the moment that woman came strutting onto the screen, Mr. Nelson just lit up and smiled. Even his blood pressure went up. He does it every time. See for yourself."

I crane my neck and catch a glimpse of Mr. Nelson on the other side of the cubicle wall. Sure enough, he's watching the screen actively, eyes almost — not quite, but almost — clear. He's bouncing his head slightly from side to side in time to the music.

"How about that. I'll have to start pre-scribing Shania Twain for all my patients."

She chuckles appreciatively as she drains urine into a disposal bucket. "So, you know, Dr. Mitchell, I'm not going to be working here much longer."

"Why's that?"

She finishes, pushes the bucket aside, and stands up with a small grimace, pressing both hands against the small of her back. "Oh, I just don't feel comfortable working here anymore." She looks around and low-ers her voice even further. "I was taking care of a patient back in May, cross-covering down in the IMU, and he died. The hospital said I made a mistake, and that's why he died."

I suddenly remember the surgery patient

who died from the pulmonary air embolus, the one Dan mentioned at his barbecue. "Carol, was that the patient who had an air embolus from a central line?"

She nods. "They said I left the cap off the line. But I didn't. I cleaned the line and put the cap back on like I'd done thousands of times before. But they didn't listen to me." She shrugs, indifferent. "I know the truth. The other nurses know the truth, too. We've all seen it a hundred times: A patient died, and the hospital needed a fall guy. I was the fall guy. Mark my words, Dr. Mitchell: Somebody has always got to take the fall."

"So what will you do now?"

"Take my pension and go somewhere else. The hospital big shots will be glad to see me go. They even helped me find a great job over at St. Luke's. I guess they were afraid I'd put up a fight or something. But I'm smarter than that — smart enough to know that it wouldn't do any good. I know what the score is. You can't fight the system."

"Well, for what it's worth, I'll be sorry to see you go." That's not entirely true. I've never been particularly close to Carol, or any of the other nurses, for that matter, but it seems like the polite thing to say.

"Thanks, Dr. Mitchell. I appreciate that."

She hustles away, and I'm left alone with Mrs. Samuelson, Shania, and my thoughts.

Okay, so you're Brad Pitt . . . That don't impress me much . . .

Somebody has always got to take the fall.

Carol's words ring in my ears as I choke down a few bites of stale pizza in my empty kitchen. Carol's story seems to corroborate what Luis and I had suspected: that Mr. Bernard was not GG's first victim. Carol and I, it seems, have a lot in common: We've both been set up by GG. Except it sounds like Carol's story is probably going to have a happier ending than mine.

I can't just roll over. All of Luis's efforts, everything he strove for, would have been in vain. I picture him on Dan's porch, cigar in hand, his face partially shrouded by the night wrapping around him, earnestly telling me that it was the right thing to do to stop her. The *honorable* thing.

I dare you to try to stop me, Steve, she had said.

Maybe I still *can* stop her. Even without Luis. I owe it to him to at least try.

But how?

I close my eyes and allow my mind to wander along shadowy corridors, to traverse the kinds of twisted, thorny paths I imagine

GG herself would trek in order to find the surest, most expedient way to put an end to this nonsense. I quickly arrive at a single, simple conclusion.

The simplest one, really. The obvious one. Ugly and cold.

I sense that, psychologically, I'm in a dark place right now. Probably the darkest place I've ever been in my life, a black place deep within the primordial recesses of my mind that I can only now access because of everything that's happened to me over the last few weeks.

I could kill her.

Direct and permanent. Not to mention what GG would probably do if she were in my position.

I'm a doctor, after all. I've got access to all kinds of nasty things. Powerful intravenous heart medications. Paralysis agents to lock up respiratory muscles. Hell, even cyanide.

Killing her would save whatever future victims she's marked down on her list.

Killing her would solve all of my problems in one fell swoop.

Or would it?

I open my eyes. My gaze strays to the other side of the table, where one of Annabelle's bibs is draped over the side of the chair. Printed on the bib, a troop of smiling, cartoon monkeys regard me in cheerful repose. Behind the bib, affixed to the kitchen wall, is a picture of the four of us — Sally, myself, Katie, and Annabelle — at the neighborhood playground, back at the beginning of the summer, before my universe started spinning on its head.

I can't kill her.

I can't kill her because then I would become her.

I'm not a cold-blooded murderer. I won't do that. I won't stoop to her level. I'm a doctor. I save lives. I don't take them. Besides, I know nothing about planning a murder and, even more important, getting away with one. I can guess that even the simplest police investigation would turn up our sex video, which would in turn point to me as a prime suspect.

No. Like it or not, if I'm going to try to stop her, I'm still going to have to play the game by her rules. Which means that, once and for all, I need to identify who she's going to target. I need to find a patient with an ICD.

So I push the pizza aside, crack open a can of soda, and open my laptop. The friendly *ping* of the operating system booting up echoes through the empty kitchen. I remotely log into ERIN. Scanning rapidly through the names in University Hospital's current census, I eliminate the patients in the hospital that GG is currently taking care of because none of them has an ICD. That leaves the patients who haven't yet been admitted. I rule out the possibility that GG would count on a patient's coming to the emergency room; she's far too meticulous for that kind of unpredictable approach.

I access the directory in ERIN that contains all of the patients who are scheduled to undergo elective surgery at University Hospital this week, beginning tomorrow morning, limiting the search to the patients GG will be taking care of. It takes me over an hour and a half of intense research, but I eventually happen upon Mr. Schultz.

Mr. Schultz is a patient who's being admitted to University Hospital Wednesday morning for routine kidney-stone surgery. According to his chart, he suffers from a condition called cardiomyopathy, or weakening of the heart muscle. He's had several heart attacks and repeated episodes of v-fib. Lucky for Mr. Schultz, the first time the v-fib occurred was at a high-stakes poker table in Vegas, where well-practiced casino employees slapped an automatic external defibrillator on his chest that saved his life (I pause briefly to savor the details of that particular story, related in the crisp and clear clinical language of the medical chart; I love it when doctors insert that kind of stuff into medical records). His cardiologist implanted the ICD a short time later.

Despite taking a list of daily heart and blood-pressure medications as long as my arm and undergoing several heart procedures to try to correct the problem, Mr. Schultz's intermittent v-fib has persisted. He also has had one of his heart valves surgically replaced and must, as a result, take a blood-thinning medication called Coumadin.

By now, it feels like my own heart is going into v-fib. My hands tremble slightly over the computer keyboard. No wonder GG was studying up on ICDs last weekend: She has access to the same operating-room schedules that I do, and I'm sure she marked Mr. Schultz as a ripe target long ago.

I take a few deep breaths, crack my knuckles, and then — just to be sure — double-check all the patients scheduled to undergo elective surgery the rest of the week, then all the ones scheduled for the following week. None of them have implantable heart devices. None of them are even remotely as sick as Mr. Schultz.

It's got to be Mr. Schultz.

Okay. Now I've identified her method and her target. So how do I stop her? And collect the evidence I need to beat her?

Think.

The overnight shift is undoubtedly when she'll strike. Mr. Schultz will need to be asleep when it happens, so that he won't realize what's going on and call for help; plus, the skeleton crew of nurses working the night shift is usually stretched pretty thin, which will make it easier for GG to slip in and out of his room undetected. Mr. Schultz also can't be hooked up to a continuous heart monitor — otherwise, the monitor will immediately sense the v-fib and alert the nurses with its automated alarms.

The most straightforward approach would be simply to park myself in Mr. Schultz's room each night for the entire duration of his hospital stay. But that would tip my hand and defeat my purpose.

Because of his blood-thinning medication and health problems, the plan is for Mr. Schultz to remain in the hospital for a total of three nights after his surgery. During the first two nights, he'll be staying in one of the specialized cardiac units, where he'll be hooked to heart monitors and under the constant surveillance of nurses with expertise in taking care of heart patients. There's no way she can effectively strike then — even if she manages to sneak into his room and access the ICD signal, any problems will immediately show up on the monitors and alert the nurses.

But for the third night, if all goes according to plan and he recovers from his surgery as expected, Mr. Schultz will be transferred to a different, less intense area of the hospital. He'll no longer be hooked up to the heart monitors or under the watchful eyes of the cardiac nurses. He'll be alone in his room for several hours at a time between routine nursing checks. Completely vulnerable.

So Friday night will be the night. It has to be. That's four days from now. I have clinic tomorrow, but if I call in sick, they'll just cancel the clinic, and that should give me plenty of time to prepare since I'm still banned from the operating room.

I yawn and glance at a wall clock. It's 2:00 A.M., and my thoughts are bogging down, like feet slogging through thick mud. I'm not quite there yet. I still need to figure out a way to trap her. I've made a lot of progress, but I'm hitting a mental wall. I need sleep. Badly.

I shut down my laptop, trudge upstairs,

and crawl into bed.

My sleep is dreamless and unexpectedly energizing.

CHAPTER 18

Tuesday, August 18

After calling in sick early in the morning, I have the entire day free to prepare my trap. It's hard work, but in the end, I'm surprised, really, at how everything comes together so smoothly. By evening, I've worked out all the details and collected the necessary equipment: a software program, down-loaded from a cardiology Web site onto my laptop, that captures wireless signals from ICDs and displays the EKG tracings in real time on my computer; and a small, top-of-the-line, remote webcam with night-vision capability, which I found in a big-box consumer-electronics store near my house.

Because of the limited radio range of the ICD signal, GG will need to enter his room; quite likely, she'll even need to stand over his bed in order to hack the software — especially if she uses her smartphone, which I'm betting she will. The plan seems straightforward enough: Hide the remote webcam with night-vision capability in Mr. Schultz's room, then conceal myself somewhere within the radius of the ICD signal, from which I'll guard him all night. The webcam and ICD will beam their respective signals to my laptop. When she makes her move, the camera should capture the visual act of her disrupting Mr. Schultz's ICD, while the cardiac software simultaneously records the wireless commands she inputs from the smart phone and the instantaneous and potentially deadly effect on his heart — all in real time. Meanwhile, I'll have a crash cart secretly at the ready to shock Mr. Schultz's heart back into its normal rhythm.

Then I'll have the evidence I'll need against GG, and Mr. Schultz will have his life.

A straightforward plan.

But not without its risks.

What if I can't jump-start Mr. Schultz's heart after she's shut it down? What if the ICD short-circuits in response to the external commands, and the subsequent heat from the burning metal cooks the surrounding heart muscle like a steak on a flaming grill? Fatal v-fib. Charbroiled heart. Those would be bad things.

But I have no other options. Neither does

Mr. Schultz, frankly: Without my help, he's a dead man. Well, okay, not exactly a dead man for certain — I could, I reluctantly concede, protect him simply by never leaving his side while he's in the hospital. But that would just make GG choose another victim. Besides, I need my evidence.

So I'll just have to roll the dice with Mr. Schultz's heart, and he and I will both have to take our chances.

CHAPTER 19

Wednesday, August 19

As with Mrs. Samuelson, my Safety Committee–mandated restrictions don't prevent me from interacting with Mr. Schultz outside the operating room. My biggest concern is making certain that GG doesn't realize what I'm up to, so I'm careful to keep a low profile, only peeking at Mr. Schultz briefly in the preoperative area once I've made certain that GG is already scrubbed in on a very long operation. I decide that it's best not to introduce myself to him so that he doesn't mention our meeting to GG.

From what I can tell, observing from the other side of the room as the staff preps him for surgery, Mr. Schultz appears to be a complete, unadulterated bastard. It's enough to make me think twice about trying to save his life. Seriously. He's 275 pounds of cantankerous flesh packed onto a five-foot-three-inch frame. His greasy, thinning hair, dyed the color of black shoe polish, is styled into an ugly comb-over that stretches ineffectually to cover the broad swathes of sweaty skin shining from his tanned pate like a copper surface reflecting bright sunlight. He has corpulent, baggy jowls, thick folds of brown belly fat that spill out from under his hospital gown and over the sides of his bed, and a wheezy, rasping voice that sets my teeth on edge. He reminds me of a huge frog; rather than lying on the gurney, he should be squatting on his haunches on the floor.

He and his wife (equally stocky and fat) treat the staff like hotel bellhops. His deep-set eyes roam suspiciously across their ID badges as he hands his Rolex over to his wife for safekeeping and peppers the nurses with questions about where they're from and where they went to school. His wife has this annoying habit of nodding and repeating each question before they have a chance to answer. I wonder if it's going to end up being a long three days.

But his surgery goes off without a hitch, and his first night in the hospital passes uneventfully.

CHAPTER 20

Thursday, August 20

Day two also goes by smoothly. Throughout the morning and into the afternoon, Mr. Schultz remains safely ensconced in the heart-patient area, alternately stuffing his face with food and screaming into his cell phone about various business deals. The monitors keep close tabs on his heart rhythm, which remains rock-solid normal. I check on him several times throughout the day, careful always to make certain that GG is nowhere in the vicinity. As afternoon wanes into evening, and the overnight nurses begin their shift, I peek into his room one last time. He's lying in bed, watching TV. His heart tracing is pristine.

On my way to my office to pick up my laptop, which I had locked there for safe-keeping earlier in the day, I pass a bank of windows overlooking the main entrance of the hospital. Glancing out at the people milling below, I stop and do a double take.

It's GG.

She's strolling away from the hospital, her arm casually draped through the arm of another med student, a good-looking guy I've seen around the hospital with a dark complexion and black, shoulder-length hair. She laughs at something he says and puts her head on his shoulder. He puts his arm around her, and she sidles up even closer.

I smile to myself. That seals the deal: There really is nothing for me to worry about tonight.

My pager goes off. A text message from the University Hospital operator blinks unassumingly at the bottom of the screen.

Mrs. Abernathy for Dr. S. Mitchell.

Mrs. Abernathy? I stare at the phone number.

Huh.

Mrs. Abernathy.

I didn't know there was a Mrs. Abernathy.

It's a little odd, and the message makes me realize that I haven't heard from Mr. Abernathy for the last few days.

My curiosity gets the better of me. I dial the number and wait through several rings. No one answers. I'm about to hang up when a hesitant voice, diaphanous as tissue paper, finally answers.

"Hello?"

"Hi, this is Dr. Mitchell from University Hospital. Is this Mrs. Abernathy?"

"Yes." The soft voice solidifies, as if taking form from a mist. "Yes, Dr. Mitchell. Thank you."

"What can I do for you?"

"Well, I just wanted to call and let you know that Ray . . . Ray, well, he passed a few days ago. Just fell over right in front of the TV, watchin' his favorite show. He . . . excuse me, Doctor."

She stops, sniffles, and blows her nose loudly, right into the phone.

I wait. Then, after a while, she says, "Are you still there, Doctor?"

"Yes, I'm still here, Mrs. Abernathy. What was it?"

"The TV show?" Suspicion steals into her voice. "Pardon me, but what kind of a question is that, Doctor?"

"No, no, Mrs. Abernathy. I didn't mean what TV show was he watching. I meant what happened to him?"

"Oh. Right. Heart attack. That's what they told me. Anyways, by the time the ambulance got here, well . . ." Her voice trails off.

"I'm sorry." The words ring hollow to me,

serving more my own selfish need to fill the awkward silence than to soothe her grief.

Her voice finds purchase again. "Never felt a thing. At least, that's what the nice young emergency-room doctor told me. What a polite boy he was. Like you. Anyways, we had a lot a good years together, me and Ray. Lot a good years." Her voice disappears back into the ether, and I wonder if it will return. It does, after a moment. "It was his time. We had a lot a good years, but it was his time. Anyways, I called you, Dr. Mitchell, because I wanted you to know that you were Ray's favorite doctor. He really liked you very much. More than any of the others."

His favorite doctor? Really?

"Ray was very particular about his doctors. He felt like you were the only doctor who ever . . . well, who just . . . listened. Cared about what he had to say. Cared about him. He never said that about any of the others. He was very particular about his doctors."

Somebody once said that movies are like life with all of the boring parts cut out. Well, if my life is a movie with all of the boring parts left in, I guess at this point I should be having a movie *moment.* A revelatory flash of self-insight when I'm overcome with sadness and regret; when I'd realize the error of my ways and appreciate the old guy for who he had been in a sentimental kind of way, and paint him with a bright postmortem gloss that reimagines him as a curmudgeonly but lovable old man.

"Thank you," I stammer. "I'm sorry for your loss." But at this particular moment, I'm not sorry. I'm about as far from sorry as you can get. Because all I can think about is how I'll never have to return the bastard's phone calls again. Or rewrite his prescriptions. Or get woken up at 3:00 A.M. at home with his stupid questions. Or sit through his verbal abuse in clinic with a tight smile and clenched fists. I'm glad he's dead, in fact. I really am. He was an evil bastard. And now he's dead. Good.

His favorite doctor.

Whatever.

The intensity of my satisfaction surprises me.

And shames me.

"Anyways," Mrs. Abernathy continues, "we're havin' a service this Sunday, and I was wonderin' if maybe you'd consider comin'. For Ray's sake. I know you doctors are always real busy and all, but it would just mean so much to me. And to Ray. I know he's smilin' at us from Heaven at this very moment."

Somehow, beneficently peering down at us from his celestial perch in Heaven is not exactly what I envision Mr. Abernathy doing right now.

"Sure, Mrs. Abernathy," I hear myself say with something that passes for sincerity. "I have a lot of things to do that day, but I think I can make it." I pause, then add, "For him." Just saying the words leaves a bad taste in my mouth.

"Will you, Dr. Mitchell? Will you? Oh, that'd be wonderful. Thank you. Thank you, sir."

Her tone brightens as she eagerly recites the name and address of the funeral home. I pretend to listen (*Uh-huh, uh-huh . . . Boyle Street . . . okay, Mrs. A . . .*) as I scribble gibberish on a Post-it note.

"I can't tell you how much this means to me. I can't wait to meet you."

"I look forward to meeting you, too, Mrs. Abernathy. See you then."

"You too, Doctor. Thank you so much."

I hang up the phone, crumple up the Post-it note, toss it in a nearby trash can, and take my laptop up to the SICU. I want to check on Mrs. Samuelson just one last time before grabbing a few hours of sleep. She's doing great and is being transferred out of the SICU tomorrow.

I walk into the SICU. It's relatively quiet tonight, at only half capacity, so there aren't many nurses around. I creep into Mrs. Samuelson's darkened room. She's snoring softly. I sink into a reclining chair, open up my laptop, and run once more through the heart monitor and imaging software. Everything looks good. Satisfied, my gaze wanders from the screen and lights on Mrs. Samuelson. She looks peaceful.

I smile to myself. For the moment, at least, I seem to have finally caught a few breaks.

I yawn and realize how *really* tired I am.

I push the recliner back and close my eyes, just for a moment . . .

CHAPTER 21

Friday, August 21

And jerk awake, totally disoriented, my
heart pounding. I thrust the recliner into a
sitting position and anxiously survey the
room, trying to get my bearings. Darkness
still presses against the windows over Mrs.
Samuelson's bed. I have a bad feeling I can't
explain.

I don't know how long I've been out. My
legs are warm and sweaty underneath the
laptop, which, despite having automatically
entered power-saving mode, radiates residual heat.

I glance at Mrs. Samuelson, still sleeping,
her breathing easy and rhythmic, like the
steady breaking of waves along a calm
beach. Somebody has drawn curtains across
the glass wall of her room, visually separating us from the rest of the SICU and the
nurses' station — an allowance for privacy
granted to patients like Mrs. Samuelson

who are doing well and no longer require intense, minute-to-minute care.

If anything, the calmness of the whole scene only increases my sense of unease.

What's wrong? Why do I feel this way?

My pager goes off, puncturing the stillness and making me jump. It's an extension in the Cardiac Intermediate Care Unit.

That's where Mr. Schultz is.

A lead ball instantly materializes in my belly. Why are they calling *me*? I tap the number into my cell phone.

"Cardiac Intermediate Care Unit. This is Karen."

"Karen, this is Dr. Mitchell, returning a page."

"Let me check to see who's trying to get ahold of you, Doctor. Just a moment while I put you on hold." There's an electronic *click,* followed by a jazzy, instrumental version of the Rolling Stones' "Satisfaction." The next twenty seconds stretch into an eternity.

Click. "I'm sorry, Doctor Mitchell, but nobody here paged you."

I really don't like the way this conversation is heading. "Okay." My mouth and tongue are so dry that I have trouble forming the words. "Since I have you on the line, Karen, how's Mr. Schultz doing?"

"Who?"

"Mr. Schultz. Room 505."

"Five oh five? Oh, right — 505. We transferred him to a regular bed, off the monitors, earlier this evening."

"What?"

"We're pretty full tonight, Doctor. We needed his bed for a patient with an acute MI. Your patient in 505 was stable, so the cardiology fellow on call authorized the transfer one night earlier than planned."

"Where did he go?"

This time, she doesn't bother to put me on hold. "Lydia, where did the patient in 505 go? Pavilion 10 West? Yes? Pavilion 10 West, Doctor. Room 1014."

Panic seizes me by the throat.

Mr. Schultz is now in a private room in a regular area of the hospital, off the continuous heart monitor, and completely vulnerable to an attack from GG. My heart is now hammering away in my chest.

"When? When did you transfer him?"

"Oh, several hours ago. Lydia paged the intern on call, and a medical student — a tall girl with a ponytail — showed up to help move the patient and sort out the transfer orders. Doesn't she work with you?"

The overhead announcement, the disembodied voice clear and dispassionate, catches me before I have time to react to this disturbing bit of news.

"Code Blue, Pavilion Ten. Code Blue, Pavilion Ten. Code Blue, Pavilion Ten."

The hospital code team is being called to Pavilion Ten.

Which, of course, means that a patient is currently dying on Pavilion Ten.

The same floor to which Mr. Schultz was sent under GG's direct supervision.

It's all happening again.

Please no. Please, God, no. Not again.

There's no time to even think. Pavilion Ten is seven floors up. I dash to the nearest bank of elevators and push the UP button. And wait. And then wait some more.

Come on, come on. I frantically thumb the elevator button over and over.

Who the hell can be riding the elevator at 4:00 a.m.?

The doors finally open, and I'm inside in an instant, jabbing at the 10 key.

The doors close. The elevator lurches upward.

Exactly one floor.

And then it stops.

The doors roll slowly open. Two young nurses get in, oblivious to my presence, loudly gossiping about a colleague, like girls between classes in a high-school hallway.

One of them, heavyset and ponderously munching on an Oreo, pushes the 5 key.

Are you kidding me? They can't take the stairs for just one fucking floor?

I rock back and forth on the balls of my feet and savagely consider telling the heavyset one that a little stair climbing might do her some good. But I hold my tongue.

After depositing the gossip girls on the fifth floor, the elevator continues to the tenth without further incident, and I'm out the doors and sprinting toward the patient-care area, looking for room 1014. I hear shouting, but don't see anyone else.

The panels next to the doors flash by: 1010, 1011, 1012, 1013 . . .

Finally, 1014.

The door is closed.

That's strange.

I fling it open, my heart in my throat, expecting the worst . . .

. . . and find Mr. Schultz fast asleep, the room as still and quiet as a tomb.

What the hell?

Mr. Schultz, jolted awake by the sound of the swinging door crashing against the wall, picks his head up off the pillow and squints at me, his squat bulk framed by the block of bright light cast across his bed by the wide-open door.

"What the *hell*?" he shouts raspily.

I ignore him, stick my head back out the doorway, and quickly scan the rest of the corridor. At the very end of the hall, several doctors and nurses are leaving the room of another patient. One of the nurses is pushing a crash cart full of medications and a defibrillator. They all look varying degrees of pissed.

"What's going on down there?" I ask a passing nurse, pointing at the clutch of people, who are mumbling angrily to one another, some yawning and rubbing their eyes.

"False alarm," he replies. "Somebody called a code on a patient who wasn't coding."

"No shit."

He grins. "Yeah, no shit." He stops when he realizes what room I'm coming out of. "Was there something you needed, Doc? I'm taking care of Mr. Schultz tonight. Is he okay?"

"Couldn't be better," I say distractedly. I should be relieved, but instead I'm completely unnerved. My mind spins feverishly, like a hamster on its wheel. What's going on? Could I have been wrong about the ICD? Why would GG ignore an opportunity like this to murder Mr. Schultz? The setup was so perfect.

Perfect.

A little too perfect, maybe?

I watch as the code team, called to a code that wasn't really a code, disperses.

I think about GG's involvement in Mr. Schultz's transfer earlier this evening, and the mysterious page to the cardiac floor for which nobody took responsibility.

Is it possible that I've been tricked? Could it be that Mr. Schultz was a feint? That he was never GG's intended target to begin with? Was GG trying to draw my attention away from someone else?

"Doc?" The nurse is still standing there, waiting for me to answer.

But then, if Mr. Schultz wasn't her target, who is? We only have a few patients in the hospital right now other than Mr. Schultz. None of them is particularly vulnerable.

Unless —

Could it possibly be —

Oh *no.*

It couldn't be.

Oh, shit.

Not her. Please not her.

"Yeah," I tell the nurse. My left arm is tingling. I ignore it. "Run a twelve-lead EKG and page the cardiology tech to come and interrogate the ICD. And don't let anyone else in the room."

I'm sprinting back the way I came before he has a chance to tell me that cardiology techs aren't usually available in the middle of the night. This time, I ignore the elevators and find the nearest stairwell, retracing my path, taking the stairs two at a time. It's all downhill, but it's seven flights, and I'm in horrible shape, so I'm panting and clutching my side as I tear through the back door of the SICU, past a couple of startled nurses, and into Mrs. Samuelson's room . . .

. . . to discover to my horror that she's sitting straight up in bed, pale as a ghost, clutching her chest with both hands, gasping for breath. The warning alarms on her vital-signs monitors are going haywire. Instead of charging boldly across the screen, tracing the sharp peaks and valleys of a normal cardiac rhythm, her heart produces a feeble, wavy line that lurches from one side of the heart monitor to the other.

She can't speak. She can't breathe. Her mouth opens and clothes reflexively, over and over again, like a caught fish flopping around on a dock. When she sees me, she reaches out with one hand, her pleading eyes bulging so prominently that they're practically leaping from their sockets. *Please, I don't want to die,* they scream silently at me. Her lips are an ugly shade of blue, the dirty shade of a fresh bruise.

Before I can react, she shudders with a horrible rattle that shakes her whole body from head to toe, arches her back and neck, and falls back on the bed, rigid as a wooden board, her eyes rolling up into her head.

For people who've never seen a grand mal seizure before, it's a terrifying sight, with the patient's arms and legs jerking spasmodically and their whole bodies thrashing around in thoroughly unnatural movements. Even now — having seen a bunch of seizures, knowing scientifically that her problem is caused by a colossal short-circuit of nerve cells in her brain, and remembering that there's nothing I can do except make sure that she doesn't hurt herself (that thing about preventing seizing patients from biting their tongues off is complete bullshit urban legend; the last thing I want to do right now is stick anything inside her mouth, least of all my fingers) — watching her flail about like a limp rag doll shaken by a child rattles me to my core.

I run to the head of her bed and cradle her head in my hands to help keep her airway open. Carol and another one of the

SICU nurses, alerted by the noise and Mrs. Samuelson's failing vital signs, join me almost immediately, their faces registering surprise mingled with cool detachment as both of them size up the scene in an instant with their practiced eyes.

"I'll call the code," Carol says, and disappears.

The seizure lasts for about ten seconds before she becomes completely, unnaturally, still. At the same moment, the heart rate on the monitor next to her bed falls to zero. I check her pulse, my fingers inching along her neck, seeking the carotid artery. Nothing. No pulse.

Struggling to keep my emotional state from unraveling like a roll of kite string being played out on a windy day, I shift positions and begin CPR, pushing down on Mrs. Samuelson's frail sternum to keep the blood flowing through her body. The other nurse grabs an Ambu bag and depresses a button that instantly collapses the air mattress underneath Mrs. Samuelson, making it easier for me to push on her sternum. She squeezes past me to the head of the bed, attaches the mask to Mrs. Samuelson's face, and calmly starts pushing air into her lungs.

"What happened?" she asks.

I describe Mrs. Samuelson's mysterious symptoms as Carol returns with two of her colleagues. More nurses and doctors arrive shortly thereafter, including the code team (who probably came directly from Mr. Schultz's room), which is led tonight by one of the more seasoned critical-care fellows. They swarm around Mrs. Samuelson, systematically stripping off her gown, checking her intravenous catheters, and hooking up additional heart and blood-pressure monitors. The anesthesia resident slips an endotracheal tube into Mrs. Samuelson's throat. The heart monitor still indicates no blood pressure or pulse.

I hand over the job of giving heart compressions to one of the new arrivals and relay my story to the critical-care fellow, Sushil, a rotund, jocular guy who's been caring for Mrs. Samuelson over the past several weeks.

"Pretty nonspecific symptoms," he muses. "Any other presenting signs? Anything else that might have precipitated a cardiovascular collapse?"

"No, nothing," I say. "She was doing great. There's no good reason why she should have crumpled so suddenly."

That's a lie, of course. There's a very good reason why this has happened, and its name is GG. I'm racking my brain now, running through all of the potential methods she might have used to try to kill Mrs. Samuelson. I have little doubt that this is her doing.

"Hey, Sushil?" the anesthesiology resident calls as he's attaching the Ambu bag to the endotracheal tube.

"Yeah?"

"There's a left subclavian central line up here that's unhooked. And look." He holds it up for us to see. There's a small gash in the side of it. "It must have ripped somehow. The line is completely open to air."

Sushil looks at me sharply.

"Do you think —" he starts.

"Yeah," I answer, the hair on the back of my neck standing on end. "Definitely. Her presentation is totally consistent with a massive pulmonary air embolus."

Sushil grimaces. "With that hole in the line being above the level of her thorax, she would have had positive pressure flow of air into the vein. So she never bled, and each inspiration would have sucked air into her subclavin vein."

I guessed wrong. GG, it seems, decided to go with the air embolus again and not the ICD.

Fuck! How could I have been so stupid? I

played right into her hands.

"Hold CPR," Sushil calls to the code team. The resident currently pushing on the sternum pauses. "Is she still in asystole?"

"Yes," answers one of the nurses, staring at the cardiac monitor over the bead.

"Okay, everyone, for now we're going to assume she's got a pulmonary air embolus until we prove otherwise. Let's place her in left lateral decubitus Trendelenburg."

Working in concert, and without blinking an eye, the SICU nurses and code team first roll Mrs. Samuelson onto her left side, then tilt the head of her bed downward so that her feet are pointed up in the air and her head is pointed toward the floor. The idea is that, by repositioning her body, we can trap the deadly air in the tip of her heart and away from her lungs. Since she's now lying mostly on her left side, the team also quickly straps a firm body board behind her back to provide resistance for the now-horizontally-oriented chest compressions.

"And administer another one mg epinephrine," Sushil says. "Let's see if we can give her right ventricle some more squeeze."

"One milligram epinephrine," the nurse by the cardiac monitor calls back as she injects the medication into one of Mrs. Samuelson's IVs.

Sushil nods, satisfied, and surveys the room. "Hey, Sheila." An idle code team resident standing in a corner of the room stirs and looks in our direction. "I need the portable ultrasound for a stat transthoracic echo. Can you go grab it for me? It's over by the nurses' station."

"Got it." She runs off and soon returns, rolling the ultrasound machine in front of her, a device that resembles a large hat rack on wheels. A large video monitor is perched on top, where the hats would otherwise be.

Sushil turns on the ultrasound machine, punches a few buttons on a keyboard located midway up the hat-rack stand, and unfurls a long cord with a thick plastic tip on one end. It's the ultrasound transducer — the part of the machine that sends and receives sound waves — and it looks a lot like the handheld, flexible attachment of a vacuum cleaner that you use on hard-to-reach places.

Sushil maneuvers his way between the code-team members working on Mrs. Samuelson. He kneels next to her, squirts a generous amount of a clear-colored material with the consistency of jelly over a spot on her chest (the thick stuff will help transmit the sound waves into and out of Mrs. Samuelson), and places the ultrasound transducer directly over the jelly, ducking regularly to avoid the resident currently administering the chest compressions.

He grunts as he examines the fluttering gray, black, and white images on the video monitor. "Oh shit. See that? That's her pulmonary artery and right ventricle. Look at all that air in her heart. It's filling the entire right side. Probably the pulmonary tree, too. Oh *shit.*"

A buzz fills the room, and the atmosphere hums with a subtle new energy.

Pulmonary air embolus.

Definitely not your run-of-the-mill code.

Still staring at the flickering screen, passing the stick back and forth over her chest, Sushil calls, "Ellen! Page the in-house CT surgery attending! Tell him we've got a massive pulmonary air embolus here." His voice remains steady, but there's an edge to it that wasn't there a few moments ago, and it cracks on the word *call.* A woman on station near the doorway of the cubicle, who I recognize as the supervising surgery nurse for the night shift, acknowledges him and quickly exits.

"Tell him," Sushil says more quietly after she's gone, as if to himself, "that I think we're going to need some help." He stands back up, eyes wide, face drawn and pale, for the first time looking truly worried. He gives an order for some more epinephrine before joining me at the foot of the bed.

"Well," he says. "That confirms the diagnosis. That is one big air embolus. I've never seen anything like it. It must be at least two hundred or three hundred cc worth of air sitting in her cardiopulmonary tree. No wonder she's not responding to CPR. Normally, we'd expect all those chest compressions to push the air bubbles into her smaller pulmonary vessels and dissipate. But — *damn,* that's a lot of air. You'd almost think somebody had deliberately injected it."

I chew on my lip and nod, my dread gathering like thunderheads before a storm. "So what do we do now?"

"We've got to get that air out of her heart," he says, absently wiping the gathering sweat from his brow.

"How do we do that?"

"Well, since CPR is failing, we could attempt aspiration of the air. I guess we could float another right-sided central line. Like a Swan-Ganz. Snake it into the right heart and aspirate out the air through that."

"There's no time," an assured Southern twang observes from behind us. Sushil and I spin around to face the on-call CT surgery attending. He's standing next to the supervising nurse, clad in scrubs.

That was fast. But of course, I remember — his call room is right down the hall. Literally right outside of the SICU. He must have been in bed.

If he was asleep, he certainly doesn't look it now. Hands on his hips, calmly working a piece of gum in slow, deliberate motions, his self-assured demeanor anchors me against the rising tide of panic in the room. His salt-and-pepper hair, worn high and tight in a flattop, is perfectly coifed. His back is straight and his chin is up — military all the way. In fact, I seem to remember reading a piece in the hospital newsletter about his being an officer in the Army Reserve who's done two combat tours in Afghanistan.

Exactly the kind of guy we need right now.

"You don't have a fluoro set up here, son," he drawls. "And it'll take too long to snake a catheter blindly. She's been in asystole for — what? Five, ten minutes now? Closed cardiac massage ain't doin' you a damn, son. She's losing neurons by the second. Even if you do manage to thread a line into her atrium, it'll take too long to suck out all that air. There's too damn much. She needs percutaneous transcardial aspiration."

Without waiting for a response, he turns to the supervising nurse. "Ellen, I need a cardiocentesis tray. The one with the eighteen-gauge spinal needle." His tone is polite; but he radiates absolute, unassailable authority. He doesn't ask Sushil or me our opinion, doesn't open the floor for debate, doesn't for a moment concede that there may be options at this point other than slamming a big-ass needle directly into Mrs. Samuelson's heart.

As an attending, he's now the senior doctor present — not to mention the one with the most experience in these kinds of situations. He now calls the shots. Sushil, of course, realizes this and humbly steps back — literally and figuratively — without another word. The nursing supervisor scurries off to grab the surgeon's equipment.

I feel a tremendous surge of relief. Now I'm back on familiar turf. Surgery-type stuff. Cold steel to heal, baby. The CT surgeon can fix her. I know he can.

Ellen promptly returns with the cardiocentesis tray. The CT surgeon sizes me up as he prepares the equipment: a scalpel, a six-inch-long hypodermic needle, an empty syringe, sterile sheets, and iodine solution.

"Steve, right?"

"Er, yes, sir." Even though I was never in

the military, I stand up more straight. I can't quite summon up the surgeon's name. I wish I could. I can barely contain my surprise that he knows mine.

"I remember when you rotated with us on the cardiac-surgery service. You did a good job. Want to lend me a hand, son?"

"Sure."

"Okay, then let's move. Quick as a jackrabbit, son. Grab you a pair of sterile gloves and prep for a subxiphoid approach. I'm going to need you to stabilize the transthoracic echo for me while I aspirate the air. Let's move!" Then, to the assembled code team, he adds, "Let's move her back supine. Quickly, folks, quickly!"

The rest of the team responds by taking Mrs. Samuelson out of her left-side, head-down position and placing her on her back again. As for me, there's no time for the kind of rigorous sterile prep jobs we normally perform in the OR before making an incision. Each moment we hesitate is more time Mrs. Samuelson's oxygen-starved brain spends dying. I throw on a pair of sterile gloves, hastily splash the iodine on her chest and upper abdomen, and spread the sterile sheets across the lower half of her body, leaving a small window that exposes the skin at the base of her breastbone. With the scalpel, the surgeon nicks a patch of the skin that's exposed through this window. Through the incision, Mrs. Samuelson's blood runs dark and thick and sluggish, indicating that it's low on oxygen.

Not a very promising sign.

"Hold compressions," the cardiac surgeon says. The code-team nurse currently performing chest compressions stops.

And, according to the heart monitor screen perched over her bed, so does Mrs. Samuelson's heart.

"Still asystolic," the surgeon murmurs. Using the ultrasound cord shaped like the vacuum-cleaner attachment, he locates her heart the same way Sushil did, but much more quickly. "Steve, hold this for me right . . . here." I grab the ultrasound cord, careful to prevent it from shifting from its current position.

The surgeon takes the needle, now connected to the large syringe, and expertly plunges it through the skin incision, aiming it toward Mrs. Samuelson's head at a forty-five-degree angle to her skin. It's the surest, quickest way to the heart from here. He promptly sinks the needle halfway underneath her breastbone.

A thin, bright, white line simultaneously appears on the ultrasound video monitor —

the tip of the needle. The surgeon moves the needle forward, deeper into Mrs. Samuelson, more slowly and cautiously now, using the ultrasound images to guide the tip through the thick outer musculature of her heart. Twice, he needs to redirect the needle tip before finding the correct path into the heart's hollow center. He positions the tip directly in the middle of the right ventricle — the chamber that blood flows through before entering the lungs — then freezes in place. Carefully holding the needle in place with his thumb and forefinger, he draws back the plunger of the syringe.

I grit my teeth.

This is it.

The syringe promptly fills with air.

"It's working," I say excitedly.

"We'll see, son," the surgeon replies flatly. He finishes pulling back the plunger, carefully unscrews the syringe off the needle, and hands the syringe to me.

"Quickly, Steve, reset the syringe for me, son."

We repeat the process three more times, each time withdrawing about 60 cc of air from Mrs. Samuelson's heart. On the fifth attempt, when he pulls back the plunger, the syringe starts to fill with blood. With breathtaking speed, he withdraws the needle, hands it to me, places his hands on her sternum, and starts performing chest compressions.

The whole process — from the time he first asked the nurse for the needle to when he began compressions — couldn't have taken more than ninety seconds.

But when the brain is deprived of oxygen, ninety seconds can be like ninety years.

Please, Mrs. Samuelson.

You can make it.

Silence grips the room. Everyone is either staring at the surgeon regularly pushing on Mrs. Samuelson's heart or, like me, gazing at the heart monitor in anticipation of what we'll see when he stops. Right now, the compressions are casting wavy, sinusoidal peaks in the line running across the monitor, like a series of rolling hills viewed in profile.

"Okay," he says after several minutes, "let's see what we've got. I'm holding compressions."

Every eyeball in the room fixates on the heart monitor.

As the wavy bumps characteristic of the chest compressions disappear, the heart curve flattens out into a line so straight it's like it was traced with a ruler.

Several agonizing seconds tick by. Nothing happens. The line remains as unbroken as the horizon.

Dammit!

I grind my teeth in frustration. I want to scream at the top of my lungs.

Fuck!

And then, just as the surgeon is about to resume the chest compressions —

It's the faintest of blips at first. Barely a minor distortion in the precise geometry of the line. But the next one, occurring a few seconds after the first, is bigger and stronger. The next one, stronger still.

And then, like the bursting of a dam, the beats are coming one on top of another, confident and sure, charging across the screen.

The electric signatures of normal heartbeats.

Those regularly interspersed hills, peaks, and valleys are the most beautiful things I've ever seen.

Mrs. Samuelson's heart is beating again.

The feeling is indescribable.

Mrs. Samuelson is alive.

She's going to make it.

I beat her. I beat GG.

Most of the ten people or so assembled in the room heave a collective breath of relief. A few smiles appear. One of the nurses pats another one on the back.

But the cardiac surgeon seems less sure. He stares at the screen for a full thirty seconds, watching her heart rhythm reestablish itself, hands poised over her chest, ready to initiate compressions again.

Her heart rate eventually stabilizes at 120 beats per minute. A little on the fast side, but still — she's had a lot of epinephrine, and considering what she's been through, it's not all that bad. Meanwhile, elated, I start planning my next move. How will GG react when she realizes her plan didn't work? Will she concede defeat? Is there a way I can gather evidence that she caused this?

Finally, satisfied, the surgeon slowly drops his hands to his sides.

"Okay. Once she's a little more stable, we can take a step back and reevaluate her status, maybe think about gettin' her down to the hyperbaric oxygen chamber to blow off any residual air —" His voice trails off.

Puzzled, I follow his gaze back to the cardiac monitor.

Mrs. Samuelson's heartbeat is slowing.

Ninety beats per minute.

The surgeon's eyes narrow.

Forty beats per minute.

He calmly repositions his hands back over

her chest.

Ten beats per minute.

The other members of the code team shift uneasily.

Zero.

The geometrically straight heart line has returned.

. All hell breaks loose again. The surgeon starts pumping her chest and calling for more epinephrine. The team redoubles its efforts, the energy in the room even more intense and focused.

But this time it feels different.

This time, it feels like she's really gone.

The surgeon agrees with my silent assessment. "She's got the smell of death on her, son," he murmurs to me. "The smell of death."

Still, he keeps it up for another fifteen minutes after that, every few minutes pausing to check if her heart has jump-started again. We give her several more doses of epinephrine.

Nothing.

The line on the monitor remains stubbornly, monotonously flat, like a highway stretching away through the desert. The color of Mrs. Samuelson's skin matches the metallic gray light of early dawn outside.

Eventually, the surgeon shakes his head

and stops. After nearly twenty minutes of continuous chest compressions, he hasn't even broken a sweat.

"That's it. We're done."

He calls the time of death.

"Well, can't say we didn't try. Thanks for your help, son."

So that's it.

Mrs. Samuelson is dead.

I lose.

"Is the family here?" the CT surgeon asks evenly, removing his gloves.

"We called them as soon as we initiated the code," the supervising nurse responds. "They're assembled in the waiting room."

Oh crap. Mrs. Samuelson's family. How can I possibly face them now?

"I'll talk to them," the surgeon says. With a loud snap, he launches each dirty glove into a nearby red-colored trash can. "But I need someone who knows the patient to come with me. Would that be you?" He points to Sushil, who's been taking care of Mrs. Samuelson since she first arrived in the SICU after her operation.

Sushil nods. "Sure. I'll come with you. How about you, Steve? You've been with them from the beginning. Do you want to come, too?"

The last thing in the world I want to do

right now is speak with Mrs. Samuelson's family. I've completely failed them not just once, but twice. I can't do it. I shake my head.

Sushil, clearly surprised, looks like he's about to say something, then shrugs and looks at the surgeon. The surgeon looks from Sushil to me, then back to Sushil.

"Okay, then. Let's go, son."

Shell-shocked and utterly defeated, I drop into a chair at the nursing station and watch as they go out to deliver the news. As the automatic doors leading into the waiting room swing open, I glimpse Mrs. Samuelson's anxious family, standing expectantly in a tight knot near the door.

The doors close.

The seconds tick by.

And then the scream — incoherent and anguished and only barely muffled by the closed automatic doors — stabs through the SICU. It feels like a white-hot knife rammed into my belly. I squeeze my eyes shut and wait for it to end.

But it doesn't. The initial scream transitions into a prolonged wail punctuated by disbelieving cries of *no* and *but she was better.* I recognize in that agonized howl the voice of the youngest daughter; and, indeed, as Sushil and the cardiac surgeon return to the SICU, I see through the briefly opened doors the rest of the family gathering tightly around her, comforting her as she sobs uncontrollably, their own faces vivid with grief.

"Well," says the cardiac surgeon flatly, to no one in particular, "that could have gone better. Good thing the preacher was there. Thanks for your help, everyone." Without another word, he wanders off toward his call room, as unflappable and cool as when he first appeared.

Sushil, on the other hand, looks thoroughly depressed and unnerved. He ignores me as he walks by, toward another patient's room. But I know what he's thinking.

Coward.

Maybe. But if he only knew what I'd done, knew that I had gambled with Mrs. Samuelson's life — and lost. Spectacularly. I prop my elbows on the counter in front of me and rest my face in my hands.

"Dr. Mitchell?"

I peer upward through the gaps in my interlaced fingers. It's Carol. She gingerly places my white coat, laptop, and computer bag on the counter.

"I think these are yours. You left them in Mrs. Samuelson's room."

"Thanks, Carol."

"Sure. You know, Dr. Mitchell, if you still want to talk to the family, we're going to let them back here in a few minutes to pay their respects before we take her — you know, downstairs."

Downstairs. Just like Mr. Bernard.

I nod and stand up, intending to slink out through the back door to avoid Mrs. Samuelson's family. I put on my white coat and absently slip my right hand into the front pocket. It hits something hard and cylindrical. I frown, puzzled. I don't normally keep things in those pockets. I close my fingers around the object and pull it out to examine it.

It's an empty syringe.

The exact type and size of syringe, common and readily available in supply rooms on every floor of University Hospital, that the cardiac surgeon had used to pull the air out of Mrs. Samuelson's dying heart.

Or the kind of syringe that someone could have used to inject a massive amount of air *into* her heart.

A note, handwritten in gentle and familiar feminine sweeps, is taped to the syringe. It reads, "S: Thanks for playing the game after all. But you guessed wrong. Remember. The Dome. Next Thursday. After M&M." There's a smiley face drawn on the bottom of the page.

An intense wave of dizziness sweeps over me. I brace myself unsteadily against the counter at the nurses' station. Carol rushes over and grabs my arm.

"Are you okay, Dr. Mitchell? Maybe you should come and sit back down."

She seems really worried; I must look like complete shit right now.

Slowly, painfully, I pull myself back up to a standing position. The dizziness passes.

"Yeah, Carol. Thanks. I'm okay," I say, smiling at her weakly. Skepticism is written all over her face. "Really, Carol. I just need some breakfast. Maybe a nap, too."

She reluctantly releases my arm and urges me to go home and get some sleep. I thank her and, distracted by the syringe, which I'm still clutching in my hand, forget completely about my plan to escape from Mrs. Samuelson's family through the back door. Instead, I shuffle slowly away from Carol (who watches my progress, hands on her hips, like a disapproving mother) through the main doors of the SICU . . .

. . . and stumble right into Mrs. Samuelson's entire family: husband, daughters, sons-in-law. They're all there in the waiting room, hugging each other, crying, and praying. I spin around and immediately reverse course, hoping none of them will see me.

"Dr. Mitchell!"

Too late.

Cursing silently, I rotate back toward Mr. Samuelson, who has disengaged himself from the main group and is approaching decisively.

"Dr. Mitchell." He takes my hand hard and holds it for a long time in both of his own, gazing into my face. His eyes are wet around the edges.

"I just can't thank you enough for everything you've done for us. From the beginning, you've just been . . . well, terrific. And now you're here, at the end, when, well . . . well, when most doctors wouldn't be."

"I . . . uh . . . I just wish I could have done more for her."

"You did what you could." He grasps my shoulders, one in each of his thick hands. "It was her time," he says sternly. "God called her home. When God calls, there's nothing else to be done."

He smiles, sadly but kindly, and releases my shoulders.

"You know, you're one of the finest doctors I've ever known. Don't think I haven't seen you in here at all hours, keeping an eye on her. Sitting at her bedside. Standing vigil." A single tear paints a silvery line down his cheek. "Don't ever change, son. You're still young, God knows, and I want you always to stay this way. Don't lose your compassion. It's a gift from God. Please don't ever forget that, no matter what the world does to you."

The rest of the family and a man I've never met gather around us. Mr. Samuelson introduces me to the newcomer as their minister, a stooped man with an elongated frame, kind face, and sparse, greasy-looking gray hair. The men shake my hand. The women embrace me. One of the daughters presents me with a thank-you card and a basketful of fresh vegetables from their farm.

"We brought this today to give to you in gratitude," she explains. "Now it's even more important to us that you take it."

Clutching the card and vegetables, I stammer my thanks, then leave them in the waiting room, hugging and crying, to be alone with one another, and with their memories of Mrs. Samuelson.

It doesn't hit me until I'm driving home from the hospital a few hours later. I'm a few blocks from my house, the basket of vegetables sitting on the seat next to me, thinking about nothing in particular, when both my hands suddenly start shaking violently, and I have trouble gripping the steering wheel. My heart slams against my chest, my ears roar, and my stomach flips over.

I jerk the car over toward the side of the road and, before it's even lurched to a stop, I'm opening the driver's-side door, leaning my head out, and puking into the street. A young mother pushing an infant in a stroller toward me on the sidewalk stops and watches me for a moment, then heaves the stroller over the curb and crosses the street, casting a few worried glances over her shoulder as she hurries away.

When I'm finished, I yank the car door closed, groaning. I wipe my mouth with the back of my hand, crank up the air-conditioning, and press my face against the vent. I gaze at my hands, which are still shaking, then at the basket of vegetables sitting on the seat next to me, and then again at my trembling hands.

Now what?

CHAPTER 22

Saturday, August 22

"What's this?" I ask, blinking away sleep and the sharp rays of morning sunlight knifing through the open front door. "I didn't order . . . I mean — I'm not expecting anything." I have trouble wrapping my tongue around the words. My head feels like a walnut squeezed between the serrated edges of a nutcracker, and the taste in my mouth is as foul as an open sewer.

The burly FedEx guy checks his watch and makes a face. "Whatever. Just sign here, okay, pal?"

I scribble my name on the electronic tablet, and he hands me a slim package before dashing back to the delivery truck idling at the curb.

Frowning, standing at my front door in boxers and T-shirt, I examine the mailing label on the package. It's addressed to me. An overnight package. The return address is . . .

Bratislava, Slovakia?

What the hell?

My stomach tightens into a knot as a flood of adrenaline washes away the last vestiges of sleep. I nervously survey my surroundings, squinting in the bright sun. *Why the hell would someone send me a random package from Eastern Europe?*

Aside from a few neighborhood kids I recognize, riding their scooters under the watchful eyes of their parents a few houses down, there's no one else around, and I don't spot any unfamiliar cars parked along our cul-de-sac.

I hesitantly run my hands over the cardboard envelope, gnawing on my lower lip, as the knot in my stomach tightens. *Irrational. Stupid. The game is over. I lost.* She played me, everyone around her, like pieces on a chessboard. The package is nothing. Completely unrelated. It's probably a mistake, or some weird marketing campaign, or a scam.

I retreat inside, bolt the door, and double-check to make sure the curtains are still drawn from last night before taking a closer look. It's thin, no thicker than several pieces of paper stacked together, and featherlight. I momentarily consider sitting down on the sofa in the living room, right next to the front door, which is where I slept last night. But the sickly-sweet smell seeping from the empty beer bottles, Chinese takeout boxes, and a half-full bottle of scotch strewn on the coffee table opposite it almost makes me puke, so I walk into the kitchen. I glance out the back window before closing the curtains.

I place the package on the middle of the table, next to the basket of vegetables from Mrs. Samuelson's family, and stare at it for a full minute. I start to reach for it, hesitate, then draw my hands back.

What the hell are you waiting for?

I rip it open and tip out the contents.

A single, small metallic key spills onto the table.

I gingerly pick it up and take a closer look. The key is silver, with a five-digit number, the words CONSTITUTION SAVINGS BANK, and an address carved in small, neat lettering into the handle.

A safe deposit box key.

I check the envelope to see if there's anything else inside. There isn't.

I lay the envelope aside, prop my chin on my hand, and stare at the key.

I'm pretty certain GG doesn't have anything to do with this. Why should she? The

508

game is over; she made good on her threat by killing Mrs. Samuelson. Is it from Luis, then? A grim token from beyond the grave? Maybe the key is some kind of fail-safe plan he had in place, just in case something happened to him. It certainly fits his style. But if it is from him, why didn't he tell me about it ahead of time? And how did he pull it off? I mean — Bratislava? Who does he know in Bratislava?

A guy like me, doing the kind of work I used to do, has a lot of useful professional connections with a lot of very interesting people.

People with unusual skill sets. People who don't ask questions.

Not that these acquaintances were enough to save him from GG. Besides, will I be able to access the box with just a key? I've never had a safe deposit box, but I don't think you can just show up with a key — I'm pretty sure you need to have identification, or something. Will they think I'm Luis? Will my name be on some kind of a list? But, then, why would he have arranged for the key to be sent to me? Why not just send me a note telling me to go to the bank?

Luis. I wince. Thinking about him makes my head hurt even more. He shouldn't be dead, and what makes it worse is that he deserved better, much better, than some frame job that besmirched his legacy, making it look like he had succumbed to the same demons he had conquered long ago in his climb out of East LA. It's not fair that he had to die that way.

If the key is from Luis, and he wanted me to use it, he would have found a way. He would have found a way to make it work.

I force some coffee, toast, and ibuprofen into my unhappy stomach, shower, and drive to Constitution Savings Bank, which is on State Street downtown, close to University Hospital. The bank is mostly empty, the expansive, marbled lobby still and foreboding and echoing, like a museum or old college library. A smattering of patrons converse in hushed tones with the employees, who outnumber the customers two to one, so I have no trouble identifying an available teller.

The formal and forbidding atmosphere only stokes a creeping sense of unease. I felt a lot more courageous at home. What if this doesn't work? I could get into some *serious* trouble, much worse than what I'm dealing with already. I have a feeling that the bank, and the police, and Luis's family (if he has one) would be extremely interested in someone snooping around the safe deposit box of a man who recently killed himself.

So each step toward the teller's window pushes my toast and coffee a little closer to my mouth.

The teller looks up as I approach the window. She's a bookish, severe-looking woman in her late forties, with gaunt cheeks, half-moon spectacles, and coal black hair tied in a bun. She reminds me of my grade-school librarian, only more intimidating. She smiles politely; but the smile doesn't reach her eyes, which are light blue, and, like the surface of the Arctic Ocean, remain frosty.

"May I help you?"

I clear my throat, which seems loud as a gunshot in the ornate stillness, and hand her the key. "I'm here to, uh, check my box."

"Identification?" she asks, examining the key with one hand while tapping on a computer keyboard in front of her with the other.

I push my driver's license across the counter. I wish I knew a few prayers because right now I sure could use one. Her head swivels purposely from the computer screen, to my license, to me, and then back again to the screen. It takes maybe ten seconds. It seems like ten hours.

"Very good, Mr. Mitchell," she finally says. "Your first time back since you rented the box, I see."

"Hmm?"

"As the co-renter for this box. Your first time back."

"Oh. Um, yeah." Inwardly, I heave a sigh of relief.

"Sign here, please."

"Hmm?"

"Sign. Here." She points to a small electronic signature pad on the counter between us and regards me over the top of her spectacles. "So we can match your signature with the one we have on file."

My signature? The one on file?

I suck in my breath and hesitate, stylus in hand.

"Is there a problem, Mr. Mitchell?"

I shake my head, purse my lips, sign the screen with the stylus, and tap the ENTER icon.

The scanner buzzes disagreeably.

My heart catches in my throat, and I feel several beads of sweat gathering on my brow, marshaling for a run down my face.

The empty smile disappears. The thin line of her mouth now matches the cold indifference in her eyes as she hits a few more buttons on her keyboard. And did she just glance over at the security guard standing watch by the door?

"One more time, please," she says, waving curtly at the signature pad and regarding me over the top of her spectacles.

I hold my breath and try again.

This time the tablet answers with a soft, friendly *ping.*

The teller's polite smile returns.

"Very good, Mr. Mitchell. I'll have Cynthia accompany you into the vault." She waves over a plain young woman, who by the rapidity with which she responds to Librarian Lady's summons and anxious demeanor is clearly a subordinate. Librarian Lady hands her my key and whispers something quietly into her ear. The woman nods and wordlessly escorts me into the vault adjacent to the counter, which is lined by rows of safe deposit boxes. She produces a second key, expertly unlocks the corresponding box using both keys, slides the box out of its slot, and guides me to a small office off the lobby that's furnished with a spare wooden desk and a few metal chairs. She leaves the box on the table and closes the door behind her as she leaves.

My breakfast tickles the back of my throat as I sit down and open the box.

I'm not sure what I was expecting. Irrefutable evidence of GG's guilt? A signed confession? Whatever I was expecting, it certainly isn't what I find.

I reach into the box and pull out . . .

. . . a cell phone.

A cheap one. It could be the twin of the one Luis gave me. In fact, I note, turning it over in my hand, it *is* the twin of the phone Luis gave me — obviously, the one he was using to send me texts.

I lay it on the table next to the box and frown. *Stupid of me.* I had completely forgotten about the cell phones. Through the signals they send to towers, cell phones can be used to track a person's location. The phones, I realize, are the only direct link between Luis and me: Even though they were prepaid, I'm sure the calls are logged by their numbers. If the police, or anyone else, had gotten ahold of this phone, they could have tracked me down to my home address through his text messages. Which, of course, would have led to uncomfortable questions and awkward situations. Now I have both phones, and the loop is closed.

Not exactly the smoking gun I was looking for; but, so far, so good. And it confirms that Luis was prepared for a worst-case scenario by keeping his phone someplace safe — someplace accessible by me, if necessary — while he was at his most vulnerable:

asleep in University Hospital.

I slip the phone in my pocket and draw the second and final item from the box: a dog-eared paperback book entitled *Eye in the Sky.* The cover shows a large, floating eye and several small human figures fleeing from it. My eyes flicker over the author line.

Philip K. Dick.

Again, like a flashback in a movie, my memory jumps back to the night on the porch.

I've always been partial to science fiction.

Luis said that Philip K. Dick was one of his favorite authors.

Don't forget what we've talked about here tonight.

Is the book a clue to something important? Something that could help me? But if so, what does it mean? I flip through the pages and immediately notice that text has been highlighted at sporadic points throughout the book with a yellow pen.

That's interesting.

Something compels me to snap the book closed and check my surroundings rather than take a closer look at the highlighted text. I'm alone, but there's a security camera, high up in one corner, keeping vigil over the room. It makes me feel exposed. So I tuck the book under my arm, walk back to the lobby, and return the safe deposit box to Librarian Lady. She hands me back my key, flashes a disdainful smile, and focuses her attention back on her computer monitor.

I pause and timidly clear my throat.

"Was there anything else, Mr. Mitchell?" She locks her glacial blue eyes on me, and the room temperature drops twenty degrees.

"I was, um, wondering — you mentioned I was the co-renter for this box."

She arches an eyebrow but says nothing.

"So, who — I mean, when was the last time my partner checked the box?"

"Your partner? Partners usually talk with one another."

"Right. He's on vacation right now. A camping trip. Very remote. No cell coverage. One of those, uh, get-away-from-it-all-type places."

"Humph." She narrows her eyes and purses her lips, but nevertheless stabs the keyboard a few more times with her finger. "Your co-renter, Mr. Reynolds, was last here on Sunday morning."

Mr. Reynolds. An alias. Not surprising. Knowing Luis, I'm sure the box can never be traced back to him directly. The bank is only a couple of blocks from University Hospital. He probably dropped it in the safe deposit box whenever he was going to be staying overnight on call in the hospital.

"You guys are open on Sundays?"

She stares at me like I'm a complete idiot. "A lot of banks are open on Sundays, Mr. Mitchell."

I stammer thanks and beat a hasty retreat from the bank.

Once I'm safely home, I leave the blinds closed, collect the other cell phone from the nightstand in the master bedroom upstairs, and unzip one of the cushions of the couch I slept on last night. I tuck both phones inside it and zip the cushion up again. I then carry *Eye in the Sky* to the kitchen, sit down at the table and, in the dim light cast by the fingers of sun prying at the cracks in the blinds, open it to the first page.

The highlighted bits of text are numbers: some written out as numeric digits, some as words. I make my way slowly and methodically through the book, writing down each of the highlighted numbers on a sheet of lined notebook paper, each number to its own line. When I'm done, there are eleven different numbers — seven two-digit and four one-digit — printed on the page. I gnaw on the tip of my pen and try to figure out why Luis would go through all this trouble to make sure that I see these eleven particular numbers.

Think.

What are numbers good for? A location, maybe? The site of another clue? GPS coordinates, in latitude and longitude, usually contain longer strings of digits: The seconds portion alone for each latitude and longitude is typically expressed to four decimal places. Nevertheless, I turn on my laptop and try shuffling the eleven numbers around in different combinations in Google Maps, but only come up with various locations in the middle of the Pacific Ocean.

I close my eyes and rub my eyeballs with the heels of my palms. Luis would have *wanted* me to solve this puzzle. He'd have tied these numbers in with something he knew I'd be able to recognize.

But what?

I crack the book and stare at each of the numbers again in turn, one by one, searching for additional details. Six of them are written out as words, five as actual numbers; two of them occur at the beginning of a sentence, three of them at the end; four of them are page numbers —

Wait a second.

Three of the numbers, and only three, occur at the end of a sentence — which means that each of these numbers immediately precedes a period. Is it possible that Luis intended for the periods to be included with these numbers? That would make for eleven numbers in all, three of them followed by a period . . .

Or, to think of it another way: *four* separate numbers separated by three periods.

My pulse quickens.

I carefully recopy the numbers, placing them all on the same line, in a single row, and insert the periods at the proper positions. Three numbers. Period. Three numbers. Period. Three numbers. Period. Two numbers.

To a computer geek like me, a string of digits like that can mean only one thing.

An Internet Protocol address. IP for short.

Every computer, printer, and other machine hooked into the Internet, or any other network, has an IP address. It suggests that Luis might be trying to guide me to a Web site. My hands tremble as I enter the numbers, with the corresponding periods, into my Web browser window.

The screen flashes briefly.

I hold my breath.

A login page appears with a prompt, in English, for a password. The rest of the page is in some language I don't understand, but it looks Eastern European. It's definitely not Russian. Polish, maybe.

Or Slovakian.

I breathe out sharply and smile.

It must be some random server Luis hijacked, most likely a secure offshore site he hacked on which he could store digital data. But what kind of data? My insides hum with anticipation. I'm as thrilled as a fourteen-year-old boy who's managed to outsmart the Internet porn lockouts on the family computer.

Until, that is, it occurs to me that Luis has left behind a twenty-character code standing between whatever is on that server and me, with no obvious clues as to how to access it.

Shit.

Luis certainly wasn't naïve or stupid enough to have used something as simplistic as a birthday, or a name, or any other easily recognizable patterns for the code. No — I have to assume that this code is composed of random letters, digits, and symbols. In which case it would take the fastest computers in the world decades to crack.

Dead end.

I pound my fist on the table.

But I'm so close.

There must be another way to figure this

out. Luis was obsessed with — what had he called it? *Compartmentalization.* He had wanted to keep vital information separate. He must have hidden the code elsewhere. The question is, where? Hoping that maybe the book itself is enough of a clue, I pull a synopsis of *Eye in the Sky* off the Internet. It sounds like a pretty weird story, with alternate universes and metaphysical ruminations on the nature of existence. But a few things pop out at me. There's the title, of course, which invokes some kind of omniscient being. And then there's a character in charge of security at a large company, who at the end of the book is revealed to have been manipulating reality for the protagonists, like an unseen puppet master.

Omniscient. Puppet master.

I snort. Those aren't bad descriptions for GG. She always seems to be one step ahead; like we're playing chess, and at each turn she already knows my next move. It's almost supernatural. Like, how the hell did she know I was sitting in Mrs. Samuelson's room before I ran to the fake code for —

Wait a minute.

How *did* GG know when I left Mrs. Samuelson's room in the SICU the night of her death? Other than me, there was no one else there except for Carol, a few other nurses, and the security guard. Nobody, including the security guard, saw her come in through the front door, so she must have slipped in through the back door of the SICU. But that means I practically would have stumbled over her in my mad rush to get to Mr. Schultz's room, when I was using the same door.

Unless she could see me run out of Mrs. Samuelson's room without actually being in or around the SICU.

Like an eye in the sky.

Or like the camera I saw in the safe deposit box room at the bank.

I've seen security cameras around University Hospital, in the large lobbies and waiting rooms on the ground floor, but never any in the actual patient rooms. Is it possible that there are security cameras in the SICU, trained on the patients in their beds? If so, one of them might have caught GG in the act. I mull that over. If there are cameras, they must be hidden, and I'm sure University Hospital Security would have something to do with them. Hadn't my friend Jason mentioned to me that he worked with University Hospital Security? Gnawing on my lower lip, I take out my phone, select Jason's number from my list of contacts, carefully compose a text message, and hit SEND.

I place the phone on the kitchen table and stare at it. I cross my arms and nervously bounce my leg up and down. The portable keystroke logger I've been carrying around, the one that uses the same technology I had used to crack GG's e-mail account, is sitting on the table next to it, so I pick it up and spin it around idly in my fingers.

Several minutes tick by.

Come on, Jason, come on . . .

The phone buzzes. I pounce on it and hungrily read the reply.

The view I see on the video is from above, as if I'm watching from a corner of the ceiling; and wide-angle, so that everything in the small room is clearly visible. It's nighttime. Mrs. Samuelson is lying in her bed, sleeping; I'm dozing next to her in the armchair, with my computer sitting on my lap. A time stamp in the lower-right-hand corner of the picture reads 4:15 A.M. August: less than ten minutes before Mrs. Samuelson coded.

What happens next in the video plays out like a string of images in a silent movie: My chin, which I see had been resting on my chest, jerks upward as I awaken and frantically survey the room. I then see myself check my pager, call the nurse, and frantically dash out the door, leaving my white coat and laptop sitting on the chair.

As I continue to watch the video, I lean forward in my chair, squeezing the life out of the armrests in anticipation as I see . . .

. . . five more minutes of footage of Mrs. Samuelson soundly sleeping.

What?

Then, in rapid-fire succession, follow the events that are indelibly, painfully scorched into my brain: Mrs. Samuelson's bolting upright in the bed, clutching at her chest as I run back into the room; the frantic and ultimately futile attempts to save her life; the cardiac surgeon calling the time of death.

Jason pauses the video and sighs. "Anything else I can do for you today, Steve? Open the personal medical files of every celebrity and politician who's recently been treated at University Hospital, maybe? Stick my neck even further out on the chopping block?" We're sitting in front of the computer in a small office in his house. He tilts back, and the squeaking of his chair mingles with the high-pitched squeals of children drifting through the open door of his study.

"What I still don't understand," he continues, "is how you knew about this surveillance system. Christ, the installation guys even made it look like they were fixing the ventilation system so the SICU nurses wouldn't suspect anything."

"I told you, Jason, I —"

"— had a hunch. Right. Because you realized security is so important in the SICU. Yes, that's the reason for the hidden cameras. But come on, Steve. Honestly. Who told you? Was it that med student you've been working with this summer? The one with the big" — he glances toward the open door and lowers his voice a notch — "tits? What's her name? Gigi? She's been doing administrative work with the Safety Committee for the past few years. I bet she somehow found out about the SICU cameras, then told you. Well, I suppose it was only a matter of time before word leaked out."

He starts muttering angrily as he logs out of the secure account he had used to remotely access the camera's video files. "I told the Security people they shouldn't have put in the others yet. Not until we had a chance to explain things."

Others? Does he mean that there are more?

"Maybe if we looked at just one more —"

"No," Jason says, emphatically. "Absolutely not. I've already broken, like, twenty major rules, what with all of the medical-liability and patient-privacy issues involved." He scowls at me. "What the hell were you looking for, anyway? What did you expect to see on that video clip? That poor lady threw an air embolism, pure and simple, because of the hole in her central line."

"I . . . I'm not sure, Jason. I had a hunch about something, but I guess I was wrong. I came to you because I thought you could help me, and because I trust you. I'm sorry. Really. I don't want you to get in any trouble."

I must look pretty miserable, because Jason's expression softens, and he sighs. "Look. I'll admit that when you texted me earlier today, my first instinct was to lie to you, deny everything, and run screaming in the opposite direction. But the security geek in me was wondering how you knew what you knew. And, besides — you're my friend. I didn't want to lie."

With a joyful shriek, Jason's son suddenly launches himself through the open doorway and into his father's lap. Laughing and struggling to maintain his balance in the office chair, Jason hugs him.

During this momentary, and fortuitous, distraction, Jason doesn't notice as I reach around to the back of his computer and retrieve my portable keystroke logger from the USB port I had surreptitiously connected it to shortly after my arrival. A little guiltily, knowing that I'll now be able to retrieve his login code to access the video files, I slip the keystroke logger into my pocket. Even though GG has already altered the videos, those files might yet come in handy.

Jason tousles his son's hair and kisses him on top of the head before turning his attention back to me. He reaches over and places a sympathetic hand on my shoulder. "But Steve. You have to understand: *We absolutely, positively never had this conversation.* You never saw this video. I'm going to come up with a legitimate reason for accessing this file, something that'll cover my ass with the Security folks. In the meantime, I think it's best if you and I just avoid each other completely for the next several weeks."

A short time later, as I crack open a beer from my fridge and collapse on the couch, I wonder how my M.D. will look on my Starbucks job application. I should have known that it wouldn't be that easy; that if GG was using the security cameras to track me in the SICU, she would have taken precautions to erase any and all trace of her presence on them. She clearly altered the tape.

I pull *Eye in the Sky* from my back pocket, where I've been carrying it all day, and flip the pages idly. Why would Luis send me to a hijacked server in Eastern Europe but not give me a way to access it? And is the server really linked to the SICU security cameras? Or to something else entirely?

I take a sip of beer and turn through the book again . . . then freeze at the inside of the back cover.

My heart skips — no, leaps over — a beat.

In the back cover of the book, handwritten in small, neat lettering, so small that I had missed it before, is a single sentence written in Russian. I'm a little rusty, so I have to go dig my old English-Russian translation book out of the basement before I'm able to translate the whole thing.

If you aren't in over your head, how do you know how tall you are?

It's something else Luis had said to me that night on Dan's porch. I pull out my laptop, and a quick Google search identifies the author of the quote: T. S. Eliot. It has to be a clue; another link to a compartmentalized piece of information, perhaps even the access code to the Web site.

Okay, so then, if it really is another clue,

what's the connection between T. S. Eliot and a funky science-fiction author who wrote about alternate realities? I pass the next several hours wading through the collected works of T. S. Eliot, trying to figure it out. A number of intriguing possibilities pop up. *The Waste Land. The Love Song of J. Alfred Prufrock. The Hollow Men. Murder in the Cathedral.* I hunt for clues in the text, but find none. Or, maybe, I find too many — the problem is that T. S. Eliot's work is so ambiguous, so rife with symbolism, that every line is pregnant with alternate meanings. Certainly there's nothing pointing me in the direction of how to crack the Web site password.

The empty beer bottles pile up as quickly as do my frustration and dejection. *Hopeless. This whole fucking situation is hopeless.* I'm getting absolutely nowhere. And I feel so . . . *alone* right now. It would be nice to have someone to confide in. But Luis is dead. And Sally, of course, due back tomorrow afternoon from Providence with Katie and Annabelle, is out of the question. Jason has, for the time being at least, disavowed me. I can't confide in Dan or any of the other doctors at University Hospital because they'll just think I'm a lunatic.

I have no proof and, as far as I can tell,

zero options.

Fucking hopeless.

I keep drinking.

I'm sitting in an exam room in clinic. Standing next to me is Mrs. Samuelson. Mr. Abernathy sits across from us, begging me to please help him with his *goddamned* prostate.

Upon hearing this, Mrs. Samuelson places her hands on her stout hips and screams at me, *Goddammit, Mr. Abernathy killed Jap bastards in the Pacific for snot-nosed little shits like you back in the Big One so why don't you do something about his goddamned prostrate already?*

Then, without waiting for an answer, she strides across the room and hands him a large red pill. It's the size of a walnut. He shoves it in his mouth and swallows it whole.

I'm cured! he shouts happily. *I'm finally cured.* He throws his hands up in the air.

He and Mrs. Samuelson hug, then kiss passionately, mouths open and tongues searching, before the scene changes, like a slow dissolve in a movie, and now I'm sitting in the hospital cafeteria with GG and Mrs. Samuelson and the kid who got shot in the penis and testicles. The kid is wearing a hospital gown and is busy changing his colostomy bag while eating scrambled eggs. He beams at me, and says brightly, "I still gots the bag, Doc!"

GG and Mrs. Samuelson nod agreeably. GG grins wickedly, and asks, "If you aren't in over your head, Steve, how do you know how tall you are?"

Someone taps me roughly on the shoulder. I turn. It's Mr. Bernard. He's wearing a hospital gown and standing next to a big IV pole, to which he's attached by a series of large IV tubes extending out of his neck. An endotracheal tube sticks out of his mouth.

He's crying.

In one hand he's holding an IV bag filled with clear fluid and labeled POTASSIUM; in the other, he's holding an identical bag labeled CEFOTETAN. He tosses the potassium bag to GG, who catches it effortlessly in her free hand.

GG pops the cap off the nozzle, puts the nozzle to her lips, and starts sucking the clear fluid directly out of the bag. Mr. Bernard offers me the cefotetan bag. I take it with my free hand, and it explodes soundlessly the moment I touch it; but I'm surprised to discover that there's no liquid in it, so I don't get wet.

His hands now freed, Mr. Bernard reaches up and pulls the breathing tube out of his throat. The tube issues a nauseating slurping sound as it exits his mouth and drips thick cords of greenish yellow mucous onto the floor. Mr. Bernard points at me and opens his mouth to speak; but instead of his voice, I hear GG's.

It's not about the patients. It's about you, says Mr. Bernard with GG's voice. Confused, I look at GG, but she's still drinking from the IV bag.

You don't care about making people feel better, Mr. Bernard/GG continues. *For you, the patients are a means to an end. It's all about you.*

Mrs. Samuelson smiles kindly as the kid with the gunshot wound calmly eats his scrambled eggs with one hand and changes his colostomy bag with the other.

And then I'm awake. I try to sit up, but the room pivots wildly about me. I dully realize that I'm still drunk. The sky outside the window is dark. My head drops heavily back on the pillow, and I'm asleep again within seconds.

CHAPTER 23

Sunday, August 23

It's really hot this morning. And humid. Especially wearing my tie and dark suit. The stench of spoiled milk — the product of a long-forgotten sippy cup abandoned underneath one of the backseats, maybe — wraps around me like a sour, stifling blanket. But I keep the windows up and the air-conditioning off. Beads of sweat gather on my nose and upper lip before leaping into space toward my lap; others slide down from my armpits, racing each other toward my hips in snaky trails running along my sides.

I find the rancid heat pleasant. It's cleansing somehow, like being in a sauna and sweating off a bad hangover. Which is exactly what I feel like I'm doing, although by now the pounding, full-blown riot in my head I woke up with this morning has quieted to a relatively tame civil disturbance,

and the ibuprofen and orange Gatorade —
the only inhabitants of my otherwise empty
stomach — have reached an uneasy truce as
I glide through the light morning traffic
toward my destination.

I'm not really sure what I'm doing. I
mean, I know where I'm going. I'm just not
sure exactly why I'm going there. All I'm
certain of is that I woke up this morning
with an urgency that cut decisively through
the painful haze of my hangover, a profound
sense of . . . unfinished business. And so
now I'm driving, my errand inspired less by
a coherent plan of action and more by some
subconscious desire to complete a task left
undone.

I wipe the sweat from my brow and sigh
resignedly. I've decided to tell Dr. Collier
everything tomorrow morning. Mr. Bernard. Mrs. Samuelson. GG. Luis. The safe
deposit box. The Web site. The book. I can't
take the chance that, while I'm struggling to
decipher Luis's final cryptic messages, GG
kills again.

I don't have a shred of proof for a story
that is, to say the very least, implausible, so
telling Dr. Collier will pretty much mean
the end of everything that's important to
me, everything I've spent the last thirteen
years of my life working toward. But the

alternative — another patient's death on my conscience — would be even worse. Much worse. My only hope is that my self-immolation will bring down enough unwanted attention on GG's head that she's never able to kill again. Like a cockroach scurrying for cover from the kitchen light, she'll have to abandon her plans for fear of being caught. Cold comfort, but it's all I have. I think that it might be enough.

And, of course, if I'm confessing to Dr. Collier, there's another person in my life with whom I'm going to have to come clean. For everything.

Sally.

I grip the steering wheel harder and clench my jaw.

That I can't even think about yet.

When I reach the funeral home, I park and join a trickle of elderly people shuffling into a modestly appointed building with a faux white colonial front decorated with fake white shutters and Roman columns with peeling paint. In the cramped lobby, an old sign with plastic white letters pushed into a black felt background directs me into a room decorated with cheap imitation wood paneling stapled to the walls and faded maroon shag carpeting. I take a seat near the back, balancing myself carefully on one of the rickety white folding chairs that are set out in neat rows. The other guests don't so much as even glance in my direction.

The memorial service is short, simple, and to the point. The minister, an energetic-appearing, cherubic guy barely older than I, talks about pride and loss and pain, and commitment and sacrifice and redemption. I listen quietly but intently, my hands folded in my lap.

"The eternal God is thy refuge," the minister finishes, "and underneath are the everlasting arms."

After the service, I wait patiently in the receiving line for my turn to pay my respects to the family. When I finally reach her, I extend my hand and smile. The smile comes naturally. It feels good. It's the first time I've smiled like that in weeks.

"Hi, Mrs. Abernathy. I'm Dr. Mitchell."

Mrs. Abernathy gently wraps both of her gnarled hands, savaged by time and arthritis, around my single outstretched one. They feel soft and warm and wise. She smiles. She's wearing yellowed dentures. She introduces me to the minister, who's standing next to her, as *Ray's favorite doctor.*

Although I don't know how often doctors go to their patient's funerals, he doesn't seem the least bit surprised to see me. He squeezes my hand, and says, "How good of you to come."

"That was, um, a nice service," I observe awkwardly. "I liked that last quote, about God's being a refuge."

"Oh, yes. Thank you." He smiles serenely. "*The eternal God is thy refuge, and underneath are the everlasting arms.* An oft-overlooked verse, but one of my favorites. Deuteronomy. Chapter 33, verse 27."

"Yes, well, very . . . uh, comforting."

I stroll out to the parking lot, thinking idly about the quote. *Deuteronomy.* The word conjures a happier time at the beginning of the summer, when Sally and I were celebrating in our kitchen, with me drinking that fantastic bottle of wine as we reminisced about our long-ago trip to San Francisco. When we had seen *Cats,* and Sally had reminded me that Deuteronomy was the only character I had related to in the entire show because it reminded me of T. S. Eliot's poetry . . .

It hits me like a brace of cold water in the face. I stop with my hand on the car door.

T. S. Eliot.

Cats.

I never sleep very well in the hospital. That fucking kitten in the call room always messes with my mind.

Makes you wonder what's behind it, doesn't it?

I suppress an idiotic urge to slap myself on the forehead. Could that be the connection? Could it really be that easy?

I jump in my car and break about twenty different traffic laws speeding to University Hospital.

They've cleaned the call room since Luis died. The bright yellow police tape draped across the door is gone. They've installed a brand-new bunk bed, and the bed linens, imprinted with the University Hospital logo, are crisp and clean and look like they've never been used even once. Which I'm sure they haven't — the word is that all of the residents are too freaked out to use this call room anymore. The rest of the room has undergone a similar makeover: The sink has been scoured, the windows washed, and the formerly dusty walls scrubbed clean.

But the poster of the kitten hanging on the clothesline remains. I make straight for it and, planting myself in front of it, size it up. The kitten glares insolently back.

The surface of the kitten poster, like the walls of the room, has recently been dusted, and it looks the cleanest I've just about ever seen it. It's otherwise completely un-changed, in the exact same spot from which it's kept its cloying vigil for the last several years, the rows of metallic screws affixing it in place to the wall.

I pull a pair of latex gloves out of my pocket, place them over my hands, and, selecting a screwdriver from the set I brought with me from the trunk of my car, remove the screws, one by one. It takes a while. I'm careful to save all the screws.

The section of wall behind the poster looks much the same as the remainder of the room, cracked and riddled with fissures. So expertly is the defect in the wall behind the poster concealed, so carefully are the edges of it worked to resemble the sur-rounding chinks in the hundred-year-old concrete, that I never would have found it with anything less than a concentrated, crack-by-crack search.

Tucked into one of the cracks, I find a folded piece of paper sealed in a plastic sandwich bag. I pry the bag from the crack, remove the paper from the bag, and care-fully unfold it. A string of twenty random numbers, letters, and punctuation marks are neatly typed on the paper.

The password.

Now I truly understand Luis's intent.

Compartmentalization. In and of itself, the password means nothing. It's only when it's coupled with the server address, which had been securely ensconced in the safe deposit box a few blocks away, that it makes sense.

And then, in the wall where the password had been hidden, I find something else.

Something that changes everything.

All thoughts of confessing to Dr. Collier disappear. A plan starts to take shape in my mind.

But there's something else I need to do first.

They arrive home from Providence just before dinner. Sally and I spend the next few hours getting Annabelle and Katie fed, bathed, dressed, and put to bed. Luckily, they're both exhausted, so neither of them puts up much of a fight.

After the girls are asleep, I lead Sally into the living room and have her sit on the couch. I pull up a chair opposite her, take both of her hands in mine, and draw a deep breath as she waits, curious and expectant.

"Sally. There's something I need to tell you . . ."

She takes it well enough, I guess. As well as could be expected. I don't really have a frame of reference since I've never confessed to adultery before.

She doesn't say anything, just stiffens, pulls her hands from mine, and wordlessly gets up from the couch. Typically Sally: calmly and coolly facing down an emotional crisis. She walks to the window and looks outside. Her back is toward me, and I can't see her face as I come clean on everything — everything except the psychopathic murderer part, of course.

"Thank you," she says wearily when I'm done. She doesn't turn around.

"For what?" I ask, startled.

"For finally being honest with me."

"Sally —"

"Don't, Steve. Just . . . don't." She sighs, crosses her arms, and looks at the floor. "Is it really over? Between you two?"

"Yes."

The next words out of her mouth cut like a serrated knife sliding between my ribs. "Tomorrow morning, I'm taking the girls and staying with my parents for a while. I need to think this through."

"I understand."

"No. No, I don't think you do." She drops her arms to her sides and clenches her fists. "That was her. In the restaurant. A few weeks ago. The woman who was with Ellie. Wasn't it?"

I hang my head. "Yes."

"I thought I caught a weird vibe between you two. Katie and Annabelle —" She shakes her head. "You know, it's bad enough, what the two of you did."

She whirls around to face me. "But if she comes near my babies again, I swear to God. I'll kill her."

I realize she's upset right now. But the look on her face is enough to make me wonder if, deep down, she really means it.

CHAPTER 24

Thursday, August 27
I'm sitting in the front row of the Dome, trying to prepare myself for what comes next, mentally laboring to grasp the enormity of what I'm about to attempt. I still can't conceive of how my life — which was going so well, so smoothly, so ordinarily at the beginning of the summer — could have taken so many unexpected turns, nor how I could have ended up contemplating the beginning of what will surely someday rank as one of the most bizarre nights of my life.

One thing is for certain: It all ends tonight. For better, or for worse, this whole terrible summer ends tonight.

The end begins with a routine administrative denouement to Mrs. Samuelson's demise: Morbidity and Mortality Report. M and M, as it's often called, is a venerable surgical tradition. In our department, it's a formal conference held on the third Thursday of each month, in the evening. Part debriefing, part quality-improvement program, and part mea culpa, it's a venue for individual surgeons to acknowledge their mistakes, the purpose of which is for the collective surgical community to discuss the complications, determine what went wrong, and try to prevent what went wrong from ever happening again. The cases are selected personally by Dr. Collier from the pool of complications that occur each month.

Surgical complications spring from many sources. A strayed hand. Bad luck. An unforeseen anatomic variation. A lapse in judgment. The fickle flesh of a sick patient. A missed diagnosis. Or, in my own case, inexperience with a particular procedure. Regardless of the cause or who's responsible, each and every surgeon takes a complication very, *very* personally.

I survey the auditorium, which is packed. M and M is always popular. Everyone in our department is here — professors, residents, med students — plus several surgeons from other hospitals. The room buzzes with conversation and short bursts of laughter. I catch a glimpse of GG, texting on her smartphone. She looks up and slips her smartphone in the front pocket of her white coat. Our eyes meet briefly, and she winks. I face forward again. Sitting in the front row with me are my fellow residents, who sip coffee and swap stories with one another. I keep to myself, focusing on the task at hand.

I nervously run my hand down the front of my newly starched white coat, tug at my tie, and try to keep from throwing up. Again. The butterflies in my stomach have already gotten the better of me once earlier this evening, and I'm hopeful that it won't happen a second time, in front of all these people.

At precisely 6:00 P.M., Dr. Collier, looking regal in a tailor-made blue pin-striped suit and red power tie, checks his watch and rises from his usual seat in the far corner of the first row. He faces the audience and solemnly stretches his hand out for silence, palm extended outward like a traffic cop making the stop signal.

The moment Dr. Collier raises his hand, a preternatural calm settles over the audience, as if the whole room just entered the eye of a storm. Conversations stop midsentence. Cell phones snap shut. Necks crane up expectantly. As is his custom each week, Dr. Collier welcomes everyone, then reminds the residents and medical students participating in the research study that we'll be receiving our next round of shots immediately after the conference in the hallway outside. Looking stricken, he adds that Luis's family opted for a private service in LA and asks that we all remember him in our own way. He then leads the assembled group in another moment of silence for Luis.

The silence is deafening, the grief palpable. I think of GG out in the audience, amidst the legitimate mourners, no doubt solemnly bowing her head; and I grind my teeth so loudly that the resident sitting next to me glances at me curiously.

Once the moment is over, Dr. Collier is all business again. He gestures toward the chief residents and settles back into his seat.

I'm up first. Somebody dims the lights as I walk to the lectern. The room remains utterly quiet. But for the sharp report of my starched white coat, which produces a crisp whooshing sound with each forward sweep of my legs, I could be walking in a vacuum. And yet the silence is ripe, crammed with an expectant, tightly wound energy, a life breathed into it by all those people stuffed into the conference room, all of whom are completely focused now on me and what I'm about to say.

I reach the lectern, clear my throat, grab the laser pointer, clear my throat, adjust the computer keyboard, clear my throat again, adjust the microphone, and try to think of something else to adjust. The knot in my stomach pulls harder.

"Proceed, please, Dr. Mitchell," Dr. Collier orders sternly.

I clear my throat one last time and advance the computer presentation to my first slide.

"Good evening. Our first case is a mortality following laparoscopic converted to open right adrenalectomy . . ."

"Louder!" a male voice calls out sharply from the depths of the audience.

I lean in toward the microphone. "Our first case this evening is a mortality following laparoscopic converted to open right adrenalectomy complicated by avulsion of the right adrenal vein and right renal hilum, myocardial infarction, fungal sepsis, and pulmonary air embolism."

I advance to the next slide, trying to ignore the way the glowing dot emitted by the laser pointer, guided by my quivering hand, is hopping around on the projector screen like a frog on crystal meth.

"Mrs. Samuelson was a fifty-three-year-old woman with a past medical history significant only for hypercholesterolemia who initially presented with bilateral lower

extremity edema and new onset hypertension."

Next slide.

I spend the following five minutes sum-
marizing the last few weeks of Mrs. Samuelson's life, succinctly and dispassionately
reducing all of her suffering to a series of
glowing lines on a PowerPoint presentation.

The operation.

Next slide.

The bleeding.

Next slide.

The heart attack and fungal infection.

Next slide.

The brief recovery.

Next slide.

The final, terrifying moments of her life.

And then I'm done. I put down the laser
pointer and look expectantly at the audience. That was the easy part. Now it's time
for the question-and-answer period. During
the next few minutes, the way I respond to
the questions that are about to sail toward
me like live grenades could conceivably help
salvage what's left of my career — or scuttle
it completely.

Dr. Collier rises from his seat and turns
partly around, positioning himself so that
he can face both the audience and me at
the same time. He clasps both hands behind

his back. "I think we can lay aside the issue of the air embolism, which is a sensitive patient-care matter currently under investigation by the Safety Committee. Let's start instead with the operation, which initiated the series of events eventually leading to this patient's demise. Dr. Mitchell, what was your first thought when you encountered that bleeding?"

My first thought was: Holy fucking shit. What the fuck have I done?

Behind the lectern, I dig my fingernails into my palms. "My first thought was to identify the source of the bleeding."

"Of course it was, Dr. Mitchell," he says, waving his brown hand impatiently. "Of course. But with bleeding that catastrophic, it's probably best to get control of the IVC first. How can you normally accomplish that laparoscopically?"

"Well, it's difficult, but possible. When this kind of vascular injury occurs, pressure can be applied to the area of injury, with dissection then performed around it to obtain greater exposure. Another laparoscopic port can also be placed to assist."

"Why was that not attempted here?"

I remember back to my initial panic on that horrible day: watching Mrs. Samuelson's blood wash across the surgical field, flailing about inside her abdomen with laparoscopic instruments, struggling fruitlessly to find the origin of the bleeding. My stomach churns, and my heart pounds. I taste bile in the back of my throat.

Concentrate.

"It was, Dr. Collier. Unfortunately, due to the catastrophic nature of the injury, vascular control was lost very quickly, and adequate visualization of the surgical field could not be reachieved."

Another voice emerges from the crowd, a cultured female one. "What about temporarily increasing the intra-abdominal pressure to twenty, or even twenty-five mmHg? That might have helped by temporarily sealing the tear."

"Yes," I say, turning toward the source of the voice, which I recognize as belonging to one of our senior faculty members. "That was not attempted."

"Why?"

"The bleeding was brisk, and our attention was focused on locating the injury."

"So, in other words, you did not think of it at the time."

I hesitate for a fraction of a second. "No, ma'am. We didn't think of it."

The room grows quiet again as they digest my answer. *So far, so good.* But I know that

I'm walking a tightrope, trying to strike the proper tonal balance between repentance and cold, forensic analysis.

Then Larry stands up and says in a clear, even voice, "This was my patient." Larry talks of the technical challenges involved with trying to peel the tumor off the IVC and his erroneous assumption that it would be a relatively easy operation to perform laparoscopically. He talks of the many nights since that he's lain awake, obsessively thinking about this case and worrying about the patient's family. He says that if he were to do it all over again, he would have used a much larger incision from the beginning and not attempted to perform the case laparoscopically.

He finishes by noting that he should also have provided more direct supervision for the residents assisting him with the operation. He doesn't mention my name.

He sits down.

Silence.

Dr. Collier and the rest of the professors nod thoughtfully. The tone of the room has changed from one of expectation and confrontation to one of empathy and reflection. Every single one of them has faced a similar situation. They've been through the fire themselves, and they understand. I get the sense that I've successfully faced a kind of initiation, a rite of passage into an exclusive club. I've faced up to my failure and learned from it so that the next patient will benefit from my hard-won experience.

"Thank you, Dr. Mitchell," Dr. Collier says. "Next case, please."

One of the other chief residents springs up to the lectern. I slide into my seat, and over the next hour discover that Mrs. Samuelson's death was but one of many bad things that had happened to the patients in our department last month. Postoperative bleeding, infections, strokes; even a surgical sponge inadvertently left in a patient after an operation — enough bad things, in fact, that before conference is over, Dr. Collier ends up using a variation of his elevator-shaft line: *Doctor, you might just as well have shoved this unfortunate woman down an open elevator shaft from the top floor of the hospital. You would have achieved the same result.*

At the end of the meeting, Dr. Collier dismisses us and reminds the residents and med students about the research-study injections, waiting to be administered in the hallway immediately outside the lecture hall. By the door, I pass by Larry, who is listening intently to one of the other residents. He hasn't talked to me in weeks. Our eyes meet. He nods slightly, twists his lips into a configuration vaguely reminiscent of a smile, and mouths, "Thanks." I nod and smile weakly in return.

The other residents and I fall into line. The old guy with the creepy smile isn't around tonight — just the young guy, who, harried and overwhelmed, fumbles and mutters under his breath. At one point, he drops one of the drug vials on the floor, and I help him pick it up as the med students (including GG, whom I notice out of the corner of my eye standing near the back of the line) and the other residents chortle and roll their eyes.

It takes twice as long as it normally does for everyone to receive their shots; the residents and students, distracted and annoyed, fidget impatiently in line. Nobody notices when, after receiving my shot, I slip back into the now-empty auditorium. The door closes soundlessly behind me. I grab my laptop from a bag underneath my seat, take it up to the lectern, plug it into the projector, and open a series of files. I then flip on a screensaver, a picture of Katie and Annabelle hugging, and return to my seat. I rummage through my computer bag, performing a final check of the rest of the equipment I brought with me tonight, confirming that everything I need for what comes next is there before shoving the bag back underneath my seat.

And then I wait.

I can't see the door to the auditorium from where I'm sitting, only the screen and lectern on the dais at the front of the room. But I can hear the murmur of voices from under the crack in the door, which soon fades, then disappears altogether. This auditorium is located in one of the oldest sections of the hospital, far away from the patient-care floors, and quickly empties out this time of evening.

Then I hear the door open, the rhythmic click of a woman's shoes on the marble floor, and the protesting squeal of an auditorium seat in the row immediately behind me as it sags under the weight of a new occupant.

"Great job, Steve. The attendings were clearly impressed. Your career seems to be getting right back on track." Her lips brush against my right earlobe, her hot breath washing playfully over the rest of my ear. "I always knew it would."

"You played me pretty well that night. With Mrs. Samuelson."

"It almost didn't work. You got back down to the SICU faster than I'd anticipated."

She starts stroking the back of my neck lightly with her fingers. Several weeks ago, her touch would have sent electric jolts down my spine; now it makes my skin crawl, but I make no move to stop her. "I underestimated you."

"You still won."

"Yes. But win or lose, it doesn't matter. What matters is patient safety."

"So you've told me. But why a pulmonary air embolus?"

"Why not?"

"Because it already had happened before at University Hospital. In May."

"I like your logic. The problem is, I didn't get the Safety Committee's full attention the first time. In May."

"What do you mean?"

She removes her hand from my neck as I twist myself around to face her.

She smirks. "After the first patient suffered his unfortunate accident, the Committee said it was a fluke. Nothing changed. I thought that was the wrong response."

"So you did it again. To Mrs. Samuelson. To make the point."

"Well, I certainly couldn't do anything as obvious as hack an ICD."

I must look as pissed as I feel, with my lips pursed and hands coiled into fists, because she pats my hand and smiles indulgently. "I take that back. I led you into that one. And to be fair, I'd been toying around with using that approach before deciding to use Mr. Schultz as a decoy. Actually, I'm impressed that you worked out all the details on your own. You don't have much of a background in cardiology."

She drapes her arms provocatively across the backs of each of the chairs on either side of the one in which she's sitting and crosses her long, slim legs. Her short white med student coat is unbuttoned and falls away from her flowered sundress, the hem of which is now sitting halfway up her bare thigh. "So," she purrs, "you decided to play the game after all, Steve. And you lost. Remember our rules."

This banter seems obscene, what with the trail of bodies she's left in her wake.

"I remember." I rise, remove my white coat, and drape it over a nearby chair. I walk to the lectern at the front of the room and check my watch. "I have something I want to show you, GG."

"I'm intrigued." She sounds anything but.

I push a button on my laptop. A familiar, soundless scene materializes on the screen at the front of the auditorium. The view is from above. Mrs. Samuelson is lying in her bed, sleeping; I'm dozing next to her in the armchair with my computer sitting on my lap. I peek at GG over the top of my laptop. She's smirking knowingly.

I look again at the video I've been feverishly preparing since Sunday, now playing to its audience of one. If my plan's going to work, I need her undivided attention for the next ten minutes; so I've increased the playback speed in order to reach the most critical portions, the ones that should really jolt her and maintain her interest, more quickly. The now familiar series of events thus unfolds in seconds rather than minutes: I awaken; I answer the page; I make a hasty exit; Mrs. Samuelson slumbers on.

"Is that it?" GG says lazily. "Because otherwise —"

The words die on her lips as a new figure creeps into Mrs. Samuelson's room. The face is clear in the vivid, high-definition image.

GG.

I steal another glance at her.

And I finally see it.

A crack in her calm façade; a fracture in that imperturbable armor of hers; a flicker of uncertainty flitting across her features. She retracts her arms from the backs of the chairs and sits up very straight, limbs tense, eyes alert, like a predator that's caught a scent.

Meanwhile, her two-dimensional avatar, wearing latex hospital gloves, unhooks Mrs. Samuelson's central line from the IV machine next to her bed. The high-speed playback renders a subtle jerkiness to GG's motions, but it's easy enough to follow every move she makes. She looks over her shoulder before pulling a large syringe out of her pocket. She attaches the syringe to Mrs. Samuelson's central line, depresses the plunger, looks over her shoulder again, detaches the syringe from the central line, pulls back on the plunger, reattaches the syringe to the central line, and depresses the plunger again. She repeats the process three more times before taping a note to the syringe, slipping it into my white coat pocket, and stealing away.

The screen darkens.

"Where did you get that?" she asks neutrally. "Is this some kind of a joke?"

The next portion of the video, also sped up, begins before I have a chance to answer. A bird's-eye view of a different hospital room now fills the front of the auditorium. A patient is asleep in a bed in the center of the screen.

Mr. Bernard.

He awakens as GG enters the room. They talk for a bit, their mouths moving rapidly and noiselessly. GG smiles and nods as she pulls a large, plastic syringe filled with clear fluid from her white coat pocket. She points to it, then to the tangle of wires surrounding the TPN bag hanging on the IV pole next to his bed. He says something. She laughs and pats him on the shoulder before donning a pair of latex gloves, connecting the syringe to the IV emerging from underneath Mr. Bernard's right collarbone, and injecting the fluid.

Mr. Bernard grimaces, and with his left hand rubs his right chest underneath the IV line. She sits down at the edge of the bed, stroking his right forearm, her lips puckered in a *shush* configuration. He closes his eyes as she continues to massage his arm. His body twitches several times, violently, then stills. GG moves her hand from his forearm to his wrist, fingers lightly touching the radial artery, and nods.

A second syringe appears in her hand, this one with a long, slender needle attached to the tip of it. She wipes a rubber-capped port at the bottom of the TPN bag with an alcohol pad, inserts the needle into it, and empties the contents of the syringe into the thick, milky white fluid. She withdraws the needle from the bag, caps it with a plastic safety tip, and places the needle in her pocket. She then checks Mr. Bernard's radial pulse one final time before depressing the bright red code-alarm button located on the wall next to his bed.

"You know what happens next," I say as the screensaver of my daughters reappears. "I could also show you the one of the first patient you killed with an air embolism. The one back in May. But I think I've made my point."

GG places her hand on her chin and stares past me at the portrait of my daughters on the screen. Her expression is unreadable. "Where did you get that second video?"

"The one of Mr. Bernard? From a University Hospital server." I step out from behind the lectern and discreetly check my watch.

Five minutes down. Five more to go.

Folding my hands behind my back, I slowly pace the length of the room as if giving a scholarly lecture to a class in the auditorium. "Through your work with the Safety Committee, you knew about the SICU cameras. But that was only the beginning of a much bigger project. What you didn't know is that, last spring, University Hospital Security secretly installed cameras in *all* of the patient rooms. Think about it:

every single patient at University under video surveillance. Because of the sensitive privacy and security issues involved, only hospital leaders and select members of the Safety Committee knew the existence of these cameras. You weren't one of them."

A paroxysm of guilt rattles through me as I reflect on how I had acquired that particular bit of knowledge, as well as the codes I needed to collect the videos from the secure University Hospital server: by analyzing the stolen keystrokes on Jason's computer. I was careful to cover my digital tracks, so that anyone who tries to trace the breach — as they surely will after tonight — shouldn't be able to follow the trail back to him.

"Why hadn't anyone looked at these videos before you?"

"Why should they have? People die in hospitals every day. There was nothing overtly, um, *nefarious* about the way Mr. Bernard or the patient with the air embolism died, certainly nothing that would have raised Security's suspicions enough to retrieve the video from the server and analyze it."

"But — what about Mrs. Samuelson? What about her video?"

"Ah. Yes. Mrs. Samuelson. We have Luis to thank for that."

"Luis?"

"As you probably know, the video surveillance system in the SICU uses an encrypted wireless network to transmit its images to a University Hospital server. Before he died, Luis had tapped directly into the wireless network and was downloading copies of the original videos."

A brilliant maneuver on Luis's part. The router for the videos was sitting behind the poster of the kitten in the call room, next to the plastic baggie with the computer password. It was connected to an ample power source and remotely linked to the Internet. "The difference between you and Luis was that while you inserted an altered version onto University Hospital's server — a very sophisticated one, I might add, so kudos for that — Luis stored the original, unedited version on a hijacked server overseas." It was a decent-sized cache of data, sitting beyond that twenty-character code on the Web site in Eastern Europe — ten days' worth of continuously accumulated, twenty-four/seven digital footage from all those different cameras. But everything was dated and time-stamped, so finding the relevant image of Mrs. Samuelson hadn't been too difficult.

She laughs. Is it my imagination, or is it

laced with just the faintest whiff of uncertainty? Uncertainty on her part would have
been unthinkable only a few short minutes
ago. "It doesn't matter. You'll never use
those videos, Steve."

"Why?"

"I still have my own video. Remember?
The one that shows you *fucking*" — her use
of, and emphasis on, that particular vulgar-
ism is unexpectedly jarring — "a woman
who just happens not to be your wife."

"I told Sally, GG. About us."

The curve of her smile flattens ever so
slightly as she spends the next several
seconds studying my face. I will my eyes to
remain locked with hers. It's an intense
experience, kind of like trying to stare into
the sun. "Why?"

"Because it was the right thing to do."
Because I owed Sally that much and had
realized that, otherwise, things would never
have been right between us again.

Her mouth forms an unabashed *O* of
surprise. I don't think I've ever seen her
genuinely caught off guard before. I gaze
calmly back, straining to keep my expression perfectly neutral, glad for the air-
conditioning vent in the ceiling directly over
my head that's the only thing preventing
my brow from becoming slick with sweat.

Then she throws back her head and laughs, long and loud.

"Nicely played, Steve. Nicely played. You took it all the way to the brink, and I blinked. You know, you really don't see it, do you? How much alike you and I are?" She shakes her head, and adds with a touch of regret, "That's why I find you so appealing, Steve. Why I still think we would make such a great team."

For a brief moment, the words hang in the air between us. Then she straightens out her dress and purposely brushes her lustrous brown hair out of her face, all business again. "So. What do you want?"

"For what?"

"Steve," she growls. "Don't insult both of our intelligences. What do you want? For keeping quiet? I'm calling your bluff."

"I'm not bluffing, GG."

"But what about your job? What's Collier going to think when he finds out about us? Your career will be *over*, Steve."

"I'll take my chances."

"You're lying." But she doesn't sound so sure.

I glance at my watch.

Anytime, now.

"Tell you what. Let me show you just one more video." I walk back to the lectern and hit the PLAY button on my computer. The picture of my daughters disappears and, with it, any remaining semblance of GG's poker face, which completely collapses, like a sand castle erased by the rising tide.

She gapes, incredulous, at the screen, on which is now projected the resident call room. It's nighttime, and the contents of the room are cast in the greenish hues of a night-vision camera. But everything's clearly visible. Bunk bed. Sink. Rickety nightstand with phone.

Everything but the kitten poster.

Luis lies on the lower berth of the bunk bed. The door opens, and a figure pokes its head into the room. There's no mistaking GG's willowy form and flowing dark hair, even with the mask covering her mouth and the lower part of her face. Her eyes glow eerily in the night vision, like a cat's reflected in the headlights of a car. The mask is attached to a thin, clear-plastic hose running to a small box clipped to a black belt at her waist. She pauses in the doorway, body taut, as if she's ready to run away at any moment. But Luis doesn't react.

I freeze the video. "At first, it didn't make sense to me how you could have ever managed to murder Luis. I mean, a big strong guy like him, probably trained to kill people using his bare hands dozens of different ways. Somehow, you engineered your way around the door lock. But asleep or not, the Luis *I* knew would have been on his feet the moment that door opened. Unless you had somehow already incapacitated him before ever setting foot inside."

I pick up the laser pointer and, on the screen, trace the mask secured snugly to her mouth and nose. "With a gas, maybe? How about nitrous oxide? Colorless. Practically odorless. Disperses quickly." I shift the laser pointer to the ventilator grate imbedded in the wall almost directly over Luis's face. "I went back and traced the origin of that shaft. You could have selectively pumped medical-grade nitrous into the call room at any number of different points. The nitrous would have initiated a state of mild anesthesia and dissociation. Not nearly enough to put him all the way under, of course, but certainly enough to take the fight out of him. Make him disoriented and vulnerable. And if the final results of the autopsy detect trace levels of nitrous in his body, as it probably will, it plays nicely with the drug-abuse cover story."

I restart the video and, like the two previous ones, the images flash by at increased speed. GG creeps up to Luis and jabs a needle into his thigh. He flails out at her, but even in this fast-forwarded version, his movements appear uncharacteristically slow and clumsy, and she springs away, well out of his reach.

Once more, I pause the video. "They found ketamine with Luis's body. Ketamine is an anesthetic. It's usually given IV, but it can also be delivered IM to patients who won't let you get close to them: like a screaming little kid who needs stitches. That's why ketamine is also an effective animal tranquilizer. The nitrous allowed you to get close enough to Luis to give him an injection of ketamine; the ketamine put him the rest of the way under. And, like the nitrous, ketamine is popular among drug addicts."

The recording resumes. Luis jumps up, hits his head on the metal railing of the top bunk, stumbles to the center of the room, and falls to the floor. He thrashes about, trying ineffectually to rise again, like a punch-drunk boxer on the mat after taking one too many hits, as GG watches from where she's pressed up against a wall.

And then Luis lies still, his eyes wide open and jaw slack. GG tosses an open duffel bag on the floor next to him, rolls him onto his back, yanks his scrub pants and underwear down to his ankles, unwraps a prepackaged central venous catheter kit she removes from the duffel bag, and drapes his left groin with towels. All the while, Luis lies there, dead to the world.

Even now, as I again watch GG effortlessly slide the fifteen-centimeter-long catheter into Luis's left femoral vein, I can't help but be impressed. She makes it look so easy. Many junior surgical residents, let alone med students, have difficulty mastering this skill. Once the catheter is secured, she pulls several medication vials from the duffel bag and injects them, one after the other, into the catheter. The rise and fall of Luis's chest slows, then stops. In quick succession, she checks each of his major pulses: the radial at the wrist, femoral in the right groin, and, finally, the carotid in the neck. She nods, drops an envelope and several vials of medicine on the floor around him, grabs the duffel bag, and leaves.

And Luis Martínez — ex-Marine and battle-hardened survivor of some of the meanest streets in the world — lies dead, in the most unlikely of places, at the hands of the most unlikely of people.

"How?" GG says quietly to Katie and Annabelle, whose smiling visages have replaced the call room on the screen.

"Luis." I turn the computer off and check my watch again. It's taking longer than I expected, and I'm running out of things to say.

Damn. Maybe I shouldn't have sped the video up so much.

I move out from behind the lectern. "He installed a camera behind the kitten poster, with the lens pointed through one of its eyes. It was streaming images to the same offshore server holding the SICU camera data." An additional fail-safe mechanism, should anything ever happen in the call room.

GG rises . . .

. . . and then sways, ever so slightly.

She places a hand on the back of a chair to steady herself. Confusion flashes across her face.

Finally.

"It's over, GG."

She laughs, but weakly, and at the same time frowns in concentration. "What — makes you say that?"

"The ketamine. It's starting to take effect."

Her eyelids, which had been drooping, spring open. Her hand flies to her shoulder.

"Yes, GG." I hold up a syringe filled with clear fluid, identical to the study medication, and labeled with the numbers *00134.* "You're not the only one with access to ket-amine. Remember when the researcher dropped the syringe on the floor out in the hallway tonight, and I helped him pick it up? Forgive me for stealing your idea, GG, but I used the opportunity to switch your syringe — the one you were supposed to receive tonight for the research study — for a duplicate one filled with 150 mg of ket-amine, enough to put a typical person down within about ten minutes." I place the syringe on the lectern and point to my watch. "It's been over fifteen since he injected you. But you're not a typical person, are you?"

She clutches the chair in front of her with both hands. "I'll . . . deny everything." She looks pained; her frown knits deep lines across her brow.

I almost feel sorry for her. Almost. But not quite. "Sure you will. Except that, very soon, you'll be sending out a dozen e-mails, compliments of me, confessing everything. They'll include copies of those videos and explain how guilty you feel and how you've decided to come clean before committing suicide here" — I sweep my hands around the room, toward the portraits of the dead surgeons gazing down upon us around the

Dome — "in one of the cradles of American surgery. Very dramatic. The media will eat it up."

"I'll tell them it was you."

"I doubt it. In a few seconds, once you're out from the ketamine, I'll be giving you a healthy dose of this." I hold up another syringe, this one attached to a capped needle. "Midazolam. A benzodiazepine. It's an amnestic. But I probably don't need to remind you of that. You're a star med student." I slip the syringe into my right pants pocket. "I figure you'll remember everything right up to the part when you went out into the hallway for the shot."

She staggers out from behind the row of chairs and collapses into a sitting position on the floor at the front of the hall, several feet away from me, swaying slightly and breathing hard.

"Why would . . . I confess? Nobody will . . . believe . . . any of that."

"Oh, I think they will. Suicide attempts in women tend to be a cry for help. Psychiatry 101. That's why women take pills and slash their wrists. Gives other people plenty of time to save them. It's the suicidal guy who decisively splatters his brain matter all to hell with a handgun to the temple." I shake my head and smile thinly. "And, besides —

are you *kidding* me? With your kinds of issues? They're going to have an army of
psychiatrists working on you for years."

"But . . . that video . . . of you and me,"
she gasps, her eyelids half-closed. "I'll them
you . . . were . . . my lover . . . tell them . . .
you were involved . . ."

"Right. *That* video." I walk over and pluck
her smartphone from her white coat pocket.
"Earlier tonight, I erased the copy you
downloaded onto the server. Once I get rid
of the original" — I wiggle the phone back
and forth — "the police — and Dr. Collier
— will never know I was ever involved with
you. You go to jail, and I get to go back to
my life." I squat down to her level, all the
better to look directly into her eyes. "Why
do you think I'm even here tonight, talking
to you? Stalling for time? I needed to steal
your phone to close the loop." I lean in a
little closer. "Besides, I wanted to see the
look on your face at the exact moment you
realized I had beaten you, you psychotic
bitch."

What comes next happens with astonish-
ing speed.

I don't even have time to be surprised as
she leaps up and charges into me. Despite
the ketamine, she's as fast and silent and
graceful as a cat.

With all of my planning, all of my meticulous preparations for tonight, a physical attack was something I had not anticipated. After all, she's supposed to be in a fucking ketamine-induced stupor by now, sprawled out on the floor in a lifeless heap, just as Luis had been. But the ketamine doesn't seem to be working.

In one fluid motion, she knocks me off-balance, and the two of us tumble backward. The lectern topples over, along with my computer and the syringe labeled *00134*. Her smartphone clatters across the floor. GG ends up on top of me and shoves her knee into my chest, knocking the wind out of me. I try to gulp some air but manage only a thin, reedy whistle, like I'm sucking my breath through a straw.

And then I'm on my back lying on the floor, and she's straddling me, pinning my arms to my sides with her long and powerful legs. I thrash my body around violently, but it's no use. I can't move. She's a lot stronger than she looks and, despite the ketamine, seems to be putting her black belt in tae kwon do to pretty good use right now.

Oh shit.

I must have miscalculated the ketamine dose. Or maybe I didn't give it enough time to work. That's the problem in a situation like this. Tranquilizers are imprecise. It's not like what you see in movies or on TV. Unless someone's hooked up to an anesthetic-gas machine, or an IV drip, there's *nothing* that will instantly knock someone out. How could I have been so stupid?

She grins down at me, looking well and truly *insane.*

"Oops," she says. "Poor Steve. I'm still awake." I strain impotently against the powerful grip of her legs. "And now . . . I'm going to kill you." She slurs her speech, speaks a little haltingly, and sways a bit, but with her hands free and mine pinned help-lessly against my sides, she can easily make good on her threat. She tightens her legs against my arms, pushing my right hand against the outside of my pant pocket.

Through the fabric of pants, I can feel the outline of the midazolam syringe I placed in my pocket a few moments ago.

"And then . . ." She licks her lips. Her ponytail has come undone, and her hair falls into her face. She flips it away with a toss of her head. It lands across her right shoulder, leaving the left side of her neck exposed. "I'm going to kill Sally . . . and Katie . . . and Annabelle." She strokes my cheek with the back of her fingers. "What do you think?"

No! I writhe and twist even more violently than before. My right arm is still trapped at my side by her left leg, but in the process of struggling, I manage to slip her grip and slide my right hand inside my pants pocket without her noticing. I wrap my hand around the syringe.

"And then," she breathes, "I swear to *God,* Steve . . . I'll turn . . . everything back on . . . *you.*"

Carefully, by feel only, having performed this task a thousand times before, I slip the hypodermic needle in my pocket free from its protective plastic sheath.

"You don't think . . . I can't . . . deal with a few pathetic psychiatrists?"

At the apex of her left sternocleidomastoid muscle, I can see the pulsations of her internal carotid artery. Just behind it, underneath the muscle, lies the internal jugular vein. If I can inject the midazolam into the vein, she'll be out within fifteen seconds. I'll never get a better shot at this.

"I'll have . . . them eating . . . out . . . of my hand."

She shifts her weight briefly as she reaches her right hand into the right pocket of her white coat.

It's all I need.

Clutching the syringe, I lurch my body abruptly to my left. It knocks her off-balance just enough for me to jerk my right hand out of my pocket, away from her leg, and stab the needle toward her neck.

For a fraction of a second, I think it's going to work.

The syringe travels in a perfect arc, the point of the needle aimed squarely at the center of her left internal jugular vein.

But it never reaches its target.

With the needle just inches short of the skin, she catches my right wrist with her left hand and slams my hand down against the marble floor. The shock of the impact sends pain lancing up my arm. I gasp and let go of the syringe, which flies out of my grip and rolls away to rest out of reach a few feet away.

She leers, and I glimpse a flash of steel in her right hand, just as it begins to curve downward toward *my* throat. But in that instant, I'm able to twist my right hand away from her left and grab her right wrist, slowing but not completely halting the forward momentum of the large, razor-sharp scalpel she's holding in her right hand.

It's not enough. The tip of the scalpel pierces the exposed skin below my left jaw and begins to dig into the soft flesh. I feel a trickle of warm, wet blood — my blood, for a change, instead of someone else's — dribble down my neck. I dimly wonder if it will leave a stain on my collar. Meanwhile, she joins her left hand to her right, using both to push down with the combined strength of her two against my one. Time slows as the focus of my entire universe becomes the scalpel.

So this is how it ends for me. How ironic. Death by scalpel.

Oddly, as I struggle to keep GG from tearing my neck open, I remain calm. There's no pain, probably because I'm pumped full of adrenaline. So, really, what's the point in freaking out? Or even putting up much of a fight? Maybe I should just let her carve me up a like a Thanksgiving turkey.

After all, my career is over. My marriage is likely over. And I'm now on the floor of one of the oldest, most prestigious teaching hospitals in the world, being attacked by a crazed, murderous medical student. I mean, if you're going to go out in style, then this is the way to do it. Right?

I only hope that, if she manages to butcher my neck, she finishes it now, here, on the cold hard floor of the auditorium. A half-ass job, with a catastrophic but only temporary interruption in the flow of blood to my brain, will simply make me stroke out, leaving me mentally incapacitated, a thirty-two-year-old vegetable gorked out in some nursing home somewhere. That would seriously suck. Not so much for me. Because, after all, if I was a drooling, brain-dead zombie fed through a plastic tube shoved into my stomach, what would I care? But for Sally. And the girls.

Sally.

Katie.

Annabelle.

No.

It can't end now. Not like this. She said she was going to *kill* them once she was done with me. I can't let that happen.

So I strain against her wrist as hard as I can, fighting to alter the destructive path of the scalpel.

But it's no use. Despite the ketamine, she's too strong, and with her two hands against my one, she has a decisive mechanical advantage. The scalpel continues its relentless journey toward the major blood vessels of my neck. I'm going to die.

Mr. Bernard, Mrs. Samuelson, Jerry Garcia — here I come.

I close my eyes and await the inevitable.

"Get off of him, you *bitch*!"

I open my eyes and can't believe what I see. Amazingly, miraculously, Sally has appeared to my right holding the midazolam syringe. She buries the needle to the hilt in the side of GG's left neck, right in the spot I had been aiming for, and depresses the plunger. I don't know what unseen force guided her hand, luck or God or whatever, but it's a perfect shot.

GG bares her teeth, lets loose a guttural growl, and deals Sally, *pregnant* Sally — shorter by at least eight inches and lighter by fifty pounds — a vicious backhand blow with her left hand before yanking the syringe out of her neck and tossing it away. Sally falls to the ground next to us, clutching her face and groaning.

And now fury blinds me to all else.

With renewed strength, I take advantage of this momentary distraction by yanking my left arm free of GG's leg. I push against her scalpel-wielding right hand with both of my hands, and in doing so am able to shove it incrementally back toward her, out of the superficial tissues of my neck. She, in turn, brings her left hand, free again after hitting Sally and disposing of the syringe, to her right.

Now, caught between two inexorable forces, the scalpel starts to shake violently in our hands, centimeters from the main blood supply to my brain. Facing each other there on the floor, limbs interlocked, scalpel at my throat, it's as if we're joined in some bizarre dance. We remain like that for what seems like hours but can't be more than five seconds, until the muscles in my arm start to cramp, then seize up.

The scalpel creeps back toward my neck.

And then, *finally,* all of those drugs pumped into her really kick in, and the tide begins to turn.

GG's arms, which had been as rigid as steel when she first jumped me, start to give way; grunting with effort, I'm able to gradually, incrementally, push the tip of the scalpel back toward her.

Then, suddenly, as if a power switch had been thrown, GG's arms go completely limp.

The scalpel clatters harmlessly to the marble floor.

And she collapses on top of me, heavy and inert.

Thank God.

I push her off and roll away, panting and groaning, the sweat streaming down my face in sheets. I crawl over to Sally, who's still lying on the ground, clutching her face. I gently pull her hands away and examine her.

An ugly purple welt is blossoming across her right cheek but, otherwise, she seems okay. Her facial bones appear completely intact, and her nose is untouched. She's shaking all over and breathing hard. She grabs hold of me, seizing me like I'm a life preserver in the middle of a tsunami, and for several minutes, we just sit there on the floor, holding on to each other, until her shaking stops.

"What are you doing here?" I murmur into her hair, rocking her back and forth. "You're supposed to be at your parents' house."

"I had my dinner with Andrea. About work. Remember? We got done early. I was nearby. I knew you had conference, and I wanted to . . . I don't know. Talk. About things. You weren't answering your cell." She points to GG's inert form. "What's all this about, Steve? I mean, I know this is . . . *her.* But I saw her attack you, and heard her talking about *killing* you. And me. And the *girls. Murdering our whole family.* And my mind, I don't know . . . I snapped. All I could think about was protecting the girls. Nothing else. So I grabbed the needle and . . ." She shudders. "But why was she talking about psychiatrists? And the police? Why was she trying to *kill* you?"

581

"It's a long story, sweetie. I am so sorry. I am so very sorry for all of this."

She takes a deep breath. "Well, we'd better call the police. Before she wakes up."

GG is sprawled on the floor next to us, eyes glassy, mouth parted slightly. A small trickle of blood is running down her neck from the needle puncture in her skin. I'm surprised it's not bigger; central veins like the internal jugular usually bleed more. Although she's gazing right at us, she clearly doesn't see us. It's a bit unsettling; like any minute she's going to jump up and grab me in a headlock. Without taking my eyes off her, I reach up to my neck. The tips of my fingers come away wet and sticky and red, but only just barely, like the kind of minor bleeding you get from a shaving nick. A quick inspection reveals that none of my blood spilled out on the floor or on GG.

Lucky.

"No."

"*No?* Don't call the police?"

"No."

"Are you *crazy,* Steve?"

"I mean, not yet. We need to get out of here first. Before we call the cops."

"*What the hell are you talking about?*"

"Sally. You have to trust me on this. Don't worry. We can get her locked away for good

582

without anyone's ever knowing we were involved." She's staring at me like I've gone off the deep end. I can't really blame her. Maybe I have. "Please, Sally. I don't have time to explain everything right now. But think of what will happen to all of us after this story gets out. Can you imagine? Once this thing goes viral? The effects on our careers? On the girls? Our lives will never be the same. *I* might even end up in jail. Think of Katie and Annabelle."

There. I've got her. That last bit about Katie and Annabelle. I can tell by the look on her face. "So . . . what do we do?" She sounds skeptical but interested.

"I've taken care of everything. I've got it all planned out. But we don't have a lot of time."

I pull myself up, wincing, my ribs and all four limbs screaming in protest. "Lock the doors to the room. And stick that chair next to the door underneath the door handle."

As Sally limps to the doors, I grab a pair of latex gloves, a rubber tourniquet, an alcohol pad, and a large syringe with hypodermic needle from my computer bag. I put on the gloves, tie the tourniquet around GG's left arm, and locate the basilic vein in the antecubital fossa, in front of the elbow between the biceps and flexor muscles of the forearm. It's a big fat juicy one, like a blue worm lazing under the surface of the skin, and I slap it gently with my fingers a few times to make it stick out more.

"What are you doing?" Sally has finished locking the doors and is watching me over my shoulder.

I wipe the skin over the vein with an alcohol pad and impale it with the syringe. "Injecting her with some more meds. Mostly narcotics. I need the world to think she was trying to kill herself in a fit of guilt." I press the syringe into her right hand, undo the tourniquet, and rise to my feet. Thin trickles of blood slowly dribble from her neck and left arm and onto the floor. I find the other syringe, the one Sally jabbed into her neck, lying a short distance away and drop it next to GG's hand.

"There. That should do it."

"Won't the police be suspicious she injected herself in the neck?"

"No. IV drug users do that all the time to themselves."

"Won't they — I don't know — get suspicious about fingerprints? Or DNA? Or something?"

"You've been watching too many cop shows. There's nothing that will ever definitively link any of this to us. We just need to keep our mouths shut and pretend we were never here. They'll never come looking. Besides, all the evidence points to her acting alone."

GG is staring through me, looking but not seeing.

"Why . . . not . . . just kill me?" she breathes. Her eyes flutter and close. Her breathing slows but doesn't halt. I palpate her carotid pulse, which is weak but steady.

I think, sadly, of Luis, that night on the McIntoshs' porch. It seems so long ago now. "Because it wouldn't be the honorable thing to do," I whisper.

I pick up her smartphone, turn off the power, and — just for good measure — remove the battery.

"*Now* what are you doing?" Sally asks.

"I don't want the GPS in her cell phone to track its location when I get rid of it." I stick the phone and battery in my pocket.

"Won't GG and the police wonder where it went?"

"Sure. But the last known location will be here at University. And University is a big place to lose one small phone. They'll figure that, in her state of mind, anything could have happened to it."

I gingerly place the scalpel, the syringe labeled *00134,* and my laptop into the computer bag, right the lectern, and take Sally by the hand. We slip out through an old maintenance door in the projector room in the back of the auditorium and wend our way through a maze of side hallways before emerging in the main corridor near the entrance to the Dome. I guide Sally to a hidden vantage point I had staked out earlier.

"The automated confession went out from her e-mail account about five minutes ago," I whisper, checking my watch. "So University Security should . . . yep. There they are now."

We watch as several University Hospital Security officers break down the front doors of the Dome and storm into the room.

She takes a deep breath and turns to me. "You know that this doesn't get you off the hook. Right? Just because she tried to kill us doesn't mean that I'm not still *really* pissed off at you."

I suppress a smile. "I understand."

CHAPTER 25

Friday, August 28

As news of the woman quickly dubbed the "Med Student Murderer" sweeps across the country, I drive to a landfill a few hours from our house and park next to two college kids wrestling a beat-up couch from the flatbed of a pickup truck. The air is filled with the sounds of heavy machinery and the cries of seagulls.

I walk to the edge of the parking lot, where a safety rail separates it from the periphery of the massive garbage pit, and toss both disposable cell phones, GG's smartphone, and the scalpel into the nearest pile of refuse below. I dropped the smartphone's battery off at a recycling center earlier today. There's no reason not to be ecologically responsible, after all.

I watch as a bulldozer pushes the pile with the cell phones and scalpel away from me, toward the center of the pit. The mountains of trash swallow the tiny mound, and it's gone, like a handful of sand sprinkled onto the grainy expanse of a desert sand dune.

EPILOGUE

It's 6:45 A.M., and I'm sitting in University Hospital's cafeteria, cradling a strong cup of coffee. The early-morning rush has begun. Nurses and lab technicians and doctors stream in and out of the food line.

I glance at my watch impatiently. The junior resident is running late this morning, and we still need to talk about the patients before I head up to the operating rooms for a full day of surgery with Dr. Collier, who asked for me personally today. It seems he wants to use our time in the operating room together as an opportunity to impart advice about my beginning my faculty job at University Hospital next year. My career trajectory, I note with more relief than satisfaction, gently blowing on the steaming surface of my coffee before taking a small sip, seems to have righted itself — thanks both to my performance at M and M conference that night, and GG's role in Mr.

Bernard's and Mrs. Samuelson's deaths.

My smartphone chimes with an incoming text message from Sally.

Can u pick up baby wipes on way home 2nite? Also — marriage counseling Sat. morning. Mom 2 watch girls.

I grimace. *Marriage counseling.* Sally wasn't kidding when she said I wasn't off the hook. I hate counseling, but it sure as shit beats divorce.

I check the time again, now growing well and truly pissed, and fire off an angry text to the junior resident. He responds that he's on his way, and I snort in exasperation.

He's not half the doctor Luis was.

My gaze falls on a large, flat-screen TV affixed to one of the opposite walls, on which CNN is recapping yesterday's events in the case of the Med Student Murderer. *The Med Student Murderer.* I shake my head. It's kind of a confusing moniker, if you ask me. Sure, it's got a certain ring to it, from the alliteration. But for the uninitiated, it's hard to tell if the murderer happens to be a med student, like GG, or if it's the other way around, and the murderer is killing med students. Whatever. It's the name that's stuck. Besides, Dr. Death was already taken.

Nancy, the lead prosecutor, stands before the judge making a statement, looking attractive yet formidable in a conservative gray pantsuit. Kind of like a cross between Hillary Clinton and an underwear model. She's got to look good: After all, it's the case of a lifetime.

The camera cuts abruptly to the defense table.

Prison has not diminished her.

In fact, clad in a bright orange jumpsuit, wrists chained, and hands sitting on her lap, she seems much bigger than either the stern-faced defense attorneys flanking her or the armed guards in uniform standing just behind her. Her ponytail is gone; her long brown hair has been shorn short, and she wears it in a plain but attractive style, in a bob that frames her serene visage. It makes her look older. She stares calmly forward, back erect, chin thrust out, betraying not a shred of emotion.

She turns and stares directly into the camera. For some indefinable reason, I can't help but feel that she's looking at me.

And me alone.

She smiles.

ABOUT THE AUTHOR

Kelly Parsons is a board-certified urologist with degrees from Stanford University, the University of Pennsylvania, and Johns Hopkins, and he is on the faculty at the University of California, San Diego. He lives with his family in Southern California. This is his first novel.

The employees of Thorndike Press hope you have enjoyed this Large Print book. All our Thorndike, Wheeler, and Kennebec Large Print titles are designed for easy reading, and all our books are made to last. Other Thorndike Press Large Print books are available at your library, through selected bookstores, or directly from us.

For information about titles, please call:
  (800) 223-1244

or visit our Web site at:
  http://gale.cengage.com/thorndike

To share your comments, please write:
  Publisher
  Thorndike Press
  10 Water St., Suite 310
  Waterville, ME 04901